TARGETS
OF DECEPTION

JEFFREY STEPHENS

VARIANCE
ARKANSAS

Timothy Schulte, Variance Publishing, 1610 South Pine St.,
Cabot, AR 72023, (501) 843-BOOK
tpaulschulte@variancepublishing.com
Published by Variance LLC (USA).
www.variancepublishing.com

Library of Congress Catalog Number – 2009928923

ISBN: 1-935142-12-7
ISBN-13: 978-1-935142-12-6

Cover Illustration by Jeremy Robinson
Jacket Design and Interior layout by Stanley J. Tremblay,
stremblay@variancepublishing.com
Edited by Shane Thomson, slthomson@variancepublishing.com

Visit Jeffrey Stephens on the web at: www.JeffreyStephens.com

To Nancy, for always being there.

ACKNOWLEDGMENTS

A mere "thank you" does not seem enough of an acknowledgment for those who have stood by me for so long as supporters, critics, ersatz editors and eternally optimistic friends—Chris Beakey, Maureen Benic, Randi Conway, Carol Garinger, Larry Garinger, Rick Gould, Linda Kaye, Jennifer Korona, Nicky Lewis, Steve Marks, Andy Moszynski, Dr. Bart Pasternak, Ginny Peluso, Carl Portale, Ron Rosa, Dennis Rowan, Ed Scannapieco, Dr. Robert Stark, Caroline Sumner, Scott Sumner, Laura Sutton, Eric Thorkilsen, Melissa Thorkilsen, Frank Wilson—I cherish each of you.

My sincerest appreciation to a very dear friend, necessarily unnamed, who told me the truth about covert operations and explained how the world is a safer place because of the many heroic deeds that can only be told in the guise of fiction.

My gratitude to Tim Schulte at Variance for his vision, Stanley Tremblay for his creativity, Rick Cutka for his expertise and my editor Shane Thomson for his insight and stubborn determination.

Special thanks to my relentless agent Bob Diforio, and to the world's absolute greatest media guru, promoter and support system, Trish Stevens.

And in the end, of course, there are Trevor and Graham and Nancy, without whom the curious passages of life would have no real meaning.

Grazie.

TARGETS
OF DECEPTION

A NOTE FROM THE AUTHOR

VX is a substance developed in Great Britain in 1952 and remains the deadliest nerve gas ever created. VX—known by its United States Army codename—is a clear, colorless liquid with the consistency of motor oil. A fraction of a drop of VX, absorbed through the skin or inhaled through aeration, can kill by severely disrupting the nervous system. Although a cocktail of drugs can serve as an antidote, VX acts so quickly that victims would have to be injected with the antidote almost immediately to have a chance at survival. VX is the only significant nerve agent created since World War II. VX is a weapon of mass destruction that spreads from impact point killing all in its path …

Foxnews.com
cfrterrorism.org
chem.ox.ac.uk

ONE

Jordan Sandor had no reason to expect this quiet autumn morning to erupt with the familiar sounds of his violent past.

It was nearly ten. The air felt crisp and cool, the calm sky bright and clear and blue. The two-lane blacktop in upstate New York was deserted, except for Dan Peters' old station wagon where Sandor slouched in the passenger seat, a casual observer of the passing countryside. He and Peters had been riding in silence when a pickup truck came into view then turned across their path.

"That's practically a traffic jam around here."

Sandor nodded. "Doesn't seem to be much doing."

"Nope, not this time of year. Summer you get the tourists, hiking, camping, and all that. Winter, they come up to ski." Peters eased the wagon along a wide curve. "Fall, some people drive up on the weekends to see the leaves turn color. Other than that you get nothing."

They passed a makeshift billboard that boasted authentic home cooking at some nearby restaurant. The poster looked so old Sandor wondered whether the restaurant even existed anymore. "You don't miss the city at all?"

Peters thought it over, surveying the barren road. "Sometimes. The places, you know. Not the people. The food, mostly. When I get a taste for good Chinese or Thai, and especially Japanese, that's when I really miss New York. No Sushi Yasuda up here."

Sandor smiled at the road ahead. "Still need your sushi fix."

"Old habits die hard."

"You were the one convinced me to try it, remember? Raw fish! Man, how many years ago was that?"

Peters didn't answer.

"Well," Jordan said after another mile or so, "I give you high marks. Looks like you've done a good job of making the transition to the quiet life."

"Quiet everywhere, except up here," Peters said, pointing to his head. Embarrassed by the confession, he fell silent again.

"You're entitled to some peace," Jordan told him.

"What I saw over there . . ." Dan paused, "it never gets peaceful for me. Sometimes I manage to ignore the noise, that's all."

The two men had fought together in the Gulf War, the first one, when they drove the Iraqis out of Kuwait, leaving behind a mess that needed to be cleaned up a dozen years later. Before that, Peters saw duty in Vietnam. He had been a career soldier, and although he was nearly fifteen years older than Sandor, Jordan outranked him when they served in the Persian Gulf.

"Well," Sandor said, "maybe peace and quiet are overrated."

"Yeah, tranquility is a bitch," Peters said, then uttered a short laugh. "So what about you? How do you like your new gig? What are you supposed to be, a reporter or something?"

"I'm a journalist, if you don't mind."

"Oh yeah, a journalist, beautiful. You talk about transition, man. I suppose you don't miss the good fight, eh?"

Sandor faced forward again. He had an uneven nose, earned in too many close-order scuffles, and a jaw etched in a strong, firm line. His complexion was tanned and a bit weathered for a man not yet forty. His hair was brown and cut just long enough to allow him to run his fingers through the waves, front to back, which he habitually did when he took time to consider a question or reflect on something that troubled him. He was doing that now, his dark, intense eyes visualizing something beyond his actual line of sight. "I gave up the good fight the day they left my men for dead in Bahrain."

"Yeah," Peters said as shook his head. "Bastards."

After his tour in the Middle East, Dan returned home to finish his military career stateside, take his pension and disappear. Jordan remained abroad, working on special assignments until an undercover team he was assigned to in Manama was betrayed. It had been more than a year since that incident in Bahrain. The day after they pulled him out and left the others behind to die, Sandor submitted his resignation from government service.

"Not everyone comes home."

Jordan nodded.

"Strange how things never work out the way you figure."

Jordan let that go too. "So what about this Ryan guy we're going to see?"

"What about him?"

"What does he think of the quiet life, now that he's back?"

"You're the journalist, you ask him."

"I will," Sandor said.

Peters rolled down his window, letting a cold breeze whip through the car.

"If this guy was really a mercenary," Jordan said, "he's got some explaining to do before I'll believe a thing he tells me."

Peters turned to his old friend and showed him a crooked grin. "Good old Jordan, Mr. Black and White. The mercenary business is immoral because you play for money. But if you put the same guy in a uniform, underpay him, and send him out to shoot someone, that makes it okay."

Sandor shook his head.

"You sure know how to wave the flag, buddy."

"Yeah, I suppose so," Jordan said. "Flag's not the problem."

Morning sunlight sparkled on the trees, an October spectacle of colors lining the road as they continued on Route 32 towards Jimmy Ryan's house.

"Close your window, will you, Dan?"

Peters chuckled as he put it up half way. He was a burly man with wide shoulders and thick arms. "Blood a little thin these days, Sandor? Winter's coming, you know. Time to bulk up." He patted his ample stomach, evidence that he no longer bothered with the physique he maintained while he was in military service.

Sandor, who was still trim and fit, eyed his friend's gut. "If it's all the same to you, I'll pass on the donuts and put on my jacket instead." He grabbed his sport coat from the back seat, pulled it on, and rubbed his hands together.

"So how well do you really know him?"

"Jimmy? I told you, I only met him last month, when he first got back from Europe."

"I thought you said he was in North Africa."

"He was. Spent some time in France, too, before he came back to the States."

3

"Uh huh. And how'd he find his way to you?"

"I met him in a bar."

"Picking up guys in bars, Danny?"

"Very cute."

"You still a Budweiser man?"

"Loyal to the end. You still going steady with Jack Daniels?"

"Ever faithful."

Danny laughed.

"You think he was looking for you, or was it just a coincidence?"

"Looking for me? I don't think so. We were watching a ballgame, talking shit, found out we were both in the Army, started gabbing about it. Save the third degree for him, will you? We'll be there in ten minutes."

"Just curious. Occupational hazard."

"I see. New occupation, new hazards. I think I liked you better in the desert."

Peters slowed down as they approached an intersection and swung into a left turn that led them onto another two-lane road. It was a narrower stretch than Route 32, but just as quiet—until a sharp *crack* rang out through the clear morning air.

"What the hell was that?" Even as Dan asked the question, they heard a second *pop*, the sound unmistakable.

"Gunshots," Sandor replied flatly.

"There's no hunting this close to 32," Dan said.

"That didn't come from any hunting rifle. Those are low velocity rounds."

As they rounded the next curve they saw, just ahead and off to their left, two cars stopped on the grass shoulder. One was a police car, the other a sedan parked in front of the cruiser. Beside the driver's door of the sedan an officer had fallen to the ground in a leaden heap.

Dan instinctively jammed on his brakes, tires screeching as the station wagon shuddered to a halt fifty yards from the two cars.

Jordan hollered a warning as a small, dark man jumped from the passenger side of the sedan and leveled an automatic pistol at them. "Move it!" he shouted. "Go!"

Dan was pulling at the column gearshift, about to throw the wagon in reverse when the first shot smashed through the windshield, covering them in a spray of fractured glass. The second round tore into Dan's right side, piercing him with the awful, numbing sensation of jagged ice slicing through his flesh before giving way almost at once to a searing shock of pain. Peters lurched backward from the impact then slumped forward onto the steering wheel. His foot slipped from the brake and the station wagon rolled slowly ahead towards the approaching gunman.

A third shot exploded through what remained of the windshield as Jordan dove below the level of the dashboard, showering them again with broken shards of safety glass. He struggled to pull his friend out of the line of fire, keeping himself as low as he could manage, even as another round whistled above him and went crashing through the side window. The car was still moving forward, now no more than thirty yards from their assailant.

Another shot sounded.

"Sonuva—"

Crack!

Sandor managed to yank Dan down, pulling him off the steering column onto the seat. Kicking his friend's feet out of the way he slammed down on the accelerator and the car surged forward with a surprising burst of power. He grabbed the wheel and tried to hold a steady course but careened wildly to the right. Jordan knew that if he ran them off the road they would be finished, so he tugged slightly to the left, judging his position with the help of a quick look above the dash. Making several reflexive adjustments, swerving left and then right, Sandor was nearly even with the two parked cars when he veered sharply left again, aiming for the gunman, who had to jump backward out of the car's path. The shooter quickly regained his balance and fired again, the bullet crashing through the rear window, sending more glass cascading across the back seat.

Jordan heard yelling in some foreign language as he reached up to tilt the rear-view mirror for a look behind.

The driver of the sedan had gotten out of the car and was waving his arms. It appeared he was ordering his companion back inside. He was tall and blond, as dissimilar in appearance from the short, swarthy gunman as he could be.

Jordan remained low, peering just above the dash now, keeping the pedal pinned to the floor, doing the best he could to put some distance between his car and theirs and wondering how he was going to survive a high-speed chase driving from the passenger seat with Dan Peters' bleeding body on top of him.

Several more shots popped behind them as he headed down the long, straight stretch of road. When it seemed the firing had finally stopped he checked the mirror again, and was surprised to see that the two men were not turning around to pursue him. Instead, they had hurried back into their car and were speeding off in the other direction, towards the main highway.

He watched as they disappeared around the curve from where he and Dan had first spotted them. Sandor knew they might turn around and come back after him, but he brought Dan's wagon to an abrupt stop and threw the gearshift into park. If they were returning, he would have no chance to outrun them unless he got behind the wheel.

"Dan, can you hear me?" He tried to raise him.

"My side," Peters muttered. "I'm hit bad."

"I know," Jordan told him, relieved to have him say anything at all. "Can you move?"

Dan nodded slightly and Jordan checked behind them again, making sure the sedan did not suddenly roar back into view, then helped Peters slide to the middle of the seat and scrambled over him to get behind the wheel. He turned to have another look back, but there was no sign of them. Not yet.

Sandor turned back to his friend, and seeing the growing stain of blood running onto the seat amidst the broken glass, pulled off his jacket, folded it up and placed it under Peters' head.

"Here," he said, grabbing Dan's parka from the back seat of the car and shaking it free of glass fragments, "hold this against your side. Hold it tight."

Jordan shifted the car into reverse, completed a high-speed turn, then sped back to the police cruiser. The sudden stop drew a groan from his friend. There was still no sign of an ambush. Jordan watched and listened intently but heard nothing except the hum of the station wagon's engine through the empty frame where the windshield had been. The quiet was eerie now, unsettling after the explosion of gunfire, the shattering of glass and the wailing of tires that had resounded along this desolate strip of highway. Sandor, now aware of the pounding in his chest, took a deep breath to steady himself before stepping quickly from the wagon. He ran around the front and knelt beside the wounded officer.

"Can you hear me?"

He gave no response. Jordan checked for a pulse along his carotid artery. He was still alive.

Sandor removed the pistol from the trooper's holster, which he found was still snapped shut. All the while he kept returning his anxious gaze ahead, searching for what might appear without warning from around the turn. He pulled at the slide of the officer's automatic, drawing a round into the breech, then climbed into the police cruiser, picked up the radio mike, and spoke into the open channel.

"We have an emergency. Officer down. Just off Route 32. Repeat, officer down. Emergency."

He released the button on the side of the microphone, waiting only an instant before a voice crackled over the speaker, and Jordan knew that for now, at least, it would be all right.

TWO

Sandor was finally alone, seated on a vinyl sofa in the waiting area of the local hospital. He had spent the day being subjected to the repetitive questions of a preliminary police interrogation, treated to a series of medical updates on Dan Peters and the wounded officer, and praised for his courage by a seemingly endless stream of strangers.

The wounded trooper, Jack Collins, was in the intensive care unit. He had only survived, according to all accounts, because of Jordan's quick reaction under fire. Dan was also out of surgery, patched up and resting quietly in the recovery room.

"Unbelievably lucky," the surgeon had explained to Jordan. "I can't begin to tell you how close this was to a lethal injury. They just missed his spine, his heart . . ."

Wincing at the lousy cup of coffee in his hand, Jordan said with a smile, "I didn't know Danny had a heart." He was hoping to be spared further torment, but the doctor would not be deterred. He described all the gruesome details of Peters' surgery before Jordan could get away and spend a few moments on his own.

Just as he settled into that reverie, he heard someone say his name.

He slowly raised his head to see a broad, stern-looking man wearing a state trooper's uniform and a chest full of medals. "Yes."

"I'm Captain Reynolds," the man said, his speech as stiff as his posture. "Jack Collins is one of my men."

Sandor stood, his lean frame of just over six feet tall bringing him eye to eye with the trooper. "Jordan," he said, offering his hand as he made a quick assessment of this authoritarian old cop.

Captain Reynolds looked like one of the tough, leathery career officers Sandor had served under, certainly a man who had experienced his share of fighting in the military. Now, years later, his weary, gray eyes said he had spent too much time in a rural area, chasing after too many drunk drivers and too many petty criminals, no longer seeing any real action. His glory days were long gone.

Reynolds' grip was firm, and he held Jordan's hand as if he didn't mean to let go. "They tell me you saved Jack's life."

"Bit of an exaggeration, I think."

"I'm not so sure. If you left him there, doctor says he would have bled to death as easily as anything else. You took a real chance, going back for him the way you did. Could've run for it yourself, right?"

Jordan was embarrassed for about the twentieth time that afternoon, and since Reynolds was obviously not the sentimental type, he figured he should put an end to this part of the discussion as politely as he could. "Look Captain, I needed a gun, and I figured Collins had one."

Reynolds showed him as tight a smile as he'd seen in a while. It was one of those official smiles Jordan would get from a commanding officer who wanted to demonstrate his appreciation for something Sandor had done, without getting emotional about it. "That's a lotta crap," the Captain said, making the statement sound as friendly as hell. "I know a combat vet when I meet one, Sandor. You didn't go back for a gun. You went back because you were trained not to leave your men behind."

"Homework, Captain?"

"Yeah, checked up on you some. Sorry I never met you overseas. Could've used you in Nam."

"Before my time," Jordan said. Then he shrugged. "Wouldn't have mattered anyway, right?"

"Probably not." Captain Reynolds shook his head. "Buy you a real cup of coffee?"

"Thanks, but I wanted to stop by to see Collins, if I can."

Reynolds nodded. "We'll catch up a little later then. I have a few questions for you."

"Right," Jordan said.

Reynolds stood there for a moment, just to let Sandor know who was in charge. Jordan thought about asking if he was dismissed, but Reynolds turned around, executing something close to a smart about-face, then walked away.

AS SANDOR STROLLED down the hospital corridor, it seemed everyone there recognized him. Small town, big news. He stopped at the nurse's station where he exchanged smiles with a cute brunette sitting behind a long, white counter.

"May I see Trooper Collins now? I understand he's feeling a little better, and I'm—"

"He's in the ICU, Mr. Sandor," she interrupted. "His only visitors should be immediate family. But for you," she added with a self-conscious tilt of her head, "I'll speak with the doctor right away."

She lingered an extra moment to smile into Jordan's dark eyes, then stepped inside a glass enclosed area behind her, picked up the telephone and, watching Jordan through the partition, made her call. The discussion was brief. She hung up and came back to the counter.

"Follow me," she said.

THE INTENSIVE CARE unit was a jungle of antiseptic technology with large, complex machinery dwarfing the patients it surrounded. Beeping sounds and audiovisual monitors animated the peaceful, yet impersonal, infirmary. The nurse led Jordan through a maze of computers and stainless steel apparatus to Jack Collins bedside.

"This is Mr. Sandor," she whispered softly, "the man who saved you."

Jordan could have done without that introduction. "They're the ones who saved you," he protested mildly as he gestured toward the equipment and staff around them. "I just kept you company till they got there." Collins looked about twenty-five, a young officer who had made a rookie's mistake. A more experienced trooper wouldn't have gone down that way, his gun still snapped into the holster.

Collins did his best to smile. He was rigged up to intravenous tubing, his head and neck bandaged, his complexion the color of the sheets pulled up to his chin. Jordan thought he looked pretty good, considering the last time he had seen him he was crumpled in a heap on the blacktop, oozing blood.

"They told me what you did," he said in a hoarse, unsteady voice. His tired eyes searched Jordan's face for something, then looked past him. "Thanks."

"Seems you're already on the mend," Jordan said cheerfully. "I just wanted to stop by, see how you're doing."

The nurse, who remained at his side, said, "He's doing fine, Mr. Sandor, but he needs his rest. Just a minute or two, please."

Jordan nodded. "Right," he said, watching her slowly walk away, giving himself a good look at her exit. "Nice girl."

"Yeah," Collins agreed. "Grew up right nearby, in Saugerties. You're not from around here, Mr. Sandor."

"It's Jordan. And no, I'm from the city. Came up to visit an old army pal, Dan Peters. Know him?"

"Not really. Think I heard the name when he moved into town." He spoke haltingly from the combination of pain and medication. "It's been a while since anyone rented the Larsen place."

"But you never met him."

"Don't think I ever laid eyes on him." Collins blinked slowly, the drugs balancing him on the edge of sleep. "I hear they did a number on him too."

"They did."

"Captain told me. Coulda been both of us, hadn't been for you."

"Forget it," Jordan said.

"How'd it go . . . down at the barracks?"

"The questioning, you mean? All right, I guess. I gave a description of the little guy with the automatic. I only saw the driver for a second, caught a glimpse of him in the mirror."

"Driver's the one who plugged me."

"Tall blond guy," Jordan said.

"Yeah. Captain tells me you gave a pretty good ID on both. License plate too. How in hell d'you manage that?"

"Instincts, that's all."

"Sure," Collins said, sounding like he was about to pass out.

"Strange looking pair, weren't they?"

Collins opened his eyes a bit. "How do you mean?"

"The little guy was Arab. The driver looked like an All-American linebacker."

"Yeah," Collins said with a slight nod. He was fading fast now.

"I wanted to ask you something, Jack. All right if I call you Jack?"

11

Collins tried to smile again, his lips dry and uneven. "Ask away."

"They tell me you stopped them for speeding. How did it happen? You give them the siren?"

"Uh huh."

"And they stopped right away?"

"Sure. Probably knew they were gonna blast me." The idea of that seemed to rouse him. "If they took off, they had to know I'd go for the radio."

Jordan nodded. That was how he figured it. "Did they say anything? Anything at all?"

Collins took a long, hard swallow. "Not a word. Sonuvabitch just nailed me." He hesitated. "I never even got my gun out of the holster."

Jordan frowned.

"Why do you ask?"

"Nothing really," Jordan said. "I just heard them yelling to each other. I thought maybe if you heard something . . ."

"Nothing." He paused again and drew a shallow, awkward breath. "Now that you mention it though . . . I thought I heard them speaking in a foreign language when I was on the ground. I wouldn't have known French from Chinese by then."

"Don't worry about it. They'll get picked up soon enough."

"The car," Collins said, his voice growing weaker as the medication was getting the best of him. "Captain said they found it."

Jordan nodded, pretending to know what he was talking about.

"Down by the reservoir. Another set of tire tracks. Second car waiting for them."

"Right," Jordan said.

"Professionals," Collins muttered.

"We were all lucky to get out of there," Sandor said.

Collins reached out and took hold of Jordan's arm. "You were the luck."

"Just one more question, then I'll let you get some rest. Know a guy up here, name of Jimmy Ryan?"

Collins started to shake his head, but it hurt too much. "No. Can't say as I do."

"Never mind." Sandor patted his hand and offered a reassuring smile. "Don't worry. Your boys will catch them."

Collins looked up at him in a way that told Jordan he knew it was a lie. "They knew what they were about," he said. "They're long gone, aren't they?"

"We'll see."

The young man hesitated, then said, "Take care of yourself."

"You too," Jordan said and turned away.

Collins was asleep before he left the room.

THREE

Sandor found Captain Reynolds just outside the ICU, where he was quietly giving instructions to two troopers standing guard in the hospital corridor assigned to protect Jack Collins.

"Captain."

Reynolds turned from his men.

"I was wondering if we could have that cup of coffee."

Reynolds told his men he would be gone a while, then took Jordan by the arm and led him down the hallway. "How's Jack?"

"Good as can be expected."

The Captain nodded. "Come on, we'll take a walk."

THEY SAT ACROSS from each other in a booth in the small diner a couple of blocks from the hospital. Reynolds told Sandor about his days in Vietnam with the 101st Airborne, information Jordan had not requested, but the trooper wanted to share all the same.

"Ran that computer check on you," Reynolds told him after he finished his personal reminiscence. "Like I said before, saw some of your service record."

Jordan waited.

"Not all of it, though. Some major gaps. Looked to me like CID blocks. Where'd you disappear to after your first tour? Military Intelligence, am I right?"

"An oxymoron," Jordan replied.

"Like 'civil servant'?"

Jordan smiled.

"So you were still in some kind of government service."

"Some kind."

"And now you're some kind of reporter?"

"Some kind."

"I'm not a big fan of reporters."

"Neither am I."

Reynolds gave him a look that told him saving Jack Collins was not a license for any smart mouth crap, not if he knew what was good for him. "So, what happened to government duty?"

Jordan looked up from his coffee and met the captain's eyes. "It got old, Captain. Too many friends got sold out by too many fat-ass bureaucrats."

"It's all part of the game, son."

"It shouldn't be a game."

"Lapsed patriot, eh?"

"No, still a patriot," Jordan said. "Just too much bullshit."

Reynolds shook his head, making a face like he just remembered something he never wanted to think about again. "Yeah, lost my taste for those games myself. Took my retirement, came back home. Got this nice job, working towards a second pension. Local politics are a piece of cake once you've done the Potomac shuffle. It's funny though, even now. Always thought I'd spend my entire life in the military."

"Any regrets?"

"Sometimes. Nine Eleven happened to all of us, know what I mean?"

Sandor nodded.

"Especially when you've worn the uniform. Made me want to re-enlist."

Sandor stared directly into Reynolds' eyes.

"So what really went down today?" Reynolds asked.

"I was hoping you'd tell me."

The captain did not reply, retaining his erect bearing as he took a drink of his coffee.

"If I knew I'd tell you," Sandor said.

15

"I wonder," Reynolds said. He shook off another thought. "I suppose I should get over to the barracks, see what they've turned up."

"Tell me about the second car, Captain, the one they had waiting near the reservoir."

Reynolds took a moment to study Sandor. "Where'd you hear that?"

"Let's just say there are a lot of rumors flying around here today."

Reynolds frowned. "They were professionals, that much is certain."

"That's exactly what Collins said."

"They had the second car waiting. Made the switch and took off, headed for God knows where."

"Were there any more victims today?" Jordan's question caught the captain halfway between sitting and standing.

Reynolds nodded slowly. "Who have you been talking to?"

"Does it matter?"

"It might."

"Okay." He sat back down. "Call it a guess, then."

"That the truth?"

"It is. I heard about the second car at the hospital. The other part is just common sense. Two pro shooters didn't come up here to nail a cop for a speeding ticket."

Reynolds nodded again. "Okay. They took out a guy, name of James Ryan."

Jordan did not respond to the mention of the name, the man he and Peters were on their way to see. Reynolds searched Sandor's expression for any sign of recognition, but saw nothing.

"Ryan just moved up here a month or so ago," Reynolds said. "We're checking it out now."

"Uh huh."

"We backtracked from where Collins first spotted the car. Didn't take much. The house this Ryan was renting isn't far from there."

Sandor waited.

"Apparently, they caused that boy some pain before they did him."

"How's that?"

"Tied him up and beat the living crap out of him. Then put two in his head."

"You been there yet to have a look yourself?"

"I'm going over, soon as I clean up some of the paperwork at the barracks."

"Mind if I ride along?"

"Not regulation, you know."

"Neither is the hole in Dan Peters' chest."

Reynolds paused. "What the hell. Need you at HQ anyway, to look through some of the mug shots they brought down from Albany, the usual routine."

Jordan slid out of the booth. "Mind if I make a quick stop first? Just want to see how Peters is doing."

"Not a problem," Reynolds said as he stood.

Jordan grinned. "Might even like to have a look around. Beautiful country you have here."

The captain fixed him with a hard stare. "You know, Sandor, I may be from a small town in upstate New York, but I'm no yokel. You follow me?"

"Yes sir," Jordan said, stopping with his jacket half pulled on.

"Relax," the captain said, giving him a slap on the shoulder. "I just want you to keep it in mind, is all."

FOUR

At the same time Jordan was having coffee with Captain Reynolds, a uniformed waiter at the Waldorf-Astoria Hotel in New York was delivering a meal to a suite on the seventeenth floor. The young man wheeled in a large tray of fresh orange juice, poached eggs, several rashers of bacon, wheat toast, and a pot of espresso. Also at hand were the pleasant incidentals this grand hotel provides—fresh marmalade and preserves, poppy seed rolls with sweet butter, and a fine setting of flatware and china. The sitting room was decorated in a sedate yet affluent style, an elegant motif harmonizing with the cool blues and greens of the drapes, warm woods, and the rich brocades of the upholstery.

"Will that be all, sir?" the young man asked.

The well-dressed Saudi gentleman seated before his mid-afternoon breakfast did not look up. One of the two men attending him pressed a tip into the waiter's hand and escorted him out of the room, closing the door behind him.

Mahmoud Rahmad removed the cloth napkin from the serving cart, then stared down at his decidedly American meal. He did not speak until his assistant returned to the room.

"The timing was truly unfortunate," Rahmad said without looking up. His

English was polished and formal, an accent produced by a British education. His features were smallish and soft, his complexion dusky, and his eyes were as dark as onyx. His black hair was combed straight back and kept neatly in place. A man in his fifties, he obviously took great care with his appearance. "However," he continued, "it was a mistake to leave them behind." He poured himself a cup of the dark coffee while his two subordinates watched in silence.

"But sir," his younger assistant protested, "Kerrigan called him back to the car. Surely Mustafa could not risk being left there."

Rahmad looked up for the first time, taking a moment before he spoke. "Mustafa was wrong not to have completed what he had begun." The young aide grew uneasy under his superior's critical gaze and lowered his eyes. Rahmad turned back to his meal. "How concerned you are for Mustafa. Do you really believe our American friend would have driven away without him?"

"I do not know Kerrigan, sir. I am sorry."

"That is quite all right. Kerrigan is a skilled operative, and he will also be made to answer for his actions. Nevertheless, the problem created still remains."

He poked at his eggs with a fork. "In England they serve kippers," he observed with a smile, which amounted to a slight parting of his lips, revealing white teeth that gleamed in contrast to his brown, oily complexion. "I came to enjoy kippers. In many things I have become infected by occidental ways." He laid down his fork, too perturbed by the notion to continue eating. "Here, for instance, we engage in thought and discussion when action is at a premium."

Rahmad sat back in his chair. "Are we certain that the man they eliminated was McHugh?"

"Yes sir."

"Very well. And they elicited everything they could from him?"

The senior aide assured him with no little satisfaction that James McHugh, who was hiding under the name of James Ryan, was made to talk before he died.

"Very well. Yet we are left with the problem of these other two men. And the policeman."

His aides nodded.

"Mustafa is certain these men did not reach McHugh first?"

"McHugh was going to meet with them this morning. Our men arrived first."

"Which is the reason, of course, they were on that road. Unfortunate timing," he said again, then shook his head.

"No sir," the senior aide disagreed. "It would only have been unfortunate if they had reached McHugh first."

Rahmad raised his eyebrows as if considering that notion. "But these men might have had previous discussions with McHugh. Who knows how much he told to the intermediary . . . what was his name?"

"Peters," the young man replied. "Dan Peters."

"Yes, Peters."

"Mustafa assures us that McHugh told Peters nothing. They were very persuasive in extracting answers."

"I am sure. And this Peters, he was only the go-between. He was to introduce McHugh to the journalist?"

"Yes sir."

Rahmad mulled it over. "Well, Kerrigan is on his way out of the country at this very moment. Mustafa is quite capable of providing for his own safety. Even so, it would be best if all witnesses were removed."

"What of the policeman?" asked the younger assistant. "He is under guard."

"Yes," Rahmad agreed. "The officer may prove more difficult to reach while he remains under special care. Amazing how this country reveres its wounded policemen, as if they should be praised rather than held accountable for their incompetence." He shook his head in disgust. "No, for now the risk would outweigh the benefit. The trooper, he knows nothing of us, or of McHugh. He has no information except the remote possibility he could identify Kerrigan or Mustafa. If he poses any such threat, we can deal with him later. Peters and his friend are the problem." He turned to his younger aide and pointed at him. "You see, there are things that experience can teach you, the most important of which may well be patience."

The young man frowned.

"For now, the other two men pose the real danger. They were to meet McHugh, which means they may know something of our operations. We must be rid of them."

"Yes sir."

"So, we must assign the situation in Woodstock to someone subtle. Peters is in the hospital. There are police everywhere, but they will not be paying any attention to him. Still, taking care of him will require finesse." He uttered a short, hollow laugh. "Perhaps we should choose another blond, blue-eyed friend for the job," he said. "No reason for our Arab brothers to receive all the bad press, should something go awry."

Mahmoud Rahmad, unofficial *charge d'affaires* for al-Qaeda espionage activities in New York, returned to the business of his mid-afternoon breakfast.

"Sir," the senior aide asked, "to whom should we refer the reporter?"

He considered that for a moment. "Find out where he lives and have his home and office searched before he gets back. Once we are sure he has nothing pertaining to our mission, we will eliminate him."

His aides nodded at his obvious logic and made ready to leave when Rahmad spoke again.

"The matter will be handed by Tafallai. He will know what to do."

FIVE

"You look positively beautiful," Jordan said as he entered the room.

"Oh, yeah," Dan Peters responded weakly, then shot a disgusted look at the intravenous tubes that stretched from his arm to the apparatus standing alongside his hospital bed. "I'd feel a lot better if I could borrow someone else's chest for a while."

"Don't look at me," Jordan said. "My chest isn't broad enough to fill your clothes." Peters was a raw-boned type, a few inches shorter but much broader than Jordan.

"Funny man," Peters groaned.

"I don't see why you're making such a fuss. Doctor says it's just a flesh wound."

"Yeah. It's my flesh, though. I feel like a pin cushion, all the needles they're sticking me with." The mild sedation left his speech slow and measured. "How's the kid?"

"Trooper Collins? He'll pull through just fine."

"Good thing for all of us you didn't get hit."

Jordan nodded. "So much for your peaceful existence in upstate New York."

Peters attempted a deep breath, grimaced at the effort then asked, "What the hell is going on here?"

"Like what?"

"Like what happened to Jimmy Ryan?"

Jordan walked to the large window that overlooked a grassy courtyard in front of the hospital. The autumn afternoon had become unseasonably warm, and he watched two young men in shirtsleeves enter the building. "You need some rest."

"I heard two nurses yapping out in the hallway."

"And?"

"Why don't *you* tell me?"

Jordan came back, moved the metal armchair beside the bed and sat down. "I'm not sure yet. It seems the two shooters were on their way back from a visit with your friend Ryan when we ran into them."

Peters worked that over for a moment, the narcotics muddling his ability to think in a straight line. "Maybe not just unlucky."

"Meaning what?"

"Gimme some time, I might sort it out. I'm kinda slow today." He shifted slightly with a grunt.

"You think Ryan told them we were coming?"

"Doesn't look that way. Collins said he stopped them for speeding."

"That so?" He took a moment to have a sip of water then settled back again. "What about Ryan?"

"What about him?"

"Come on, damnit."

Jordan leaned forward in his chair and, speaking very softly, said, "Way I get it, they did a number on him . . . before they killed him."

"Christ."

"Listen, I haven't told the police we were on our way to see him. Better not share that. Not yet. All right?"

"Why?"

"It could mean more trouble for us than we need right now."

"More trouble than getting shot?"

Jordan smiled. "I'm going out to see Ryan's place with Reynolds, the trooper in charge."

"He asks you something, you gonna lie?"

Jordan sighed then sat back. "I won't be volunteering anything."

"Yeah, I guess not," Peters agreed. "So what about me?"

"What about you?"

"You going to keep lying to me?"

"I guess that depends."

"On what?"

Sandor pushed his hair back with the palm of his hand. "You go first."

"What the hell do I know—"

"That's what I'm asking."

Danny's pallid complexion seemed to flush for a moment. "You figure someone found out we were going to see Ryan?"

"That's what I figure."

"Look, I admit our timing was lousy. You think it's more than that?"

"That depends on what else you have to tell me."

Peters struggled to keep his focus. "I told you already. I met Ryan after he got back from Europe. Real quiet guy at first. Met him in the local saloon drinking beers. Got to talking about the service . . . you know how it goes. What branch of the service are you in? What division? Where did you tour?"

"Go on."

Peters' words came a little more easily now. "He was like a lot of the guys who did time overseas, except more so. Always looking over his shoulder, like an old gunfighter."

"And how old was this old gunfighter?"

"Not sure. Somewhere between you and me. Anyway, we got friendlier, talked about Nam and the Gulf. He told me he did a tour in the Orient before doing a stretch in the Middle East. He said he saw a lot, wanted to put some of it on paper but couldn't write a lick. He was thinking about contacting some reporters. That's when I told him about you. A week or so later, he says he wants to meet you."

"Just like that? He was going to dictate his memoirs to me?"

"I told him you were the best."

"At what?"

Dan answered with a frown. "When he got back to me, he said he'd been to the library, looked up a couple of pieces you'd written. He thought you might be the right guy to help him."

Jordan nodded. "I guess I should be flattered."

"Hey, I'm already in pain here, all right. Cut me some slack. Anyway, he said he had some dynamite you could put a match to. Worked with people who knew about al-Qaeda, Qadaffi, Iraq, illegal arms trade, biological and chemical weapons, you name it. Told me he also knew a lot about former GIs who sold out."

"And you figured he was one of them."

"Yeah, that's what I figured."

"And now you figure that these two hit men found out Ryan was talking to you?"

"If they didn't know before, they must know now, right?"

Jordan nodded. "I would assume so. They worked him over pretty good, according to Reynolds."

"Reynolds?"

"I told you, the captain heading up the investigation." Jordan had a look at his friend. "You're out of steam, pal. Get some rest." He stood and placed his hand on Dan's arm.

"Okay, but you gotta know this includes you too now. I mean, if Ryan spilled his guts, he wasn't just talking about me."

"I realize that"

"Whatever Ryan told them, he knew I was bringing you there today, right?"

"I understand."

"You've got to be careful."

"All right, all right."

Peters opened his eyes a bit wider. "So when do you tell me the truth?"

"Later. Take a nap."

"Screw a nap, I want some answers."

"I'm working on it, believe me."

"Give me a break. This guy didn't want to see you because you could write an article for him. He wanted to see you because of your old connections in Washington."

Jordan offered no response.

"When Ryan said he checked you out, he found more than the articles you wrote. Am I right?"

"Maybe."

"So . . . what's going on?" Peters asked.

Jordan reached out and pinched his cheek. "When I figure it out, you'll be the first to know."

"Come on, Jordan. You owe me."

"Owe you? You owe me, pal. I saved your life."

"Bullshit!" Dan bit his lip, catching his breath, then forced a weak smile through a surge of pain. "Nothing but a flesh wound. You said so yourself."

SIX

Operations Officer John Covington received a call in his Langley office about the shootings near Woodstock, New York. He was apprised of the inquiries being made by local authorities, his own sources having already concluded that the dead man was indeed James McHugh. But that identification came too late, both for McHugh and for the Central Intelligence Agency. Covington's team had been searching for him, and under the Foreign Intelligence Surveillance Act they might have learned something sooner through wiretaps and other covert technology. Unfortunately, since the media was all over the government for using FISA to justify domestic spying, intelligence-gathering efforts were severely curtailed on all fronts. So now McHugh was dead and the best the CIA could hope for was that his death would somehow provide them the next lead they desperately needed.

Covington was a slightly built man of fifty with thinning hair, thin lips, and a slender nose that caused Jordan Sandor to once wonder aloud whether those stingy nostrils allowed in enough air to prevent brain damage. He was wearing his customary white button-down shirt and conservative tie to go with a conservative suit and his conservative manner. Whatever romantic image the public had of the typical CIA agent, Covington provided an accurate picture of the men who actually operated inside the Agency, his appearance and demeanor more like an accountant ready for a tough audit than a man poised for dangerous, physical action. He was part of the large corps of administrative personnel who supported the activities of the men and women in the field who risked their lives in anonymous endeavors that sometimes succeeded, but often failed.

WHEN THE CALL came through on his private line, David Fryar knew it had to be trouble. Only a handful of people had the number, and its use was intended only for emergencies. Emergencies were never good news.

He picked up the phone. "Fryar."

The man on the other end did not waste time with a polite greeting. The caller, instantly recognizable to Fryar, demanded, "What the hell happened to those shipments yesterday?"

Fryar fumbled for the right words as he began to explain the customs issues the company faced in getting the shipments out, but the man stopped him.

"Our friend is extremely upset."

David Fryar was president of Loubar Technical Assistance Corporation, a rapidly expanding manufacturer of specialized electronics, with offices recently opened in Paris and Hong Kong. That expansion, and most of its success, was due to the patronage of Fryar's "friend," Vincent Traiman.

They met a few years before, when Fryar was a vice president at Loubar, which was then a struggling electronics firm. Traiman was an operative at Central Intelligence who possessed considerable knowledge of technology, an understanding of foreign markets, and numerous contacts in the Middle East. They had been introduced at a promotional party being hosted by Loubar in Paris, then traveled together to Jiddah when Traiman suggested he might have some valuable contacts there.

Fryar quickly learned that Traiman was already familiar with Loubar products. The company was on the cutting edge and Traiman believed the company could have a bright future, especially in countries where he enjoyed some influence. He told Fryar that only three ingredients were needed to ensure success. First, increased sophistication in the area of surveillance and quasi-military appliances, such as those used in the deployment of chemical weapons, with which the company had been recently experimenting. Second, an aggressive sales force that could provide an appropriate presence throughout Europe, Asia, and the

Middle East. Third, and most interesting to David Fryar, his new friend believed the company needed a change in leadership.

Traiman was both a clear thinker and capable of bringing his plans to fruition. Within a year the former president of the company, a decidedly uncooperative man with limited global vision, met with an unfortunate automobile accident. After some corporate in-fighting, Fryar became head of the company. Under his stewardship the sales force amassed an impressive record of increasing revenues, and Fryar had remained at the helm since, with the Loubar Corporation continuing to grow rapidly in income and international stature.

Along with that success, however, came certain risks. Traiman left government service and became involved with indeterminate principals who were developed into lucrative customers of Loubar. Since the products being sold were often on a proscribed list for shipment to certain unfriendly foreign countries, great pains had to be taken to route these goods through acceptable ports, to describe the contents with special care, and to otherwise cover tracks.

A recent order had proved especially troublesome. So much so, in fact, that before it could be released for shipment to Marseilles, Fryar had interceded and held up the transit papers. He feared that this time Traiman had stepped too far over the line, even for Fryar, and he knew there would be hell to pay for his decision.

"I know he must be disappointed," Fryar said to the caller. "Please tell him that it was a difficult decision, but the matter deserves special attention."

"A difficult decision," the man replied in a mocking tone. "I don't think so."

"We need to review the matter."

"We need the shipment."

Fryar was silent.

"Mr. Groat will be contacting you. You can review it with him." And with that, the line went dead.

MARK BYRNES WAS waiting in his office when Covington arrived to make his report. Byrnes was a handsome man of about sixty with well-defined features, his graying hair cut short and combed close, his blue eyes shrewd in a way his subordinates often found unsettling. He was a product of Harvard and Oxford, the diplomatic corps and State Department, not to mention the breeding of a wealthy family that was as close as America comes to aristocracy. Byrnes had recently been rewarded for his hard work by a promotion from deputy director of operations stationed overseas to deputy director of operations in Washington. He was a man who always knew what he was about.

Covington entered the DD's office and, after polite greetings, Byrnes asked a few questions. Covington's answers were satisfactory.

"So then, you're up to speed."

"I am," Covington agreed.

"This is the only thing I want you working on right now, John. And I want you there right away. McHugh's death may give us the best lead we've had in weeks."

"Yes sir," Covington said.

The deputy director took a look around his large, warmly appointed office. The walls were covered with photographs of Byrnes and the President, Byrnes with various congressmen, and Byrnes with heads of state. He waited as Covington also had a look. It was a reminder of how far he had moved up the chain of command.

"What do we know about Andrioli?" the DD asked.

"We have no lead on his whereabouts. Not yet."

"Even with McHugh dead we still have a chance to get to him"

"Yes sir."

"We're running out of time on this operation, John. We can't announce to the media that there are new security threats without a single positive shred of information in hand."

"I understand."

"I hope you do. I truly hope you do. Now get to New York and find out what you can."

JORDAN SPENT THE late afternoon at the state trooper barracks. A police artist had driven down from Albany and Sandor worked with him to refine the descriptions he had given earlier. They also reviewed a new series of mug shots on the computer, after being granted access to the federal database. They struck out there, but Jordan was not surprised. The more they searched, the more evident it became to him that the two shooters were men who flew below the radar.

For now, he kept those thoughts to himself and struggled to be as patient as he could manage. Matters for the local authorities were fairly chaotic, one of their own having been shot. That was their principal focus. There was also discussion about Ryan, about taking his body to Kingston for an autopsy, and Sandor listened as three junior officers debated the necessity of such action. After all, the youngest of the three argued, there was clear evidence that Ryan had been beaten before getting plugged with two shots from close range. They understood that an autopsy was standard procedure, the trooper said, but what was the point in tearing the corpse apart just to confirm what they already knew?

Sandor had answers he was not giving. The ballistics expert would be interested in the slugs they recovered. They would need to confirm that the shooters on the road had also taken out Ryan. There would also be questions about chemicals that might be found in the dead man's system, and Sandor assumed they would find traces of so-called truth drugs.

While the local law enforcement team debated the possible reasons for the sadistic beating of Ryan prior to his murder, Jordan was certain that he and Dan Peters knew why. Whatever story Ryan had to tell, as Ryan himself had said to Peters, it was dynamite.

The rest of the available police force, including men and women borrowed from neighboring towns and the state, were scurrying around looking for clues, and surveying the roadside scene of the shooting. As far as Sandor reckoned, they were trying to close the barn door after the horses had galloped away.

"You ready, Sandor?" Reynolds came up from behind, all business in front of his men.

"Ready, sir," Jordan said.

THE PLACE RENTED by Jimmy Ryan was a tiny house set back from an unpaved lane that shunted off an access road leading to Route 32. As Reynolds had explained, it was not far from the spot where Collins and Peters had been shot. Jordan simply nodded, realizing he and Dan had only been a few minutes and a couple of miles late.

The dirt driveway kicked up a cloud of dust as Reynolds brought his cruiser to a halt. Two troopers were waiting on the small front porch as the captain and Sandor got out of the car.

"This is Sandor," the captain said. "Guy that helped Jack."

The officers said hello, then offered their thanks.

"So, what have we got here?" Jordan asked.

Neither of the troopers replied.

"Let's have a look," Reynolds said as he led him into the house. The two officers remained on guard at the door.

Dusk was replacing day, and there wasn't much in the way of lighting in the main room. All the same, Jordan made out the scene immediately. Ryan's body had been removed hours ago, but the chair was there, as were the fragments of rope that had bound Ryan to the wooden seat. Splotches of dried blood stained an oval loom rug.

"Nice, eh?"

Jordan nodded. "I guess you got photos of all this. Before they took him out, I mean."

The captain responded with a withering look, and Sandor was reminded again of what sort of commanding officer Reynolds must have been.

"Sorry," Jordan said politely. "Of course, you did."

"Several rolls of film, a videotape, and a hundred digital images, if you care to know."

"Right."

Sandor and Reynolds slowly circled the chair in which Ryan had died, viewing the scene from all angles, each of them envisioning what had happened there.

"No sign of forced entry," Reynolds told him, "but around here, who locks the door? Even so, I get the feeling he knew these guys. No sign of a struggle, no overturned tables, no nothing."

"Maybe. On the other hand, they might have walked in, guns drawn, taken him before he had a chance to react."

Reynolds grunted. "Main question is, What was the point? Look at this place." He extended his arm like he was displaying the third-place prize on a game show. "What the hell would they possibly want? And no sign that the place was searched. Unless he had the Hope Diamond sitting on the table there, what would they be looking for?"

"Information," Jordan said.

The two men stared at each other for a moment.

"Only thing that makes sense," Sandor said.

Reynolds nodded. "They certainly beat the hell out of the poor bastard, that much is obvious."

"Rule out sodium pentathol."

"What's that?"

"Some of the guys talking about the autopsy."

"Yeah," Reynolds agreed. "You don't pump a guy full of truth serum and then beat the hell out of him."

"My thought exactly. Coroner will tell that tale."

"So, not much to see, right?"

Jordan moved slowly around the small area that encompassed most of the modest house, the living room, dining table and the entry to the kitchen. "I assume your men have searched the place," he said over his shoulder.

"Thoroughly."

"Find anything interesting?" he asked as he took it all in, looking for something that might be out of place.

"Nothing," the captain said. "Except one item we thought was odd."

Sandor turned towards him. "I'm all ears."

"This off the record?" Reynolds asked with a wry smile.

"Only if you insist."

The captain came toward him. They were standing face to face at the doorway to the small kitchen. "One of those electronic tickets," he said in a quiet voice, "the kind you get off a computer. Hidden in his dresser. Plane ticket to Paris."

"As in France?"

"Strange thing. For a guy living in this kind of a shack, I mean. First class ticket, leaving tomorrow. And a hotel reservation."

"Going back," Jordan said to himself.

"What's that?"

"Nothing. So you tracked it down?"

"We did. The ticket was booked in the name of James McHugh. Hotel reservation also in the name of James McHugh."

"McHugh? And you ran his prints through—"

"The federal databank. Yeah."

"Don't tell me."

"Our friend Jimmy Ryan was actually one James McHugh."

Sandor did not appear surprised, a fact not lost on Reynolds. "I can tell by the look in your eyes it gets better than that, Captain."

Reynolds nodded. "McHugh was ex-military. His service record looked a lot like yours."

"Meaning?"

"Name, rank, and social security number. Did his duty and *puff*. Finished business. Guy no longer exists after that."

"Uh huh. So we're not talking about a robbery here."

"Not even close." Reynolds hesitated. "And something tells me you knew that before we walked in."

Sandor gave no answer to that. "And when you brought McHugh's name up on the computer?"

"I'm sure all the bells and whistles were going off down in Washington."

"Agreed."

The two troopers at the door were straining to hear the discussion, but missing most of it as Sandor and Reynolds became quieter with each exchange.

"I imagine the feds'll be coming in on this in no time," Jordan said.

"I believe that's affirmative," the captain said. "So what say we cut the crap and you tell me what you know about all this?"

Jordan shook his head. "No more than you do."

The captain leaned even closer now. "That's not good enough, son. I've been up front with you. Now why don't you tell me something I don't know?"

"Like what?"

"Look, I got one man in the morgue, two men in the hospital, and by some incredible coincidence you and the dead man turn out to be some kind of former spooks—all this in a town where six speeding tickets in a week is a crime wave."

"What a mess," Jordan said, doing his best to sound sympathetic.

"That's it? I give you everything I got before the feds show, and all I get from you is 'what a mess'?"

Sandor stared at him without speaking.

"You said something about him going back. What makes you think this guy was ever in France? You told me you never met him."

"And I never did. But I also never said I didn't know anything about him."

"Which makes you better informed than I am right now."

"I'm not trying to be difficult, Captain. There are some things I have to do first."

"Me too, like investigating a murder and two attempts."

"Give me a little time and—"

"I don't have time, Sandor." Reynolds stared into Jordan's eyes, the younger man's unblinking gaze a match for his own. "Something tells me you're gonna need a friend around here pretty soon. You took care of Jack and so you're entitled to something for that, but don't count on it for too much. I can get unfriendly real fast. I think you're jerking me around."

"All right," Jordan said. "Let me sort some of this out, then I'll get back to you."

"You'll get back to me? That's not good enough, Sandor."

"I'm asking you to trust me."

Reynolds lifted his trooper's hat and passed his hand over his thinning scalp. "You're not making it easy."

"I understand, Captain."

"All right," Reynolds said with a rueful expression, "but as far as I'm concerned, you're on a short timeline."

Jordan nodded, then looked around the room again as if he might have missed something. "What did you say the name of that hotel in Paris was?"

Reynolds smiled. "I didn't say." He pulled a note pad from his pocket. "It's called . . . the Pas de Tour," he said, butchering the pronunciation so badly that he had to spell it out. "Mean anything to you?"

"Just that your French is as bad as mine," Jordan replied with a smile.

Reynolds shook his head. "Anything else?"

"Not yet," Jordan said. "Not yet."

SEVEN

It was dark by the time Captain Reynolds had one of his men give Sandor a ride back to Dan Peters' house. Jordan figured the young officer knew less of what was going on than he did, so he managed to keep their discussion brief and close to the surface.

Jordan thanked the trooper as he dropped him off, grateful to be done with everyone and everything for now. It had been a long, draining day and, alone in Dan's small home, he realized how tired he was. He decided to sleep there, then get an early start for home the next morning. He fixed himself a ham and cheese sandwich and, as he was finishing a second bottle of Dan's Budweiser, he telephoned his best friend, Bill Sternlich, in New York.

Sternlich was an articles editor for the *Times*. He and Sandor had met over a decade ago, when Bill was on assignment to the Washington bureau, and Jordan was working for the government. Now they were both in New York, their friendship having stood the test of years, not to mention their philosophic differences.

Professional considerations sometimes made it an uneasy alliance. Jordan could never reveal much about his work and what little he shared with Bill could not be printed. That was the first irony of their friendship. The second was the disparity between Sternlich's liberal beliefs, engendered so relentlessly by the editorial leanings of his newspaper, and Sandor's own individualistic views, which would better be expressed by Ayn Rand than anything on the *Times* Op-Ed pages. The final irony was Jordan's abrupt departure from the Agency and his subsequent decision to enlist in the Fourth Estate, albeit on a freelance basis. Sternlich had given him help, even getting a couple of Sandor's pieces published in the *Times'* Sunday Magazine section.

The main point for Jordan and Bill was that they were friends, which meant something special to each of them.

"You really okay?"

"I'm fine," Jordan said. "Friend of mine, Dan Peters, took a bullet in the side. The trooper was hit pretty hard too. We were lucky to get out."

Neither man said anything for a moment.

"I need a favor, Bill."

"Hey, I'm totally shocked," Sternlich said with one of his short, asthmatic laughs. Their recent history was a bit lopsided in the area of favors given and received. "For a minute there I was afraid you called to ask me to lunch. Or just to say hello. I wouldn't want to die from the shock."

Jordan ignored the sarcasm. "I need some information on a James McHugh. Likely to be classified. You'll probably need to go through one of your government sources."

"Will I?"

"You'll have to move fast, though, before it comes out that the Jimmy Ryan that was murdered up here today was actually one James McHugh."

"That right?"

"Yes. You've got the scoop. Print it right after you get me the dope on this guy."

"And why, may I be so bold to ask, don't you just call one of your old cronies in Langley to get this *whatever*, this deep background information?"

"Even guys I still trust there will balk. I was involved in the shooting."

"Mind if I ask, then, why I would I want to do this?"

"Who knows? Full-length article?"

"My by-line or yours?"

"I'll flip you for it." Sternlich forced a derisive laugh. "Come on Bill, I need your help. I have a feeling there's something big going on here."

Sternlich issued a long, theatrical sigh into the phone. "I don't know what I can do, but I'll take a run at it."

"You're a pal."

"And what am I supposed to be looking for?"

"I'm not sure. Not exactly. See if you can find out where he's been the past couple of years. Check out his government service. Get addresses, prior contacts, phone numbers, identification numbers, the usual tap dance."

"Uh huh."

Jordan could tell that Sternlich was writing things down, a good sign. "And Bill, see what connection he had to Paris."

"Paris?"

"I'm coming back tomorrow. Call you in the morning."

"I may have to trade favors to get this. You understand that?"

"Of course."

"You'll owe me for this one."

"No problem."

"I mean it, Jordan."

"I need this Billy. I wouldn't ask if I didn't."

JORDAN LEFT WOODSTOCK early the next day and drove south, the bright October sun rising to his left as he headed towards New York City. He guided his aging Land Rover along the sweeping curves and extended straightaways.

Jordan's mind raced as he drove in silence, the radio and his cell phone turned off. He gazed out at the road ahead, realizing that the danger he had faced yesterday would only intensify in the hours and days ahead.

Whatever James McHugh had known, his gruesome death was proof of its importance. His murderers had inflicted a sadistic beating, and when there was nothing left for McHugh to save, strapped in that wooden chair facing certain death, he would have done anything to spare himself those final moments of pain and degradation. He would have revealed anything his murderers wanted to know, including his intention to meet with Sandor and Peters, which left them both as marked men.

HE ARRIVED IN the city, pulled his car up to the curb in the "No Parking" zone in front of the old brownstone where he lived on West 76th Street, then placed an expired Press Card in the windshield. He ran up the front steps and, unlocking the front door to the building, he entered the vestibule and grabbed his mail. His eyes adjusted to the filtered light as he climbed the stairs to his third floor apartment, rifling through the bills and advertisements as he went.

38

He got to his apartment, put the key in the door and stepped inside, still concentrating on the mail in his hands. Then he looked up.

The place was in shambles.

Jordan left the door open behind him as he moved farther inside, his nerves on alert as he placed his mail on the foyer table and warily stepped into the living room. It appeared that everything had been turned inside out. His brown tufted leather couch was sliced open, clumps of stuffing scattered all over the room, the brass and glass cocktail table shoved against the wall, two chairs and a mahogany cabinet turned over, even the Oriental rug lifted and yanked to the side. Where looking through a cabinet would have sufficed, the drawer had been pulled out, turned upside down and smashed.

Sandor moved cautiously to the bedroom. If possible, it looked even worse. The mattress was slashed, closet and dresser taken apart, clothing scattered all over the floor. He stepped inside the closet, reached up to a hidden compartment above the top shelf, and pulled away a false panel. He was relieved to find the contents, which consisted of small arsenal, intact. He lifted out his Walther PPK .380 and drew back the slide far enough to see the first round was chambered.

He remained quiet, his movements studied. He could not be certain the intruder had gone. He checked the bathroom and the small kitchen, ready for an assault from anywhere in the apartment. The second bedroom, which he used as his office, was also a disaster. His filing cabinets had been emptied, the leather chair knocked over, his antique roll-top desk searched, papers strewn across the room. The intruders had ripped through and savaged the most intimate details of his private life. His writing, letters, even personal souvenirs had been examined and destroyed.

He walked back into the living room, slowly surveying the damage. It left the apartment with an eerie coldness, as if he himself had been stripped and beaten by faceless strangers then left alone to suffer the violation and indignity.

When he was convinced he was alone, he went back and slammed the front door.

Make no mistake about it, he told himself, *these people are killers, and whatever they want, whatever they believe Jimmy McHugh might have told you, they'll sure as hell kill you to get it.*

Jordan went to the bathroom, placed his gun on the counter, and leaned over the sink to splash cold water on his face. He had a look in the mirror, staring at himself for a moment, studying his dark features, preparing himself.

Back in the bedroom, he sorted through the clutter of shirts and trousers that were scattered across the floor. He had shaved and showered at Dan's earlier that morning, but was still wearing clothes from the day before. He picked up a pair of gray slacks, a long-sleeved, black polo sweater, and found his favorite black loafers. He quickly changed then returned to the living room, righted a chair, and sat down to make a call. As he reached for the telephone, he saw the line had been cut.

"Sonuvabitch," he said.

EIGHT

Rahmad's assassin, Tafallai, was strolling down 76th Street. It was a quiet street by New York City standards, rows of brownstones lining both sides, trees planted in pavement cutouts, circled by short, wrought-iron grating. He moved at an unhurried pace, alert to any movement around him, as he approached Sandor's building.

When he received the call informing him that his target had returned home, he had stopped at a Korean market and purchased the largest bunch of flowers they had.

He stopped and had a look up and down the street. There was nothing to make him suspicious, no indication that the police had responded to a call about the break-in. He resumed walking until he was directly in front of Sandor's building, then he turned and headed up the stairs.

JORDAN HAD PACKED his black leather overnight bag with a few articles of clothing and most of the contents he retrieved from the hidden compartment in his closet, including the Smith & Wesson .45. The smaller handgun, a Walther PPK .380, was already tucked into the back of his waistband.

He needed to make a couple of calls before he left town and, although he had a clean cell in the bag that he had never used before, he didn't want to use that line. Not yet.

Florence Carter was an attractive black woman who lived directly below him, an actress of stage and screen whenever she could get the work, a waitress the rest of the time.

It was not yet noon, and she was home.

Jordan told her he was having phone problems. She let him in and said he should make himself comfortable.

"You need some privacy?" she asked.

"No, I don't think so. But thanks."

She offered him something to drink, but he passed.

"Say, Florence, you didn't hear anything going on upstairs last night? Or early this morning?"

She shook her head. "I was working last night. What sort of thing you mean?"

"I was away overnight. Thought someone might have been in my apartment."

"In your apartment?"

"It's nothing. Just my phones are out. Service guy might have come by or something."

"No. Not that I know of. My phone is fine."

"Good. Well, I'll just be a couple of minutes."

"Take your time," she told him.

Jordan sat on the couch and picked up the cordless telephone. When he checked his answering service, there were several messages, including a voicemail from Reynolds in the past hour.

His first call was to Sternlich.

"How bad?" he asked after Jordan had told him about his apartment.

"Like a small tornado ran through my place."

"Call the police, Jordan."

"No. Not yet, at least."

"What are you waiting for?"

"I had enough of the *gendarmes* yesterday."

"And what happens when these intruders make a return visit?"

"Maybe I'll ask them to clean up."

"I think you ought to make yourself scarce for a while."

"The idea had crossed my mind. What've you found out for me?"

"Nothing yet. I'm a reporter, not a magician."

"You're not even a reporter anymore. You're an editor, remember? Use your connections and get me some answers."

"I'll work on it. Please call the police."

"First I'm going to see Beth," Jordan told him.

"Beth?"

"We have a lunch date. Thought maybe I should keep it."

"Why not?" Sternlich said in frustration. "Give her my best."

"I will. Just call me when you have something."

Jordan hung up and began dialing a new number.

"I owe you a buck, Florence. I've got to call upstate."

"Don't be silly," she said as she answered a buzz from the front door of their small building.

Jordan was transferred three times before he finally got through to Captain Reynolds. "I have some news for you from down here," he said, then described what he had found when he returned home. "Please don't tell me to call the locals. You and I know this is no ordinary B and E."

Reynolds didn't disagree. "But you should have the place photographed and dusted for prints."

"I haven't touched much, believe me. I'd just prefer to put that on hold for a little while."

"Reason?"

Jordan thought it over, but was distracted by the conversation Florence was having over the intercom.

"I'm getting enough attention right now," he told Reynolds. "Might be better if these clowns don't know I've been to my apartment yet."

"That assumes you're not being watched," Reynolds warned. "And these are not clowns, Sandor. You know that already. I've got to advise you to report this. Off the record, I never heard a thing about it."

"Agreed, and thanks."

"Isn't that something?" Florence was talking to herself. "Who'd be sending me flowers today?"

"How're the patients doing this morning?" Jordan continued.

"Early report, they're both stable. Your friend is in better shape than Collins—"

"What did you say, Florence?" asked Jordan.

"—may be safer up here—" Reynolds was still talking.

43

"Flowers," she said.

"—got men all over the place—"

"What's that?" Jordan asked over his shoulder.

"I said—" said the captain, beginning to answer Jordan's question as though it had been meant for him.

"Not you."

"What?"

"Hold on, Captain," Jordan said, then turned to Florence. "Is it your birthday or something?"

"No."

"Were you expecting flowers from someone?"

"Jordan, what's going on?" Captain Reynolds' voice sounded tinny coming from the receiver.

Florence saw the look in Sandor's eyes and her smile instantly vanished. "No. No, I'm not."

"Is your door locked?"

"No," she said, feeling scared and not knowing why.

"Lock it," he ordered her. "Now."

She was suddenly so frightened that she couldn't move, so Jordan raced across the room and bolted the door himself.

"Jordan? . . . Jordan—" Reynolds' voice was growing anxious.

"Captain," Jordan said into the phone, "I think I've got an unwelcome visitor on his way upstairs. I'll call you back."

"Call the poli—" Reynolds barked, but Jordan had already hung up.

"Listen, Florence," Sandor said, "just stay cool and quiet and we'll be all right."

"This has something to do with last night, right? Your apartment? The telephones, like you were asking?"

"Just stay calm, we'll be fine." Even as he spoke the words, he remembered.

The look on his face froze her. "What is it?"

"My door," he said. "I left my door open." Jordan also remembered the .45 he had left upstairs in the leather bag. He cursed himself—a year in from the field and as rusty as an old hinge.

"Look—" she began, but Jordan help up his hand again.

"This guy who says he has flowers, he may be looking for me. He probably rang your buzzer to get into the building. One out of eight apartments, right? If he was really bringing you flowers he'd be knocking on your door by now."

The look on her face told him she understood.

"Take the phone, go into the bathroom, lock the door, and call the police. Tell them there's a burglary in progress. Tell them the man is armed. Give them the address. Then get in your bathtub and keep down till I tell you to come out. Got it?"

Florence nodded, then took the phone and punched in 9-1-1 as she hurried into the bathroom.

NINE

Tafallai was already in the building, walking up the stairs with a bouquet of flowers in his left hand. He stopped two steps below Florence's landing when the metallic sound of a deadbolt sliding into place resonated in the hallway.

Was her door being opened or locked?

Tafallai trusted his instincts, relying on his ability to evaluate danger. And to survive. Would this woman unbolt her door but not open it? Perhaps if she were waiting for him to knock. But something didn't feel right.

He laid down the flowers and gripped the butt of his automatic, drawing it carefully from the holster, the barrel lengthened by a silencer. Then, keeping low to ensure that he could not be seen from her peephole, he advanced to the head of the staircase, where he stayed in his crouch and waited. There was nothing but silence throughout the building.

In the small entry foyer he had tried ringing two other apartments with female names on the directory, neither answering, before he buzzed Florence Carter. Single or married, old or young, he knew that women generally abandoned caution at the prospect of a flower delivery. Florence Carter and the bouquet was his entry ticket into the building.

He planned to deliver the flowers, with a note from "Your Secret Admirer." Then he would begin downstairs as she closed the door behind him. She would have no suspicion of him, no cause to retain even the vaguest recollection of his appearance as she took the flowers into her flat and read the note. Once she shut her door, he would turn and head back up to Sandor's apartment, dispose of his target, then return to the street and lose himself in the crowd.

But now something felt wrong. His man had reported Sandor's return, which meant Sandor would have discovered that his apartment had been vandalized. But no police had been to the building yet. *Why?*

The sound of the deadbolt had persuaded him to move swiftly. He would forego the delivery and head directly to Sandor's flat. He turned back for the bouquet and used the flowers to hide the automatic, just in case the woman opened the door. If she did, he would tell her he had trouble finding her door. Tafallai nodded to himself. This was the move.

FLORENCE STOOD ANXIOUSLY in the sanctuary of her cramped bathroom, worrying in the silence, expecting a sound, an action, a voice. She was whispering into her cordless phone, urging the operator to hurry.

Jordan was standing at Florence's front door, straining to pick up any hint of movement in the stairwell. He felt the sensations he knew well, the dryness of mouth, moist hands, and pounding chest. For a moment he wondered if his imagination had run wild. He told himself he would have quite a laugh over this one when it turned out to be nothing more than a flower delivery. But if someone was delivering flowers, where was he? *How long does it take to walk up two flights of stairs?*

Jordan looked through the peephole and saw nothing.

TAFALLAI CLIMBED FAR enough up the next set of steps to see the landing. There was Sandor's door standing ajar.

He froze for an instant, like an animal on the prowl suddenly confronted by an unexpected situation, using the moment to weigh every possible implication before initiating his next action. When he moved again he kept as low as possible, creeping to the head of the stairwell. He put the flowers down and extended his weapon slightly, keeping it close to his side where he could not be easily disarmed by a sweeping move. But no attack came as Tafallai cautiously and efficiently moved inside and searched the apartment, stepping lightly, still aware that Sandor might be waiting.

It did not take long for him to confirm that Sandor was not there. He spotted the leather bag on the bed, had a quick look inside, and smiled at the sight of the automatic. Wherever Sandor was, he was unarmed.

Tafallai then realized that Sandor's flat was directly above Florence Carter's. Only scant minutes had elapsed since he heard the bolt turn on the floor below. His instincts told him that Sandor was in the apartment he had selected for his means to enter the building. He picked up the bouquet, left Sandor's apartment, and moved quietly back down the stairs.

THE ONLY SOUND Jordan heard was the faint creak of floorboards from his apartment above. He was angry at himself for leaving his door open and, for a fleeting moment, considered bolting from Florence's apartment and making for the street. But that wouldn't take the girl out of harm's way. If he took her with him, with such a slight lead, they would become too easy a target, especially if the man upstairs had backup waiting outside.

There was also the option of taking a run upstairs, but Jordan could not be sure where the man was or which of them would get off the first shots. And again, he had the girl to think about.

Then he heard the dull sound of steps heading back down the stairs and knew it was too late now to do anything but stay where he was. Jordan was loath to do nothing while waiting for the police, even it if was the obvious move. It simply was not his style. He would prefer to confront the man, to see if he was one of the shooters from the day before, to learn what he could. He realized that once the sirens came wailing down the street, his opportunity would be lost.

So Jordan stood by the door and waited and listened and struggled to come up with a way to protect Florence and still make a move.

TAFALLAI CREPT QUIETLY down the stairs, resuming his crouch, until he was in the middle of the landing. He reached up quickly and, using the flowers to muffle the sound, shattered the small overhead light fixture with a swipe of his Glock 9mm, sending tiny bits of glass to the floor and bathing the landing in a shadowy darkness before he knocked on Florence Carter's door.

"Miss Carter. I have your flowers."

There was no response.

"Miss Carter. It's the man from the flower shop." He knocked again.

JORDAN HEARD THE dull *pop* of the light bulb breaking. A quick look through the peephole revealed nothing but darkness. He was startled at the sudden knock at the door and a man's voice calling Florence's name. The accent was foreign, the voice sure and unhurried.

Now he and this man stood face to face, separated only by the door. Who knew how long it would take the police to respond at this time of day? Even with sirens blaring, the traffic would be a mess. It might only be ten minutes, but it might as well be days. Jordan considered turning the bolt and yanking the door open, but the door opened in, not out, which would give the other man the edge if Jordan was going to charge at him. He had no choice, he decided, but to hold his position.

"MISS CARTER, I cannot just leave the flowers here." The voice betrayed a growing impatience. "You must sign for them." Tafallai knocked again, then grabbed the knob and gave it a short, firm twist. The woman who had buzzed him into the building was not answering, which meant he was right—she was not alone in the apartment. She was with Jordan Sandor.

JORDAN WATCHED AS the knob jimmied back and forth. The moment of silence that followed was shattered when Tafallai slammed his heel against the door. He wanted to draw Sandor to the door in front of him to brace it shut. He gave a second hard kick. And a third. Then he fired three shots, the rounds spitting through the silencer and splintering their way into the wooden door.

Jordan dropped to his knees at the sound of the muffled explosions, the crackle of fragmenting wood, the impact of slugs flattening on the fireproof metal insert reinforcing the door. He lunged to the side at the next thrusting kick against the weakened door. He stayed on his knees, his body straining to keep the door secure against another assault.

Tafallai fired two more shots, this time targeting the lock, the bullets caroming so loudly off the brass that Florence uttered a scream from the bathroom, provoking Tafallai to spend his last four shots in the nine-round clip.

The old door held fast.

"*Ibn himar!*"

SANDOR ADJUSTED HIS position, mindful of what might come next. The man might have explosives, or he might change to armor-piercing shells that would rip through the reinforced door. He listened, the momentary silence more frightening than the fusillade that had come before.

TAFALLAI REPLACED THE clip in his automatic and fired another series of shots.

Police sirens could be heard in the distance, and whether or not they were coming for him, he would not take the risk. He cursed loudly, knowing that for now he had failed. He had wasted too much time, performed too haphazardly.

He fired two more shots at the center of the door as he turned away, then ran down the stairs, past the flowers scattered on the landing. He replaced his Glock in its holster and, closing his coat, he strode down the steps and onto the street, disappearing around the corner just before a New York City Police squad car arrived on the scene.

ONCE JORDAN HEARD the shooter run downstairs, he replaced the Walther in his waistband and let Florence out of her bathroom. He managed to calm her enough to explain that they were now safe. "It's all over," he told her. "He's gone. Help is on the way." He started to pull away, saying he was going upstairs to check his apartment, but she grabbed his arm.

"Wh—where are you going? Don't leave!"

"Listen—"

"You can't leave me here!" The more Sandor tried to get free the more she tightened her grip.

"Listen to me!" For reasons he could not explain to her, Jordan wanted no part of the local authorities, not now. Someone was trying to kill him, and he needed to get out of there before he got tied up in hours of questioning and bureaucratic time wasting. And the longer he waited the less chance he would have to follow his attacker. "The police are coming. They're here. Just outside," he said, pointing toward the window. "You can hear them."

Florence began to loosen her hold on Jordan as the sirens grew louder and more reassuring. He gently but firmly removed his forearm from her grasp and rubbed the marks her fingers had imprinted on his flesh. He sat her on the couch and went to her refrigerator and poured her a glass of wine to calm her nerves.

"It's all right now. The police are here," he told her again. He was out of time and had no intention of spending the next twelve hours down at the local precinct answering questions and looking at another ream of mug shots while explaining things he had no interest in explaining.

"Look," he said, "I have to go."

Florence was too numb to speak. She remained on the couch, barely managing a nod.

"I'll be right back," he assured her. He made a motion to leave and she began to protest, but was too exhausted to offer any resistance. Jordan did his best to give her a comforting smile then headed out, shutting her splintered door behind him.

He raced upstairs to his apartment, pulled on his jacket, grabbed his leather bag, and went to his front door.

The police could be heard coming up the stairs to Florence's landing. He waited and watched from the shadows as the officers surveyed the evidence of the shooting, drew their weapons, and knocked on the shredded door. The moment they entered her apartment would be Jordan's only chance to get out of the building, and he took it. Once he heard her door close, he hurried down the three flights of stairs, then slowed to a saunter as he headed outside.

He looked up and down the street, but there was nothing unusual except the double-parked police cruiser. There was no one to follow, no leads to pursue.

He turned for Columbus Avenue, where he hailed a cab and headed south toward Midtown.

TEN

Dan Peters had dozed fitfully in his hospital bed, the discomfort of his wound and the intrusions of doctors and nurses throughout the night making it difficult to sleep. All of this was complicated by the confluence of memories and dreams that kept his mind spinning, awake or asleep. The memories would not go away.

It was daylight now, he noticed, but that made no difference. He was still trying to sleep.

His eyes opened slightly when yet another young doctor came into the room and stood over his bed. He adjusted the intravenous apparatus that fed him a steady flow of glucose solution and antibiotics. Peters closed his eyes again, not seeing the doctor inject a clear substance into the tube that ran from the plastic sack of fluid into his arm.

"Have a good rest," the doctor said. Peters was happy to hear the suggestion. Maybe they were finally going to leave him alone for a while.

The doctor walked out of the room, nodding at a nurse who approached as he made his way down the long corridor. She responded with an automatic smile what was gradually replaced with an uncertain look. She slowed and turned to see him reach the end of the hallway and turn the corner.

When two uniformed troopers came out of the elevator, he stopped, made a show of looking at some papers he was holding, then made a gesture with his hand as if he had forgotten something. He turned back, stepping quickly around the corner and through the entrance to the stairway.

One of the troopers followed him until he disappeared around the corner. He took a quick look into Peters' room, but saw nothing unusual there.

The nurse came out of another patient's room, and the trooper stopped her. "Hey, who was the doctor who just came out of Peters' room?"

She shook her head. "I don't know him," she said. "I've never seen him before."

"Call for a doctor right away. Have Peters checked out," the officer said, grabbing his radio and breaking into a trot back for his partner. "All stations. We've got some suspicious activity on three," he reported into the walkie-talkie. "Cover the lobby and check the elevators for an unidentified man, dressed like a doctor. Five ten, Caucasian, brown hair." The best he could do after a brief glimpse.

The young man they were looking for was already running down the interior staircase, removing his white lab coat as he went, the syringe still in the pocket. He dropped the coat to the floor as he neared the door to the lobby and then removed the wig he was wearing, his blond crewcut in stark contrast to the longer, darker hairpiece. He adjusted the brown sport coat he had worn underneath the white jacket and put on a pair of eyeglasses. As two troopers were responding to the radio alert from upstairs, he stepped calmly into the lobby. He appeared not to notice two officers rushing to the elevators and three others running to the stairwell.

They were too late. Dan Peters' murderer reached the exit, stepped outside the building, then strode quickly to a waiting car that sped him away.

ELEVEN

Jordan arrived at the Algonquin early for his lunch date with Beth. He made himself comfortable in one of the faded armchairs and settled down to wait. He usually enjoyed the serenity of this old hotel, pleased for the moment to wrap himself in the solace of plush cushions and a stiff drink. He also appreciated the connection between this venerated room and the literary lights of days past, something Bill Sternlich found endlessly amusing.

Sandor was lost in thought, plotting his next move. Then, shaking his head at a bad idea, he heard, "Hello Jordan."

Her voice startled him. He hadn't noticed her come up from behind.

You're out of practice, he warned himself.

He turned and said, "How long have you been there?"

"Boy, that's some greeting," she replied. "I just got here." She looked down at the table. "Whiskey? Kind of heavy before lunch."

"Tennessee whiskey," he corrected her as he stood, then gently kissed her cheek. He caught a hint of perfume, recognizing her fragrance, wondering why he hadn't noticed it as she came up behind him. The scent evoked a flash of re-membrances, the moments of laughter and anger and passion, her soft, warm body next to his, and ultimately the realization again of why it was so difficult to let her go. "It's early, I know, but it's already been a rough day. Sit down."

Beth Sharrow took the chair opposite his, easing herself gracefully into the seat. She was always graceful. "Bourbon." she said thoughtfully. "I think I'll go with something a little less potent."

For a moment he lost himself in the hazel eyes and confident but curious smile he knew so well.

"You look like you're in a trance," Beth said. "Not wearing your hero's laurels very well, are you?"

"My heroics are yesterday's news, unfortunately. Boys in the office having fun with this?"

"I wouldn't know."

"Come on, Beth."

He had met her years before on a visit to the New York office of the CIA, where they housed office personnel, communications experts, and a huge retinue of computer geeks. Jordan thought Beth was one of the best analysts in the Agency.

"Al Tamucci started a pool," she admitted, referring to one of the computer techies he knew.

"For what? For when I'm going to buy it?"

"No. For when you're coming back to work for the Company."

"Not likely," he said.

She nodded. "How's Dan."

"He's a tough old s.o.b. He'll be all right," he said, then followed that with a quick shake of his head and a faraway look, as if deciding whether to reveal something he wasn't ready to share.

Beth recognized the look. "What is it?"

He hesitated, then said, "Someone broke into my apartment."

"What?"

"I didn't want to tell you on the phone."

Beth's smile had melted into a look of concern. "When?"

"Not sure. Yesterday. Last night. Early this morning. They wrecked the place, whenever they were there."

An elderly waiter in a dark, red waistcoat came by and asked if the young lady would care for a cocktail.

"Uh, a white wine, please. Chardonnay, if you have that."

"White wine," Jordan teased. "Here, at the Algonquin?"

"Please, Jordan, tell me what happened."

"All right, but Dorothy Parker must be spinning in her grave."

The waiter was still standing there.

Jordan glanced down at his glass. He said "I'm fine for now," and the man trudged off to get Beth her wine.

"I don't know what happened," Jordan told her. "I don't even know if it's related to yesterday."

"That's nonsense and you know it. There are no such things as coincidences, isn't that what you taught me?"

"Did I say that?"

"Why would they be after you, though?"

"I don't know yet."

"I thought the problem upstate was just . . ."

"Bad timing? An ill wind? Wrong place at the wrong time?"

She shook her head. "I wish you weren't so amused."

Jordan took a swallow of the caramel-colored liquor. "I'm not amused," he said, "believe me. You should see my living room."

Beth searched his dark brown eyes for some sign of fear, but there was none. There was only that look of fascination that had always infuriated her so. "What did the police say?" she asked.

"I haven't called the police yet."

"Why?"

"I will, but not yet. There are some things I want to find out first."

"Jordan, you've got to call the authorities."

"The authorities? Kind of vague advice there, Beth. Maybe I should call the Company and have them traipsing around my life again."

"Maybe you should."

Jordan shrugged. "What's the difference when I call? My couch will still be a goner when I get home tomorrow?"

"Tomorrow?"

"I thought going back there today might be a bad idea."

"You're right," she agreed, then paused. "You can stay at my place. If you'd like."

"Thanks." He lifted his glass again, but didn't drink. "I wouldn't want to interfere with any of your plans."

"Give me a break, Jordan."

He smiled at the sudden flash of anger. "Thanks, really, but I should go upstate today and see Danny, check out what they've found so far. I'm not sure what I'll be doing after that. Maybe I should call an interior decorator."

She shook her head again in that disapproving way he found both charming and annoying. "You know, Jordan, I'd feel a lot better if you seemed less entertained and a little more concerned."

The waiter returned with her wine, which provided Jordan momentary escape from her critical gaze.

"Believe me," he said as the waiter ambled away, "I'm concerned. For starters, I got shot at yesterday. My friend actually *was* shot. And now my apartment looks like a bomb hit it." He held up his glass and said, "Here's to safe roads ahead," then waited her out until she gave up staring at him and took up her wine. They touched glasses and he drank off a fair sized gulp of his Jack Daniels. "Hey, come on. It's bad luck if you don't drink after a toast."

She sipped some of the Chardonnay, then replaced the glass on the small, wooden cocktail table. "You're not a field agent any more, Jordan. You're not an agent at all. You're flying solo on this, unless you come in."

"That's not happening."

"All right. So tell me the truth. What were they looking for in your apartment? You?"

"I don't think they were searching for me when they slashed my mattress open."

She frowned. "What, then?"

"I really don't know. Papers or something, that's my guess. Something I don't actually have, if you want to know."

"Papers having to do with what?"

"That's what I need to figure out."

"Why not let me take this in? Let us figure it out. Stay with me for a few days, let our people do what they can do."

"I'm not ready for that yet. And you've got to consider that whoever broke in will eventually come looking for me. How safe would it be for you if I led them to your door?"

"Well then you need protection. This isn't your fight anymore, Jordan."

"You may be right," he said. Then he leaned forward and took her hand in both of his, softly kissing her open palm. "With everything that's happened, I'm just glad to see you."

She took her hand back slowly. "Sure. So let's get down to it. You didn't keep our lunch date today, with everything that's happened, just to tell me how much you've missed me. What do you want?"

"Want? I wanted to see you."

Beth sighed. "All right, now you've seen me. What else?"

Jordan sat back and looked at her. "Well, you might get me some information."

TAFALLAI HAD BEEN waiting for the call. The team that was tracking Sandor told him they had picked him up again when he got in the cab on Columbus Avenue, followed him to 44th Street, and saw him enter the Algonquin.

Tafallai arrived and made eye contact with his spotter, dismissing him, and then quickly surveyed the area. There was no sense making an attempt on Sandor in a crowded hotel. Instead, he entered a small poster shop directly across the street from the hotel, pretending to browse through photos of old movie stars. From there he kept an eye on the entrance to the Algonquin and awaited his next opportunity.

JORDAN AND BETH agreed it was best to skip their lunch, once he promised to go directly to the police before returning upstate. It was a lie, of course, and he suspected that she knew it. All the same, she agreed to find out what she could about James McHugh. Jordan promised to call her as they said goodbye in front of the Algonquin. Beth closed her coat for the short walk back to her office. Then he gave her a kiss and sent her on her way before turning east toward Fifth Avenue.

The autumn afternoon carried a damp, gray chill, so he turned up his collar and hunched his shoulders as he walked along 44th Street. It was wonderful, he mused, how a couple of drinks and the cool air had him believing that he would figure something out before it was too late. Now he needed to clear his head for more serious considerations, pleased to be taking the short walk.

Beth disappeared around the corner at the Avenue of the Americas. But before Jordan had gotten fifty yards from the hotel, a black sedan pulled up to the curb beside him. A beefy man in a dark suit stepped out and blocked his path.

The car was so obviously a standard US government-issue vehicle that it didn't even occur to Jordan to reach for his automatic. He simply watched as the man held up an identification card and badge.

"Mr. Sandor," he said, "you need to come with us."

TAFALLAI HAD WATCHED Jordan and Beth part company on the street. He waited a few moments then left the shop. He had just begun to follow Jordan when he saw the black sedan pull up to the curb and a man, obviously some sort of government agent, intercept Jordan. Without hesitation, he reversed direction and went after Beth.

TWELVE

Sandor stood there, staring at the man without speaking.

"Mr. Sandor, I'm Agent Springs. FBI." The man was about five feet ten and sturdily built with short hair, dull features, and an even duller affect. He was still holding up his identification when he repeated, "You need to come with us."

"Is this about the parking ticket?" Jordan asked.

Agent Springs responded with a frown. As Sandor knew only too well, unlike the sedan, a sense of humor is most definitely not standard US government issue. "We need to speak with you, sir. Immediately."

Jordan told him he would just as soon speak with him another time, but neither Springs nor the second agent, still seated at the wheel of the car, were budging.

"Please get in."

Sandor nodded. "Right. Why don't you make an appointment with my secretary, and I'll be happy to meet with you. Say, next Thursday."

"We prefer you come with us now, sir."

"Prefer, as in, 'you're under arrest'?"

Springs' demeanor was as insipid as his eyes. "You're not being arrested."

"Well, good. Then you won't mind if I make a quick call and change my plans. I'll only be a minute." Without waiting for a reply, Jordan smiled and turned away, stepping towards the front of the Harvard Club. He pulled his cell phone out of his leather bag, powered it up and dialed Captain Reynolds. When the call was answered on the third ring, he said, "Jordan Sandor here. Looking for Captain Reynolds. It's urgent."

"Mr. Sandor? Yes, hold on," the trooper told him.

This time, the captain picked up the call at once. "Sandor? I've been trying to reach you."

"I figured that. The feds have arrived, right?"

"Yes, but that's not why I've been trying you. I'm sorry to tell you, I've got some bad news."

"I'm listening."

Reynolds paused. "Mr. Peters is dead."

He felt all the air leave his chest in one sudden rush. Then he steadied himself and tried to keep his voice quiet. He stole a quick look at Agent Springs, who remained standing there, not moving. "How the hell can he be dead?"

"Doctors don't know what happened yet. They're going to do an autopsy. It appears he had a massive coronary."

"What?"

"A doctor was spotted coming out of his room this morning, someone the nurse on duty had never seen before."

"Did they catch him?"

"No. Whoever he was, he got away."

"Drugs?"

"Guy in forensics says his IV might've been injected with something. We should have an answer by tomorrow morning. Maybe even tonight."

"Look. I can't come up now. I was going to but the feds are here to take me in."

"You'll be better off," Reynolds said. "They're all over us too."

"Why? What are they telling you makes this federal?"

"Off the record?"

"As agreed. You're telling me my friend is dead. I need to know."

"Maybe two friends, right?"

"No," Jordan said. "I told you the truth about Ryan or McHugh or whoever he was. I never met him."

"Right. Well, all they'll say is that it has something to do with national security. That's the way they're playing it, anyway."

Sandor nodded to himself, but did not respond.

"They told me I'm not supposed to discuss the case with you. Not even about Peters."

"Perfect. And I bet you just love being pushed aside by a lot of DC suits."

"My poker face is probably off a little. One of my boys gets shot in the neck, a local guy is murdered and now they say another has a suspicious heart attack."

"Suspicious? You're kidding, right?'

"I don't need you rubbing my nose in it too."

Jordan gave no answer, which was apology enough for Reynolds.

"They threw us aside like we're the Hardy Boys, just a bunch of hicks getting in their way."

"And now they're here for me."

"I'm not surprised. Are you?"

"No."

"You and your friend, you were on your way to see McHugh, am I right?"

"That's what they said?"

"That's what I think."

"Okay, off the record, as you like to say. We were."

"And whoever these people are, they took out Peters, then came after you in New York."

"Looks that way."

"Why? Not because you and Peters were witnesses. Collins was a witness too."

"Collins is under guard."

"Peters would have been under guard too, if you had leveled with me."

Sandor felt the slap of his accusation. "That's unless you believe Danny had a heart attack."

"Crap," Reynolds said.

"That airline ticket you told me about. It was round trip, right?"

"It was."

"In the name of McHugh?"

"Right."

"What airline?"

"Air France. They confiscated it along with everything else we had on the case."

FBI Agent Springs cleared his throat. Jordan turned to him and held up his forefinger. "I better go," he told Reynolds.

"I've got one tidbit might interest you."

"I'm listening."

"Did you know McHugh had a sister?"

"How would I know that?"

"Just asking. She arrived this morning, after we talked. Drove up to the house, met two of my men protecting the crime scene. Got here before the FBI took over."

"A visit from his sister a day after he's shot?"

"That's all I know. Feds took her away for questioning as soon as they got into town."

Jordan nodded. "Thanks."

"Remember, Sandor, you didn't hear any of this from me."

"You and I are fine, Captain, believe me."

"Good, cause now I gotta advise you to go with them."

"Trust me, at the moment I don't have any choice."

"And we didn't have a conversation about any of this, just so we're clear."

"Crystal." Jordan thought about the leather bag he was carrying, with the automatic zipped into the inside pocket, together with his cash and passports. He wondered how long it would be before the FBI searched him and everything he had with him. "What about Danny's autopsy?"

"I'll let you know."

"You're a good man, Captain."

"I think you are too. Hope I'm not wrong."

"That's it then?"

"That's all I got. Maybe the boys in the button-down shirts can tell you more."

Jordan signed off, then made a show of dropping his cell phone so he could bend over and take the Walther automatic from his belt and slide it inside the bag.

Dan Peters was dead, he told himself, barely able to believe it. *Probably took him out the same time they came for me.*

He did the best he could to collect himself, then turned and walked back to the waiting car. "So," he said to Agent Springs, "want me to drive?"

THIRTEEN

Mahmoud Rahmad was seated behind a large, polished rosewood desk in the opulent Park Avenue office he used while in New York. He was glaring at his two aides.

"Perhaps you are correct, sir," said his younger associate, "but Tafallai believes it is only a temporary delay."

Rahmad shook his head. "There are no delays in such matters. There is only failure." His ebony eyes flashed with anger. "I want to know who has taken Sandor into custody. And where they are holding him."

"Yes sir."

After a moment of silence, Rahmad asked, "Why are you still here?"

The aides exchange a glance and the younger of the two says, "Tafallai believes we will be able to find him."

Rahmad responded with a bitter smile, his young aide reacting by shifting uneasily in his seat. "And how can that be, my friend? Tafallai has twice failed at his assignment, and now what? He wants to conduct a personal manhunt, is that it? I assure you it will be at his expense, in every sense."

The older assistant, who was leaning on a credenza off to the side, spoke up now. "Tafallai has a lead."

"Ah. Through what divine intervention?"

"Sandor met with a woman, sir. Tafallai saw them together. He is following her now."

"Tafallai should have acted when he saw them together."

"Perhaps so, Rahmad, but the risks were great, and the opportunity did not present itself."

"The opportunity did not present itself," Rahmad mocked him. "Opportunities are created, they do not come gift-wrapped my dear man." He stood and turned away from them, looking out his window to Park Avenue below. "Risks," he said, still not facing them. "Risks to whom? To our friend Tafallai?" He turned back to them. "Proceed. By all means proceed. Traiman has a schedule to keep, and I will not be the one to hold it up."

VINCENT TRAIMAN WAS the man to whom Rahmad reported, a former American agent who was now working for al-Qaeda, and who was presently hiding in North Africa. In his final assignment for the Agency, before his defection, he had served as Jordan Sandor's field supervisor.

During his tenure with Central Intelligence, Traiman was known to be both resourceful and ruthless, a determined man who inspired apprehension from subordinates and superiors alike. Those fears were vindicated more than four years before when he betrayed the Agency and his country, turned rogue, and disappeared into Libya. He took with him a briefcase filled with non-sequential hundred dollar bills, a series of numbered Swiss accounts and a folder full of illegal arms deals. He also had a notebook containing the names and address of American contacts and undercover agents throughout the Middle East, just for insurance. His intention to turn traitor was some time in the making.

Traiman was a man with a pragmatic sense of history. He understood that the promise of socialism around the world had been revealed as another Big Lie, not even lasting a century. He had witnessed the triumph of capitalism up close as the Soviet Union fell, the Iron Curtain was torn away and the bloc of repressed, satellite nations disintegrated, leaving each to regain its autonomy. But then Arafat, Qaddafi, Saddam Hussein and the leaders of al-Qaeda preached a community of Arab brotherhood, and Traiman saw the coming of a new world order.

He realized that only the naïve and uninformed could possibly believe the concentration of wealth enjoyed by the oil-rich Middle Eastern nations would be shared in a Pan-Arab vision. Dictatorships, monarchies and elite oligarchies ruled the region. There was no real hope for the struggling, suffering masses while oppression, starvation and tyranny, all wrapped in the name of Allah, suffocated them in the narcotic of religious and ethnic fervor.

Traiman saw all of this as an opportunity, and he sold out his own country to reap the benefits of the myth being perpetrated by Islamic extremism. Up to recent times, these Arab nations were bit players on the global economic stage. However, as the need for oil expanded exponentially, their influence grew and they began to promote their own twenty-first century version of world domination. Power through the control of energy, through the intimidation of their own people and through the exportation of terror abroad. None of the princes, generals and statesmen from these countries, or the mercenaries they hired, suffered the deprivation or self-sacrifice they advocated for their zealous constituents. The ideology they espoused was nothing more than a device to satisfy their own greed. It was not a new theme, but there were far-reaching implications in a world that had been rapidly contracting in size through technology, communications, advanced arms and nuclear proliferation.

Traiman recognized his chance during a tour of duty in Saudi Arabia, where he made contacts that sustained him in his efforts to build a force of professional assassins.

As part of his departure strategy, Traiman arranged for the assassination of his top agent, Jordan Sandor, knowing that once his defection was confirmed, Jordan would be the first to come after him. Rather than risk becoming the target of the most talented operative in the CIA's counter-terrorism unit, he made a pre-emptive strike. His plot failed, but by then Traiman had already vanished behind a wall of Wahhabi protection.

A couple of years later, Traiman engineered an incursion in Bahrain that, as a bonus, once again drew the involvement of Sandor. However, as before, his former charge escaped unharmed. Now, after having coordinated a number of small attacks in Israel and Western Europe, he was preparing a major assault for which he was to be handsomely compensated, and only a few of his closest associates had any idea of the magnitude of the personal rewards he would receive.

He was a man who gave new meaning to words like mercenary and traitor. He was also a man whose existence the Agency could not afford to publicly acknowledge. Nevertheless, he occupied one of the top spots on the secret list of most-wanted terrorists compiled by the CIA, MI6 and the Mossad. He was wanted, as they say, dead or alive.

FOURTEEN

The two FBI agents drove Jordan to an office building on West 48th Street, not far from the building where Beth Sharrow and her fellow CIA analysts worked. A whole team of security guards met him in the lobby. They checked his ID, asked him to remove his shoes, and instructed him to place his bag in a gray plastic tray at the end of a conveyor belt leading into an x-ray machine. "Is all this necessary?" he asked, thinking of the Walther, the .45, the spare clips and cash he had stowed inside.

"Please place the bag in the tray, sir." The guard's tone of voice made it clear that compliance was nonnegotiable.

Sandor did as he was told and was guided through the upright metal detector as his bag moved slowly along. As it disappeared into the x-ray machine, Jordan watched the guard seated before the visual display raise his eyebrows as the image must have come to a halt in the center of the monitor. The guard standing behind him placed his hand on his sidearm and, stepping around the console, extended his other hand toward Sandor and said, "Please step aside, sir."

"I don't understand—" Jordan began, stalling for time.

"Step aside," the guard repeated, unsnapping his holster, "and place your hands behind your head." The rest of the security team followed suit, assuming defensive postures, hands on their weapons. The guard in charge touched his earpiece and spoke quietly but firmly, and waited.

Jordan was playing out a variety of possible scenarios and none of them were good.

"Stand down," the security chief suddenly ordered his detail. "All clear." And handing Sandor's bag to Agent Springs he said to Jordan, "I apologize for the inconvenience, sir. You may proceed."

Of all the scenarios Jordan had envisioned, this was not one of them.

Special Agent Springs escorted him upstairs in the elevator and down a corridor to a small conference room on the seventeenth floor. There was only one person in the room when they entered, and he did not bother to look up when Jordan was ushered in. "Have a seat," he said as he continued making notes in a file.

"Sure," Sandor said. "Don't rush yourself on my account."

Sandor's tone caused the man to glance up at him now. "I'm Special Agent Prescott, and I'm in charge here," he said. "I know who you are, and I'm not in the mood for any of your bullshit. I said have a seat, so have a seat."

Jordan grinned, then made his way to a chair against the wall and sat down.

Agent Springs was standing in the doorway, about to leave. "Will there be anything else, sir?"

"That'll be all," Prescott said.

As Springs turned, Jordan called after him. "How do I get my bag back? Government going to give me a voucher for it?"

Springs looked from Sandor to his boss but said nothing. His expression made it clear what he'd like to do to Sandor with a voucher.

"Springs will hold onto your belongings," Prescott said.

"Oh good," Jordan said. "I feel so much better now."

Springs hesitated. Then he left the room.

Jordan watched as Prescott returned his attention to his file. The conference room was rigged with an array of government equipment. By the look of things, the set-up was pulled together in a hurry. Two telephones were on the table where Prescott was working; a computer station was positioned to the side, the screen flashing code numbers, skittishly awaiting further input; a fax machine was perched on a box against the wall; a recording machine was in place; three or four devices Jordan did not recognize were lined up off to the side; and a series of cables ran from all this electronic paraphernalia, under the tables, into a strip of surge protectors.

He figured Prescott was with the FBI's Counterterrorism Division. It was obvious that whatever the feds were doing here, they had only recently set up shop. But they obviously meant business.

Jordan knew that Prescott's peremptory affect was intended to reinforce the fact that he had all the power, Jordan had none, and on a whim he could toss him in a hole so deep he'd need a steam shovel to dig himself out. He was a typical field office chief, and his attitude, as Jordan knew, was standard federal issue. Sandor had been through it all before, on both sides of the charade, and had developed an unwavering dislike for the Prescotts of the world. The entire act was the work of small, unquestioning minds, the consequence of an inability to articulate reason, leaving no choice but to resort to the "because I said so" justification for their actions. As far as Jordan was concerned, no desk jockey had ever won a race.

Everything about Prescott was predictable, even his clothing. His suit was medium gray, his shirt was white with a button-down collar, his tie was red with little blue dots. He looked middle-aged, assuming people live to be a hundred and ten. His nose was wide, his complexion sallow and marred, his eyes pale and hard and cold.

"So you're Jordan Sandor." Prescott put down his pen and removed his reading glasses.

Jordan saw no need to respond.

"We appreciate your cooperation."

"My cooperation?" Jordan smiled. "Your appreciation is evident from the greeting I got downstairs." He did not mention his surprise at the fact that Agent Springs had held onto his leather bag after it was passed through the metal detector without removing either automatic. "Now that I've reached the inner sanctum, you might want to search me again. I may have a stick of dynamite somewhere your boys didn't look."

"Standard procedure. You know that. The important thing is that you're here."

"Well, just in case this interview is being recorded for posterity, I wasn't given much of a choice."

"You want us to get a subpoena, I'll have one in five minutes."

"I believe you. So as long as I'm here, let's talk about Danny Peters."

"We're sorry about your friend—"

"I'm sure."

70

"But I'll set the agenda for this discussion."

"Look, I've had a rough couple of days, so let's get down to it. Why is the FBI investigating a roadside shooting?"

Prescott leaned forward, which was an empty sort of gesture at intimacy, since Jordan was seated ten feet away. "Mr. Sandor, I realize what you've been through, but I'm going to be the one conducting this investigation, not you. Your questions will have to wait."

"I can ask, right? It's still a free country, as they say, isn't it Mr. Prescott?"

Prescott responded with an undisguised look of contempt. "I already know all about you, my friend." He tilted his head towards the computer station. "Your recklessness. Your insubordination. Some of it is fairly intriguing, I must say."

Even in the new order, where intelligence agencies were supposed to work together through the recently created Terrorist Threat Integration Center, Sandor realized that whatever information came up on the federal database would still be laundered to wash out the details of any of the classified work he did for the CIA's Joint Counterterrorism Center. It was actually somewhat amusing that these subjective assessments would have survived the cleansing process.

"Let's get this clear from the get-go, Mr. Prescott. I'm not here to intrigue you, and I'm not your friend. My friend was Dan Peters. He was shot in the chest for no reason at all yesterday morning and turned up dead this morning in a local hospital, with a stated cause of death that a first-year intern wouldn't believe. So you tell me what's going on or you can go back to your Big Brother data bank and I'll find my own way out of here."

Prescott curled his upper lip above his uneven teeth, as if he just detected a bad smell. "Have it your way. We've heard from the coroner." He held up a sheet of paper. "Faxed in while you were on your way here. Preliminary blood tests indicate Mr. Peters' coronary was chemically induced." He looked at the report. "They suspect a massive dose of a potassium nitrate solution was injected into his IV, which would cause a fatal coronary reaction in less than a minute." He glanced up at Sandor. "It says that this sort of potassium compound wouldn't leave the kind of trace other drugs might have, but they're still working on it."

The news was not unexpected, but it hit Jordan hard. He felt his eyes burn, and he took a deep breath.

"How well did you know Peters?"

"We were friends," Jordan said, feeling lousy talking about him in the past tense. "Fought together in the Gulf War."

"I know all that. I'm asking how close you were, how much you knew about his activities since he moved to upstate New York."

Jordan was thinking about Dan, not really paying attention to Prescott. Then, as if finally hearing the question, he looked up and said, "Not much. We spent a lot of time together when we served in the military. Only kept in touch on and off since then."

One of the telephones on Prescott's table rang. He answered it. "Yes? I see. Are they here now?" Prescott did not bother to disguise his annoyance. "All right, show them in." He placed the receiver back in its cradle. "We're going to be joined by, uh, others."

"Should I guess, or are you going to tell me who?"

Before Prescott could reply, the door to the conference room opened and John Covington entered, followed by one of his men, Todd Nealon. The door was closed behind them.

"Hello Jordan," Covington said pleasantly as he stepped to the front of the room. He looked the same as the last time Sandor had seen him in Washington, at the debriefing after the mess in the Persian Gulf. His fine features and cropped hair gave him the look of a bank manager, not a senior CIA operations chief.

Nealon was taller and slimmer than his boss. He and Sandor had met in the past, and Sandor had not been impressed. He was not likely to be impressed by an operative who had yet to earn a position any better than John Covington's lackey.

Jordan said, "You'll excuse me if I don't get up."

Nealon sat in a chair near the door, and Covington walked over to Prescott, whose confusion was apparent as he got out of his seat to shake hands.

"You know each other?" Prescott asked.

Covington explained that he and Mr. Nealon were from the State Department, attached to a unit involved with international liaison work. "Mr. Sandor was assigned to our delegation at one time."

Prescott nodded, as if that meant something to him.

It was all Sandor could do not to laugh at the bogus job description.

"It's been a while, Jordan," Covington said, taking a seat halfway between Sandor and Prescott.

"You don't call. You don't write. Not even a Christmas card since you stood me up in Bahrain," Jordan said.

Covington shrugged indulgently. "Things don't always turn out the way you expect."

"No, I suppose not. It would have been nice, though, if someone told those

guys in Manama exactly what they could expect. I mean, they did get their heads blown off, for whatever was expected, right?"

Covington calmly turned back to the FBI man, saying, "I don't want to interfere with your investigation, Special Agent Prescott, but I wonder if we might have a few minutes alone with Mr. Sandor." As an inducement, he offered his pale imitation of a smile.

The effort was wasted on Prescott, who had already guessed that Covington and Nealon were not with the State Department, doing international liaison work, and that the background on Sandor, as reported to him by the computer, had been sanitized beyond recognition.

"Not so fast," Jordan interrupted. "Did anybody search *them* before they came in here?"

Ignoring the sarcasm, Covington assured Prescott they would only be a minute.

Prescott studied Covington, knowing he could not refuse the request, but doing his best to appear as though he was actually weighing his reply. After all, he was in charge here. "Fine," he said. "But we've got to move this along. We're wasting time."

"Of course," Covington agreed genially. He and Nealon even stood as Prescott left the room. A proper show of respect. Jordan remained in his chair. When Covington sat down again, he turned toward Sandor, trying to read something from his impassive expression.

"Nausea," Jordan said, "if that's what you're wondering about."

"Look, I told you before, and I'll say it again. We didn't know what you were up against in Bahrain."

Sandor shook his head. "You hung those men out to dry. You left them behind because they were politically inconvenient. And what happens? Byrnes gets a promotion to deputy director, you get a gold star for the effort and those poor bastards get dumped in an unmarked grave by al-Qaeda. Tell me, Covington, what's wrong with that picture?"

Covington's shoulders slumped as he blew out a long breath. "And what if you're right? We were all following orders, including me."

"Following orders?" Sandor shook his head. "If that isn't the lamest answer you could give, I just don't know. You want some time, see if you can come up with something better?"

"Look, the DDO was told to pull the plug, and that was that. What difference does it make what we say about it now?"

"What difference, John? I'm the difference now. You're here because you need something from me, and I wouldn't cross the street to save your life."

Covington resumed his stiff posture. "Maybe not. But my life is not what's at stake here, is it?"

"Oh, I see. You're going to scare me?"

Covington shook his head. "You're too stubborn and too reckless to be afraid, Sandor. I've had the privilege of seeing that first hand."

"But you need my help."

"Your help? Is that why you think I'm here?"

"I'll tell you what I think. I think that guy upstate had information you wanted. And now he's dead, and you're hoping I know something."

Covington stared at him. "And do you?"

"If I did, why would I want to tell you?"

Covington started to say something, but Jordan stopped him. "Save your breath. I'm finished dealing with you people," he said and started to get up.

"Are you?" Covington asked. "I hope not. I truly hope not for your sake."

FIFTEEN

Rahmad received an urgent summons from Tripoli. Traiman wanted to see him immediately, and so arrangements were made for him to fly back to Libya that night, via Paris, on his Saudi diplomatic passport.

Another message sent from Traiman was channeled from North Africa to a man who called himself Robert Groat. He had been waiting in a hotel room in Washington, DC, for his orders and was now instructed to go ahead with his visit to David Fryar, president of the Loubar Corporation. Groat decoded the e-mail, and then made his preparations for that conference. He retrieved his aluminum attaché case from the closet, laid it carefully on the table and opened it, removing the papers and files and placing them aside. He then lifted a false panel, exposing the tightly packed contents and a series of wires that ran to a digital sensor. He pocketed a small remote device, activated the sensor, then replaced the panel, the papers, and closing the case, went on his way.

"MR. FRYAR, THERE'S a gentleman here to see you. His name is Robert Groat." David Fryar's secretary was speaking into the intercom. "Mr. Groat says he has an appointment, but I don't show anything in my system." The well groomed, middle-aged woman was obviously embarrassed at the possibility of her inefficiency, and looked up at Groat with an apologetic smile.

Groat was a short, well-muscled man, with a thick neck and gray hair that made him appear older than his fifty-three years. He nodded at the woman, neither forgiving her gaffe nor criticizing her for it. He was simply nodding.

"That's all right," Fryar replied over the speaker. "Show him in."

David Fryar was the president of Loubar Technical Assistance Corporation, a rapidly expanding manufacturer of specialized electronics, with offices recently opened in Paris and Hong Kong. Groat had come to the corporate headquarters and, indeed, was without an appointment. He knew Fryar would see him anyway.

The secretary escorted Groat into Fryar's paneled office, where he was standing behind his desk, waiting.

"Could I get you something, Mr. Groat?" the woman asked. "Coffee, water?"

Groat took a moment to survey the oversized room, his heavy-lidded eyes giving the false impression that he was either tired or uninterested. He sized up the man who came from behind his desk to greet him. Close to sixty. Overweight and comfortable. Eyes and chin gone weak with success. His posture a bit stiff, apparently concerned about this meeting, his handshake tentative. "No, thank you," Groat finally replied to the woman.

As his assistant turned to leave, Fryar went back to his chair. Groat slid his metal attaché case under the desk then sat down.

"They said I would be hearing from you," Fryar said. "I didn't expect you so soon."

"There was no reason to wait," Groat replied in a monotone that expressed his indifference to the task at hand. "As soon as they saw the problem develop, they sent me here straightaway."

"Problem?" Fryar's anxious gaze wandered about the room. "Does Traiman think there's a problem?"

"Yes. Interference with our shipments is always a problem."

Fryar was not prepared for this meeting, not today. He had not been sleeping well since learning of the problems with the latest cargo destined for the Middle East. Although the cargo was routed through Marseilles, its ultimate destination had been exposed. He agonized over the possible discovery by Customs officials that this shipment of electronic materiel was being illegally forwarded to a prohibited port, not to mention the consequences of what a full investigation of his company might reveal. He was even more troubled that his decision to hold back the freight was too impulsive. He knew that dealing with Vincent Traiman could be worse than a government inquiry. Far worse.

He had worried over this since he received the phone call from one of Traiman's salesmen—that's what they were called, salesmen—informing him that they were extremely upset that he had halted the shipment of two containers of highly sensitive surveillance equipment. Fryar was told he would be hearing from their regional representative, Robert Groat. Fryar had not had a full night's sleep since.

Fryar was aware, of course, that the orders placed by Traiman's salesmen would ultimately find their way to the Middle East. The itineraries for these shipments were always obscured by a series of documents and intervening transports that concealed their intended destination. These interim transfers, and a complex network of bills of lading, provided Loubar a veneer of innocence while circumventing federal laws making such shipments of quasi-military equipment illegal. Every shipment was positioned for delivery to a lawful port and described as non-military in content.

Over the past few weeks, however, Traiman had stepped up the timing, demanding a more direct approach. That was the cause of the error, Fryar believed. One of the forwarding documents had been discovered by an executive in the shipping company, making it apparent that the merchandise was intended for Libya. Discreet inquiries were quickly made through an intermediary, but it was apparent that the man could not be bought off. That was when Fryar feigned ignorance of the true destination for the shipment and made the decision to postpone the exports.

Now, being visited by Vincent Traiman's emissary, Fryar wondered whether he had made the wrong choice. What if the shipment had been sent? Traiman could have dealt with the trans-Atlantic shipper later. Some arrangement would certainly be made. Fryar and his company could have pleaded ignorance, or they might have claimed they had no involvement in the actual transfer of the goods once they arrived in Marseilles. After all, this was the same rationale that had assuaged Fryar's conscience for the past three years. His products were shipped to European ports. What was done with them after that was not his concern. His real concern was Traiman.

Now, as Groat sat watching him, Fryar struggled with his predicament. He tried to explain how difficult it would have been to justify a release of the product once the intended port had been uncovered. He attempted to enlist

Groat's aid in resolving the dilemma to everyone's satisfaction. He offered to work out the issue, not realizing that it was already too late, not realizing that he, David Fryar, had become the issue.

"This goes far beyond the usual request," Fryar gave by way of explanation. "The risks are considerable."

"Yes, of course, of course, but one must be prudent too. There is real danger here."

"For whom, Mr. Fryar? For you?"

"For all of us."

Groat shook his head slowly. "The danger for all of us exists only if you continue to block these shipments."

Fryar's eyes betrayed true understanding of his dilemma, and Groat answered with a look that told him how well he understood men like Fryar, men who had no sense of allegiance and dangerously short memories. He listened as the flabby executive offered another nervous justification for his actions. It was interesting, Groat reflected as Fryar rambled on, how some men will accept prosperity without assessing its true cost, while others will scrutinize both success and failure with an eye to the causes and effects of each.

Fryar was a scientist-turned-businessman who enjoyed an elevated position of power and wealth he had never imagined. Prestige, luxurious living, fast cars, expensive homes, even women. With the enthusiasm of an irresponsible adolescent, he failed to look beyond his pleasures, to assess the consequences of the bargain he had made. And why should he? As Groat had already observed, men like David Fryar had short memories.

"Excuse me," Groat said, interrupting the litany to which he was paying no attention. "I think we should come right to the point."

"Why, uh, yes, yes, of course. Go ahead."

"The shipments have been held past their embarkation dates. The integrity of our operation depends in part on your company." He paused then added, "It depends on your company honoring its commitments." His voice bore no inflection, the message delivered without emotion. "The goods must be released and we must be assured we will not have this problem in the future."

His words hung in the quiet of the overdressed office like a cloud about to burst. Fryar began to explain his concerns again, his desire to cooperate, his fear of what might occur. He held his hands up, palms facing Groat, as if he was preparing to fend off a blow. Then he placed his hands on the desk and said, "I simply don't see how we can release these shipments right now."

Groat allowed that last statement to settle over them. What he knew, and Fryar did not, was the truth of Vincent Traiman's plan. What Groat knew, as one of very few men privy to Traiman's scheme, was that Loubar's technology was critical to the execution of Traiman's scheme. What Groat also knew was that Traiman was not willing to wait. "Is that the answer you want me to take back with me?"

"No no, of course not," Fryar said. He left his seat and walked to the window that overlooked the Capitol. "What can I do?" He seemed to be asking the question of the city that lay before him.

"Release the shipments. We understand the crates are ready."

"Yes," he admitted, "that's right."

"Inform the shipping company that the goods are to be delivered to Marseilles. We give you our assurance that once they arrive in Europe, Loubar will have no participation in the transfer beyond the original destination." Now Groat stood and picked up the telephone.

Fryar stared at him. "I need to think this through. To make arrangements. I'll take care of it tomorrow morning, first thing."

Groat's voice turned cold. "Call now," he said. "Unless you call now, in front of me, I'll have no choice but to report your position to Mr. Traiman. I think you know that would be a mistake on your part."

The threat had been made and now the two men studied each other in silence, until the receiver began beeping. Groat replaced it, but remained standing, staring at Fryar.

"Very well," the older man said dully, the defeat in his voice and his posture. He returned to his desk, took his seat and picked up the phone. Groat stood over him as he made the call. He gave instructions that the delayed shipment be released immediately and was about to hang up, but Groat interrupted. He insisted on speaking to the supervisor in the Loubar shipping department himself.

Fryar felt the anger well up in his chest, but when he looked at Groat he saw in the man's eyes that he had no choice. He handed him the phone, and Groat waited for the supervisor to get on the line, then quickly confirmed that the shipment would be in transit that night. Fryar was too upset to recognize the familiarity of their discussion, or to guess the truth - that the supervisor Groat had asked for was already on the Traiman payroll.

"You did the right thing," Groat told him as he put the phone down. "We have other matters to discuss, but I'm out of time." He turned to the door.

Fryar began to speak, but Groat cut him off. "I'll be in touch."

In the front lobby, down the hall from the office, Fryar's secretary bade Mr. Groat a good day.

"Thank you," he said. "Mr. Fryar would like to see you."

She thanked him and he walked off, heading directly for the elevators.

Fryar's secretary took a moment to collect some papers from her desk, turned to her employer's office, then knocked on the door and entered. She found Fryar seated in his chair, staring out the window.

"Yes?" he asked.

"Mr. Groat said you wanted to see me."

Fryar shook his head, still distracted.

His secretary was standing there, waiting for a response, when she noticed the silver attaché case. "What's this?" she asked.

GROAT RODE DOWN in the elevator alone, stepped quickly through the granite-floored lobby, crossed the street and hailed a cab. As a taxi pulled up, Groat reached into his coat pocket and pressed the button on the remote he was carrying, a device smaller than a pack of cigarettes. Almost instantly, the explosives hidden in Groat's attaché erupted with a deafening roar, shattering the full-length, plate glass windows, sending a deluge of metal and glass and wood to the street below. Flames followed the falling debris, climbing the building's blackened façade, and fire spread throughout the large office above, consuming the entire space in a searing blaze.

"Holy shit," the cab driver said as Groat climbed into the back seat.

The driver craned his neck for a better look at the cascading mix of smoking fragments. "I don't know what's going on, mac, but I'm getting' the hell outta here before somethin' falls on my car."

"Good idea." Groat gave the driver an address in Georgetown and eased himself into the seat, not bothering to look back at the confusion and panic that was growing behind them as they pulled away.

Driving along the Potomac, the cab driver chattered on about the explosion. At some point in the midst of his mindless speculation about the blast he paused.

"Yes," Groat responded to the silence, "just awful."

The taxi pulled up to the curb in front of Clyde's Restaurant. Groat paid the driver, then stood there and watched him drive away. He turned in the opposite direction and walked around the block. He tossed the remote transmitter in a public waste can, pulled out his cell phone, and punched in the numbers of an office at CIA headquarters.

As soon as the voice on the other end answered, Groat said, "I know the group responsible for the explosion today." Then he recited the address of an apartment in Washington where three Arabs from the extremist Wahhabi sect were in hiding.

This was the last part of Groat's current assignment: to betray his own team of terrorists waiting for instructions from Vincent Traiman for a mission they would never carry out. Only Traiman knew that he would expose them. And only he and Traiman knew the reason why.

Groat ended the call, tossed the cell phone into another trash can he passed, then hailed a taxi and headed for the airport.

SIXTEEN

"You've got more to worry about than me," Jordan said, seated in Prescott's office with John Covington and Todd Nealon.

"Meaning what?" Covington replied wearily.

"Meaning . . . that for you to be involved means something big is going on."

"I'm here to monitor the investigation. Let's just say the Company is an interested party."

"Ah, John Covington, always the Company man."

"And Jordan Sandor, always the crusader in pursuit of justice, always holding the higher moral ground."

Jordan leaned back and stared at him. "How is Byrnes? Still as warm and fuzzy as bullet-proof glass?"

Covington responded with a blank stare.

"Bet he misses me," Sandor said with a slight smile.

"If he does, he'd be the only one."

"Now that hurts."

"You're a pain in the ass, Sandor. We're better off with you gone."

"You may be right. But since you're the ones who flew up from Washington to see me, why not let me in on what we're dealing with here?"

"*We* are not dealing with anything, and I'm not authorized to divulge a single shred of information to you. You're inactive, remember? You want to talk, you go ahead. You want to dummy up, I'll have the FBI hold you as a material witness till you're sucking jell-o through a straw, which would suit me fine."

"Come on," Jordan said with a short laugh, "that tough guy act didn't work for you ten years ago, why try to sell it now? Maybe you should let Nealon have a go at it."

Covington and Nealon exchanged a glance.

"It seems I tripped into a whole vat of your problems," Sandor said, "and now I'm involved, whether you like it or not. You can bully me, which we both know isn't going to cut it, or you can ask me to help, which irritates you more than a little bit. Either way, I figure you've got something you want me to do." He turned to Nealon and grinned. "That the party line?"

Nealon did not reply.

"No. Not this time," Covington said. "You've been on ice for more than a year. You're not on the team anymore."

"We finally agree about something."

"Good. So tell us what you know about James McHugh."

"Who's McHugh?" Jordan asked, not revealing what Captain Reynolds had told him about Ryan's real name.

Covington gave him a look that said he wasn't buying it. "McHugh was the other man who was murdered in Woodstock."

"Ryan, you mean?"

Covington frowned. "His name was McHugh, as you no doubt know by now. We think he had sensitive intelligence we needed. Our guess is you were after it too."

Sandor saw no point in denying it so he said nothing.

"Why don't you start by telling us how you were introduced?"

"Dan Peters set it up. I never got to speak with the guy." Jordan shrugged. "I don't even know what he had."

Covington paused. "For once I believe you."

The way he said it, Jordan suddenly had the thought that it might have been Covington who orchestrated the break-in of his apartment.

"So, where does that leave us?" Jordan asked.

"I'm not authorized to divulge that."

Sandor got up and walked around the room, needing to do something before he punched Covington in the jaw. When he sat down again he said, "You're playing me, John."

"Why don't you tell me about the shooting in your building today?"

"Just a florist with a bad attitude."

"Way I hear it, they'd already turned your apartment into a recycling station."

Jordan sat there staring at him.

Covington leaned forward, resting his forearms on his thighs. "McHugh was a combat vet. He comes home. Civilian life doesn't take, so he heads back to Saudi Arabia, gets recruited by a bad group out of Libya. He becomes one of the play-for-pay boys, working field ops, training these scumbags. Probably the same cell that killed those college students for Qaddafi, went after our ambassador in Italy, took out the *charge d'affaires* in Paris. McHugh was making a buck, pretending to himself that he was just a guy doing a job until one morning he wakes up and reads the headlines about Nine Eleven and presto, this isn't just a video game in the desert anymore. He waits a while then bolts for home."

"So, they wanted him. We wanted him. They got to him first."

Covington drew a deep breath and let it out slowly. "Did you ever speak with McHugh? Did he ever tell you anything at all?"

Sandor stared into Covington's cold, pale eyes. "I told you the truth. I never met him. Peters was taking me to see him yesterday. You know the rest of that story."

"Never spoke with him?"

"Never. So let's have it. Who was he working for?"

Covington sat upright in his chair, resuming his wooden posture. "We think he was working for Vincent."

At first, Jordan could not bring himself to respond. His mind raced back to a thousand old images as he tried to reel his thoughts forward again. He ran his fingers through his hair, then scratched the back of his neck. "Traiman?" he finally said.

"We think so."

Jordan felt his jaw tighten.

"McHugh was working for that bastard?"

"Imagine, someone you hate more than you hate us—"

"You mean someone I hate even more than *you*."

"It's clear now you have nothing we need." Covington closed the file he was holding. "You can go."

"That sonuvabitch tried to kill me."

"Yes, he screwed you. He screwed us. He screwed his country. But this is not your battle anymore—not since you walked out. Stay out of it."

"Stay out? I couldn't be deeper in it."

Covington waited for Sandor to finish. "Our friend Prescott is going to ask you some questions. He doesn't know what kind of work you did with us, and he doesn't need to know."

"Still happily sharing information among the federal agencies, I see."

"In this case it could compromise our plans."

"While I'm dodging bullets."

"You're not my problem, Sandor. Maybe the Bureau will place you in protective custody if you like, or you can go somewhere and hide until we sort this out."

"That's a good one."

Covington's cell phone began ringing, but he ignored it until it stopped. He stood there, looking down at Jordan. "We're done here. Do us both a favor and answer Prescott's questions, then stay the hell out of our way."

The two men stared at each other, the silence broken by the sound of Nealon's cell phone ringing.

Nealon flipped his phone open. "Nealon." He listened without speaking. And, when he finally responded, it was brief and to the point. "Yes sir, I'll tell him."

He ended the call and couldn't help glancing at Sandor before he spoke to Covington. "We need to talk, sir," he said.

Nealon and Covington went to the far corner of the room. Nealon whispered for a few moments, and Covington's look of surprise was no act as far as Jordan could tell. Then they turned to him.

"What now?" Jordan asked.

Covington hesitated then said, "You'll see it on the evening news anyway." He shook his head. "There was an explosion in an office building in DC. A few people dead, several injured."

"Where?"

"A company called Loubar. Deal in high-end electronics."

Jordan knew the name, recalled it had something to do with a series of controversial military contracts. "Anything else?"

"An anonymous tip led to the capture of three men, believed to be a hit team sent by al-Qaeda."

"Also in DC?"

Covington nodded. "Nealon, let Prescott back in now." And turning to Jordan, he added, "You handle him however you want. If you get in the way of the feds' investigation, they'll charge you with obstruction and lock you up. Just in case you were wondering."

Sandor watched as they headed for the door. "You're a real piece of work, John."

Covington turned back to him. "As far as the Company is concerned, you are a liability, which puts you in a different category of risk, if you catch my drift."

Sandor smiled at the threat. "You're still the same pathetic, little paper pusher," he said, then watched Covington and Nealon walk out the door.

SEVENTEEN

Tafallai must not fail again. He knew the consequences. He also realized that his target was now alert to his efforts, and the authorities were involved. The situation had to be resolved before Rahmad returned to New York. He had to act, and time was short.

Tafallai had never failed before. In one capacity or another, he had been involved in a number of political assassinations. Not murders, but wartime executions of the enemy. Some assignments had been so expertly conceived and implemented that the deaths had been ruled accidental. Others had been brutal, such as the bludgeoning of a Saudi student in California or the shooting of the Qaddafi liaison who had become too comfortable with Western ways. In these instances, Tafallai was instructed to use unequivocal methods. His charge was plain—to leave a clear message for others who might be tempted to imprudent action.

In the case of this American, there was no need for subtlety, nor was there any particular reason for his death to bear warning to others. In the matter of Jordan Sandor, the means would be justified by the end.

Tafallai sat in a coffee shop across the street from the building where he had tracked Beth earlier that day. It was a tall, modern-looking edifice, and when he had followed her into the lobby, he discovered it was home to several floors of federal offices. He had watched as she used a magnetic card to pass through security and disappear into an elevator as he casually browsed the directory on the wall. The building was far too secure for him to make his move there, but this woman was his best lead for now, so he reported in to Rahmad, remaining in the area until just before five, when he found his way to a table in this diner. Now he stared out the etched-glass window into the darkening shadows of evening, and waited.

MAKING HIS RETURN, Prescott strutted in ahead of Covington and Nealon, his bearing and expression intended to convey a message to Sandor—that Prescott was still the man in charge.

Jordan was amused, realizing that of the four of them, Prescott understood the least of what was at stake. All the same, the two CIA officers obligingly submitted to Prescott's show of authority, reminding Jordan yet again why he had chosen to turn his back on these bureaucrats and their corrupt and, ultimately, lethal games.

Covington was at his obsequious best, an act Sandor had had occasion to witness in the past. Covington agreed with Prescott's assertion that the FBI had jurisdiction over the matter, and was certainly in the best position to conduct the investigation. He maintained his ruse about the State Department, giving his assurance that they had only intervened because of the coincidental involvement of their former employee, the insubordinate Jordan Sandor. Covington and Nealon were there to assist Prescott solely for whatever purpose the Bureau might regard as helpful.

They were soon joined by an FBI agent who operated the recording device and, as Prescott pursued his interrogation of Sandor, his questions only confirmed the shallowness of his understanding. Jordan saw no reason to educate him. If the Agency wanted to keep the Bureau in the dark for now, that was their business. He answered the questions, volunteering nothing. Covington suggested an occasional question, but steered wide of anything that might actually lead to the truth of his relationship with Sandor. Jordan did not interfere, allowing Covington to maintain the deception.

Prescott inquired into the shootings upstate, Sandor's intended visit to McHugh's home, the trashing of Jordan's apartment and the attack that afternoon. Prescott reached into a file and read off a series of Arabic names, none of which Sandor admitted recognizing as he memorized the list for future reference.

At the conclusion of the interview, Jordan was invited to stay overnight at a nearby hotel.

"Invited?"

"Let's say you are being requested to stay."

"You're locking me up, is that the idea?"

"No, I wouldn't put it that way," Prescott replied testily.

"Just how would you put it?"

"It will only be for a short time," Covington interrupted, giving his best imitation of a concerned tone. "You are in serious danger. Your apartment has been vandalized, you've been the target of an assault and your safety is obviously compromised. Mr. Prescott is offering his help. There are agents available, and a night or two under guard might be the best thing for all of us."

"For all of us? I suppose being taken into custody is a fitting reward for saving a cop's life."

"You can stow that hero bullshit," Prescott snapped. "That may go over big with your new friends upstate, but as far as we're concerned, you just showed up at the wrong place at the wrong time."

"Who am I to disagree?" Jordan shrugged. "That's it, then?"

"That's it."

Jordan stood to face him. "They have a penthouse suite at this hotel?"

AGENT SPRINGS LED Sandor down to the underground garage and got into the FBI sedan.

"No motorcycle escort?"

Springs grunted.

"I get the feeling you don't like me."

"Not much, no."

"Any reason? My face, maybe? It's been known to annoy people from time to time."

"You're an inconvenience, that's all."

"And you don't like acting as my babysitter."

Agent Springs allowed himself a slight grin. "Not what I signed on for, no."

"Fair enough. How about I make it up to you? I'll buy you dinner. On the government account, of course."

The grin faded.

"Lighten up," Sandor said. "You allowed to drink on duty?"

THE HOTEL THEY were using was on Times Square, just a couple of blocks west. Springs checked Sandor in. Then, to Sandor's amazement, he handed him his leather bag.

Jordan declined the desk clerk's offer to get him help with his luggage. "I can handle this," he said, holding up the satchel.

Springs took him to the elevator and they got in together. "You need this to get off at our floor," Springs said, placing a plastic room key in a slot that cleared access in the elevator to the concierge level, where the contingent from Washington was staying.

"No penthouse suite, eh?"

Springs frowned and said, "We've arranged for room service. If you want something to eat, just dial the operator."

"Right," Jordan said. "So I guess dinner for the two of us is out, then."

They got off the lift and found their way to Sandor's room without further conversation. Springs held out the electronic key, which Jordan took and opened the door. He turned back to Springs, who was still standing there, then looked down at the agent's hand. "You're not expecting a tip, are you? I mean, I carried my own bag."

Springs gave him a look that told him how happy he would be to close the hand Jordan was looking at and plant it squarely on his chin. Instead, he turned and strode away.

Jordan switched on the light, locked the door behind him and went to the small desk near the window. The first thing he did was check the contents of his leather bag. To his surprise everything was there, even the two handguns. He sat down and thought that through.

The interview with Prescott and Covington had been more informative than he had expected. Using the ballpoint pen and note paper provided by the hotel, Jordan wrote the names Prescott had asked him about:

Zayn

Mahmoud Rahmad

Suaramar

Mustafa Tagliev

Talal Abdullah Driann

Ibraiam Abass

Most of them meant nothing to him. Not yet. But it was a start.

He went over to the bed and lay down, studying his list, trying to connect the names with any of the research he had done during the past several months. Mahmoud Rahmad, Saudi diplomat, as Jordan recalled, was the only familiar name. The only name, that is, except for the one he had not written down.

Vincent R. Traiman. Sandor's former field supervisor in the Agency, who had disappeared four years ago, only to emerge as a paid al-Qaeda operative who was allegedly behind a string of terrorist strikes in Israel and Europe. Traiman had reportedly engineered the illegal arms deals that facilitated those attacks, all the while living under the protection of Qadaffi in Libya.

After the invasion of Iraq and removal of Saddam Hussein, Qadaffi claimed to have seen the light and made a show of laying down his arms and abandoning his anti-Western rhetoric. Whether his conversion was real or just a convenient pose based on self-preservation, his regime made no admission that Traiman had ever been holed up in Tripoli. Traiman's whereabouts were currently listed as unknown, but rumor had it that Traiman had overstayed his welcome in Libya. Sooner, rather than later, he would be on the move.

Now, as Jordan watched a television news report on the explosion at the Loubar Corporation in Washington, he remembered a covert investigation, a couple of years back, into shipments of electronic matériel from Loubar that the Agency believed were connected to Traiman's mercenary operations. Nothing was ever proved, but the suspicion persisted. And now, the day after McHugh was murdered, someone took out the headquarters of Loubar, and an al-Qaeda cell in the Capitol was exposed.

Jordan knew that these three events must somehow be related, and he knew Traiman well enough to know that they had his fingerprints all over them. All he had to do was connect the dots.

EIGHTEEN

The evening had begun to grow dark, late autumn breezes blowing a chill through the angular ravines that define the sharp contours of space between the buildings of Manhattan. Tafallai noticed neither the weather nor the passers-by. As people hurried along, he casually finished another cigarette, dropped the butt to the sidewalk and sauntered slowly into the human stream as it moved up the avenue.

Beth Sharrow joined the flow of pedestrians as she began her walk uptown. Pulling her coat closed around her neck, she kept a brisk pace as she tried to make the lights at each corner. She had not heard from Jordan all afternoon and was anxious to get home. Perhaps she would find a message there.

Tafallai had the appearance of another young man who had come to the States to make his future. He looked like an academic, perhaps a graduate student in his mid-twenties, which was in fact the basis for his visa. His skin was olive-toned, his hair curly, long and unkempt. He was not physically imposing, standing only five foot six, slight of build, fine featured. He wore a crew neck sweater and jeans, and a tweed sport coat that hid the 9mm automatic slung in a holster pulled tight against the left side of his chest.

Such a large city, New York. So congested, particularly at this time of day, that the relentless rhythm and nearly frantic movement of the people furnished him cover and provided opportunities to observe. It was just a few years after the attack on Nine Eleven, but his swarthy complexion and Arab features aroused no special notice in New York. Americans have short memories and very little sense of history, he told himself.

He kept a safe distance, watching as Beth stopped only once, in a small grocery store. She walked the entire way to East Sixty-Fifth Street, making it that much easier to follow her. Perhaps he would be doubly lucky and find Sandor waiting at her apartment. That would be too much to ask. He would be satisfied with the answers she would provide. That should be enough.

As Beth approached the entrance to the apartment building, he suddenly quickened his pace, reaching her just as she got to the front door. She felt him coming up from behind and turned to face him.

"Jordan sent me," he said before she could speak. "I've been waiting across the street for you."

"Jordan?"

"Yes. He told me you could get him a message if he and I lost contact." His voice was filled with the urgency of the imaginary message. "I haven't been able to reach him since noon."

Beth eyed him with obvious suspicion. "What exactly did Jordan say?"

Tafallai recognized the look, knowing he could not chance further discussion out in the open. In a deft move, he pulled his automatic from inside his jacket and pressed the point of the silencer hard against her ribs before she could react. "What he said, was that if you don't open the door right now, I'll kill you where you stand." As they stood face to face, a passerby might have thought them a young couple in love.

Beth froze, her left arm clutching the small plastic bag of groceries, her right hand holding the front door key. The training she had received was no match for the 9mm. She stared down at the weapon, her face a mask of fear.

Tafallai grabbed the key ring from her. "Stay very close to me, you understand? And don't try anything heroic."

Beth looked into his dark, lifeless eyes, neither moving nor speaking.

"Go," he said.

Beth forced herself to speak. "I'll scream."

"I doubt it. Believe me, you're not important enough for me to worry about. Now move or I'll kill you where you stand." He unlocked the front door and shoved her into the small vestibule. "Where's your apartment?"

"Fourth floor," she said hoarsely.

The car came, and it was empty. He shoved her in, pressed 4, then spun her back around to face him. "Anyone in your place?"

Beth shook her head.

"Don't lie to me," he said, showing her the automatic at eye level.

She shook her head again, and they waited in silence until they reached the fourth floor, Beth staring at the barrel of his gun.

As the elevator door slid open, he grabbed her roughly by the arm and forced her to walk to her door, the automatic again pressed into her side. She fumbled through her keys, finding the one that fit the lock.

They entered the apartment, a large studio with a small foyer that widened into a space that served as both sitting area and bedroom. He closed the door behind them, setting the latch in place. The lamp she always left on in the entry was the only light. It appeared to him they were alone.

He shoved her into a chair, the grocery bag falling to the floor, a tomato rolling across the carpet. He had a quick look around the small apartment, all the while training the gun on her as he moved swiftly in and out of the entryways to the kitchen and bathroom. "Let's keep this simple," he said. "Where is Jordan Sandor?"

"I don't know," she replied in a voice that was so choked with fright it was barely audible.

Tafallai responded by stepping quickly towards her then lashed out, smacking her hard across her cheek with the back of his left hand. Her head snapped back and she grabbed her face with both hands.

He leaned over her, roughly jabbing the barrel of the Glock into her sternum. "You were with him today. Where is he?"

Beth began to cry, her sobs of helplessness nearly strangling the words she tried to speak. "I . . . don't know. I swear it. I . . . I don't know."

He reached down, grabbed her by the collar of her coat and pulled her to her feet. He snarled into her terrified face, then struck her again, this time sending her reeling backwards. She spun, fell face down, sprawled on the edge of her bed.

"This can't be worth it. *He* can't be worth it." Tafallai came at her from behind. "Now tell me what you know, and we'll have an end to this."

Beth did not respond. She was incapable of uttering a reply, sobbing hysterically as she crawled onto the bed, struggling desperately to get away from him.

But he was right behind her. He pulled her by the shoulder, turning her around. She stared up, her eyes transfixed on the gun. In a violent sweep he crashed the barrel of the automatic against the side of her jaw, the sickening sound of her bone fracturing beneath the blow. She screamed out in anguish, and he reached for a pillow and shoved it over her face.

Beth clutched at the pillow, gasping for air, pain reverberating through her skull in a deafening mix of panic and agony.

"Is it worth it?" he demanded, his voice angrier now. He yanked her coat open, then ripped at her blouse and bra as she struggled to push him away. "Is it worth it?"

Beth writhed convulsively. All that mattered now was getting him away from him, but this small man was much stronger than he appeared. He pulled the pillow away from her—it was stained with blood from her swollen mouth and jaw—and threw it to the floor.

She shrank from him, curling up, fetus-like against the carved mahogany headboard.

Tafallai leaned forward, his eyes meeting hers in the dim light. "Tell me," he hissed at her through clenched teeth.

She could not focus, her body cold with shock. "Woodstock," she muttered. "It's all I know." She spoke slowly and with difficulty. "Woodstock," she mumbled again.

"When?"

"Today."

"You're lying," he said, raising his hand above her shattered jaw.

"Leave me alone." She was whimpering uncontrollably, her entire body trembling.

Tafallai shook her by the arm, pointing the gun at her face. He realized he would get nothing more from her. "This is the last time I'm going to ask you. Where is he?"

Beth's hazel eyes widened, perhaps sensing she had come to the end. She stared at him, only for an instant, then screamed, "Leave me alone," collapsing under the pain of the effort.

When she heard the sound of wood shattering and metal twisting from her doorway, it seemed a distant event to Beth, a surreal moment of violent action she was witnessing from afar. The door had come crashing open, two men bursting through. Tafallai turned to fire at them, but he was too late. The small apartment erupted in a barrage of gunfire and bloodshed. Not hers, Beth was beginning to understand, but his. The spray of blood was his—his blood.

The first man through was already standing over Tafallai as the second pulled the blanket from the bed and covered Beth.

As he leaned forward she shrank away in terror. "Miss Sharrow," the man said, "we're here to help you. Are you all right?"

She reached up and wrapped her arms around the man's neck, then wept as he lifted her from the bed.

"It's okay," the agent told her. "It's going to be all right."

"She's in shock," a third man said as he came in. "Get her the hell out of here."

"They call an ambulance yet?"

"Yeah."

The two men looked to the first agent, who was now kneeling over Tafallai's body. He was shaking his head.

"No good," he said. "He's dead."

"Damnit," said the third man. "Covington isn't going to like it."

NINETEEN

Jordan had not eaten since he munched on peanuts and cashews at the Algonquin. He considered room service, calling for a rare steak and a bottle of whatever they claimed to be their most expensive red wine. But, deciding he didn't feel like sitting alone in the room, he dialed the operator to see what sort of restaurant was available downstairs. He was not surprised to find that his call went directly to an FBI hookup.

"Well," he said, "do you think you can at least get me a decent table?"

Yes, the agent told him humorlessly, he was free to go down to dinner. Then hung up.

WHEN JORDAN LEFT his room, he was greeted by a brief nod from an agent stationed in the hallway. Whatever Prescott and Covington were up to, they were serious about keeping tabs on him.

He rode down in the elevator and then strolled through the lobby, keeping an eye out for familiar faces, friendly or otherwise. He entered the restaurant and went straight for the bar. It was a dark room with reflective ceilings, sparkling walls, and black lacquer cocktail tables—all about as cozy as stainless steel. Still, Jordan was happier here than sitting upstairs.

He ordered a Jack Daniels Single Barrel on the rocks and had a seat.

He knew he was being watched. He also knew that any attempt to leave the hotel would create havoc. Even so, he longed for one of the comfortable armchairs at the Algonquin.

His drink came and he took a sip, the first burning taste cutting through a long day's thirst. *Maybe I should skip dinner altogether*, he thought. *Maybe I should just get good and drunk.*

He was turning that idea over when he noticed a woman approach. She stopped a few barstools away, standing there, staring at him. She looked to be in her thirties, her trim figure clad in tight jeans and a fitted black v-neck. Her arms at her sides. Her hands empty. She had sandy colored hair and unhappy eyes. In the dimly lit bar he made her for a working girl. He gave her a little frown then looked straight ahead, hoping she would get the idea that he wasn't the type.

She approached him, and he was about to suggest that she peddle her story elsewhere. Before he had the chance, however, she asked quietly, "Are you Mr. Sandor?"

He looked her up and down now. She had a nice shape, an extremely pretty face, and pale blue eyes that seemed even sadder than they had from a distance. "Who's asking?"

"I'm Christine Frank," she said. "Jimmy McHugh's sister."

THE TELEPHONE RANG. Covington was in his room on the concierge level, hanging up the few things he had brought from Washington. It was Nealon. He explained that Beth Sharrow had been attacked but was in stable condition.

"How the hell did that happen?"

"They had just arrived," Nealon told him. "Two men were being positioned inside, one at the front. As soon as they heard her scream, they went through her door."

"And the man?"

"He's dead, sir. He was armed. We had no choice but to fire."

Covington sat down on the edge of the bed. Holding the phone in one hand, he rubbed his face with the other. "Any ID on him?"

"Not yet."

"Check all sources. Find out what you can about him. See if we can connect some dots here."

"Yes sir."

Covington put down the hotel phone, reached for his cell and placed a call.

JORDAN HAD TURNED on the barstool to face the young woman. "You mind spinning around once? Slowly."

"Excuse me?"

"I've been kind of unpopular lately," he said. "I don't need another stranger making an unfriendly visit. Not up close and personal like this."

She blinked, not moving.

"The way those jeans fit, I don't think I need to frisk you, but just to be sure . . . if you don't mind."

Christine responded with a confused look. "Are you asking me if I have a gun or something?"

"Or something, yes." Jordan was holding his drink, watching her. "A gun, a bomb, a blackjack, a hidden microphone. Anything at all. Yes, that's what I'm asking."

She forced a smile and, although it took an effort, he thought it was a very good smile. It managed to light up her entire face just for an instant. Even her doleful eyes.

She did a pirouette for him, even lifting her sweater just enough to expose some of her midriff which, as far as he could tell, was also pretty good. There were no wires, and there was no gun.

"All right?"

"I'm sorry," he said. "Sit down."

She took the seat beside him.

Her features were cleanly drawn, her lips full, her tousled blond hair worn to shoulder length, a natural color for her fair complexion. Her pale blue eyes were tinged with red and a bit swollen. There was a slight scar over the left brow that gave a hint of character. She rested her hand on the bar, her fingers moving up and down to some beat that had nothing to do with the piped-in music playing in the background.

"Relax," he said. "Can I get you something?"

"No."

"I was going to have dinner. Thought I'd eat at the bar, if you're interested."

"No, thank you."

"A drink?"

She thought it over. "All right."

The bartender came over to see what was going on, especially after Christine did her little one-step rumba.

"New jeans," Jordan said to the man. "She wanted me to see how well they fit."

The bartender appeared unconvinced. "Can I get you something?" he asked her.

"Yes, please. Uh, whiskey sour. Straight up. And sweet."

"Right," the man said, took another look at the two of them before shoving off to mix the drink.

"Whiskey sour, sweet and straight up. You're a real boozer, I can tell."

"Not really, no," she said.

"So you're McHugh's sister?"

"Half sister."

"I'm sorry about what happened."

She looked down at her hands, and he thought she might start crying.

"Sit down," he said, and so she perched on the stool beside him.

"I heard you were here for questioning," she said, almost in a whisper. "Like me."

"How did you hear that?"

"The state trooper from Woodstock, the one in charge there."

"Uh huh."

"Then the officers who brought me here. They said you were staying here too."

"They told you I was here?"

"Yes. I mean, they didn't say it was you. They said there was someone else they were 'helping,' but I knew it was you from the uh . . ."

"I know, the trooper upstate."

"Right."

"So how did you know who I was?"

"The trooper described you."

"I guess Captain Reynolds has quite an artistic way with words. You made me right away."

"No, actually. You're the third man I've approached in the past hour." She gave him another look at her smile. "I think that's why the bartender is watching me."

"He's not the only one."

She looked over her shoulder at two agents seated at a small table between them and the exit to the main lobby.

"I noticed them when I came in. And they're letting you run free in here, picking up strange men at the bar?"

"I wouldn't put it like that."

He took a sip of whiskey. "So they offered you protective custody?"

"Yes," she nodded anxiously. "At first they were nice about it. The men upstate. I told them I didn't need any protection, but they insisted and drove me down here. I was in a daze after finding out about, you know, about Jimmy. They said there were men in New York wanted to question me. So that's what they did, all afternoon. Question me. Then they told me I should stay here overnight—for my own safety—and think things over." She began to stall out.

"Go on," he said.

"I don't know what I'm supposed to think over."

"You could have just gone home."

She shook her head, as if he made less sense than they did.

She was pretty good, he thought, *but Covington could have done better.*

The bartender brought her drink and Jordan asked for another.

"You sure you don't want dinner?" Sandor asked her.

"I don't think so. I'm not hungry."

"Well, here's to better days," he said, holding up his glass as he watched her sip at the tart cocktail.

"I went to Woodstock to see Jimmy," she said, then demurely wiped her lips with a paper napkin.

Definitely not much of a drinker, Sandor noted.

"When I got there, I found out what happened." She looked at him, her blue eyes wide, her posture considerably more relaxed than when she first walked up to him. She let out a long, audible sigh as she pushed flaxen strands of hair from her forehead.

Jordan shrugged and finished off his Jack Daniels in a gulp.

"So what do you want?"

She hesitated. "I want to leave. I have to leave."

"Call a lawyer. You're not accused of any crime, right? Why come to me?"

She shook her head slightly, as if to say she was not sure. "I don't know. I thought . . . from what the captain upstate said about you and what they said here . . . I thought—"

"That I would help you."

"Yes."

"I know it sounds crazy—"

"That it does. So what exactly am I supposed to help you do?"

She looked at him again. "I want you to help me to get out of here. I have to go someplace. And even if you don't want to go with me—"

"Go with you?"

"Yes."

"Uh huh. Look, Miss Frank, people have taken to shooting at me the past couple of days. Your brother and a very good friend of mine are already dead. I'm the last guy in the world you want to be standing next to right now. No offense, but maybe protective custody isn't such a bad idea."

She stared at him hard. "But you don't believe that, do you?"

Now it was Jordan's turn to stare. "No," he admitted, pushing some of his hair back with his hand. "I don't."

"But you don't believe me either. I can see that."

"Under the circumstances, I'm sure you can understand if I'm a little skeptical of everyone right now. Whoever you are, you've got to tell me something that might persuade me to help you. Wherever it is you think you're going."

"All right," she said, looking around, then leaning towards him as if she were about to plant a kiss on his cheek, she whispered in his ear. "Jimmy had a friend."

TWENTY

Jordan and Christine took a table in the grill room beside a large wall of dark tinted windows overlooking Times Square. She spoke as quietly as she could, Jordan regularly urging her to lower her voice, knowing that Covington, the FBI, or both, could be remotely monitoring the conversation. The two agents, still seated near the entrance to the bar, did not appear all that interested, except perhaps to block any attempt they might make to leave the place. Even so, Sandor knew they could easily be a decoy.

As he worked on his whiskey and listened, Christine told him about her brother.

James McHugh fought in Vietnam and Cambodia with one of the last groups of Green Berets out of Saigon. He made it home, but his experiences in Southeast Asia cast a shadow he could not outrun. He had seen young American soldiers murdered and crippled in rice paddies and bomb-pocked fields. He left every vestige of his own youth and innocence over there. The reward for his pain and sacrifice was an ungrateful homeland, filled with people who hated the war and behaved as if the veterans themselves were somehow to blame. He found himself in a society driven by a seemingly endless contest for more and greater material comforts, and he could not find a way to compete.

Drink and pills had gotten him through the days and nights as he sought to fit into the new order. Finally, when he thought he might never sober up long enough to regain a sense of purpose, an old comrade-in-arms contacted him about work in the Middle East. The positions being offered were strictly non-combat, involving personnel training, equipment and weapon education, flight instruction and technical assistance. The money was good, and tax-free. Why, his friend asked, pay taxes to a country that has no use for you after it sent you to hell, not caring whether you ever came back?

McHugh followed his friend to Libya.

In the beginning things had been fine, or so he wrote to Christine. He was earning good money, had a certain level of authority and, most important, he had a reason to get up in the morning. He did not tell her the truth about his work, not in the beginning. He claimed he was working for a foreign company. Eventually he confessed what he had been doing, admitting that that he had rationalized his role by being far removed from the actual consequences of his actions. He was a purveyor of military knowledge, nowhere near the bomb blasts in Jerusalem, the assassination attempts in Yemen, the plots to upset the uneasy balance of power throughout the world's most volatile region.

He visited the compound at Bab el-Azziziya, where Qadaffi's disingenuous array of Bedouin tents were actually surrounded by a fortress of walls, bunkers and a sprawling military complex. He went into the desert to training grounds where mock attacks were acted out like rehearsals for a bad action movie. McHugh was not part of the fighting, or so he told himself, even as his doubts were assuaged with money and alcohol and women—all of which were made available to him and his fellow mercenaries in a society where liquor and pornography were contraband.

And so he stumbled forward through the years . . . until one night, when he was watching a cable newscast about the war in Iraq, a report about the soldiers being killed by terrorist assaults . . . until he heard the report about a decorated captain, an old friend, who had been blown to pieces by a roadside bomb . . . until that instant, when he was confronted by everything he had managed to ignore up to then. And then there was Nine Eleven. In a few blinding moments, he was compelled to open his eyes to the contribution he was making to this devastation.

He did not react immediately. Biding his time. Continuing to perform his duties. Waiting several months before requesting leave for some R & R in

France. He contacted Christine, whom he had not seen in more than a decade. She was going on her summer vacation, on leave from her position as an assistant professor of art history at Penn State. He invited her to visit, to tour the museums of Paris, providing a rationale for his excursion. He received permission from the quasi-military order of command, then in June flew to Orly, with the secret intention of disappearing forever.

"That was a couple of months ago," Christine said. "When we got together in Paris, that's when Jimmy told me everything he'd been doing in North Africa."

Jordan nodded. "Go on."

"When he invited me to Paris, he told me he was going to be on vacation. Then, when I got there, he told me he wasn't going back, that he wanted to come home. He was scared. There was fear in everything he said, everything he did. That's when he left Paris."

"And you left with him?"

"No. I flew to Madrid and stayed there for two weeks. He insisted on it, paid in advance for everything—the hotel, plane tickets, everything. He wanted people to think we were going there together."

Jordan shook his head as he contemplated the risk she had unwittingly taken. If her story was true, her brother had placed her life in danger by involving her in his scheme to escape. "And before Paris, you hadn't seen him for more than ten years?"

"Hadn't had a letter from him in more than three."

"Okay. So what happened after Spain, when you got back home?"

"Nothing. Not for a couple of months, anyway. I had no way to find him, no idea where he was. Then I got a call from his friend. He asked me to go to Woodstock and see Jimmy. You know the rest."

"You knew this friend?"

"I only met him once, in Paris this past summer. When he called me the other day, he said Jimmy was in trouble, that he needed my help."

Jordan had another good look at her, allowing a brief silence to fall over them as he studied her pale blue eyes for any sort of tell. "So," he finally said with a sigh, "who are you, really? Who sent you to me? Prescott doesn't have the imagination. It would have to be Covington. But frankly, I expect more of him."

Christine began to speak, but he held up his hand. "Wait. Let me get this straight. You were supposed to tell me this last bit, about your brother's friend. Then we're supposed to compare everything the two of us know and run off into the night to avenge your brother's murder. How am I doing?"

Christine's eyes filled with tears and she began to cry. She sobbed in a quiet,

105

soulful way that Jordan was sure she had calculated for maximum effect.

"Save it," he said, having another pull of his whiskey. "I don't melt at the sight of a woman crying. No hard feelings, but the whole act is wasted on me." He handed her a napkin. "Just go back to wherever you came from and tell them it was a nice try, but it didn't work."

She took the napkin, lowered her head and wiped her eyes. Watching her, he had to wonder. If she was acting, she was very good.

"Come on," he said. "Knock it off."

She looked up at him, her eyes red and swollen again. "I don't understand." She spoke in halting fashion now, struggling to take a deep breath. "Those men, they said you were going to leave, that you'd never stay here. That's why I tried to find you. Why would I lie about all this?"

"Why would you lie? There are all sorts of reasons, believe me. But let's assume you're for real. What do you expect me to do?"

"I hoped you would help me."

"I'm listening." She nodded, and Jordan knew that if he was being taken, he was being taken but good.

"Okay," Christine said, "this other man—"

"Don't say any names," Jordan cut her off.

Christine nodded. "This other man, he was Jimmy's best friend over there," she said. "He was the one who took him to Libya in the first place. Now he's here, in the States."

"I'm still listening."

"These people—the people that killed Jimmy—they'll be after him too."

"And you and I are supposed to save him."

"There's more to it than that."

"Then why not tell the feds?"

"I can't. Don't you see?"

"I'm afraid I don't."

"He told me that if Traiman doesn't kill him, the government will."

The mention of Traiman's name got him to sit up straight in his seat. "No names, right?"

"Sorry. But he was their boss, or whatever, the man they worked for."

Jordan felt his spine stiffen even more. "And what do you expect to do for this other guy?"

"Warn him? Help him? I don't know. He and Jimmy wanted to speak with someone, someone they could trust."

"And that was supposed to be me?"

"I think so."

"And you knew my name before you got here." It wasn't a question.

"Yes," she admitted. "I knew your name."

"From Jimmy's friend?"

"Yes."

"Who got my name from your brother?"

"I'm not sure."

"But he needs your help. Our help."

"He does."

"And he has information he's willing to share with me."

"I believe that, yes."

"Where is he?"

"Will you help me?"

Jordan sat, staring at her. She knew Traiman's name. She knew his name. She told the tale and, if it was not entirely credible, it wasn't the worst setup he'd ever heard. He had to figure she was either a plant from Covington or a trap set by the men who had murdered McHugh and Danny. Either way, he had to know.

"Let's eat something first," he said. "I'm starving."

TWENTY-ONE

Covington was still in his hotel room when Nealon called back.

"We're only getting parts of their conversation," Nealon told him. "They're speaking very quietly. We'll have to go back and filter out the ambient noise on the tape."

"Cut the techno crap, Todd. Where are they?"

"They're still in the restaurant, sir."

Covington sucked air through his clenched teeth. "I mean, in their conversation."

"Sorry. She said McHugh had a friend. She wants Sandor to help her find him."

"Did she give him a name?"

"No sir. Sandor told her not to use names."

"Any location on this friend?"

"Not yet."

"Well stay with it. And keep me informed. Move Prescott's men out of the way if you have to."

"Yes sir."

"But gently. Move them gently."

"Yes sir."

SANDOR HAD A salad, a rare sirloin steak and drank off the best part of a bottle of Opus One. Christine only picked at her salad and barely touched her lamb chops.

As Jordan stood to leave, the two government agents at the far table turned toward him.

"*Upstairs,*" Jordan mouthed towards them, pointing toward the ceiling. He extended his hand to help Christine from her chair and told her, "No reason to have them jumping up and pulling out their guns."

He wrote a large tip on the bill and charged it to the room, then took Christine by the arm and led her back through the bar to the elevators.

"I assume you're staying on the concierge floor with the rest of the spooks."

She reached into her pocket and pulled out the plastic pass key.

"Good," he said. "I've got some calls to make. Then we'll get together again."

CHRISTINE INSERTED THE plastic card into the slot, and they rode up in the elevator. She leaned against the mirrored wall and lowered her head.

"Tired?" Jordan asked.

She nodded.

He moved close to her, whispering directly in her ear. "I want you come to my room in thirty minutes. Bring whatever you need to take with you. No suitcase, just a purse and whatever you can stuff in it."

She nodded again.

"We'll tell them we're going back down to the bar for a nightcap."

The door to the elevator slid open and the guard near the elevator on their floor was still there waiting for them as they stepped out.

"Good evening," Jordan said to him as they walked by. The agent said nothing.

Christine was staying a few rooms down from his, and he walked her to her door.

"Try and relax," he said. "Take a bath or something."

She gave him a curious look.

109

"Women like taking baths when they need to unwind, right?"

She smiled, and he decided that whoever she really was, he definitely liked her smile.

"Stop by in half an hour," he told her in a voice loud enough for their guard to hear. "We'll have one last cocktail." When she was safely inside, he returned to his room, shut the door behind him and flipped the security bolt.

As he stood there, alone in the quiet, his first thought was that something was wrong. All wrong. Covington would never allow this girl to get to him unless he wanted it that way. She had far too much information, including Traiman's name. And why would they permit him to keep his bag with everything intact?

Jordan grabbed the leather satchel from the desk, tossed it on the bed and went through it. Everything was still there, including the cash, the extra passports and his clean cell in the false pockets inside. That didn't mean it had not been searched. It only meant they were willing to let him keep what he had, at least for now.

The obvious question was why. The answer was just as obvious. They wanted him out there, a moving target in search of Jimmy McHugh's friend. And Christine was somehow a part of that plan.

He used the hotel phone to make his first call. "Captain Reynolds, please." It was nearly midnight, and the officer on duty told him the captain could not be reached. There was none of the small talk or cooperation he had had from the other trooper that afternoon, even after Jordan said the matter was urgent. It was apparent that Reynolds' unavailability had nothing to do with the time of night. Someone had cut off that line of communication.

His next call was to Sternlich. Bill picked up the phone on the first ring.

"Sternlich."

"Sorry to call you so late, Billy."

"Forget it. I wasn't sleeping. I've actually been trying to reach you for hours but your cell phone is off."

"I thought it would be better to keep it shut down for now." He did not tell him that he assumed the line was already being tapped.

"Have you heard about Beth?" Sternlich and his wife had known Beth Sharrow from the time she and Jordan had begun seeing each other.

"What about her?"

Sternlich described the attack on Beth.

Sandor paced back and forth in the small room, the phone in one hand, the receiver in the other. He finally stopped moving and sank slowly into the club chair. "How is she?"

"Pretty bad, Jordan. Broken jaw. Shock. A real mess. Good news is they say she'll be all right."

"Lunch," was all Jordan could think of to say.

"What?"

"I met her today for drinks. We were supposed to have lunch, remember? They must have followed me. Used her to get to me." The compassion he felt for Beth quickly passed into anger. "What about the sonuvabitch who—"

"Dead."

"Damnit."

Sternlich did not reply.

"Any word on who he was?"

"Nothing yet. Not that I've heard."

"Where is she?"

"Mt. Sinai. But a visit from you is out of the question. For her sake as well as yours."

Jordan nodded at the phone. "Have you spoken with her?"

"She's under sedation. I'll go over in the morning."

"Right." Jordan gazed numbly out the hotel window at the brightly lit New York City skyline. "So here I am, all over again," he said. "And that sonuvabitch Covington didn't even tell me."

"What?"

"Nothing." He knew Covington's men were listening on this line. His comments were for their benefit. "You get anything for me on that thing I asked you about? Just say yes or no."

"Not really. I feel like a doped-up mouse in a rigged maze. Information roadblocks everywhere, courtesy of Big Brother, which tells me you're onto something important. And dangerous."

"I would say so."

"But you're okay?"

"So far. I'm with McHugh's sister. She's telling me a tale, but I don't believe her. I think they're setting me up. I need to get a couple of drinks in her, then see what she has to say." Sandor clearly wanted Covington's men to hear that. "And Bill, drop this thing I asked you about. I'll take it from here."

"You sure?"

"Absolutely." He was concerned he had already involved Sternlich too much. "Just let me know what you hear about Beth."

"I will. Where are you now?"

"I'm in protective custody, courtesy of the feds."

"Well that's good, anyway."

"I'm not so sure. Meanwhile, this is the number where you can call me," he said, reciting the hotel line and room number."

"All right. I'll call you in the morning."

"Thanks pal," Jordan said, then hung up.

Peters. McHugh. And now Beth. All that was left to him was to search for a man whose name and location he didn't even know. A man who might lead him to Vincent Traiman. Hopefully Covington's men would buy his story that he was taking Christine downstairs for more drinks in the hope of getting her to tell him the truth.

He stripped off his clothes, took his toiletry kit from the bag and went into the bathroom. He brushed his teeth, shaved, then stood in a steaming hot shower, at the end of which he turned the water cold, taking his breath away as it washed away the effects of the bourbon and the wine, reviving him for what he knew would be a sleepless night ahead.

He toweled off, went back inside to his bag and pulled the second cell phone from one of the side compartments. He had to assume both cell phones had been tapped, but this one had an encryption chip that scrambled outgoing numbers and made it all but impossible to decipher the conversation. When Langley scrambles a call, even Langley has a tough time making sense of things. He also assumed Covington had the room bugged, so he went back to the bathroom, turned on the shower and the sink, which should provide enough background noise to muddy up the sound of a quiet conversation. Then he punched in the numbers for his contact's private line.

"Yes," the familiar voice answered.

"Sandor here."

"I was beginning to wonder."

Sandor gave a brief report, including his discussion with Christine. He spoke as quietly as he could.

"What do you think about Christine Frank?"

"I'm not sure. She might be for real."

"Her background check hasn't turned up anything irregular."

"So I'm going to run with it, then."

"Good."

"What about the interrogation?"

"I didn't get much from them. Just a list of names," Jordan said, then recited them. "You didn't tell me about Traiman."

The line was quiet.

"Stay focused, Jordan."

"Yes sir."

Jordan hesitated. "I heard about Beth."

"I'm sorry about that, Jordan." There was only the slightest pause. "When do you move?"

"I'm out of here, tonight. I'm taking the girl with me."

"Good. We're running short on time."

"What about the three al-Qaeda you picked up in DC today?" Jordan asked.

"We're working on it. We don't think they had anything to do with the explosion at Loubar. They also don't seem to know much."

"Want me to come down and take a run at them?"

"If I thought it would do any good, I'd get you here tonight. They were on a need-to-know basis. Or that's what it looks like. They were waiting for instructions."

"Then someone flipped them for another reason."

"That's what we think."

"Who?"

"We're working on it."

"Let me know what you find out."

"Of course. You do the same."

"Only you," Jordan said.

"Only me. At least for now. We can't trust anyone else."

"It may be a while before I can call you again."

"I understand. You be careful. On all fronts."

"Yes sir."

"Remember, this is not personal—you and Traiman."

"Right."

"I mean it."

"I'm clear on that, sir."

"And Jordan . . . it's good to have you back."

Sandor rang off, then nodded into the darkness, reflecting for only an instant on an abandoned career revived.

TWENTY-TWO

It was half past midnight when Christine Frank left her room. The agent on duty eyed her suspiciously as she strolled down the hall and knocked on Sandor's door. Jordan came out into the hall and gave a short wave to their sentry. He received no response.

Once they were in the room, Jordan closed the door and motioned her into the bathroom. He shut that door behind them, then turned on the hair dryer provided by the hotel and laid it on the vanity counter. It roared and rattled against the marble, making the racket he intended to mask their discussion.

"We don't have much time," he told her.

She nodded.

He stood with his back against the wall, arms folded. Christine was dressed in dark blue slacks and a baby-blue crewneck sweater. She had fixed her hair and made up her face, using little in the way of cosmetics as far as he could tell. It was a good look for her.

"So," he said, "let's have it. Speak quietly and give me the whole thing."

Christine took a deep breath.

"Jimmy's friend was a man named Anthony Andrioli. I met him in Paris. He and Jimmy were in the service together. Tony was the one who introduced Jimmy to the Libyan connection. And when Jimmy left France, Tony also disappeared."

Christine said that she had not told this to any of Prescott's men, fearing that Andrioli faced the same danger that led to McHugh's death. She did not tell them Andrioli had contacted her to say that Jimmy was living in Woodstock. She had never even mentioned his name. She had lied but somehow, she explained to Jordan, it seemed the right thing to do at the time.

She understood that Andrioli and her brother were in some kind of trouble. That much was clear to her in France. When Andrioli called her, he said that the threat came not only from the people in the Middle East who were hunting them, but from the American authorities as well. McHugh and Andrioli were criminals, but they had valuable information. They told her that they had made an attempt to trade what they knew for protection, but the government contacts they reached out to had turned them down. Now they were afraid to trust anyone.

"Why me, then?" Jordan asked.

"I honestly don't know. I only know what Tony told me on the phone."

"Which was what?"

"That Jimmy was going to meet with you. That he was going to ask you to help them. I told you, that's how I knew your name. That's why I asked the captain in Woodstock about you."

If she was telling the truth, and Covington was using her to draw him into the game, Jordan was going to take his chances. If she was working for the men who were trying to kill him, and had already murdered McHugh and Peters, he realized that by letting her into his room he would likely be dead already. At least it was a starting point. The compact Walther PPK he had taken from his bag and secured against the small of his back was a reminder of that uncertainty.

"Suppose I buy your story," he said as he carefully studied her, his expression and tone severe as he asked. "Where is Andrioli now?"

"You'll go with me?" she asked.

"Answer the question."

She hesitated. "Florida," she said. "Fort Lauderdale."

He nodded, the din of the hair dryer blowing and vibrating against the hard countertop filling the small room, frustrating any sort of eavesdropping Covington or Prescott might have arranged. "Tell me where he is and I'll go. You'll be safe here. All things considered, protective custody is the best place for you right now. I can take whatever message you want me to deliver."

"No," she said. "I'm scared of these people. Besides, Tony doesn't know you, but he'll speak to you if I'm there."

Sandor nodded. "Fort Lauderdale," he said.

"Yes. Like I said, he and Jimmy had information. Important information. But they don't trust anyone."

"You said that already."

"Sorry."

"Except this guy Andrioli will trust you, right?"

"I think so."

"Even though you only met him for five minutes in Paris."

"He was the one who called me. Told me to check on Jimmy. He was the one who gave me your name."

"You said that already too."

"You're not making this any easier for me."

"If he's got my name already, why do you need to go along?"

"I told you. He'll trust me."

Jordan shook his head. It was all wrong.

She looked directly into his eyes, the din of the clattering hair dryer echoing off the walls of the small bathroom. "Please, can we get out of here?"

"We can try," he said.

"Will we?"

Jordan grinned. "We're going to the bar—"

"The bar?"

"Yes," he said. "I want them to think I'm taking you down to the bar to get you drunk."

"Get me drunk—?"

"That's what I want them to think, all right? Are you always this difficult?"

She nodded.

Jordan turned off the dryer and opened the door. He took her by the arm and led her to the bed. He motioned for her purse, then dumped out its contents. It was a large handbag. She had stuffed in clean panties, an extra top and various sundries. He took his soft, black leather satchel, removed a few unnecessary items, then folded up the sides of his bag and buttoned them in place so it appeared smaller, a feature that came in handy from time to time. He moved close to her and whispered, "This is your purse. You carry it."

They left the room, walking at a leisurely pace to the elevator. A new guard was on duty. The midnight-to-eight shift, Jordan figured.

"We're going downstairs for a nightcap," Sandor said with a smile. "No decent cognac in the mini bar, you know?"

The guard did not smile. "Kinda late, isn't it?"

"Hey," Jordan replied, "you guys can actually speak. I thought this was like Buckingham Palace. Beefeaters. No talking." He pushed the down button on the elevator.

The guard picked up his two-way. "I said, I think it's late."

"Well gee, thanks for the concern pop, but it's never too late for cognac."

The elevator bell rang softly and the doors opened. The guard got to his feet.

"Give me a break," Jordan said with a shrug of his shoulders. "How far can we go in an elevator? We'll see your teammates in the lobby." He held Christine's hand and gently drew her into the lift. "Don't wait up," he said to the agent as the doors closed. The man was already speaking to someone downstairs.

Jordan hit the button for the lobby. Then, as the doors slid closed, he also hit the buttons for floors three, two and one. He looked down at her shoes. "Can you run in those?"

"Run? Sure, if I have to."

"Down stairs?"

"Whatever you say."

He took the bag from her shoulder. "We won't have much time. They won't be suspicious when it stops at three, but when it stops at two and then one they'll be all over us."

When the elevator stopped at three, he grabbed her wrist and pulled her out, heading in a trot down the hallway towards the exit sign. At the end of the corridor he pushed the stairwell door open and led the way down the steps past level two and one and then past the main floor, continuing downward, to the first basement level.

"Come on," he said, urging her to keep up. They reached the lower landing, where Sandor was relieved to find the door open for re-entry. They would have lost too much time if they had had to find another way out. By now the elevator would have made its extra stops and opened in the lobby. The car would be empty, and Prescott's agents would already be searching for them.

They entered a long concrete-lined passageway where the kitchen and room service facilities were located. He turned to the right and they took off.

There was still a skeleton hotel staff on hand at this hour, and a heavy-set black woman in her fifties poked her head out the door to see who was running down the hall.

"Hello," Sandor said pleasantly, coming to a halt. "We need a quick favor."

The woman gave them a suspicious look. "I'll bet."

"We're not running out on our hotel bill, believe me. I'm rescuing my sister from her boyfriend."

"Sister, huh?" the woman replied.

"Yeah. Her boyfriend's a bastard. Beats her. Won't let her go." As he spoke, Jordan pulled a hundred dollar bill from his pocket. "All we need is a back way out of here," he said, holding up the money.

"I could lose my job," the woman said.

"Who'll ever know?" Jordan asked, pulling a second bill out and giving the woman a closer look at the two portraits of Benjamin Franklin.

"Well," the woman said, "I'm not about goin' anywhere with you two, see? But I can tell you the best way out."

Jordan pressed the money into her hand. The woman quickly folded the bills and stuffed them into the pocket of her apron.

"Right there," she said, pointing down the length of corridor. "Third door on your left. Take the stairs down one more flight to the garage, then take the first door to your right and go back up the ramp to 44th Street. You'll run into Louis—he'd be the only one on duty now at the cashier station. You just tell him Celia sent you. He'll let you by without no trouble."

"Thank you, Celia," Jordan said as he turned to race down the hallway.

"I'm not Celia," she called after them. "Celia's a no account pain in my ass. But Louis likes her. And if there's any trouble, it'll be her neck." Then she turned and went back to work in the kitchen.

They followed her directions down another level where they found the entrance to the underground garage. Jordan stopped.

"Hold it." He put out his arm and held her back. They stood in the doorway as he surveyed the large parking area. "Security cameras. Up there." He pointed to a stationary camera off to their left. "We need to get around that one. They'll already be checking the monitors."

"Then what? Can we run up that ramp?"

"They might have agents outside by now," he told her. "I have no idea how much manpower they've thrown at this detail."

"What are we going to do?"

"Only two choices, far as I can tell. We can go on foot—take our chances, hope to get lucky . . ."

"Or?"

"Or, we can steal a ride."

118

He led her into the garage, heading to the right, staying low behind the parked cars, out of the line of site of the security camera. Sandor chose an older model Ford Taurus nosed in to the wall and dropped his bag to the ground. He cupped his hands around his face and peered through the driver's window and saw the blinking red light telling him the alarm system was armed. He checked the car on the other side of him and saw it was also locked. This was a self-park garage, and he would use a bit of self-help to get them out of there. "No problem."

He opened his bag and removed a flat piece of metal with a rounded hook at the end from his cloth-covered tool kit. In a few moments he had the hood open and the alarm system disarmed. He used the same tool to unlock the driver's door. Then he slid under the dashboard, pulled out the ignition wires and started the car while Christine kneeled on the ground beside him. "Come on," he told her, and she climbed across his lap to the passenger side.

Jordan backed the car out, drove up the ramp and stopped at the cashier station. He rolled down his window. The clerk inside the glass booth was a trim black man who appeared to be in his early forties. He asked for the parking receipt.

"You must be Louis," Sandor said.

"I know you?"

"No, but Celia told us to ask for you."

A slight smile came to the man's lips.

"You see, Louis, we've lost our receipt and we're kind of in a hurry. She said you could help us out."

The man's smile vanished. "She did, eh? And how do I know you're not stealing this here car?"

Jordan turned to Christine. "You hear that, sweetheart? Isn't that rich." He turned back to Louis. "Let me ask you something? If I was going to steal a car from this parking lot, why would I choose this old heap?"

Louis nodded at the logic of his argument. "All right," he said as he began to lean forward, "but lemme see your car key. So I know you ain't pullin' the wool, if you see my point."

"Of course," Jordan said but, instead of reaching for the non-existent key, he picked up the Walther and leveled it at Louis' face. "I'm sorry Louis, but if you move a hair, I'm going to have to shoot you in the head. And believe me, I would really prefer not to have to do that."

With his other hand, Jordan pulled a hundred dollar bill from his pocket. "You see, Louis, we have a problem and not much time to work it out. So here's the drill. You raise the crossbar and get out of your booth. You take this hundred dollars and run up the ramp where I can see you. All we need is a minute. Then you can come back here and call the police or whoever you've got to call. In the meantime, you get to keep the hundred.

"So what's it going to be, Louis? I'm all out of time, and I would really hate to have to blow your head off."

Louis started to move.

"Eh eh eh eh," Sandor responded, waving the gun at him. "No panic buttons, Louis."

"Easy man, I'm just gettin' outta the booth."

"Raise the bar first. And Louis, if I hear an alarm go off, I'll come after you. Maybe not right now, but Celia knows where you live."

The bar came up, Louis stepped gingerly from his booth, grabbed the C-note from Jordan's hand and took off like a deer in rut up the ramp.

Jordan stepped on the gas and turned east on 44th Street.

TWENTY-THREE

John Covington was trying to catch a nap in his hotel room, fully clothed, on top of the quilted bedspread when the telephone rang. It roused him from an uneasy sleep. He had the receiver in his hand before the second ring.

"I just got the call from downstairs, sir. He's gone."

Covington nodded into the darkness. "Good."

"It seems Washington was right about him," Nealon said.

Covington bristled at the suggestion that the deputy director, not he, had made that evaluation.

"He's a loose cannon, isn't he, sir?"

"Sandor was never a team player," Covington said. "Now he's not even on the roster."

"Yes sir."

"What else?"

"Sandor tried to reach Reynolds. They shut him down. Then he spoke to his friend, the reporter at the *Times*. He knows about Beth Sharrow."

Covington considered that for a moment. *It might help.*

"We think he made another call, on a cell phone. We couldn't get that one, too much background interference."

"Let me know if you get a trace."

"Yes sir," Nealon said.

"So it's Sandor and the girl."

"She sure won't make for unattractive company for him, will she, sir?"

Covington had enough of Nealon's unenlightening observations. "Did they leave on foot?"

"No, they stole a car from the hotel garage. We're trying to get a lead on them now."

"Excuse me? You're telling me you lost them?"

"Prescott's men lost them, sir."

"I instructed you to move his men aside, not shove them in a ditch."

"We did our best to stay with them, but Prescott's agents were the gate-keepers. Sandor gave them the slip."

"Do we have any information on the car?"

"We do, but it's no help. It was abandoned a few blocks away."

"And then what? Cab, subway, on foot, what?"

"We're tracking that down. You think they'll stay in New York?"

"That's what I need you to find out," Covington replied angrily. "Get on it. And once you pick up the scent again, remember, Sandor will be looking for us, so give him room to move. I don't want him to see us. At least not yet. I want him to spend his energy finding Andrioli, not shaking our team."

Covington didn't wait for an answer before hanging up. He switched on the lamp and stood up, having a look out the window at New York City below. Sandor had taken the bait. He probably wouldn't trust the girl. Not at first. He might not even buy any of what she had told him. All Sandor had to believe was that there was danger and that he could protect her.

As Covington knew, it was a role his former agent would find irresistible. And then, perhaps, he would lead them to Andrioli.

AFTER SANDOR HAD exited the parking garage and turned the Taurus onto 44th Street, he checked the rear-view mirror and saw two agents in front of the hotel. One was on a radio transmitter, the other frantically looking around. He saw one of them point at the car, not certain whether they had guessed right or if they had just received a call from inside the hotel.

Jordan maintained a steady speed, reaching Sixth Avenue where he took a quick left and then another left on Fifty-Third Street. He pulled to the curb and left the car running next to a fire hydrant just east of Seventh Avenue. He told Christine to get out, grabbed his bag and exited the sedan. Shoving the Walther in his pocket he took her hand. They ran to Broadway, then north to 57th Street, where Jordan hailed a cab.

COVINGTON GOT ANOTHER call from Nealon. The FBI had given him some worthless details about the Taurus that Sandor had stolen. They located a man who spotted the couple leaving the car and walking west, toward Broadway. Other than that, they had nothing.

Once it was clear that they had lost Jordan, Covington had no choice but to telephone Washington.

The deputy director was not pleased to be called at one in the morning, especially to be given bad news.

"You're telling me between the FBI and the Agency combined, you lost him?"

"Yes sir."

"Without a single lead on where he's going?"

"So far, that's the situation."

"Unbelievable," Mark Byrnes fumed. "This was supposed to be a long leash, Covington, not an open cage!"

"Yes sir."

"Well, do something about it."

"Yes sir. What about involving the Bureau?"

"What do you think? We have no choice now. Explain the predicament. Tell them to call in their Homeland Security liaison. And try to be diplomatic about it."

"Yes sir."

Byrnes took a deep breath. "You heard about the takedown of the three-man cell, just a couple of hours after the explosion at Loubar?"

"I did."

"Interesting timing. And doesn't it strike you as odd that the informant had a direct number for the Agency? Used that, rather than calling the police or the FBI?"

"The thought had occurred to me," Covington said.

"Yes," the DD replied, musing over the possible implications of that seemingly small issue.

"They could have someone inside, sir. Is that what you're thinking?"

"It's not the most obvious conclusion but yes, that was my concern."

"These men are being interrogated now?"

"Of course."

"Maybe that will lead to something."

Byrnes paused. "We'll see. So far we've gotten nothing. But I intend to become involved in the questioning."

Covington did not voice his surprise at the DD becoming hands on at that level.

"Bottom line," Byrnes said, "find Sandor and find Andrioli."

"Yes sir."

"And Covington . . ."

"Sir?"

"No matter what else goes down, we need Andrioli alive."

"Yes sir."

The DD ended the call without further comment.

JORDAN HAD THE cab take them to a motel he knew, just across the Grand Central Parkway from LaGuardia Airport. It was the sort of motel where the clerk at the front desk was accustomed to the sight of a man and a woman arriving after one in the morning, knowing it was none of his business. Jordan paid for the room in cash—which was also none of the clerk's business. He handed Sandor a key to a room on the second floor and bid them a good night.

Jordan and Christine found the room and let themselves in. It was square with a large, well-used bed against the wall, one chair, an old television bolted to the top of the dresser, and a nightstand. Jordan went to the telephone, set his bag on the floor and began making arrangements for a flight to Fort Lauderdale the next morning.

"Nine o'clock," he said over his shoulder. "That's the first flight I could get us on."

"At least we can get some rest," Christine said. "I haven't slept for two nights."

Finished with the airline, Jordan phoned Federal Express to get an address for the nearest drop box. Next, he called information and got a number and address for a commercial mailbox center in Fort Lauderdale. When he was done, he propped up two pillows and lay down on the bed. Christine sat down beside him.

"So," Jordan said, staring up at the ceiling, "you want to tell me why you're really here?"

She fluffed up her pillows and leaned on her arm, facing him. "I don't know what you mean."

"What I mean is, Prescott wouldn't have held us, at least not for long. You could have contacted anyone you chose—an attorney, a family member, a friend. People must have known you were coming to New York. Captain Reynolds could have helped. You would have been safe. They weren't going to throw you in a dungeon. You could have found a way to contact Andrioli."

"No," she said, "you're wrong. We won't be able to reach him unless we go there and find him."

"That's it? That's your whole explanation?"

"Yes," she said, her voice beginning to tremble. "If you don't believe me, why are you here?"

He turned towards her. "I haven't got anything better to do."

"That's reassuring."

"Look, I'd like to believe you. If you're telling the truth, I have every reason to get on that plane in the morning and help you search for Jimmy's pal. He may have information, as you say, and I want it. Two men are dead, one of them a friend of mine, another in the hospital. And I'm beginning to feel like a moving target in a carnival game. There's a connection somewhere, and your guy Andrioli might know what it is." He let her think about that for a moment, then added, "Of course, if you're lying, there might even be more reason to stay close to you."

"That's it, then?"

"That's it."

"So I'm either a liar or not." The look of sadness in her eyes seemed genuine enough to him. "That's why you're here?"

"That," he said, "and your smile."

She lowered her head, not bothering to attend to the tear that ran down her cheek. "I only met you a few hours ago, and all I've done is cry."

"I've noticed." He sat up to have a better look at her then reached out and tenderly wiped her face with his fingertips. "This is the second hotel room we've been in together and all you do is cry. Could ruin my reputation."

Christine forced a slight smile.

"That's better," he said.

Their eyes met, just long enough for the intimacy of the moment to become uncomfortable. She turned away.

"Come on," he said, "we'll get this all sorted out." He gently pushed the hair back from her face. "It's what I do, you know."

She allowed herself to relax into his arms. "I know," she whispered. "Tony told me."

"Told you what?"

"He told me that's why Jimmy was going to meet with you. That you were a reporter or something, but that you really were something else before."

"Andrioli told you that?"

She nodded and Jordan found himself wishing he could speak with Dan Peters one more time. He pulled away slightly, not speaking as Christine studied his face, the strong line of his jaw, the determined look in his eyes.

"You really can help, can't you?"

"Yes," Jordan said. "I think I can."

TWENTY-FOUR

Mahmoud Rahmad reached Tripoli, via a flight from Paris. He was met at the airport, then traveled by limousine to the progressive center of this historic city, oblivious to the dazzling architectural counterpoints that defined this country in transition. Modern design was mixed with traditional structures, less a blend than a dissonant metaphor of the internal struggles this nation faced. Though a man with considerable appreciation for aesthetics Rahmad was concerned with the more immediate issues at hand.

He arrived at his destination, a contemporary office building situated in the heart of town, and he proceeded at once to the top floor. The elevator rose without pause to the highest level where he emerged into a richly appointed reception area that displayed the occidental taste of its inhabitants. Although most of the international espionage activities in Libya had long been coordinated from the Villa Pietri, this penthouse was another sort of operation. Rahmad was ushered into Vincent R. Traiman's private office.

Traiman was in his middle fifties, with short, dark nappy hair and reptilian eyes. He was not quite six feet tall, with broad shoulders and strong arms. His features were blunt and hard, possessing something of the brutality of a pugilist and the roughness of a former linebacker. He had, in fact, played football in his college days. From there he enlisted in the service, eventually rising to the rank of captain in the United States Army. Later, he worked as an aide in the diplomatic corps before being recruited as a field operative for the CIA.

While he was with the Company, Traiman used his experience and training to land several assignments in the Middle East, where he cultivated influential friends and contacts along the way. He also found a way to amass a small, private army.

The United States government provided unwitting assistance to Traiman's enterprise, having created a sub-class of sociopaths among the combat veterans from Southeast Asia. These soldiers had been part of the elite teams trained to become vicious jungle killers, snipers and close-order assassins. After being continually exposed to the threat of death, these men were incapable of resuming their normal lives after the fall of Saigon.

Some came home ill-equipped to carry on with their prior lives, falling victim to the haunting memories of war. Others re-upped, seeking in military service that sense of danger that had become their personal opiate. But the American Armed Forces could no longer provide what they needed. Even when the United States had wars to fight, they were now different wars. The Gulf War of 1991 was typical of this new era of conflict. Scud missiles and Stingers took the place of boots on the ground. The public had no stomach for sending men overseas to fight in battles perceived to be the problems of other countries. Vietnam had changed all that.

These impatient warriors were not willing to wait more than a decade for the United States to launch its next offensive in Iraq. They became increasingly frustrated, breaking rules and violating laws. Those still in the service became insubordinate to younger, higher-ranking officers who had no idea what real fighting was about. And each of these malcontents had his name and serial numbers entered into the all-knowing computers of the United States intelligence community.

While he was still with the CIA, Vincent R. Traiman had had access to those computers. He knew who these men were, knew that they were candidates for the platoon he intended to build. To the most talented men who were unable to leave the thrill of war behind, he offered lucrative contracts. He used his position not only to create personal profit through illegal arms transactions, but also to build his own forces. These were men he could enlist, not to risk death for God, country or ideology, but for money. And a renewed sense of purpose. And the sheer excitement of battle.

When Traiman left the CIA, he did not resign. He simply disappeared, drawing on the protection of his own palace guard as well as the resources of al-Qaeda. Ironically, he had never armed himself with so much as a pocket knife.

"YOUR OMISSIONS HAVE become dangerous, Rahmad." Traiman's manner was always direct, his speech a potent economy of words. "You will have to rectify these errors."

"This work has already begun."

"Has it? Then how could you have missed the significance of Jordan Sandor's presence in Woodstock?"

Rahmad hesitated, then said, "We have placed a team on Sandor."

"Yes, I know. And does this team know that Sandor is no longer in government custody?"

Rahmad did his best to conceal his surprise. Just before he left New York, he was informed that Sandor had been taken by the FBI. Now Traiman was suggesting that his intelligence sources in Libya were better than Rahmad's, right there in New York. "We suspected that he would be released," he lied. "Our team is on this."

"Are they? We'll see. Are you also aware that Tafallai was killed last night in New York? In the process of attacking a woman Sandor worked with at the Agency?"

"I've been flying all night. I—"

"Yes, I understand that. But in the meantime, your principal concern remains unresolved."

"Andrioli," Rahmad said tentatively.

"Of course."

Now Rahmad's eyes avoided Traiman's critical gaze. "I must be honest and report that our men have been unsuccessful in locating him. If McHugh knew where he is, our men were not able to extract this information."

Traiman's laughter had no trace of humor as it cut through the tension of the interview. "Very noble of you, Rahmad, to admit the failure of your men. And what of you? What part do you have in this failure?"

The Arab did not respond. He suffered Traiman's anger in silence, still averting the cold gaze that bore down upon him. He only looked up when Traiman stood and walked to the wall of windows behind his desk.

"It has become increasingly difficult to recruit skilled men." Traiman spoke as he looked out at the city, his back to Rahmad. "We have had to increase salaries and bonuses, and to give assurances we prefer not to give. Revelations from our friend Andrioli could compromise our plans, not to mention the efforts of the teams we have already put in place. The longer he remains at large, the greater the risk."

"I understand."

"We are at a crossroads, Rahmad, and time is a luxury we do not have. You understand that too, I presume."

"I do."

Traiman turned to face him. "It happens that I do know where we can find Mr. Andrioli. We have a team ready to depart for the United States today."

Once again, Rahmad was rocked by Traiman's superior intelligence sources. "Where?" he asked, straining to sound composed.

"Don't be concerned," Traiman said with an abrupt wave of his hand.

Rahmad wanted to know where Andrioli was and how Traiman had learned of his location, but held his tongue.

"You will meet with the team this morning. Right now. They will debrief you. Tell them everything you know about Andrioli. Give them all the information your men have gathered."

"Of course," Rahmad agreed quickly.

Traiman replied with an impatient look that said he no longer expected much from Rahmad. "Our teams are moving into place in New York and San Francisco. They're already situated in London and Rome. However, we received some other bad news. The group in Washington has been compromised."

"I am aware of that," Rahmad said, grateful to finally be told something he already knew, even if he had learned of it from Fox News before leaving the States. "A tragedy."

"Yes," Traiman agreed. Although Rahmad doubtlessly suspected that he was behind the explosion at Loubar, there was no reason for him to suppose that Traiman had orchestrated the betrayal of the team in Washington.

"How were they discovered?" Rahmad asked.

"We're investigating that now. Their cell is being blamed for the explosion at Loubar."

"Is that possible?"

"Of course not."

Rahmad's eyes narrowed as he said, "Their capture must have been a blow to our friends here."

Traiman nodded, not revealing to Rahmad that he had been the one behind the exposure of the hit team in Washington, "Yes, a shame, but all part of the business we have chosen. For now we must deal with the technical supplies being shipped from Loubar. Since the problem with Mr. Fryar has been resolved to our satisfaction, we'll need to monitor the situation until a new chief executive of that company is selected."

"Of course."

Traiman also kept to himself the pressure he was receiving from Qaddafi's regime to leave Tripoli. He was becoming a political liability, and was preparing to abandon his bunker in Libya for a yacht that would take him to anonymous safety on the Mediterranean. In the meantime, the release of the shipment from Loubar would be enough to buy him some needed time.

"Your assistance may be required in that process," he told Rahmad. "If you are contacted by a man named Groat, you are to give him your full cooperation."

TWENTY-FIVE

It was nearly two in the morning by the time Jordan and Christine had finished talking. She claimed not to know anything more of importance than she had already shared with him, but Sandor encouraged her to go over everything again, filling in some blanks along the way.

Jimmy McHugh was actually her half brother, which explained their different last names. He was more than ten years older than Christine. Born when their mother was a teenager too young to take care of her baby. Jimmy was raised by foster parents, and Christine never knew of his existence until after both of her parents had died. Christine, who believed she was an only child, had come to live in the care of her mother's sister, Aunt Sarah in Wilkes Barre. It was Aunt Sarah who told both Christine and Jimmy the truth. Jimmy, who was already in the service, had begun writing to his sister from Vietnam. Christine met him a couple of times after the war, but he was moving around a lot in those days, and they lost touch again for several years.

Christine had difficulty speaking about her family, at times unable to look directly at Jordan as she recounted her personal history. Jordan helped keep her on track, not expressing his continuing skepticism, eventually leading her back to her final meeting with McHugh in Paris.

Christine said that she had begun to hear from Jimmy again less than a year ago. There were some phone calls and letters from overseas. Then a few months ago he had written and asked her to come to France.

When she visited her brother in Paris, she really believed it was going to be a family reunion and a vacation. "The day after I arrived, that's when he told me the truth. At least most of it. He said he needed help to get away from the people he was working for. That's why he sent me to Madrid. He wanted them to believe we were going to visit the Prado and all that, with my being an art history professor."

"You mentioned."

"Well, an assistant professor."

"Right. But he put you in harm's way. They could have come looking for you to find him."

She was sitting up against the padded headboard now. "I know," she said. "What else could he do? He needed me."

Jordan realized he was becoming angry at this dead man's thoughtlessness and the selfish risks he took at her expense. Then he thought of Dan Peters, and of Beth, and exhaled slowly. "I guess he did," he said.

"He still does," she said softly.

He let that go. "And you didn't share any of this with Prescott?"

"Not really. I just told him that Jimmy was my brother. He didn't seem very interested in my past."

"What was he interested in?"

"Mainly about anything Jimmy told me, how I came to be visiting him, that stuff."

"Did you tell him about Paris and Madrid?"

"Yes. But actually, it was the other man who asked me about it."

"Covington?"

"Yes."

"What did you tell him?"

"Everything except about meeting Tony."

"Did you talk about helping him?"

"I told you, I never even mentioned his name."

"Did they?"

She shook her head.

"Well, we'll find out how much help we can be to Mr. Andrioli in a few hours. Let's get some rest."

She got up from the bed and pulled back her side of the covers. "I don't have anything to sleep in," she said.

Jordan stood up and turned down the other half of the bedspread. "How about I turn around, you get yourself ready and climb under the sheets?'

She laughed. "What a prude you are, Mr. Sandor." She began to undress. "You going to just stand there and make me feel ridiculous?"

"Sorry," Jordan said, his back to her now. He stripped down to his underpants, then dialed the automated wake-up call mechanism. He climbed under the sheets and switched off his light as she did the same on her side of the bed.

"Just one last thing," he said quietly into the darkness. "Who is Tony to you? Really."

"I told you. He's Jimmy's best friend."

"That's it?"

"That's it."

"And you're willing to risk your life to get to him, to warn him?"

He waited until she finally said, "No. That's not what this is about. Not for me. Jimmy wanted to do something. He and Tony, they have information they wanted to give to someone they could trust."

"And that's us."

"Yes," she whispered.

"All right."

"But what you just said. About risking my life."

"Yes?"

"It's hard for me to think of it like that. I still can't, you know?"

"I understand."

They let the darkness fill the quiet for a while.

"It's hard for me to believe Jimmy is gone," she said.

Jordan didn't respond.

"You'll watch out for me, won't you?"

"Yes, I will. Now try and get some sleep. Tomorrow's going to be another long day."

He heard her utter a sigh. Felt her relax a little beside him.

He wanted to believe her, but he didn't. She had just lost her brother, and yet she hadn't even mentioned a funeral. Her family saga was sketchy at best, delivered in a staccato fashion that spoke more of invention than remembrance. He believed that she was truly frightened, but he still wasn't convinced he knew what was driving her.

PRESCOTT FOUND COVINGTON in the hotel lobby. It was the middle of the night. Neither the late hour nor his sour mood helped Prescott's lousy complexion and homely face. There were no polite greetings as he approached.

"Well?" Covington asked.

"Still nothing," Prescott admitted.

"I wish I could understand this. I really do. You were alerted that they were on the move and you lost them fifty yards from the hotel."

"Save it," Prescott barked back at him. "You can throw your weight around someplace else. My people know their job."

"Of course."

"We're working on a lead. They may have been spotted on foot, heading up Broadway."

"Look, don't misunderstand. I'm not here to criticize the Bureau's procedures. But we have a shared problem. We need to find them, or it'll be an embarrassment to both of us."

"Not to mention a danger to the Frank girl, if your friend Sandor is allowed to run amuck."

"Yes, that too," Covington replied, sounding less concerned than Prescott had expected, but he let it go.

"So when are you going to drop this State Department bullshit and tell me why the CIA is involved?"

Covington pressed his thin lips together and nodded. "You need to make a phone call," he said. "And so do I."

TWENTY-SIX

As Sandor struggled to find a couple of hours' sleep in the middle of the New York night, Mahmoud Rahmad was completing his interview with two men who had been brought to Vincent Traiman's office in the heart of Tripoli.

One was an American, tall and trim with straight, dark hair and pointed features. The second was an Englishman, who stood a bit shorter than his companion, with reddish hair, a wide nose and pale, inert eyes. They were each neatly attired in suits and ties, ready to pose as corporate types who would soon be en route to the United States.

Traiman was in attendance as Rahmad provided the details of the information he had gathered on McHugh, Andrioli and the events of the past two days in New York.

The two assassins listened without speaking, their taciturn manner nettling Rahmad.

"McHugh did not know Andrioli's location," Rahmad told them. "McHugh's sister was their go-between." He looked from the American to the Englishman, but neither reacted. While Rahmad shared what he knew, he also wanted information from them. That was his business, after all. Information.

He had no way of knowing that these men were under strict orders from Traiman to reveal nothing. Neither was even authorized to disclose their ultimate destination.

Rahmad proceeded with his monologue, going over things twice at Traiman's prompting.

Then Traiman stood and announced the interview was at an end.

He and Rahmad bid the men good fortune, then had them escorted to a car for the ride to the airport. There, they would board a flight to Paris, the first leg on their journey to Miami International and then Fort Lauderdale.

AT FIRST LIGHT, Bill Sternlich got out of bed without waking his wife, pulled on his old, white terrycloth bathrobe and shuffled his way into the kitchen to put on a pot of coffee. His laptop was on the table, and he connected to the internet. As he waited for the water to boil, the screen on his computer came to life, and he checked his e-mails to see whether any leads on Jordan's requests for information had come through. Sandor had told him to drop the search, but curiosity was a professional hazard. There were several messages, none related to his requests on James McHugh. He scrolled down, stopping at an e-mail from an unfamiliar source. The transmission was marked "Urgent!"

He opened it and stared at the screen. The note read:

The girl was a warning to those who interfere.

You have been warned.

SANDOR AWOKE IN the unfamiliar surroundings of their room at the La-Guardia motel. He quietly slid out from under the sheets, canceled the wake-up call and grabbed his clothes from the chair. He showered and dressed before Christine was up.

He had his leather bag in the bathroom, and carefully removed the S & W .45 and the Walther PPK with their extra clips. He wrapped each gun in a hand towel, stuffed them back in the satchel and opened the door.

She was still asleep. He stood over the bed, watching her for a moment. He was a professional. She was a liability. He would take her to Florida and try to find Anthony Andrioli. After that, he would have to cut her loose.

"Come on," he said, gently shaking her by the shoulder, rousing her into consciousness.

Christine looked around, confused for a moment, then smiled at him as she raised her arms and stretched. "I was having the strangest dream."

"Tell me about it on the plane. It's time to get ready." Jordan pulled on his jacket and picked up his bag. "I'll be back in a few minutes."

"Where are you going?"

"I've got to take care of something."

She looked worried.

"I'll come right back," he repeated. "Bolt the door behind me."

Sandor walked the five long blocks to the FedEx drop box he had called for the night before. The box stood in front of one of the better hotels near the airport. He opened the top slot holding supplies, pulling out one of the large Tyvek envelopes and a mailing label. He wrote out the address of the drop-box center in Fort Lauderdale he had looked up, using the name from his second passport as the recipient. He also used a false name and address for the sender and checked off the box that read "Bill Recipient." Then he pasted the label to the envelope.

Jordan stopped and had a look around. People were already coming and going at this hour, but no one was paying any attention to him. He pulled the two towels from his satchel, placed them in the envelope, sealed it with the adhesive strip and dropped the package with a thud into the metal deposit box.

Sandor knew there was no chance to get his weapons past security at the airport, even if he checked the leather bag through. The high-resolution screeners would have their sirens blaring in an instant. It had been too late last night to get them out for delivery this morning, and he would not have been happy about giving up the protection anyway, just in case he had been followed to the motel. Sending them ahead was his only chance to get them down South, although he would not be able to retrieve them until tomorrow, assuming they would not be intercepted in transit. He might have other options for securing a weapon once he was in Florida, but he couldn't be sure.

Jordan's immediate problem was that he was unarmed now with so far to travel and so much ahead of him. He felt naked.

He hurried back to the motel through the chilly morning, mulling over what still remained in his leather case.

He had his real passport; the second passport in the name of Scott Kerr; two clean credit cards in the name of his alias; a dummy passport form that could be made up with a photo and name, as the need arose; almost ten thousand dollars in cash, which he had already been using, a hundred dollars at a time; both cell phones, which may or may not be compromised at this point—he had to assume they were—and a small address book with names, phone numbers and a series of codes that might yet come in handy.

He inhaled deeply and exhaled slowly, his breath forming a small cloud in the cold air before him as he walked briskly along, wondering if he was already being followed.

PRESCOTT AND COVINGTON sat down for an early breakfast in the hotel restaurant. Their meeting a few hours before, after losing Sandor's trail, had not satisfied the FBI man, and he demanded a full briefing.

"I've been authorized by the Agency to advise you of certain facts," Covington began. There was neither explanation nor apology for the deception he had employed up to that moment. "McHugh was wanted by our CTC group for questioning. Sandor is one of our former operatives who became involved, strictly by happenstance."

"Bullshit," Prescott said.

"Excuse me?"

"I said bullshit. And I mean it on at least two counts. First of all, you spooks don't have any former operatives. The CIA doesn't have a retirement plan for field agents. And his being there was no coincidence. I also made my phone call, and Homeland Security wants you to give me the full background on everything you've got. This is a domestic issue, Covington, and CIA has no jurisdiction."

"That's your story," Covington said and picked up the menu.

Prescott reached across the table and pushed the menu aside. "It's a little late to be throwing your weight around. We lost this guy because of you. Your men interfered with our containment detail, and I need to know how you want me to fill out my report. Should I say that you wanted him gone or that you're just an idiot?"

Covington blinked. He was smaller and more narrowly built than Prescott. He was not a man comfortable with physical anger. He placed the menu on the table. "Sandor is on the move because he stumbled onto something, and we're using that to assist us. He and Miss Frank may have a lead on someone we need to find. An associate of McHugh's. Whether you choose to believe me or not, Sandor is no longer working for us."

As far as Covington was concerned, this was an accurate statement. At the moment, there was only one man in the CIA who knew otherwise. "The fact is, he and the girl are in grave danger, but we are willing to take that risk, given the serious matters at stake."

"*You're* willing to take the risk? You guys kill me. Did anyone ask Christine Frank if she's willing to take the risk?"

Covington stared back at Prescott.

"So that's it?" Prescott demanded. "That's the full level of cooperation we get?"

"That's all that I'm permitted to divulge at this time."

"I see. And are we supposed to be looking for them?"

"Yes. You are. As you said, this is CONUS jurisdiction, right?"

Prescott grunted. "So you gave them a lead, they spit the bit and now it's my problem. Is that the way this is going down?"

Covington gave no answer.

"And where do we think they're ultimately headed? Paris?"

Covington's narrow eyes widened slightly.

"That's right. You're not the only one with intelligence sources. We know all about McHugh's plane ticket to France."

"Have you alerted the international airports?"

"I've made the necessary communications, yes."

"JFK, Newark?"

"Logan and DC as well."

"What about domestic flights?"

"We're working on that. A little tougher, of course, but doable."

Covington hesitated.

"What is it?" Prescott demanded.

"Is the Bureau ordering them captured or just followed?"

"You tell me, since this seems to be your show."

Covington looked away from him. "We want them out there," he admitted, then picked up his menu again.

IF A MANHUNT had been mounted to find them, Jordan saw no evidence of it when they got out of their cab at LaGuardia.

He correctly guessed that Covington would thwart any attempts to apprehend them, at least for the time being. Sandor was not worried about benign surveillance. His concern was enemy action. Amidst the busy, early morning pedestrian traffic inside the terminal, he was alert to any indication they were being watched. He glanced at the faces of strangers, particularly those who were standing still rather than moving. He eyed guards and airline personnel as they walked past or looked in their direction. But he spotted nothing unusual as they made their way through the terminal to the automated ticket machine.

He felt particularly vulnerable without a weapon, exposed in the wide-open, pre-security check-in area, where anyone could be armed. He retrieved their tickets from the machine, using one of the credit cards in the name of Scott Kerr. For now, Christine would have to use her real name and identification. They would rectify that, however, once they got to Florida. For now, he could only hope that his name was the one they would be tracking and that he would make it through.

They joined the long, slow line for screening. If they were going to be stopped, Jordan expected it to happen here or at the boarding gate. A TSA agent stood at the beginning of the queue where Sandor displayed their first class electronic tickets. Christine showed the man her driver's license. Jordan held up his passport, opened to the first page.

They moved ahead to join the line, waiting silently as the procession crept along. When it was her turn, Christine went through the metal detector without incident. Jordan placed his bag on the conveyor belt, removed his silver M-clip from his pocket and the steel-banded Rolex Daytona from his wrist and placed it in the gray plastic tray. He stepped through the frame of the machine. It made no sound. He picked up his money and watch, then waited for his bag to slide through on the conveyor belt.

"Could you step over here please," a small, Hispanic woman in a dark blue uniform said to him as he picked up the leather overnight case.

Jordan turned and followed her off to the side, where she instructed him to place the bag on a Formica-topped table.

"Is there a problem?" he asked with a polite smile.

He received no smile in response. "Please sit down and remove your shoes."

Christine was standing twenty or so feet beyond the checkpoint. Jordan gave her a reassuring look, nodding across the wide corridor at a man who was being put through the same drill. He sat down, removed his shoes and watched as the woman passed them through the scanner again.

She brought back his loafers and asked him to unzip the bag.

Sandor was pleased he had taken the time to secrete his additional passports in the false pocket along the inside of the case. The scanner would have picked them up as a bunch papers, but if the guard pulled them out and saw multiple identification documents it would cause a problem.

The woman gave the contents a cursory inspection, then told him he could go.

Jordan slipped on his shoes, picked up the bag and joined Christine.

He took her by the arm and they proceeded through the terminal.

"Routine," he assured her. "I'll probably get stopped at the gate too. Don't worry. Just a random check. Sometimes your number comes up, that's all."

They purchased magazines and coffee, then found seats near their gate. "This is the first time that I've felt safe since we got here," Christine said.

Jordan nodded, not admitting that he would not relax until takeoff. All the same, it was mildly reassuring to know that no one other than airport personnel would be armed on his side of the electronic gates.

When boarding began, Jordan was pulled aside again for a quick search. He chatted amiably with the security guard, all the while scanning the surrounding areas for unfriendly faces.

Once the cursory examination of his bag was completed, he and Christine joined the other first class passengers, settled into their comfortable leather seats, then waited anxiously until the plane filled up and the door was closed.

When the jet made its way to the runway and began its rapid acceleration along the tarmac, Jordan felt his body relax for the first time that morning. He knew they would be in danger again when they landed, but for the next couple of hours he could rest.

He wondered again how much of a risk his traveling companion might be. Then he let the thought go.

He was asleep before the plane completed its ascent.

TWENTY-SEVEN

Fort Lauderdale was warm and humid, but Jordan was not slowed by the change to a tropical climate. They had disembarked without incident, and as they stepped out into the Florida sun, Sandor felt refreshed, his reserves of energy restored.

He removed his sport coat and took Christine's jacket, folding them into his bag which he enlarged by unsnapping the sides. They took a cab and headed for the marina.

The address Christine had for Andrioli—which Jordan would only have her tell him once they were on the plane—was a numbered boat slip along the Intracoastal Waterway at New River Drive. The taxi moved along the sun-bleached streets to Las Olas Boulevard, the main thoroughfare adjacent to the canal. Christine had directions that would lead them from there to the docksite of the boat where Andrioli was staying.

At Sandor's request, the cab driver let them out at a corner about a quarter mile from New River. They stood there for a few moments, Jordan looking up and down the street.

"What are you thinking?" Christine asked him. "You didn't say a word the entire ride over here."

"It just strikes me as odd that you have his address, that's all."

"What's that supposed to mean?"

"Just what I said. This guy is in mortal danger. He's hiding from his own government, not to mention the people who killed your brother. It just seems strange that he'd be giving out his address like he was having a cocktail party. He could have given you a cell phone number, a contact address. That's what I mean."

"What you're really saying is that you still don't believe me."

"Come on, we can't stand here all day. Let's walk."

Christine remained where she was. "Tell me. Do you believe me or don't you?"

"No," Jordan said. "Not completely."

Christine's angry look told him she was all done with sadness, at least for now. "Why are you here, then?" she demanded. "Why?"

Jordan's eyes narrowed. "The truth?"

"Of course, the truth."

"Because it doesn't matter whether or not you're lying to me. You're the only lead I have right now. I'd just as soon not step on any land mines along the trail, that's all."

The frankness of his response seemed to diffuse her anger. Her voice softened again as she said, "I'm not lying to you. Jimmy didn't want to know where Tony was, just in case, in case . . ."

"I understand."

"I was the contact."

Standing there in the Florida sun, as the reflection of the bright morning danced off her sandy-colored hair and her clear blue eyes gazed up at him, he wanted to trust her. But too many years of training and too much experience in the field told him that he should know better. "It's all right," he said in a soothing voice. "We're here to find this guy. Let's find him."

They exchanged a momentary look that became a truce.

"All right," she said with a nod, and they walked on to their unscheduled appointment with Anthony Andrioli.

TRAIMAN'S MEN WERE scheduled to arrive in Florida that evening. Their plane, having departed from Paris, was already cruising high above the Atlantic as

Christine and Jordan strolled along the cement pier that ran beside Fort Lauderdale's inland canals.

But the assassins sent by Traiman were not coming for Jordan. They were not even certain he would be there. These two well-dressed men, seated comfortably in their business-class seats, were coming to find Anthony Andrioli.

Traiman did not like losing men, particularly those he had recruited himself. Competent men. Men who knew more about his plans than was comfortable for them to know, now that they had departed his organization. In his world, there was no provision for early retirement. He certainly agreed with Special Agent Prescott about that.

In the instance of the hit team in DC, however, he had arranged to betray those men himself. They had been dispatched to Washington as part of a program of coordinated assassinations. They had been awaiting instructions on their targets, the dates for action and the precise plans for implementing the murders of several high-ranking legislators. When they were arrested, they were still looking forward to receiving their orders.

But there were no orders coming. And there was no program of coordinated assassinations. Traiman had sent these men as a decoy, planning for Groat to turn them in as soon as his mission at Loubar headquarters was complete. These Arab assassins would be arrested, blamed for the explosion, interrogated. One or more of them would crack—Traiman was counting on that—and the Americans would then believe they had discovered a new al-Qaeda conspiracy involving several teams of assassins being sent to the United States to murder political leaders.

But there was no such conspiracy. The authorities would run off in all the wrong directions, spending their energy and resources protecting congressmen and cabinet secretaries, entirely missing the essence of Traiman's real plan. And no one would know the truth.

No one, Traiman feared, except Anthony Andrioli.

When McHugh and Andrioli disappeared from Paris, Traiman began by making conciliatory gestures. He offered them special inducements through an intermediary in France to bring both men back. McHugh and Andrioli were well aware of how generous such enticements could be—the money, women and drugs that were virtually without limit. They were also aware of how Traiman would ultimately make them answer for their disloyalty.

When neither man responded to these entreaties, all indications were that they had returned home. Traiman assigned Rahmad and his US based espionage network to find and remove them. They had now been successful in locating

McHugh, but McHugh was never as bright as Andrioli. McHugh made stupid mistakes, using the telephone, contacting people. Once they tracked him down, the methods employed by Kerrigan and Mustafa to get him to talk were direct and brutal.

Under torture, McHugh admitted his suspicions that the assassination teams sent by Traiman were diversionary. That there was another offensive being planned for the United States and elsewhere. But he admitted that he lacked any knowledge of the details.

Andrioli was another matter entirely.

Traiman was therefore obliged to put the mission on hold until he could determine the extent of the damage the second of his two traitors might cause by revealing what he knew to American authorities. The interference of David Fryar at Loubar with key shipments had caused another temporary setback. As Traiman realized, his Arab associates were not patient men, and their intolerance of the delay was growing.

That was the reason Traiman summoned Rahmad to Tripoli. Every now and then, a face-to-face meeting was necessary, if for no other reason than to remind his subordinates of his influence.

Even though some time had been wasted on the journey east, it would be paid off in the effect of the visit. Mahmoud Rahmad needed to have the importance of this task emphasized, his own expendability underlined.

Rahmad would be sent back to New York to fulfill his other responsibilities and, soon, Anthony Andrioli and the growing stain of his betrayal would cease to be a problem.

TWENTY-EIGHT

The boats on the New River canal were docked broadside, bow to stern, secured with spring lines, their hulls cushioned by bumpers against the concrete bulkhead. Jordan and Christine strolled along the northern embankment, silently reading each transom, searching for the name Christine had for Andrioli's boat. which was all she had. The name of the boat and the general location of the dock.

They moved without speaking, Jordan's sense of uneasiness amplified by the fact that he was unarmed. He walked with his bag slung over his shoulder. Christine stayed right beside him as they passed an assortment of cabin cruisers and sailboats. As each boat came into view, their anxiety intensified. Perhaps Andrioli had abandoned the vessel, or moved to another marina. He might have put out to sea. Christine might have the name wrong.

The midday sun now conspired to heighten their discomfort, the cloudless sky offering no relief. They were fresh from the chill of autumn in the north, and the early feeling of comforting warmth was replaced with a sweltering heat. Sandor found himself wishing he could change from his long-sleeved knit shirt.

They had just passed a two-masted sloop called the *Excess* from Wilmington,

Delaware, when the stern of the next vessel, a power boat, came into view. It was about forty feet long, of white fiberglass construction with teak trim. It bore the name *Winsome II.*

Christine stopped, but Jordan took her arm and urged her forward, the two of them continuing past the boat in silence.

Sandor was a stranger to Andrioli. He knew he could not step aboard the vessel without risking a sudden and violent reaction. Christine would have to make the approach. That much was certain.

As they passed the bow of a cabin cruiser docked ahead of Andrioli's, Jordan said, "Look, we have no way of knowing what the situation is in there. He may not be alone. He may not be there at all. He may have other visitors already, we can't be sure."

They stopped and Jordan turned to have another look at the *Winsome II.* It appeared very quiet. "How well do you really know him?"

"I told you. I met him in Paris, with Jimmy."

"And he'll recognize you?"

"Of course."

"So you'll have to go first. I'll wait just off to the side. There," he said, pointing to a bench along the walkway.

Jordan knew they had already been standing there long enough. "All right, go to the stern and call for him. Quietly. First name only. And be careful. First sign of trouble, anything that bothers you, you take off. Understand?"

She nodded and turned towards the boat, then looked back again. "What should I say to him?"

"Say hello. Tell him you're in trouble and ask to come aboard. Tell him your brother's dead." The last statement sounded harsher than he intended. "I'm sorry. Look, just let him hear your voice. Let him have a look at you. I'll be waiting right there."

Jordan walked away, stopping beside the wooden bench, watching her. *Damn,* he thought, *I would feel a lot better if I had a gun.*

The *Winsome II* was a solid looking sport fishing boat with an enclosed wheelhouse, flying bridge and deep-sea rigs. There was no activity that Sandor could detect. No sign of movement above or below deck. Maybe Andrioli was out. Maybe he really was gone.

He watched Christine lean forward and knock on the hull near the aft railing. She knocked again and, when she received no response, moved forward to have a look inside through a porthole of the main salon. She knocked again. There was no reply.

Jordan moved towards her now. Something did not feel right. When he moved up behind her, she nearly jumped with fright.

"You scared me to death!"

"He's not answering?"

"I called his name, but I didn't want to yell it out."

Jordan looked behind them, up and down the quay. "Call your own name," he said.

"What?"

"Tell him who you are."

She leaned closer to the opening into the stern cabin. "Tony," she called out softly. "It's Christine. We're here to see you."

She said it again and they waited.

"Move two steps back," a voice from somewhere inside the vessel responded now, "and keep your hands at your sides. Nice and natural now, the both of you."

Two steps back would put them squarely in front of the salon porthole. Jordan thought about diving to the ground before a shot could be fired, but that would leave Christine an easy target. He hesitated. Whoever was inside could have taken them out already, if he was willing to shoot them right there, in the open. He dropped his hands to his sides. "Come on," he said, taking her by the wrist and pulling back.

They stepped away from the railing then heard Christine's name spoken in an astonished tone from the disembodied voice. "Come aboard, both of you. But leave your hands where they are. Especially you, cowboy."

"Hold it," Jordan snapped, taking hold of her arm again, before she could step forward. "We're not moving anywhere until Christine gets a look at you."

There was silence. Then a curtain was pulled back at the porthole of the main salon, below deck, and a face appeared. The man peered cautiously from beside the short drape. Even with a growth of beard and shaggy hair, Christine knew him at once.

"Tony," she exclaimed with relief.

"All right," he barked in military fashion. "Get aboard. And buddy, you leave your hands out where I can see 'em," he said, his accent retaining a tinge of his Southern upbringing. "Christine, you take the bag."

They stepped past the opening in the railing, through the wheelhouse and down the stairs to the main sitting area below. If Andrioli trusted Christine, it was belied by the Heckler & Koch USP 9 with the long, silenced barrel he leveled at them as they entered the cabin.

Andrioli was a wiry man somewhere in his fifties, his age tough to judge from the unkempt growth of beard and sloppy attire. His white polo shirt was dirty and wrinkled, and the khakis he wore looked as though they'd been slept in. He studied Jordan and Christine with sad brown eyes as they stepped into the main salon.

"Sorry for my crude idea of hospitality," he said. "Close that hatch behind you and latch it."

Jordan did as he was told.

"All right, lemme have a look see." He motioned Christine to drop the bag, then pressed the barrel of the automatic into Sandor's back as he gave him a quick, but expert, frisking. He inspected the contents of the leather case, mostly feeling around for anything sharp or metallic. Then he searched Christine, all the while holding his pistol at the ready.

"Not exactly a warm-hearted reunion," Jordan said.

"Afraid not. These are troubled times, you know. Sorry Christine."

"It's all right," she said. "We understand."

"Whatever," he replied coldly, obviously beyond caring about anyone's understanding. "Go ahead, siddown."

Jordan and Christine sat on the settee facing their host, who settled into the captain's chair in front of the chart table. He laid the gun in his lap. "Smoke?" he asked them as he pulled out a pack of Marlboros. They both declined. "Filthy habit, I gotta admit." He lit up and took a long drag. "So," he said to Christine, "who is this character and what's up with Jimmy?"

She looked at Jordan, hoping he would respond.

"This character," he said, "is Jordan Sandor. I'm the guy your friend Jimmy wanted to meet."

"You're Sandor, eh?"

"Right. And, in case you hadn't heard, your friend Jimmy is dead."

Andrioli's eyes moved slowly away from them, more pain in his expression than surprise. It was obvious he had not heard about McHugh. There was nothing to make the murders in Woodstock a national story. Unless Andrioli had an active source of information, which he probably did not, he would be in the dark. From the looks of the man, he was going it very much alone.

"Poor Jimmy," he said at last. "How?"

Sandor answered him. "Two men, one a small, dark-skinned Arab, the other a tall, light-haired American." Jordan searched his face for some sign of recognition. If Andrioli had any ideas, he wasn't sharing them yet. "They tied him to a chair, beat him senseless, then put two in his head."

Jordan's description was purposely harsh, but the vivid description of his comrade's death didn't seem to faze Andrioli. Instead, he turned to Christine and asked, "You all right?"

"I suppose so."

"Lousy sons o' bitches."

"Jordan is the man Jimmy was going to talk to before, well, before—"

"I know that, assuming this is really Sandor."

"The same people who did this, they've also come after Jordan."

That got Andrioli's attention. He shot a quick glance at Sandor, but said nothing. He looked back at Christine. "What about you?" Andrioli asked her.

"You mean has anyone—"

"Yeah, that's exactly what I mean."

"No. Not at all."

"Well then, what the hell are you doing here?" Andrioli's anger surprised them both. "Jimmy should never have gotten you involved in this bullshit. I told him he was wrong to have you come to Paris in the first place, the selfish little bastard. What in hell are you doing now, getting mixed up in this?"

"I wanted to help, that's all."

"Hold on a minute," Jordan said. "Let's back up here."

"Yeah," Andrioli agreed, "that's a good idea. Why don't you start by telling me what you know about all this."

"Funny, I was just about to ask you the same thing," Jordan said. "Of course, you do have the gun. Why don't I go first."

BILL STERNLICH SAT at the desk in his office, staring at the screen. He received no reply to any of the inquiries he had made for Jordan, except for the warning that found its way to his personal e-mail address at home. The lack of response from his usual sources was odd, to say the least. Based on what Jordan had told him, he was certain there would have been some Homeland Security report. He found none.

One thing was obvious—Jordan was back at his old job. Sternlich was sure of that. But the total information blackout was extraordinary. Whatever his friend had happened upon was bigger than either of them had first suspected. At least it was bigger than Jordan had told him.

He picked up the telephone and dialed Jordan's cell phone number for the fifth try that morning. This time, he didn't bother to leave a message.

TWENTY-NINE

Jordan described the events of the past three days, from the shooting in Woodstock and the murders of McHugh and Peters, to the attempt on his own life, the ransacking of his apartment and the apparent attempt of the government to hold them in protective custody. Sandor had already concluded that Andrioli was no amateur, and if he wanted the man's help, it wasn't going to work for him to hold back what he knew so far.

Andrioli interrupted occasionally to ask for details. He wanted more precise descriptions of the two shooters in Woodstock. He was interested in the questions put to Jordan and Christine by Prescott and Covington.

Sandor answered everything, withholding only the fact of his former career with Central Intelligence. He also stayed with John Covington's claim that he and Todd Nealon were from the State Department.

The information Andrioli found most disturbing was the evidence that Jimmy had made arrangements to return to Paris. Was he planning to flip again? Was he going to back to save himself and sell out his friend? It was difficult for him to contemplate any of that, especially in front of Christine.

Andrioli brought out some beers, passed them around and laid his gun on the chart table. He took two large gulps from his can then eyed Jordan with obvious suspicion. "That it?"

"Those are the headlines and the back stories as far as I know," Jordan said. "Mind if I ask a few questions now?"

"You can if you want, but I'll tell you up front, the more you know, the more dangerous this gets."

"Your pal Jimmy didn't worry about that when he asked to meet me, which is why I'm here in the first place, right? And you two didn't worry about it when you got Christine involved in all of this." He let that thought linger. "Anyway," Jordan said, "how much more dangerous can it get? They've tried to kill me twice already."

"You've got a point there," Andrioli conceded without a trace of sympathy. "But they failed. You happened to get in their way in Woodstock. That was bad luck. They tried to clean you up at your apartment, but they missed that chance. Maybe they'll let you be," he suggested, but there was no conviction in his voice.

He sat back, slowly stroking his scraggly, auburn beard, drawing his hand across his mouth thoughtfully, as if trying to convince himself that these killers might actually abandon their interest in these unclaimed victims.

Jordan could see in his eyes that he had dismissed the idea, so he decided to change the subject. Try to get him talking about what he knew. "So, what made you choose a boat in Fort Lauderdale? It's pretty exposed for a man in hiding, isn't it?"

"Maybe." Andrioli permitted himself a brief smile that brightened his gray features. For a moment. "Not exactly the old Hole-in-the-Wall in Wyoming, is it?"

"Not exactly. No."

Andrioli took another long gulp of beer. "That's all right. Haven't you ever read 'The Purloined Letter'? I thought you're supposed to be a writer."

"Sort of a writer. I know the story."

"Hide in plain sight, right? When we split up, Jimmy ran for the mountains. Bad move, if you ask me. That's why I never told him where I was going. He was a good guy, but he wasn't the sharpest knife in the drawer." He glanced at Christine. "Sorry."

"I understand," she said softly.

"Look, I figured those sons o' bitches were gonna find us no matter where we hid. They trap you in the mountains, you got no one around and nowhere to go.

I figured I'd be better off on a boat. I can take off if I have the chance. Or I can slip over the side into the canal. And I'm surrounded by a slew of people here all the time.

"These bastards are vicious, but they're not stupid. The two that took out Jimmy, they were pros. They're not about to get caught or killed just to do a job. The more careful they have to be, the better chance I have to make a move. I came south, went to a broker and rented this thing for six months, paid cash in advance. Easy as that."

Jordan watched Andrioli throw back another mouthful of beer. Unremitting fear had taken its toll on this man. His eyes seemed constantly alert to peripheral dangers. Exhaustion lined his face. His body seemed perpetually tense. Even worse, Jordan knew, was the realization that he had been the cause of his own inevitable destruction.

"Who were they," Jordan asked him, "the two who took out McHugh? Were they Traiman's men?" It was the first time either of them had mentioned that name.

Andrioli managed a hearty laugh. "That's good, cowboy. Very good." He leaned forward in his chair. "Look, I didn't invite either of you to this party. You told me what you could. Best thing you can do now is blow the hell out of here and get as far away from me as you can."

"Thanks for the advice, but we're not going anywhere. You and Jimmy had something to tell me."

"That right?"

"That's right. And I'll tell you what else. If we walk out of here now and any-one catches up with us, they'll figure we know too much already. So we're cooked either way. You think it'll be tough for them to force Christine to tell them where you are?" Christine winced at the thought, but the two men ignored her. "Even if you leave here today, you'll be a hell of a lot easier to track when they have a starting place."

Andrioli stared into Jordan's determined eyes. "Tell me again those names they ran by you."

"All right if I get the list from my bag?"

Andrioli grinned. "I'll get it." He picked up the bag. Jordan told him where to find the list. He fished it out and handed the paper to Sandor.

"Zayn."

Andrioli nodded. "I know that name. Iraqi. Former Republican Guard of the late Saddam Hussein regime. Recently joined up with Traiman, from what I hear."

"Mahmoud Rahmad."

"Yeah. Saudi. Runs Traiman's operation in New York. Diplomatic passport. Friend of the al-Qaeda boys. Slimy bastard."

"Suaramar."

"Hmmm. Never met him, but I know the name. I think he works with Traiman in Syria."

"Mustafa Tagliev."

"He's an agent for the CIA, NSA, some bullshit. They probably threw his name in there to keep you honest."

"American?"

"Nah. Works for the US, though."

"What about Tallal Abdullah Driann, you know him?"

"Sure. He's Qaddafi's liaison, worked on everything Traiman was running out of Libya. Now that Qaddafi claims he wants to be a good guy, he'll sell out Driann in a heartbeat, especially if the world finds out what's been going on over there."

"Plausible deniability."

"You got it."

"The last name is Ibrahim Abass."

"Yeah, I met him once. He's Traiman's direct contact with al-Qaeda. Bad guy. Most dangerous guy on your list."

"Where is he?"

"No idea. Showed up in Tripoli once in a while, not often. Lately the word has been that Qaddafi's people are trying to push the entire Traiman operation out of the country. He could be one of the group promoting that agenda, but Traiman's not an easy man to shove around."

Jordan nodded. "And this Rahmad, you say he's in New York."

"Usually."

They were quiet for a minute as Andrioli took a swig of his beer. "You know, no matter what they said, there's no way the feds wanted you two in protective custody."

"What makes you say that?"

"Come on, you seem like a smart guy. You think if they wanted to hold you, you wouldn't still be there?"

"I don't know," he lied. "We made a pretty good run for it, right?"

Christine, who had been quiet for most of their long exchange, nodded. "We did," she agreed. "You could see them on the street. They were looking for us."

"Looking, sure. But not holding you. See what I mean?"

Sandor nodded. Andrioli was a bit rough around the edges, but he was no fool.

"What does that mean?" Christine asked.

"Well," Andrioli said as he scratched his short, untidy beard, "it probably means they had you followed here."

THIRTY

The jetliner landed in Miami, where Traiman's men disembarked and entered the international arrivals building. They stood in different lines, one an American citizen, the other a visitor from Great Britain. The immigrations officers gave them and their papers a cursory once over. The passports were in order, and no questions were raised. They made their way through customs without incident, then into the arrival lounge where they were met by a driver holding up a cardboard sign with their assumed names.

They followed the chauffer outside to a waiting Lincoln Town Car attended by a second man who took their suitcases and held the back door open. There were no greetings beyond an exchange of curt nods. When all four men were comfortably seated inside, the car took off for the ride up the coast to Fort Lauderdale.

"Where are the goods?" the American asked.

The man who met them in the terminal reached for the hardshell case at his feet, then passed it to the back seat. The American flipped the latches and opened it, finding two Sig Sauer P228 9mm automatic pistols nestled safely in foam rubber. He lifted one out and handed it to the Englishman. He removed the second, checking the fifteen-shot clip. There were extra clips, fully loaded, and each man pocketed two. There were also two small packets of C-4 explosive with detonators and infrared remote devices.

"You have the address yet?"

"We have a lead on a boat on the canal," said the man in the passenger seat.

"A lead?" the tall Englishman asked.

"Don't worry," the driver said. "We'll get you where you need to be."

The two killers sent by Traiman completed their breakdown and inspection of the weapons, then stared out the windows as the sedan motored north to the Fort Lauderdale exits. They circled around to Las Olas Boulevard, not far from the corner where Jordan and Christine had arrived by cab earlier in the day, turned from the main street into a public parking lot situated directly behind a low-slung row of shops and restaurants that fronted on the main street.

They pulled to a remote end of the lot where the car came to a stop. The driver turned off the headlights and engine. Then they waited.

THIRTY-ONE

Andrioli had relaxed a bit from the beer and the company. He told them it had been a while since he had a conversation with anyone that had lasted longer than it took to order a pizza. He described the solitary life he had been living for the past couple of months. His only real sense of freedom came when he undocked his boat and set out for the calm, open sea. He admitted he was often tempted to just keep going. Only two things brought him back: the commitment he and Jimmy made to stop Traiman—that was the first reason. The second was the uncertainty of where his journey would end.

So he described how he would return to his slip, make midnight visits on foot to the twenty-four-hour grocery store, then spend sleepless nights, trying to sort out whatever future was left to him. It was difficult to go it alone. No one else could understand the pressure or the fear. No one except McHugh. They were two fugitives in search of escape. Looking for the right approach. The right contact.

"Now that Jimmy's dead," he said, "there's no more reason to wait."

Jordan let him talk, waiting for his monologue to lead back to Traiman and the work they had done in the deserts of North Africa. Andrioli was not so easily manipulated.

"If there's no more reason to wait," Jordan said, "why not tell us what this is all about? What have you got to lose at this point?"

Andrioli stared at him again then turned to Christine. "You believe he never met Jimmy?"

"I do."

"But you were on your way to see him," he said to Jordan. Andrioli was working it over one more time.

"McHugh asked to see me. Dan Peters put us together. Like I told you, I never got there." Jordan turned away, shaking his head. "How many times you want to go over this?"

"Your friend, Peters. He had to be working for Covington," Andrioli announced flatly. "It's the only thing that fits."

"Covington?"

"You said Covington claimed he was from the State Department. Well he's not. He's CIA."

Sandor did his best to appear surprised. "Run that by me again."

Andrioli finished off his beer, set the can down and gave Jordan a dubious look that told him he wasn't buying his act. "John Covington is a CIA chief. He's been after Jimmy and me since before we got back. He was the man we got referred to, when we first tried to make a deal from Paris. He didn't think we had enough to sell."

"Which leaves us where?"

Andrioli shrugged. "You know who Traiman is." It was a statement, not a question.

"I have an idea."

Andrioli smiled, as if he knew something else he wasn't ready to share. "Lemme help you out." He got up, taking his automatic with him, and brought them another two cans of Budweiser from the small refrigerator. He tossed one underhanded to Jordan. "Traiman used to be an American agent. I don't know what kind. Special Services, CIA, something. He took a powder a few years back, went turncoat on them. Now he runs a training camp for terrorists. He also brokers weapons and technology deals in the Middle East."

Jordan nodded. "So they say. Where did you and Jimmy fit in?"

"We were like instructors, basically. Trained all sorts of scum that Traiman brought into the fold from all over the place." He returned to his seat, placing the gun back atop the teak chart table. "It was wild, since we didn't speak anything but English. We had interpreters, never even needed to learn the languages, and believe me, there were a lot of different nationalities. Like a bizzaro United Nations, if you know what I mean. All upside down. We were highly paid drill sergeants. More than that, even. We taught those sons o' bitches everything."

Neither Jordan nor Christine uttered a word in response.

"You hear about the explosion in Washington yesterday?"

"I read the story in the morning paper," Jordan said, "on the flight down."

"Yeah, I saw it on the news. The company was Loubar," Andrioli told them. "Manufactured all types of paramilitary technology, bio-chemical stuff. If you saw the article, you know the deal. Anyway, president of the company died, along with his secretary and a couple of other people. The guy's name was Fryar, David Fryar."

"Should I take a guess?'

"Go ahead."

"He was Traiman's man in Washington."

"One of them," Andrioli said. "Probably stepped outta line. Asked for more money. Or worse."

"Such as?"

"Held up the shipments, maybe. Traiman's on a timetable right now. He needs to move his teams into the States, and he needs the equipment."

"What kind of timetable?"

Andrioli lit another cigarette and inhaled deeply before going on. "I'm not sure. Last spring Traiman was assembling some of his best men for assignments in the States. Assassination teams, that's what he trained them for. For here, and in Europe too."

"Who are the targets?"

"Who would you think?" Andrioli asked with a frown. "Heads of state, politicians, whatever."

"And this wasn't coming from Qaddafi?" Sandor asked.

"No way. Traiman is way beyond him. Old Muammar got religion after we bombed the shit out of Baghdad. He gave it the old 'No más.' Threw in the towel. I think that's when they first told Traiman his lease was up."

"So Traiman's not in Tripoli anymore?"

"Let's say if he is, he won't be welcome there much longer. Don't know if he still has enough pull with the bad guys to buy a little time."

"Al-Qaeda?"

"Yeah. Especially now, because it's going to get really ugly."

"How? With these hit teams?"

Andrioli shook his head. "Nah, I think those squads are a decoy."

"A decoy? For what?"

Andrioli eyed him warily. "Not sure, but I know they're moving something bad into place."

"Something bad?"

"Chemicals. Biological weapons."

Sandor's eyes narrowed. "Biological weapons? What kind?"

"Don't know."

"When do they make their move?"

"Not sure of that either." Andrioli took another drag on the cigarette. "When Jimmy and I split, we threw a monkey wrench into their scheme, if you see what I mean."

"I'm not sure I do."

"I have to paint you a picture?" He took another swig of beer. "When Jimmy and I took off, Traiman couldn't be sure how much we knew, or where we'd go with it."

Jordan waited, watching Andrioli take a puff of his Marlboro. When he lifted his can of beer to have another drink Sandor lunged across the cabin, driving his left elbow into Andrioli's chest, then grabbed the automatic with his right hand and twisted it free. Beer splashed all over Andrioli's shirt and face as Jordan spun to the side, coming up with the pistol in hand.

"Nice move," Andrioli said as he righted himself and wiped some of the beer away. "Man, I'm outta practice."

"All right, enough of this good ol' boy bullshit. Let's get some real answers about what you know, shall we?"

THIRTY-TWO

Traiman's men decided it was dark enough. There was no one in view. This part of town was far from the night action along A1A near the Fort Lauderdale beach. Anyone they passed would pose little in the way of risk or subsequent identification. They got directions from the driver then made their pick-up plan. They went over everything twice before the two men stepped out into the balmy night air and made their way to the quay where they would find Andrioli's boat.

The American knew Andrioli, having spent time with him outside Tripoli during the operations briefings earlier in the year. The Englishman had met him once. Traiman had selected these men for this clean-up task since neither was a friend of Andrioli's, but either could readily identify him. Prior personal contact was superior to a photographic survey, particularly since the target had likely altered his appearance. There were physical characteristics that could not be easily disguised, and these men were trained to penetrate such camouflage.

Ultimately, the risk that Andrioli would recognize either or both of them was immaterial; everyone understood that Anthony Andrioli would be awaiting this appointment, that he was serving time on his own death watch.

There was no crisis of spiritual confidence, no conflicting loyalties, no apprehension about the consequences of their actions. They were hired and trained as assassins, and the part they played in the rising tide of international terrorism, even when it involved a fellow combatant, was not their concern.

The American was a sharpshooter and, even by the standards of his trade, a particularly vicious killer. He had been schooled in martial arts and could be as deadly with his hands as he was with a gun. The Englishman, like his companion, was an expert marksman. He was also skilled in the use of explosives, hence the inclusion of C-4 and detonators in their arsenal.

If they took Andrioli alive, their instructions were to find out what he knew, using any means they chose. Then they were to eliminate him.

"THAT'S QUITE A move for a reporter, cowboy."

"United States Army, *cowboy*. I had training from a pretty good drill instructor myself."

Andrioli wiped his shirt with his hand and drank off what was left in the can of Bud. "Yeah, I know."

"You know what?"

"I know you're not just some reporter. Why the hell you think Jimmy picked you, because you're Ernest Hemingway?"

Jordan stared at him.

"We were with Traiman long enough. We heard all the old war stories. You were his fair-haired boy, back when he was doing his part for Uncle Sam. When he went AWOL, you were also the guy who got away."

"What's going on?" Christine asked Andrioli then turned to Jordan. "What is he talking about?"

"Nothing—"

"Come on, Sandor, drop the act. Traiman tried to have you done four years ago. Then he almost had you in Bahrain. You were a heartbeat from being buried neck high in the Sahara Desert."

"Jordan?" Christine burrowed her gaze into Sandor's eyes.

Jordan sighed and, stretching his neck, tried to rub out the tension with his free hand.

"Little over a year ago, our friend Sandor here was part of an undercover operation in Manama," Andrioli explained. "That's the capital of a small sheikdom called Bahrain located in the Persian Gulf, just off the coast of Saudi Arabia. Way we heard the story, Sandor was assigned to meet with four locals from Qatar, another little country on the Gulf, who claimed to have information about an al-Qaeda cell. Sandor was supposed to work with these informants to organize a raid on the al-Qaeda camp and take as many of the terrorists alive as they could while destroying the operation."

He was looking at Jordan now. "Traiman's men got word and kidnapped the locals from their hotel rooms in broad daylight before the CIA assault team was in place. Sandor arrived a half a day too late, then called for backup, intending to rescue his team. But Covington, who Sandor still wants to claim is with the State Department, refused the request, aborted the mission and ordered Sandor brought back before the United States was embarrassed by anyone finding out about an American military operation being planned smack in the middle of Bahrain. Tends to create some bad feelings, you start waging war in someone else's country."

"And those four men?" Christine asked.

"They were turned over to the terrorists. You can guess what happened to them. Anyway, Sandor resigned from the government and walked away." He looked at Jordan and asked, "Did I leave anything out?"

He did not respond.

"Is this true?" Christine asked Jordan, looking at him with an odd mixture of anger and admiration in her eyes. "Is it?"

When Jordan gave no answer, Andrioli said, "It is, believe me." Then he turned back to Sandor. "So now what? You gonna shoot me?"

"That depends."

"On what?"

"On the answers I get."

"Shit, why not just shoot me? Probably be doing me a favor."

Christine began to stand up, but Jordan said, "Sit down," without taking his eyes off Andrioli.

"Jordan—" she began.

"I said sit down, and I mean it." She lowered herself back onto the upholstered banquet.

"So," Jordan said, keeping his attention focused on Andrioli, "here we are. You know who I am and I have a pretty good idea of who you are. Talk."

"What's the point? Jimmy and I went down this road and ran into a dead end," Andrioli said. "It's like I told you. We made calls from Paris to people we knew through our contacts. We wound up with Covington and he told us to pound sand. To start with, he didn't seem to believe anything we said. Even if it was true, he said we didn't have enough to buy what we wanted."

"Which was what?"

"Money, immunity, witness protection. You know the drill." He looked at the empty beer can and flipped it onto the chart table.

"Easy," Jordan warned him.

"Okay, okay. Don't get excited." Andrioli smiled at Christine. "He's tough."

"Have you tried to speak with someone other than Covington?"

"Sure we did," Andrioli sighed. "Everyone we talked to figured it the same way—we were telling a tale just to make a deal, get immunity, whatever. How could we prove anything? What did we have to show them? Covington was the only one who seemed interested in giving us a tumble, but then he turned to bullshit too. That's when we took off."

"And so I was another contact, is that the idea?"

Andrioli nodded. "Maybe the last one. That was the idea, anyway. Peters to McHugh and now to me. Tinkers to Evers to Chance." He smiled. "Did Danny tell you he knew me?"

Jordan shook his head at this latest revelation. Now things were beginning to make sense. "I never even heard your name until Christine gave it to me last night."

"Good man, Peters. Served with him for about six months. I'm sorry he got in the line of fire."

"Me too. So your idea was what? To convince me to pitch it to someone for you?"

"That was one idea."

"Why me?"

Andrioli allowed himself a slight grin. "You know why. You've got an inside track. And you're the only person I know hates Traiman more than I do."

Jordan nodded. "You have another idea if we can't sell the first one?"

Andrioli shrugged and offered a crooked smile. "Yeah. Now that the team was arrested in DC, my story starts to make sense, right?"

"Run that by me again."

"The bogus hit squad they just grabbed on a tip. Who do you think the tip came from?"

Sandor nodded but did not reply.

"Still, I figure if they haven't bought what I've told them up to now, I've got to get more to sell."

THE TWO KILLERS strode purposefully toward the canal, each intent on his responsibilities. Each understood what had to be done.

They continued along the concrete dock without speaking. The American reached inside his jacket and felt for his automatic. The Englishman did the same.

Sandor had often wondered at the blindness of such men, their inability to perceive the irony of their position—that someday their roles with Andrioli might well be reversed. Experience had taught Jordan that armed conflict had an immediacy that did not permit for reflection or doubt. Hesitation is fatal.

And so these executioners moved on, the time for thought having succumbed to instinct as the transom of the *Winsome II* came into view up ahead.

As they came even with Andrioli's cabin cruiser, the American gave a discrete signal to move on. Without breaking stride, they kept walking, coming to a stop after passing several more boats.

"Well then?" the red-haired Englishman asked quietly.

"I don't like it."

"The setup?"

The American nodded. "Bow to stern. Too open. And spring lines. We make a move to board, he'll feel us as soon as we step on deck."

The Englishman nodded. They were standing face to face, a hundred feet beyond the forward railing of the *Winsome II*. Even so, they spoke in a whisper.

"And we don't know what he has rigged up."

"What about blowing it?"

The American shook his head. "No good, not unless we know for sure he's inside. We can't be sorting through the pieces afterwards."

The Englishman frowned. "Agreed."

167

THIRTY-THREE

When a soldier spends enough time in active combat, he develops auxiliary senses. Awake or asleep, he becomes alert to sounds that do not quite fit with the character of other noises. Even an unusual silence can snap him to attention.

Jordan asked a question, but Andrioli was listening to something else. He held up his hand and rose slowly from his seat.

Sandor immediately sensed it also. He stood, turning to Christine, his finger to his lips.

There had been two sets of footsteps, shuffling by the boat, disappearing into the night. Then they heard the footsteps again, coming back the other way, not really conscious of them until they came to a stop.

Jordan moved next to Andrioli, who was checking to see that the blackout drapes on all of the portholes of this main salon were pulled shut. "You have any other guns here?" Jordan whispered.

Andrioli nodded, pointed to the aft cabin, holding up one finger.

"Get it," Jordan breathed in his ear.

Andrioli stepped quickly to the rear of the vessel, quietly unlatched the door to that cabin, went inside, and then emerged with a Browning 9mm.

The footsteps had ended somewhere near the bow. Andrioli pointed in that direction and Jordan responded with a brief nod.

Sandor saw that Andrioli was holding two extra clips for his Browning. Jordan held up the H&K with its long silencer and motioned to Andrioli's hand.

Andrioli disappeared into the aft cabin again and quickly returned with a box of 9mm shells. He handed it to Sandor. The two men were side by side, straining to hear what was going on above deck.

"They're either going to board us or blow the boat," Jordan said in a barely audible voice, his mouth close to Andrioli's ear. "We've got to move now."

Andrioli nodded. He tapped Christine's shoulder and gestured toward the rear cabin. It would be the safest place for her, he said, once the action began.

Christine turned to Jordan. The steely look in his eyes told her not to debate the instruction.

As she started to move, he whispered, "Keep down, no matter what. Don't come out unless one of us calls you."

Christine hurried into the aft cabin, and Jordan closed the door behind her.

Andrioli held up two fingers.

Sandor nodded his agreement. There were two men. They were at the front of the boat right now, but would doubtless split up. Jordan knew that he and Andrioli were running out of time, but if they acted too soon, or moved in the wrong direction, they might be cut down before they had a chance to mount a counter-attack. He reached for Andrioli's arm and drew him toward the short stairway that led to the wheelhouse. "Open the latch as quietly as you can. I'll go forward, make some noise there. Just get it unlocked then stand aside. When I come past, I'll blow through the hatch. You follow me out."

Andrioli nodded.

"There's no margin for error. Shoot to kill."

Andrioli nodded again and watched as Jordan moved forward to the salon.

THE RED-HAIRED ENGLISHMAN finished rigging the two explosive devices and handed the larger one to his partner. He fastened the C-4 near the railing of the bow, while the American stepped to the outside of the quay, taking a circuitous route to the rear of the boat where he attached the main charge to the aft hull, just behind the wheelhouse deck. Their plan was simple. The first, small explosion would bring Andrioli out. If they couldn't finish him off with a bullet, they would ignite the second charge, and Andrioli and his boat would be history.

The Englishman stepped away from the bow, choosing a vantage point near a thick wood piling where he would have a clear shot at anyone coming through the main cabin or out through the hatch on the foredeck. He had his automatic in hand, keeping it under his jacket as he waited for the American to finish.

There was a noise from inside the boat, up towards the forward hatch. He snapped his head in that direction, then gave a quick whistle to the American, who jumped back and pulled out his Sig Sauer.

JORDAN HAD SMACKED his hand twice against the inside bulkhead of the forward cabin. Then he sprinted back through the main salon, vaulting the steps to the pilothouse in a single motion, slamming his shoulder hard into the door that Andrioli had unlocked, bursting through in a sideward roll, hitting the deck with a thud. He scampered behind the instrument panel tower just as the Englishman detonated the small charge attached to the front hull, the explosion sending a spray of fiberglass, teak and other debris into the air and across the dock.

The American saw Sandor first and, having the better angle from the rear, he opened fire immediately, sending three shots spitting through his silencer that shattered fiberglass and ricocheted inside the wheelhouse.

Jordan fired back at the American, who took cover next to the boat docked behind them.

Andrioli had emerged from below, diving to a position alongside the wheel and firing his automatic at the crouching American to their rear. His weapon was the only one of the four not equipped with a silencer, and the reverberating report of the Browning echoed inside the wheelhouse.

The Englishman, seeing Andrioli emerge, shot two rounds through the plastic windscreen, whistling just above his target's head.

A woman somewhere inside the sailboat to their stern let out a scream, and people along the canal began coming above decks to see what was going on.

In the noise and confusion, Sandor gestured to Andrioli to cover the forward shooter, then crawled on his stomach towards the transom. He climbed over the port railing on the water side and crept along the catwalk until he came to the end. There, he spotted the second explosive against the side of the hull. He couldn't tell if it was set for remote ignition or timed detonation, but he knew that touching the charge might set it off either way.

He peered around the transom until the American, crouching behind the next boat, rose slightly to fire another shot. Sandor saw the man was holding something in his left hand and, figuring it was the remote, he leveled his gun and fired. The first shot hit the American in the arm. The second caught the side of his neck, spinning him around until he was in full view. Jordan fired again, striking him in the chest and dropping him to the ground, dead, before he could detonate the aft charge.

Sandor wondered if there was other plastique in place, or if the second shooter could set off the C-4 attached to the transom.

The first explosion had caused a fire to break out in the forward cabin, and Jordan knew they had little time before the flames on board reached the fuel tanks or another explosion was detonated. The smoke alone would eventually drive them into the open. He had no line of sight on the man up front, but continued to move along the stern of the boat until he was at the corner of the starboard side, at the dock. He heard Andrioli's Browning send off three more shots in rapid succession and, using that cover to leap from the water deck onto the concrete path, he squeezed off two shots at the Englishman, who was squatting low behind a bulkhead piling. One splintered the pole. The second glanced off the man's shoulder, turning him into a better line of fire.

As Sandor pulled the trigger on that last round, however, he heard the nauseating, metallic click of the slide snapping open. "Damnit," he cursed himself for not keeping track of his ammunition.

The Englishman also saw what happened and righted himself for a shot at Jordan, who now jumped back towards the cover of the burning *Winsome II*, reaching in his pocket for more shells.

But Andrioli had also seen Jordan come up empty. He stood and fired off the new clip he had just slid into the Browning, driving the Englishman backwards with four bullets ripping into his chest and face.

Jordan peered above the aft railing and nodded at Andrioli. "Thanks, pal."

"Any time."

"Get Christine, my bag, anything else you need, and let's get the hell out of here. There's more plastic against the stern and there may be other charges. Don't know if it's on timers or what."

Andrioli leaped down the four steps into the main cabin and rushed into the aft stateroom. Christine was standing there, terror in her eyes, her body rigid with fear. Andrioli pulled out an attaché case he kept in the locker below his bunk, then grabbed Christine roughly by the arm. As they raced through the salon, he picked up Jordan's bag and made it above decks.

"Come on," Jordan urged them. "Let's move."

A growing crowd inched nearer the scene, but Jordan loudly warned them back.

"Someone call the police. Call the fire department. Get the Coast Guard out here," he yelled at the crowd. "And back up. This boat is going to explode."

That sent the crowd moving backward.

Andrioli and Christine jumped onto the dock, even as sirens began to sound in the distance. Andrioli walked up to the Englishman he had shot. He was face down, so Andrioli turned him over with the toe of his boot. "I knew this dirty sonuvabitch. I recognize the other guy too."

"You've got nice friends," Sandor said. "Let's get the hell out of here."

THIRTY-FOUR

Koppel knocked on the door of the room in the Mayflower Hotel in Washington. As instructed, he had come alone.

The man who greeted him was not at all what Koppel had expected. He was Koppel's age, nearly sixty, but unlike Koppel he was tall and trim and had a patrician bearing. He looked more like a corporate executive than a government agent, and his piercing gaze made Koppel instantly uneasy.

"So good of you to come," the man said, stepping to the side to allow Koppel inside.

Martin Koppel proceeded warily, having a quick look around, surprised to see that no one else was there.

Shutting the door behind them, the deputy director of the Central Intelligence Agency offered his hand and said, "I'm Mark Byrnes."

MARTY KOPPEL HAD seen better days. Back in the seventies he had emerged as a golden boy of American finance. He had run hedge funds that were among the darlings of Wall Street, helping to make any number of wealthy people wealthier. Whether he was financing dot com start-ups or investing in blue chip companies, Marty Koppel knew what worked.

Then Marty lost his touch.

The eighties had come and gone. And so did the bull market. Regrettably, Marty was not a man who took short positions. He had fought the new trends as long as his capital held out, then watched helplessly as his stock market investments shriveled up as quickly as a winning streak at a Vegas craps table.

By the time the nineties rolled around, his instincts had completely betrayed him, his golden sensibilities having morphed into a cluster of mistakes. The high-tech hedge funds he rode up the Nasdaq wave had all turned to dust, taking with them his assets—and those of his investors. Marty had become an instant dinosaur. A modern, up-to-the-minute, techno-age anachronism. He had leveraged everything he owned and lost it all. What was worse, he became a star in one of America's greatest sporting events—witnessing the spectacular rise and disastrous fall of a celebrity. The people who had enjoyed his champagne and eaten his caviar now found him a pathetic boor, avoiding him with the same eagerness they had once expended to court his attention. All the while bearing witness to his slide into oblivion.

There was a sad irony to all of this, since Marty had taken pains not to make enemies as his wealth and fame increased. Having grown up poor in the Kingsbridge section of the Bronx, he was mindful of the admonition about the people you meet on your journey up and down the ladder of life. It was a puzzle to him, therefore, that so many took so much pleasure in watching his demise.

But recently, through a friend of a friend, Marty had been introduced to an opportunity for funding new investments. An admirer of his aggressive style was interested in teaming with Koppel on something new, something *au courant.*

There followed the mandatory string of telephone calls and lunch meetings at tony restaurants in New York. Then Marty was invited to meet a man named Robert Groat, the direct representative of a consortium of European investors. Or so he claimed. The principal money man, it was explained to Koppel, was a wealthy recluse who lived on a yacht in the Mediterranean. Mr. Groat had informed Marty that his client was particular about whom he met or spoke with, and that he regarded secrecy as the highest priority in his business dealings.

Koppel was not interested in the man's social idiosyncrasies, nor was he curious about his religious affiliations, eating habits or sexual preferences. Koppel readily vowed his discretion, and made arrangements to travel to Europe to meet the money man.

It was only after those plans were made that Koppel was contacted by another party interested in his new opportunity—a representative of the United States government. Marty was invited to a meeting the next day, the intimation being that his presence was required, not requested.

"YOU'RE THE GUY I spoke with on the phone?"

"I am."

"And we're alone here?"

"Absolutely."

"No tapes, no recording. Just you and me."

"That's right."

"And you want to talk with me about what, exactly?"

Byrnes offered a tight smile. "I can see your reputation is well deserved. You're a man who likes to come right to the point."

"That's me," Koppel said, having another look around as if he expected a more lavish room to be provided for this meeting. "It's not exactly a thrill to have the feds call you down to Washington, if you know what I mean."

"Of course," Byrnes said. He did not offer Koppel a seat. They were standing, face to face. "We have information that you're about to enter into a business arrangement, setting up a domestically based fund for national and international investments, correct?"

"Who's asking?"

"I am."

"And who are you, exactly?"

"Let's just say that I represent the federal government, as you have suggested. That should be enough for now."

Koppel wasn't so sure, and he shook his head slightly. "Okay, let's say you're right. I'm starting a new company. That against the law or something?"

"Not necessarily."

Koppel didn't like the man's tone. He also didn't like that they were still standing. Marty was short, heavy and decidedly out of shape. He would be perfectly happy to sit down. "What is this about, taxes?"

"No, Mr. Koppel. It's about the fund you will be establishing. I've been informed that it will be financed by overseas investors. Am I correct?"

Koppel saw no reason to deny what they obviously both knew to be the truth. "Yeah, you got it," he said.

"And the investments you are to make will largely be placed in short positions with respect to various commodities, stocks, derivatives and so forth. In common parlance, your investors want you to bet that the market prices will fall in the near future."

The extent of this man's information took Koppel back a step. That was exactly what he understood as the intention of Mr. Groat's bearish client or clients, whoever they were. How this man knew that was quite beyond him. "The plans of my clients—"

"Of course," Byrnes cut him off. "I understand. We have a matter of ethics to deal with."

"We sure do," Koppel told him.

"Good. I just wanted to be certain I was dealing with a man of character. Please," he said, finally pointing to one of the two chairs in the room, "have a seat. It appears we have a great many things to discuss."

THE CROWD ALONG the New River Canal, gathering closer to the burning vessel, was too concerned with the dead men on the quay to pay much attention to the three people fleeing from the scene. Andrioli led Jordan and Christine up a short set of concrete steps, around the back of the dock and down the street to a nearby parking lot.

He took them to a beige Toyota Corolla, unlocked the door and told them to get in.

"Won't they spot us?" Christine asked.

Andrioli ignored the question as they climbed inside. He pumped the accelerator, turned the ignition key and listened as the old sedan shuddered to a start. "Don't worry about it," he said, then threw the car into gear and turned out of the lot onto Las Olas Boulevard.

Once they were on the main street, Andrioli was careful to maintain the legal speed limit as the blare of sirens from police cars and fire engines grew louder. "Here they come," he said.

Andrioli was driving away from the commercial area of the city, towards the night action near the beach. He turned off Las Olas as soon as he could, the sound of the onrushing rescue vehicles receding now as they headed for the canal.

"You've got a plan to get us out of here, I take it?"

Andrioli nodded at Jordan. "I do. Just chill out and let me handle this."

Christine was seated in the back, the two men in the front of the car. Even in the balmy night air, she began to shiver.

"You okay?" Jordan asked.

"I'll be fine," she told him.

"So," Andrioli said, not taking his eyes from the road, "way you handled that, I guess everything they said about you is true."

"Don't believe everything you hear."

"I knew a lotta guys in the service, never coulda taken my gun from me, or moved like you did back there."

"That so? Well, just in case you forgot, I would have had my head blown off if you hadn't come up and taken out the second shooter."

"You counted wrong, that's all."

Sandor allowed himself a grim smile in the darkness. "I knew the H&K carried fifteen shots. You'd think I could have counted to fifteen."

"Uh uh," Andrioli said, allowing himself a smile. "You counted right. Last chamber was clear."

"What?"

"An old trick of mine. Call it an insurance policy."

Jordan shook his head.

"Hey, only the paranoid survive."

"Seems I've heard that line before," Jordan said.

They reached the fringes of the town's main activity, where Andrioli turned into a small complex of squat buildings just two blocks from the shore road. He pulled into an enclosed parking garage, coming to a stop inside.

"This is what they call the moment of truth," Andrioli said.

"Meaning what?"

"Meaning, we're either going on together from here, or it's *hasta la vista*. Up to you."

"How about we make a call to Washington, first? We don't have to turn ourselves in, not yet. But we can tell them what you know. I've got some friends I can reach."

"I'll bet you do," Andrioli replied. He stepped on the gas again, pulling around a cement post and coming to a stop in a parking space there. They got out of the car, the sickly glow of the weak, florescent lighting making Andrioli appear older and more exhausted than before. "You just don't get it," he said, slamming the door shut.

"Get what?"

"Covington and his people. The way they're using you to get to me. What the hell," Andrioli said, as if speaking to himself. "You're probably part of this already."

"Part of what?" Christine asked across the top of the car.

"I don't know," Andrioli said with a dismissive shake of his head.

"Look," she said, "if Jordan was here to hurt you, would he have risked his life just now?"

"He didn't have much choice, did he?"

"Of course, he did. He had the gun, you didn't. He could have given you up to those guys."

Andrioli was not convinced.

"I asked him to come here with me," she reminded him. "All this, this . . . whatever this is, it wasn't his idea."

The two men were staring at her now.

"So, wherever we're going, whatever we're doing, right now I think it's fair to say that we're going together."

Sandor and Andrioli looked at each other, not speaking.

"Well?" Jordan asked him.

Andrioli scratched his beard. "That car over there is mine," he said, pointing to a navy blue Chevy. "You and Christine take it, drive out slowly and wait on the street. I'll dump this car down the block, then come back to meet you." He opened his attaché case and removed a set of keys and tossed them over the car to Jordan. "Go ahead."

Jordan caught the keys, still watching him.

"And then what?" Christine asked. "Where do we go from here?"

Jordan knew the answer. "Paris," he said.

Andrioli nodded. "He's right," he said to Christine, without taking his eyes off Jordan. "We're going back to Paris."

THE DRIVER AND his companion were sitting in the Lincoln Town Car when they heard the explosion. Their orders were to bring Traiman's men to the canal, then take them back to the airport. They heard the gunfire in the distance, but did nothing. They had no instructions to interfere. For now they just sat and waited for two passengers who would not be returning.

THIRTY-FIVE

"You ever wonder what they're thinking," Andrioli asked, "in that last second? You know what I mean."

Sandor knew precisely what he meant. "I have," he admitted.

"You seen a lotta guys die, have you?"

"More than my share," Jordan admitted.

"Yeah. Me too."

They were heading up the interstate from Florida toward Georgia, Andrioli at the wheel. Switching cars had gotten them safely out of Fort Lauderdale. Even if Covington's men tracked them to the shootings at Andrioli's boat, it would be a while before anyone could identify and locate the old Toyota. And where would they look after that?

"I have no wife, no kids," Andrioli said into the darkness. "All that stuff about your life passing before your eyes. I always figured you would think about your wife and kids. I don't know." He pulled out a cigarette, lowered his window a bit and lit up. "You married?'

"No," Jordan said. "Never."

"No kids then."

"No."

Andrioli took a long drag of the Marlboro and blew it towards the open window. "What the hell would you see, then, when the lights are going out?"

Jordan had a look at the man's profile, the uneven nose, the prominent, bearded chin. "I have no idea," he said. "Will it matter?"

"It might," Andrioli said. "If there's no God or anything, I figure those last seconds, that becomes your heaven or your hell, right then and there. It may be all you get."

Jordan peered over his shoulder. Christine had curled up in the back seat and was sleeping under his sport jacket.

"You have a passport?" Andrioli asked him.

Jordan told him he did.

"Your own name?"

"No, I'm covered. Don't worry."

"What about Christine?"

Sandor had another look in the back seat. "We should leave her in Atlanta."

Andrioli nodded. "I guess so." He let another few miles go by before saying, "You came to see me without a weapon."

"I did."

"Kind of risky, wasn't it?"

"Not any more than trying to get them through at LaGuardia."

"No shit," Andrioli said, thinking of their narrow escape.

"I sent a package to myself. Won't come until tomorrow morning, back in Lauderdale."

"Great. A day late and a gun short."

"I guess so."

"Well forget it. I can work it out when we get to France."

Jordan watched him drive the car, neither man saying anything as they covered a long stretch of highway.

Andrioli took a long drag on his cigarette, blew out a cloud of smoke, then broke the silence. "Hey, about that thing that went down in Bahrain."

"What about it?"

"I had nothing to do with it. I mean, we heard about it afterwards, but McHugh and I weren't involved. Okay?"

"Okay."

"It's not like I even knew who you were. You were just the name of some guy from Traiman's past. Anyway, I wanted you to know I had nothing to do with it, in case you had any ideas about that."

"Okay," Jordan said again, taking a moment to have another look at Andrioli. "So why are you really going to Paris? Why not just make a stand here?"

"It'll never be safe for me here. You just saw that. Jimmy already bought it. This is a business deal at this point. I've got something they want, and if I get just a little more of it, it might save my life. Strengthen my negotiating position, if you see what I mean."

"I'm listening."

"Traiman believes Jimmy and I knew more than we did. The government's not so sure. If Traiman gets to me first, I'm dead. If the government finds me, they'll see I don't have enough to deal with and they'll lock me up. Either way, I'm finished."

"What do you really have?"

Andrioli turned to him. "I already told you everything I know. I truly did. And it's not enough."

"Okay. So, what's in Paris?"

Andrioli looked out at the highway and took a long drag on his Marlboro then let it out slowly. "Answers," he said. "Answers."

THIRTY-SIX

John Covington had flown back to Washington for a meeting with Deputy Director Byrnes. The DD was in his office, waiting.

"Coffee, John?"

"No thank you, sir."

The director removed his reading glasses and began gently massaging the bridge of his nose with his thumb and forefinger. "We may finally be getting someplace," he said with a weary sigh. "It's about time."

"Yes sir. Things developed quickly in Florida."

The DD nodded. "I received a call from the Bureau. Needless to say, they were not happy about your antics in New York."

Covington knew that Byrnes was sensitive to criticism about governmental agencies not sharing information in the post-Nine Eleven world. He was surprised at being awarded the blame, however, since he was following the DD's orders. "It had to be done."

"Yes, of course it did. There's too much at stake to risk their interference. In any case, there may be less of an issue than they think."

"Sir?"

"This matter wasn't going to remain within the Bureau's jurisdiction for long," the DD said.

"After the debacle in Fort Lauderdale, I don't think Andrioli will make a run back to North Africa."

"Where then?" The DD took a quiet sip of his steaming black coffee, effortlessly raising the cup to his lips without compromising his posture.

"France would be a better guess." Covington told him. "They found a plane ticket at McHugh's house. First class to Paris. It was in my report."

Byrnes nodded, and Covington waited for him to say something. He did not.

"So sir, do you think he and Andrioli were planning to go back?"

"What do you think?" Byrnes asked.

"It doesn't make sense."

"It might, if they thought they could make a better deal there than they could get here."

"I suppose you're right."

"Perhaps there are others involved."

Covington nodded.

"What about Sandor?" the DD asked.

"We've pushed him this far. Knowing him, he won't be able to resist."

Byrnes nodded without taking his eyes from Covington.

"You don't really believe Andrioli has enough information to interrupt Traiman's plans, do you?" Covington asked.

Byrnes leaned back in his chair. "Not based on the preliminary interrogation of the three men we arrested. And we're not likely to get more from them at this point."

"Are they explosives experts?"

"There was no evidence of that in their Washington apartment. The arsenal we found in their apartment was designed for sniper attacks, not the construction of bombs. They've been questioned separately, of course. Each denies any involvement in the destruction of the Loubar office building."

"I see."

They discussed the implications of having apprehended the team of potential assassins. Then Covington returned to the subject of his assignment.

"Do you think we're wasting our time on Andrioli, then?"

"Not at all," Byrnes said. "Whatever he has—whatever he can get—we want it. We also want to see where he goes. The path he travels may have more value than anything he can tell us."

"If he has so little intelligence data on these ops, why is Traiman so intent on removing him?"

"I believe it may have more to do with Vincent than with Andrioli." Byrnes had worked with Traiman for years. "Vincent was always a cautious man."

"And what if Traiman's people reach Andrioli first?"

"They'll kill him. We saw that yesterday in Florida. That is, of course, unless he has something to trade."

"And the risk assessment?"

"We clearly stand to gain more by pushing him than bringing him in, at least for now."

"What about the girl?"

"The girl . . . yes." The DD raised his right eyebrow slightly. "What options does she have? She may be too frightened to move on her own."

"Yes," Covington agreed, "I suppose you're right. They might leave her behind."

"It's possible," Byrnes agreed. "I assume you've reviewed the CTC reports on the teams Traiman sent into Western Europe."

"I have," Covington said. The Counter-Terrorism Center had confirmed the movement of men believed to be involved with Traiman. They were currently running down the specific locations and identities.

"The press is going to get hold of this," Byrnes said. "There are leaks we can't plug. They may even be coming from the other side, as part of their terror campaign."

"You think al-Qaeda would use advance teams to advertise their plans?"

"Possibly. This is about terror, after all. The governments involved have increased security measures for the heads of state, particularly in the U.K. and Italy. The Secret Service is obviously on high alert."

"They believe this is for real?"

"We all do," Byrnes acknowledged solemnly. "Traiman is doing an effective job of gearing up without allowing us to pinpoint the source."

"Or the targets."

"Yes. The President has his hands full with Iraq, Iran and rest of this mess. He can't afford another domestic catastrophe on his watch. The war, the stock market, the fear. The American people have had enough. And you never know how the Arab nations will align themselves."

"Petropolitics."

The DD permitted himself a grim smile. "The Arabs love to hate one another, but they're uniformly resistant to outside interference." He thought that over and then asked, "So where are we on locating them?"

Covington shifted in his seat. "They left Fort Lauderdale right after the shootings. We're trying to pick up their trail now."

"What about the shooters?"

"Two of Traiman's men, or that's what it looks like. We sold it to the local authorities as a drug deal gone bad. The Bureau helped with that."

"And Sandor?"

"As I said, we're canvassing the airports. Got a lead on a car switch. Trying to trace that now."

"Keep your eye on Paris," Byrnes told him again.

THIRTY-SEVEN

Morning broke in a glare of hazy sunshine that seemed to mock their loss of sleep. Night had become day, but it was less a transition than a milestone on their journey.

They stopped for breakfast at a Waffle House, just off the highway outside Macon. A short, unkempt waitress, who looked even wearier than they felt, took their order and brought them each a cup of steaming coffee.

"I heard you." It was the first thing Christine had said in quite a while.

"Heard what?" Andrioli asked, taking a sip from the heavy, ceramic mug.

"You expect me to stay behind, don't you?"

Neither man responded.

"When were you going to tell me?"

"Christine . . ." Andrioli began, then stopped, not sure of what to say.

"You've seen how dangerous these people are," Jordan said quietly. She was sitting beside him in the small booth, and he turned toward her, placing his arm around her shoulders. "You wanted to find Tony, and we have. Why would you put yourself in any more danger?"

"Why would you?" she asked defiantly. "I'm involved in this as much as you are."

Jordan knew it might be useful to have a woman with them. He also knew the risks they would be taking.

"These people are killers," Andrioli said as casually as if he were commenting on the coffee. "You've seen it firsthand. They murdered Jimmy, and they'll keep after me wherever I go. If either of you are with me, you'll be in the line of fire."

"Don't you think I'm in the line of fire now?"

The two men exchanged a knowing glance. She was, of course, correct. Christine and Jordan had become targets, whether they went with Andrioli or not. Traiman would regard them as contaminated by the information he might have given them. Just as Dan Peters was terminated, as a collateral risk, Christine would be in their sights, one way or another. Sandor also realized what they did not—that Traiman had ulterior reasons for eliminating them.

"All right," Jordan said. "But any time you want to bail, you just give us the signal."

"Not me," she said. "I'm in this till the end."

THEY DROVE ON to Atlanta, where Andrioli located a shop offering instant passport photos. Christine had her picture taken, then got back in the car. Meantime, Andrioli used his passport and false credit card to buy a cell phone.

"I've got some arts and crafts to do," Andrioli told Jordan. "You drive." He climbed in the back seat, opened his attaché case and began working on a passport for Christine. Jordan got behind the wheel.

"You carry blanks?" Christine asked as she watched him applying her photo to the first page of a forged US passport.

"Comes in handy, as you can see. Not much trouble using one of them when you leave the country. Hassle getting back in with it, though." He looked up at her as they shared the obvious thought—that they might never get that far.

As Jordan drove, Andrioli went back to expertly affixing the photograph to the page before applying a stamp. He handed it to Christine and had her sign it.

"At least they won't be able to track us by our real names," he said, taking the passport back to finish his work. "The first thing they'll do is run flight rosters through the IATA computers. We'll travel separately. You two as a couple. I'll book as a single." Andrioli then used his new cell phone to make the reservations—two phone calls, different credit cards. Jordan had his Scott

Kerr passport, and an American Express card issued in the same name.

They made another stop, at a luggage store, where they bought a matching set of suitcases. Jordan and Andrioli agreed it would be less suspicious if they checked in for an international flight with baggage. They purchased a few items in a clothing shop then left the city, resting for a few hours until dusk in a park overlooking a small lake.

THEY ARRIVED AT the airport, left the car in the short-term lot and went through the contents of Jordan's black leather bag and Andrioli's attaché case. They knew they had to leave the two automatics behind. As they walked to the parking lot exit they placed the guns in a nearby trash can, making certain no one was watching as they covered them with newspapers, then moved on.

"I feel naked," Andrioli said.

Jordan smiled. "Second time for me in two days. I've been throwing away some very nice hardware." He slapped Andrioli on the shoulder. "Look on the bright side. At least we don't have to worry about a weapons charge."

His encouraging demeanor belied the tension he felt rising up the back of his neck as they approached the terminal. If anyone had followed them, or if someone were waiting at the airport, they would be captured. Or worse.

"I think we should call Covington," Andrioli said.

Jordan stopped. "Covington?"

"I told you, he was the point man when Jimmy and I tried to come in."

"But you told me he wouldn't deal. He turned you down."

"It's worth a try, if I can talk our way out of this."

"It won't work," Sandor told him.

"I still think we should try."

"And as soon as we call, he'll trace us. They'll pick us up. You'll be done."

"They'll never trace this cell phone. Not it if we're quick."

Jordan knew that whatever phone number Andrioli had for Covington would be hooked into the satellite links at the Global Response Center that could pinpoint their location within ninety seconds. He decided not to divulge his own knowledge of Covington's secure line. "All right," Jordan agreed, "but it's a waste of time."

"Why?" Christine asked.

Jordan was not prepared to give that answer, not yet. He understood that Covington wanted them in the hunt, that he would reject any deal Andrioli tried to make at this point. "Just a feeling," he said. "Let me do the talking. And time me. Give me seventy-five seconds."

Andrioli's eyes narrowed slightly, but he handed Jordan the phone. They were at the edge of the parking lot, across the access road from the international terminal. Andrioli opened his case and pulled out a number. Jordan recognized it as one of the sterile lines the Agency kept for outside contacts. As he had guessed, it was also a line easily tapped for tracing through GPS locators.

Jordan dialed the number and listened to it ring.

"Covington," the familiar voice answered.

"Jordan Sandor."

"You and who else?" he demanded brusquely.

"I'm standing here with Tony Andrioli and Christine Frank. Christine and I are paying Tony a visit here in Fort Lauderdale."

"I heard about the shootings."

"Good. Then you know Andrioli is telling the truth when he says he's got something to deal."

"Where are you?"

Jordan didn't answer. Instead he turned to Andrioli. "Covington sends his regards."

"I realize you can't talk. Just tell me if you're leaving the country," Covington said.

"First, we need to know where the Agency stands on helping us. We were almost killed last night," Jordan replied into the telephone.

"So you're on the move."

"Naturally," Jordan said. "You don't want us sitting out in the open for target practice, do you?"

"Are you going to Paris?"

"Look, Andrioli has information. He's willing to trade it for protection."

"We don't bargain with traitors, and we're not convinced he has all that much to sell."

Jordan looked to Andrioli again. "Covington says you can turn yourself in and they'll put in a good word for you at sentencing."

Andrioli responded with a grim smile.

"He says you can shove it," Sandor replied to Covington. "If the best you can offer is the deluxe cell at Leavenworth, he'll take his chances on the outside."

Covington said, "Tell him he's got to give me something with real substance I can take to the director. Meantime, Sandor, I need to know where you're going."

Jordan only repeated the first part of Covington's remark, to which Andrioli just shook his head.

"Tell him to pound sand," Andrioli said. "That's what he told me."

"He says you should pound sand," Jordan said into the phone.

Christine pointed to her watch. She mouthed the words, "*Thirty seconds left.*"

"This guy is setting you and the girl up for trade bait." Covington tried a different tack.

While that thought had already occurred to Jordan, it surprised him to get the advice from Covington. He was not the type to caution his operatives, even former operatives, when it might scare them off. Perhaps it was that uncharacteristic gesture that gave Jordan the idea. Or maybe he had the idea already. "One more question. Why did you send those two men to kill us last night?"

"What!" The surprise in Covington's voice was as genuine as the look on Andrioli's face.

"*Twenty seconds.*"

"They could have been your men as easily as Traiman's. Andrioli recognized one, said he worked for the Agency in Paris." Andrioli had not said any such thing, but he let Jordan play out the hand.

"What is this?" Covington demanded.

"Why would Andrioli lie to me?"

"I just told you why."

There was a short silence on the line then Jordan said, "No deal then?"

"*Ten seconds.*"

"Sandor, where the hell are you? Are you going to Paris? Yes or no."

Jordan hesitated.

"*Five seconds.*"

Covington had just confirmed what he had suspected since he managed to escape the hotel in New York. The Agency wanted Andrioli, not for what he knew, but as bait for bigger prey.

"We're moving again—" Jordan said.

"*Three seconds.*"

"—and you just blew—"

"*Two.*"

"—your best shot—"

"Jordan!"

"—to make a deal." Without a goodbye, he snapped the phone shut, disconnecting the call.

"Cutting it a little close, don't you think," Christine said.

Jordan shook his head. "And I had so much more I wanted to say."
Andrioli was obviously disappointed.

"What did you expect?" Sandor asked him.

"I'm not sure anymore."

"Come on," Jordan said, "let's go check in. We could all use a drink."

THIRTY EIGHT

Jordan and Christine checked in first. Andrioli stayed back near a bank of phones, pretending to make a call as he watched them receive their boarding passes without incident. He then made his way to the first class check-in and was quickly provided his ticket.

He was not far behind them in the long, slow security queue. Another agonizing wait until they got through to the other side.

They found a small cocktail lounge near their gate and ordered drinks.

"Notice anything?" Andrioli asked.

"Not a thing," Sandor told him.

For now, Jordan believed that no one was certain where they were or where they were going. Although Covington suspected they would soon be en route to Paris, and probably attempted to track the cell phone call, Sandor had to assume he was on his own. Jordan asked for Andrioli's phone.

"Who are you going to call?"

"What's the difference now?"

Andrioli didn't like the answer.

"A friend in New York. He's okay. We may need a contact person."

Andrioli reluctantly handed over the telephone and Jordan pulled a number from his pocket. He turned away from his companions and quickly punched in the numbers. A trooper in Woodstock, New York, answered the call, and Jordan asked for Captain Reynolds.

"Tell him it's Jordan Sandor," he said, then waited.

"Sandor," Reynolds growled in his best combat voice when he came on the line, "they tell me you've become a fugitive. Where the hell are you?"

"I can't tell you that Captain, but I have to ask you to do something for me."

"You are a brash young man," Reynolds said.

"Look, I have no one else I can trust. Is this line clean?"

"Clean? It better be."

"You have a pencil?"

"I'm listening," the captain said.

Jordan quietly recited a phone number. "You got it?"

"I got it."

"It's a secure line. Call that number, and just say that all three of us are on our way. Would you do that? Just say all three of us are on our way."

There was silence on the other end.

"Captain?"

"I'm here, Sandor."

"Will you do that?"

"Give me one decent reason I should."

Jordan shook his head. "Because I'm asking, that's all."

The captain paused again. "All right."

"Thank you, sir," Jordan said.

"Be careful," Reynolds said, then hung up.

The next call Jordan made was to Bill Sternlich.

"Where are you now?" Sternlich asked, after Jordan briefly described the Fort Lauderdale shootings.

"It's better if you don't know. In fact, I've got to keep this call short so they can't run a trace. How's Beth?"

"Getting better. Pretty banged up, I can tell you, but she'll be fine."

"Is she under guard?"

"You bet."

"Good," Jordan sighed. He had moved off to the end of the bar, farther out of earshot from his traveling companions.

"I finally got some dope on your pal McHugh. Guess it's too late to do you any good, eh?"

"Not at all. What've you got?"

"Not much, except he's a Code Orange on the terror alert barometer. Records sealed and all that. Most of his dossier is classified, still regarded as a national security issue. I even got a threatening little e-mail message warning me off the search."

That brought Sandor up short. "Be careful Bill. These people are serious."

"I believe you."

"I'll call you when I can."

"Listen, Jordan, I did get one little tidbit you might find interesting."

"I'm listening."

"There's no record James McHugh ever had a sister."

JORDAN AND CHRISTINE sat in business class. Andrioli was up front, in first.

Less than an hour after they took off Christine was asleep. Sandor watched her, wondering again what she was about. He knew Sternlich would be following up on her name and background, even though he told him not to, but whatever he uncovered might be another fabric of lies. But devised by whom?

Jordan stared out the window as the plane passed through the clouds in a darkening sky. He tried again to get some much needed rest.

IT WAS JUST past daybreak when they landed. They navigated their separate ways through customs and immigration, then met up on the taxi line. There the three of them climbed into a cab that wound its way around the curves of the French *autoroute* past the recently constructed, multi-level buildings that had become part of the landscape of suburban Paris.

"No problems?"

Andrioli shook his head. "Customs opened the suitcase, but I told them I was here to buy some clothes. You know the French. They love that bullshit."

The cab cruised along the highway that belted the city in an uneven circle.

"What do we do first?" Christine asked.

"First, I visit an old friend," Andrioli said. Then, speaking French with an accent Jordan knew must be like fingernails on a blackboard to their driver, Andrioli gave the man his itinerary.

They would make a brief stop on the Boulevard Raspail before heading to the hotel Pas de Tour on the Rue des Saints-Pères. This was the small hotel on the

Left Bank where Jimmy McHugh had made a reservation the day before he died.

"Is that a good idea?" Christine wondered aloud. She was sitting between them. She looked to Andrioli for an answer.

Andrioli was thinking about something else, tugging on his scraggly beard, staring out the window. "Is what a good idea?"

"Going to that hotel." She lowered her voice, just in case the driver's English was better than it seemed when they entered the taxi.

"You afraid we'll be in danger?"

Christine nodded vigorously, as if to say how obvious her concern should be to both of them.

Tony smiled. "A little late to be worried about that now." He took Christine's hand and patted it gently. "I'm sorry, but we're already up to our asses in alligators. No time to be worried about jumping in the old swimming hole. The only thing we've got going for us is surprise, the oldest ally in the book of war. They don't expect us to be coming at them, which may be our best chance. If we try to run and hide they'll find us, and we'll end up all over the front page of *Le Figaro*. Am I right, Sandor?"

"I'm afraid so," Jordan agreed.

Andrioli responded with a short laugh. "By the time we reach the city, half of Traiman's men in Europe will already know we're in town. We need to make a show of force. The only chance we have is a direct attack, correct?"

This time Jordan gave no answer.

"Way I see it, we've got to rattle their cage, show them that we can get inside their organization. We have to shake something loose to get the information we need."

"Then trade it with the US to stop Traiman and buy Tony his freedom," Sandor said, finishing his thought.

"Something like that."

"And who do you think is going to make that deal?"

"Come on. Covington knew we were on our way to Paris. That's what he said to you on the phone, right?"

"Yes," Jordan admitted.

"Good. So, if we're going into the trenches together, no more secrets, all right?"

"All right," Jordan said.

They turned to Christine.

"What secrets could I have?"

"Everyone has a secret," Sandor said.

She turned away from him without a response.

THE CAB STOPPED at the address on the Boulevard Raspail. Andrioli told the driver to wait. "I'll be right back," he said, climbing out of the cab, taking his attaché case with him. Before he shut the door, he leaned in and spoke quietly to Jordan. "If you hear anything—any trouble—or if I'm not back in ten minutes, get the hell outta Dodge. You hear me?"

Jordan nodded. Andrioli stood up, shut the door and disappeared into a small apartment building across the street.

When he was gone, Christine asked Jordan, "What did you mean? About my having a secret."

"Just what I said. No one lives without a secret."

She shook her head but did not speak. When she looked up at him, her sad, moist eyes were met by his cold gaze.

"It doesn't make you a bad person," he said with a grin that softened his features but did nothing to hide the suspicion in his eyes.

She was about to say something, then hesitated.

ANDRIOLI REMOVED A set of keys from his case, used one of them to get into the building, and took the stairs two at a time till he reached the third floor. There were four flats on the landing. He paused in front of the door on the left, listening.

Nothing.

He placed his attaché on the floor and, standing off to the side, knocked twice and waited.

Nothing.

If they were waiting for him, he had no time to finesse a quiet entrance. Using another key, he turned it in the lock, the click as loud as an explosion in the quiet. In one motion he turned the knob and thrust the door open, bursting into the small apartment like a fullback going through the line. Low, hard and fast.

Nothing.

There was no one there.

He hurried into the kitchen, kneeled down and reached under the sink, feeling for a small package he had taped there two months before. Just as he detached the parcel he heard something behind him. He spun quickly, coming to his feet as he dropped the bundle and raised his hands to the ready.

Nothing.

He nodded at the dim silence, waiting, his muscles tense, his eyes alert. Then Emil's cat scooted across the floor and jumped onto the counter beside him.

"THERE'S SOMETHING YOU'RE not telling me," Christine whispered.

Jordan shook his head. "There's a lot I'm not telling you, which makes us even." He checked his watch and had a look across the street. "Don't worry," he said. "We'll have time to catch up."

"Will we, Jordan?"

He looked at her again without answering.

"You still don't believe me, do you?"

"No," he said. "But I want to. I want to very much."

ANDRIOLI EMERGED FROM the building. He looked up and down the street, then hustled across to the taxi and told the man to drive on. He placed the attaché case on Christine's lap and opened the top so the driver could not see what he had inside. He showed them the two US government-issue Colt .45 automatics and a box of cartridges he had removed from the package upstairs. "My friends and I always kept at least one safe house," he said. "Jimmy and I left these behind." There were two other small boxes, still wrapped in paper, for which he offered no explanation. At least, not yet.

"That was dangerous," Jordan said. "What if someone was waiting?"

"What choice did we have?" Then in a whisper, he added, "Unarmed, we're as good as dead anyway."

He leaned towards them and said, "Here's the deal. I'll get out on the Boulevard Saint-Germain. There's a small café on the corner. I'll wait there. You and Christine take the cab to the Pas de Tour. When you walk in you ask the clerk for a double room with a bath. No matter what he says, even if he's telling you he doesn't speak English, you interrupt him immediately and say 'Room Forty-seven.' You got that? Room Forty-seven."

Jordan nodded.

"He'll give you a key. The hotel isn't very big, but it's got two tiers separated by an outdoor patio. When he gives you the key, don't hesitate. Pick up your bag and walk through the glass door out onto the patio."

"Where's the door to the patio? We want to look like we know what we're about, right?"

"It's just to the right of the desk. Small lobby, can't miss it. Walk across the patio to a second glass door, directly opposite. Take the stairway on the left up to the room."

"Forty-seven."

"Not necessarily. He might give you another room in the back tier. Our best shot is if someone is already in Forty-seven."

"Why?"

"Don't worry. As long as you ask for number Forty-seven, he'll understand. That's just the password."

"What if there are no rooms available?"

"There's always a room. But if he gives you any bullshit or gets on the phone, you just tell him you have no time to wait and get the hell out of there. Don't run, don't act nervous. Just leave."

Jordan nodded. "Will he ask for our names? Or our passports?"

"No. Now, once you head for that rear staircase the clerk will definitely call his contact to tell him one of Traiman's men has arrived. From that moment on, you're in danger. There are probably others in the hotel already. They tend to check each other out, just to keep score, if you catch my drift."

"Got it."

"Leave your suitcase in the room and use some of this." He picked up one of the small packages and tore back the paper to show Sandor the C-4 plastic explosive. "I assume you know what to do with this."

Sandor gave him a look that said no explanation would be required.

"All right. Once you get to the room you set this, then you head right back out. And I mean right away. Whether or not you get to the front desk before it blows, you make sure you give the clerk the name Mr. Forest. Tell him this was a message from Mr. Forest."

"Forest."

"Right. Then you go on over towards the church up the street, the Saint-Germain-des-Prés. Everyone knows where it is."

"I know it," Jordan said.

"Good. I'll meet you there."

Jordan nodded.

Andrioli took one of the automatics, still hidden from the driver by the top of the open attaché. He made a quick check of the weapon, then took an extra clip from the case and placed the gun and the spare magazine under his jacket.

"I take it you're expecting a welcome committee to form right away."

"I am," Andrioli said.

"Then Christine should be out of the way."

Andrioli thought that over.

"I'll put her in a cab," Jordan said. "You can wait somewhere very public," he told her. "If one of us doesn't come for you in an hour, you head straight for the US Embassy."

Christine saw that Jordan was not about to debate the point. "All right. Where?"

Jordan leaned towards them and whispered, "I'll pick a public spot, somewhere on the Champs-Elysées."

She nodded.

"One last thing," Andrioli said. "The two towers in the hotel are connected by a walkway on the top floor. Just in case you hit a snag in there you can go up, across and down. It'll bring you back to the lobby. At least you won't be pinned in the back of the hotel. It's pretty quiet back there, and help is hard to find."

"Thanks for the encouragement," Jordan said.

"Don't mention it. How's your French?"

"Dead awful."

"Good enough. When you walk in, you speak English to the clerk. No problem. But in the back of the hotel, if you can't fake the French, both of you should keep your traps shut."

"Why does Christine have to come in at all? Why not let her out here?"

"You'll attract less attention at first. You'll need the head start because when the clerk calls in with your descriptions, they'll know who you are. Get in, rig the plastique, then get your butts outta there. Understand?"

Jordan understood but he didn't like it. It was Andrioli's show for now, and for now Sandor would play it his way.

THIRTY-NINE

The taxi turned past the Hotel des Invalides and onto the Boulevard Saint-Germain. Andrioli told the driver to circle past the corner of the Rue des Saints-Pères, then had him stop in front of a café that was busy with morning customers.

"Now you two be careful," he said as the car pulled up to the curb, allowing himself a tense smile. "All of a sudden I feel like I'm Mother Goose." He turned back to the cabbie and told him to drop his friends at the Pas de Tour. The Frenchman was obviously annoyed by all the detours, so Andrioli paid the fare in advance and gave him a large tip, which managed to erase the man's Parisian frown. Andrioli closed his attaché case and handed it to Jordan. "Good luck," he said as he stepped out into the morning air.

Jordan did not have time to watch Andrioli enter the café. As soon as the door slammed shut the cab took a wild right turn across several lanes of the broad boulevard and lurched down a narrow street, stopping about halfway down the block in front of the hotel.

Christine stepped out and Jordan followed. They took the two suitcases from the trunk while the cabbie, his fare already in hand, made no pretense at helping them with their bags. As soon as they shut the trunk, he sped away.

The façade of the Pas de Tour was set in the middle of the street, an inconspicuous place one could pass again and again without ever realizing it was a hotel. Jordan handed Christine the lighter valise, then picked up Andrioli's attaché case and, slinging his leather bag over his left shoulder, pushed through the wooden door and entered the lobby.

The clerk's desk was near the rear, over towards the left. The small lobby surprisingly deep and rather narrow. That explained the two tiers, Jordan thought. One in front for the general roster of guests, the one in the rear reserved for special patrons. As he approached the desk, he could see the patio and the glass door to the side, just as Andrioli had described it.

"Room for two," he said without offering a greeting. "With bath."

The clerk was a short, stocky, middle-aged man with an inexpressive face bathed in tedium. "I am sorry, *monsieur*, but—"

"Room Forty-seven." Jordan's brusque interruption was greeted by nothing more than a slight furrowing of the man's brow. Then, as the clerk reached below the desk, Jordan felt his body tense, the hard metal of the Colt pressing against his side beneath his sport coat. But the bored Frenchman brought up nothing more threatening than a key.

"*Cinquante-sept, monsieur.*"

"No," Sandor replied firmly, "I said Forty-seven."

"I am sorry, *monsieur*, this is not available. Fifty-seven," he said in his heavily accented English and held out the key.

Jordan nodded and took the key. The clerk made no request for a credit card, identification or passport. Sandor motioned for Christine to proceed out the rear glass door to the patio. As he followed her, the clerk called after him.

"*Monsieur*. The messages. In what name will you accept messages?"

Jordan kept moving, letting the door swing shut behind him.

They stepped quickly across the tiled terrace, their footsteps echoing in the quiet of the enclosed courtyard. An elderly couple was having their morning coffee, not bothering to take notice of the new arrivals. Once Jordan reached the other side, he found the rear stairway. It was darker than in the lobby.

"I'm afraid," Christine said, her voice trembling in the dismal silence of the hallway.

"Come on," he said softly. "No English, not until we get to the room." He placed his arm around her shoulders, urging her on.

DEPUTY DIRECTOR BYRNES was seated in the office of his boss, Michael Walsh, the Director of Central Intelligence. They were linked by secure video-conference with the Secretary of Homeland Security, the Secretary of Defense, the President of the United States and his National Security Advisor. Byrnes had been given the floor to provide a briefing on the current status of the counter-terrorist operation involving Vincent Traiman. When he concluded, the Secretary of Homeland Security began to speak, but the President interrupted him.

"I want to be sure I understand this, gentlemen, because a lot of this is news to me."

"Yes sir," Byrnes responded, knowing it would be his obligation to answer the President. And to take the heat.

"I've read the reports on this rogue agent, Traiman. I'm up to speed on that. Now you're saying he went after two reverse defectors—Americans—who flew the coop and wanted to come home."

"Yes sir. They tried to make a deal."

"But as I understand it, you passed on it. Although, I'm still not sure I understand the reasons why. Then one of them is murdered in New York, and the other almost gets blown to kingdom come in Florida. Have I got this right so far?"

"Yes, Mr. President."

"And all this time, these two men might have had valuable information specifically related to movements of these teams of killers Traiman is running."

"We are not clear about the extent or accuracy of the information they possess. Or possessed."

"I see." The opportunity to watch the look of displeasure on the President's face made the interview far worse than a simple telephone conference would have been. The commander-in-chief was not a man who tended to hide his feelings, especially when he was dissatisfied with his subordinates. "So then, while we have a real and present threat to our national security initiated by this sonuvabitch in Libya, or wherever he's hiding at the moment, not to mention the danger to targeted allies in Europe, you guys fiddled around instead of bringing these boys in. And now, one of them is dead, while the other is on the run someplace in Europe."

"Paris, Mr. President."

"France. Perfect. Our ultimate fair-weather friend. Meantime, we've got an explosion here in Washington, a terrorist cell discovered down the block from the White House, the media demanding to know what the hell is going on, and I'm not clear what the hell we're doing to defuse the situation."

"Yes sir."

"And then, to add to this chaos, we have one of our most capable operatives, who no longer works for us because we let him down a year ago, running around without giving us any idea about where he's going or how he intends to proceed. Have I got this now?"

"Yes sir."

"Well then, Mr. Byrnes, why don't you explain to all of us how you can justify these actions, with everything that's at stake here. I can't have my people raising the Terror Alert levels with nothing but a hunch to back it up."

The deputy director took a deep breath. "Mr. President, please understand that I know full well what is at stake, and that I would never play fast and loose with the security of our country, or of my own men, for that matter."

"Thank you for the speech, Mr. Byrnes. Now, how about a straight answer?"

"Yes, Mr. President. First, our intelligence sources inform us that Mr. McHugh and Mr. Andrioli had incomplete data on the current offensive being planned by Traiman for al-Qaeda. Second, we have reason to believe that Andrioli still has contacts in Paris who can provide the missing pieces to the bigger puzzle on these threats. Our hope is to follow him upstream to more informed sources."

"Is that it?"

"No sir. We are extremely close now on at least two fronts. One is an operation intended to neutralize Traiman by bringing him out into the open where he can be apprehended. The other involves Andrioli and his efforts to obtain the additional, critical information on these terrorist plans."

"What chance does this Andrioli have, acting alone against al-Qaeda?"

"He is not alone, sir. I can assure you, Mr. President, as I have assured the director, I have teams in place on these operations." Byrnes would disclose a general description of those arrangements, but he was not ready to divulge the full extent of Jordan's involvement, not even to the President. "For what it's worth," he said, "Sandor was one of our very best men, as you've mentioned. Whatever he's up to, I can vouch for the fact that he would never betray us."

"Well that's very comforting, Mr. Byrnes. Anything else on that score?"

"Yes sir. We have word that Sandor's with Andrioli now, in Paris, even as we speak."

FORTY

Vincent Traiman's office was crowded with people or, more accurately, was as crowded as he ever allowed his office to become. He was seated behind his large, contemporary desk of glass and steel, silently surveying the group as if he were some benign corporate executive.

His key aides had been included in the conference, marking the significance of this meeting. Traiman would typically isolate his staff, doling out information on a need-to-know basis. But today, all of them needed to know.

Mahmoud Rahmad was in Traiman's office. Also present were Tallal Abdul-lah Driann, Colonel Qaddafi's *charge d'affaires* for matters related to Libya's role as host to Traiman's operation, and Faisal Ridaya, the head of Libya's European propaganda lobby. The Colonel now steered clear of any direct communications with the terrorist cabal, limiting his involvement to the briefings he received at the Bab el-Azziziya barracks or his offices in the Villa Pietri. Having occupied the self-styled role as Great Leader for more than three decades, Qaddafi was working hard to revise his image as the Mad Dog of the Middle East, President Reagan's accurate judgment of him in the 1980's. Lately he had adopted a lower profile, assuming the appearance of a mature and moderate statesman, undertaking a public relations push the liberal media in the West was eating up.

As evidence that this new image was a charade, Driann and Ridaya were accompanied to the meeting by Ibrahim Abass, Traiman's direct liaison with al-Qaeda.

"I have handled the situation with Loubar," Traiman informed the gathering. "Our current shipment has been released." He did not disclose the true nature or purpose of the shipment.

"We understand that," Ridaya responded with a knowing look. He was an educated man, sophisticated and experienced in the world markets, with entrée to Europe's most exclusive circles in commerce, politics and society. "Unfortunately, the untimely death of Mr. Fryar was the subject of some discussion and speculation in the foreign markets," Ridaya pointed out to his host.

"Speculation is only valuable in the political arena," Traiman replied. "It is of no consequence to me."

Ridaya nodded graciously. Grace was a necessary quality in his work, even when he would have preferred a more sincere reaction. "Is it not speculation to suggest that Loubar will be able to fulfill the outstanding contracts?"

"No," Traiman responded in a firm tone. "It is a statement of fact. The outstanding orders will be honored."

"Very well. We shall be guided accordingly."

"Now then," Traiman continued, "it appears our operations in the United States have been less covert than anticipated. The Secret Service has apprehended the team in Washington. Our teams in New York and San Francisco are worried about exposure and await further instructions."

No one inquired as to the reasons for the failure in Washington. No one asked how the team had been compromised.

"What of the preparations in Europe?" inquired the al-Qaeda delegate, Ibrahim Abass.

"We are moving those men into place."

"And the rumors of the two who defected from your organization?"

Traiman responded to Abass with an admiring nod. Other than Traiman himself, he knew that Abass was the most dangerous man in the room, with the most effective intelligence network. "Your sources are to be commended."

Abass offered no reply.

"One of these men has been neutralized."

"Had he compromised your plans before he was removed?"

"No."

"You are certain of this?"

"We are."

"And the other man?"

"We know that he has attempted to deal with the American government, but his efforts have been rejected. He lacks enough information to cause us any real problems. For the moment, he's nothing more than a nuisance that we are in the process of handling."

"A nuisance," Abass repeated with an abrupt wave of his hand. "This sort of bungling is more than a nuisance, Mr. Traiman. We have worked too long and invested far too much with your organization to have it jeopardized at the last moment by a nuisance."

"The operation is not jeopardized," Traiman told them all, his tone remaining confident and restrained.

Ridaya asked, "Why were these men not eliminated in the first instance, when they were located in the United States?"

"As I've said, one of them was removed as soon as we found him. The other eluded us, for a time, but has now returned to France."

There was some muttering around the room. Ridaya's expression confessed his surprise. "He has come back to Europe?"

"He has. And our people are working on the matter as we speak."

JORDAN AND CHRISTINE headed up the carpeted stairs, finding there were only two rooms on each floor. When they got to the third landing, they hadn't taken two steps down the hall toward their room before a door opened in front of them. Christine froze.

Two men came out, talking to each other. As they walked toward Jordan and Christine, Jordan turned her toward the door next to them. He bent forward to disguise his height and to cover his face. He made a show of looking for the key in his jacket pockets as the two men passed behind them without stopping. As they took the stairs down to the next level, Jordan glanced quickly to his side.

Even in the darkness of the hallway, he knew them at once. The second man was the driver of the car in Woodstock. The tall, blond-haired American. Jordan knew him as surely as he reached for the cold handle of the Colt automatic.

The men had not paused or, if they did, Jordan had not seen it. He waited to hear them reach the next landing below, then grabbed Christine again and led her up the stairs as quickly and quietly as they could move.

Maybe Andrioli was right. Perhaps surprise was on their side. Traiman would never expect them to be there. Why would he be looking for Jordan and Christine in the dimly lit hallway of his own hotel?

As soon as Jordan and Christine reached Room 57, they made their way inside. And the moment Jordan shut the door behind them, Christine broke down and began to sob. Jordan took her in his arms and held her close. "Go ahead," he said, "I don't blame you a bit."

IF RIDAYA WAS satisfied with Traiman's assurance that the Andrioli matter was being handled, Abass was clearly not. Nor was he constrained by the dictates of Ridaya's political correctness. "These would not be the same people who have failed up to now, would they?"

"Of course not. The men who failed in eliminating Andrioli have paid the ultimate price for their incompetence."

Abass stood up and walked towards the edge of the large desk to face Traiman. "We realize that you do not share the vision or the passion or the commitment of my people. For us there is the *jihad*. For you, only a capitalist motivation which is foreign to our holy crusade. You are, what you Americans so quaintly call, a gun for hire, a necessary evil in our war against the greater forces of sin. When you speak of paying the ultimate price you betray your misunderstanding of all we live and die for. Do I make myself clear?"

Traiman looked up at him, his dark eyes meeting the ebony gaze of the Arab terrorist, neither of them blinking. "I understand only this," Traiman said. "In this life, we are rewarded for success and punished for failure. In the new order, if and when it comes, I will have succeeded and my position will be secure."

"Perhaps so. For now, with the loss of our team in Washington, we need the others to be put in place."

"Of course," Traiman agreed, knowing that no such arrangements would be made.

Then Abass leaned forward. "And we need to know about the shipments you have been arranging."

Traiman did what he could to conceal his surprise, sorry he had not already sent Rahmad back to New York. He filed away the notion that this was something he would have to take care of soon. "Those arrangements have nothing to do with our current plans. They have been set in motion for a future project I am developing."

Abass waved Rahmad aside and offered up a sneer that was as close as he ever came to a real smile. "We are most interested to hear of your future plans, but for now I am concerned about the success of the planned attacks. The exposure of our team in Washington was an unfortunate loss we do not expect to suffer elsewhere. Do I make myself clear?"

Traiman was not about to back down. He also knew well enough that this was no time to confront Abass. "What reason would you have to doubt me?"

"Up to now you have provided munitions, technology and intelligence gathering. The raids you have organized were minor skirmishes. We are embarking on a greater scale of action, and we must have assurances that our operations will succeed."

Traiman had to do his best to appear committed to the success of these operations, especially as he knew that he had worn out his welcome in Libya. Contrary to what most of the others believed about his teams of assassins, Traiman had a far more sinister scheme in play.

"Believe me, Ibrahim," Traiman said, addressing the al-Qaeda henchman in this familiar way, his tone becoming friendly as he reminded himself of his real goal, "I am as committed to the success of these plans as you are."

FORTY-ONE

Inside their room, Christine sat on the edge of the bed, watching as Sandor busied himself with the contents of Andrioli's brief case.

There was no remote detonation device for the plastique. All he had was a primitive fuse, which would afford them only minimal time to leave the hotel before the explosion. He tore off a small piece, went into the bathroom, placed it in the sink and lit it to get a sense of the burn time.

"Well," he said as he came back into the room, "at least it appears to be a slow burner. Should give us enough time to get clear."

She gave him a look that begged him to say he was only teasing.

"Once I set this charge and light it, we're going to have to move."

Christine nodded. "All right," she said. "Just tell me what to do."

"The clerk has likely gotten word out by now. They may send someone to check us out."

She stood as he placed the C-4 along the heater unit, where it would do the most damage. He was on his hands and knees, running the fuse along the floor, not concerned if it set the rug on fire before it burned all the way down. The important thing was for the charge to be properly ignited.

When he was finished, he looked up at her. "You ready?"

She nodded.

"All right. Once we leave the room, there's no turning back. Stay close to me, no matter what happens." He stood, grabbed his black bag and handed her Andrioli's attaché. He picked up the .45 and shoved it in his jacket pocket. Then he lit a match. "Here we go," he said, and lit the fuse.

They left the room, quietly shutting the door behind them. Then, almost immediately as they began down the stairs, they heard the sound of a door opening below them. Jordan pulled Christine behind him and felt for the handle of the .45.

They waited for an instant, listening as a door closed. They heard what sounded like two men heading down the steps.

The staircase was narrow and winding, well suited to the bell tower design but not intended for more than one person moving up or down at a time.

Jordan motioned for her to stay put, then eased his way silently down to get a better look. He waited to hear them reach the next landing below, then he hustled back to Christine, grabbed her hand and pulled her up the stairs, moving as quickly and quietly as they could.

"Come on. They don't know we're here yet," he told her. "But as soon as they get to the front desk they'll be coming back for us."

He continued racing upward, Christine right behind.

They reached the top level, where they found the passageway Andrioli had described.

If we had gone directly down and through the atrium, we would be on the street by now, Jordan told himself as he thought of the fuse burning away in Room 57.

He gave Christine a gentle shove, following her as they sprinted ahead, stopping at the archway to an enclosed bridge that connected the two towers, spanning the length of the patio below.

Jordan, holding the automatic in his right hand, found himself thinking of *Al-Sirat,* the bridge Muslims walk over to see if they will go to paradise or to hell. More slender than a spider's thread and sharper than a sword, according to Islamic tradition, it was a span only the good passed over swiftly enough to reach heaven.

He took Christine's hand again and began running, quickly traversing the narrow overpass, reaching a door at the other end. He hesitated, listening. It was quiet, so he pushed it open, the gun at his side as he stepped out onto the top-floor landing. He looked quickly in each direction. No one was there. The stairwell below was silent.

As they raced down the stairs, Jordan remained in the lead. He checked over his shoulder to ensure that she was close behind, attentive to any sound that might tell him Traiman's men had circled back to find them. The steep, winding staircase offered them no protection as they approached the end of each flight. These small landings were the only places a pursuer could hide, unless they had positioned themselves inside one of the rooms.

They came around the last turn without seeing anyone, but Jordan realized the gravest danger awaited them in the lobby.

He stopped at the bottom of the staircase, behind the door that led directly into the deep, narrow foyer. Christine was beside him. They paused for a moment, Sandor visualizing the layout of the area, imagining how he would position a backup team if he were preparing the attack. He would place one behind the counter, another in the corner near the entrance. He decided he would base his move on that, knowing he must move immediately. The two men they saw in the rear tower had likely begun to search for them, and they could be anywhere in the building by now.

"Stay low and close," he whispered to her, then pushed through the door in a running crouch, his gun extended. He came to a stop beside the desk.

The clerk, who was handing a key to another guest, froze in place and stared at Sandor wide-eyed.

"Don't make a move," Jordan said, pointing the gun up at the clerk's face as he quickly scanned the room.

The guest, an Englishman who had either begun the day with an early bracer or was ending a long night, had trouble getting his eyes to focus on the gray gunmetal of the Colt. "Say, what is all this?" he asked unevenly.

"Shut the hell up and get on the floor," Jordan barked at him.

The Brit immediately dropped to his knees, either grateful to be taken out of the action or badly in need of rest.

Before anyone made another move, they were rocked by the concussive sound of the explosion coming from the rear of the hotel.

The clerk began yelling something in French, but Jordan trained the barrel of the automatic at his eyes. "Out," he hollered.

The portly man moved cautiously, his eyes on the gun that remained leveled at him as he moved.

"Keep watch on the glass door," Jordan said over his shoulder to Christine, referring to the entranceway to the patio behind them. "Come on," he yelled at the clerk, grabbing him roughly by the arm then twisting him around to use him as a shield.

"Jordan," Christine whispered. "I think I hear something."

Sandor stopped, the sound of hurried footsteps in the distance coming from the front stairwell they had just used. "Let's go," he said, pushing the clerk towards the front door. "You first." He shoved the man through the front door and out onto the Rue des Saints-Pères.

As the door swung open, the man stumbled. Jordan let him go. The clerk fell to the ground on his back. Christine was right behind them.

Jordan leaned over the stout little clerk, the automatic now hidden under his jacket. "Mr. Forest, you got that. Any messages for Mr. Forest, you hold them for me."

The man stared up at him, his look of bewilderment mixed with fear and rage.

Jordan pulled out their room key and dropped it onto the man's chest. "Mr. Forest. You got that?"

The man nodded without speaking.

"Good, because I don't want to have to come back here and find you. *Comprende?*"

When the clerk nodded again, Jordan took Christine's hand and ran towards the Boulevard Saint-Germain.

At the corner of the Rue des Saints-Pères and Saint-Germain, Jordan flagged down a passing taxi.

"Take this cab to Fouquet's," Jordan told her. "Sit there as long as you feel safe, but if Andrioli and I don't show in an hour, don't wait any more. Take a cab to the US Embassy. Tell them you've got to speak to someone at Langley about Jordan Sandor." He reached into his pocket and pulled out two phone numbers he had written out. "The first number is in Virginia. Just add 4-3-4 at the end. Tell them you've got to be connected to that number. It's an emergency. You got it? Don't write it down, just remember it. You add 4-3-4. Tell them everything you know."

"All right. What's the other number?"

"Add a 212 area code and a 5 at the end."

She nodded.

"That's my friend's number. Bill Sternlich. He'll help you."

The taxi driver was becoming impatient. "*Monsieur,*" he said, leaning toward the passenger window, "do you want the cab?"

"Yes yes," Jordan said. Turning back to Christine, he handed her some folded one hundred dollar bills and said, "Now go."

"Will you be all right?"

He looked over his shoulder. He could not see very far down the street as it curved in an arc before the hotel. "I'll be fine," he told her. "Now get out of here."

She took his face in her hands and kissed him. "I'll be waiting. Don't worry."

Jordan smiled. "I'll be there. Now go!" he said to the driver, slamming the door shut and heading off without looking back.

FORTY-TWO

The fair-haired American named Kerrigan came into the lobby first, his smaller, darker partner right behind. The desk clerk, who was brushing himself off after shouting a loud string of French expletives down the street at Jordan and Christine, had lumbered back inside. The Englishman remained kneeling at the base of the front desk. He began to utter a rueful, "I say," but the effort was stifled at the sight of another automatic weapon, this one being brandished by the tall American.

The concierge did not have to be coaxed into describing everything that had happened, including the message left by Sandor. Normally, he was paid for information, but this time he was only too pleased to help, giving every detail. He finished by saying that the man and woman had gone off to the right, towards Saint-Germain.

Kerrigan and his partner cautiously opened the front door and stepped outside the hotel. They moved slowly at first, looking up and down the Rue des Saints-Pères several times before splitting up, each taking a side of the street as they began to stride purposefully towards the Boulevard. Kerrigan's partner, on the far side of the arched lane, got a look at Christine in the cab as it pulled away. He was surprised to see Sandor remain behind.

He signaled Kerrigan, who crossed over in time to spot Sandor before he disappeared from view, off to their right. They saw that he was alone, moving at a brisk pace in the direction of the Rue de Rennes.

It was a chilly autumn day, the streets busy with the morning traffic of students, artists, tourists and local habitués of the Left Bank. They needed to follow him, but a public scene would be a problem. They would have to find a better place to take him out.

When they reached the corner, they had a line of sight on him again. Kerrigan saw him cross the wide Boulevard and they waited, giving Jordan a more comfortable lead, then went after him.

ANDRIOLI NODDED TO himself as he viewed the proceedings from his ringside seat in the corner café across the way. Hiding behind a newspaper, he watched Christine leaving in the cab, Jordan heading off to their appointed meeting place and the two trailers following in a carefully choreographed ballet of pursuit.

Andrioli waited until he saw Jordan safely cross the Boulevard in the direction of their rendezvous, the cathedral known as Saint-German-des-Près. He stood up, left a tip for his espresso and croissant, then stepped out into the brisk morning air. He did not recognize Kerrigan or his partner, but he made them immediately. He knew how Traiman worked and expected a two-man team. Andrioli doubted they had backup in place. Not if they were onto Sandor this quickly. Jordan and Christine had obviously surprised them by coming to the hotel, and there hadn't been enough time to activate another pair of hitters.

He stood on the corner for a moment, watching, but saw no signs of anyone else in the hunt. Andrioli timed his move to cover Jordan's back. Left on his own, the two assassins would surely kill Sandor within a matter of minutes. But Andrioli knew where Jordan was going, and that gave him the edge.

Rather than traveling along the bend of the avenue where they might spot him, Andrioli walked quickly to his left, then made a right on Rue Jacob. He moved with purpose, criss-crossing the narrow street twice, prepared for what might still be coming from behind. He held his attaché case tightly in his left hand, his right gripping the Colt beneath his coat.

After walking full circle around the church, Andrioli turned up the Rue Saint

Benoit and stepped into a dark, quiet doorway on the side of the ancient stone cathedral. From there he could not miss them. Not if Jordan came this way.

Sandor did not disappoint. He hurried along the Rue Bonaparte, not breaking stride. He was fully exposed now but if he stopped, or even hesitated, his pursuers would know he had reached a meeting place. Or even worse, an ambush.

Instead, Jordan continued past the side of the church and through the small square, as if heading for the quay along the Seine. Andrioli waited, but no one appeared. He did not want to risk showing himself, but Jordan was leaving his line of sight. He hesitated, knowing that he would put them both in danger if he made a move from his doorway.

Jordan did not even glance in his direction as he walked by, keeping his gait brisk, passing within feet of Andrioli as he turned right towards the back of the cathedral.

That was when the first of the two men appeared. Just as Jordan was entering the tiny Rue des Beaux-Arts, the smaller man came into view around the far corner. He was pulling a gun from inside his jacket. He appeared to be alone.

It was the smart play, of course. His partner had likely circled back, anticipating Sandor's course. Or he might have gone toward the river, or even hidden in one of the other recesses along the cathedral wall on the opposite side. Andrioli knew he was past waiting now. Once Jordan was completely out of his sight, he could not cover him.

"Traiman," Andrioli hollered, and the man on the Rue Bonaparte instinctively turned to the sound of the shout. It was all Andrioli wanted. A split second to freeze him, and to give Jordan an instant to react. Andrioli stepped from the doorway, squeezing off two shots. The bullets whizzed through the silencer he had attached and, finding their target, spun the man and dropped him to the ground.

That extra moment was all Sandor needed. In one agile motion he drew his automatic from his belt and dove to safety in a nearby doorway. Quiet returned to the street with an eerie suddenness.

Jordan, squatting in the sanctuary of his portal, peered out at the small square adjacent to the church. Neither Andrioli nor Sandor could see each other now, and neither of them had a bead on Kerrigan. They were both vulnerable, since Kerrigan would have spotted where the shots had come from. He would also have seen where Sandor had positioned himself. There was also the problem of the man lying in the street, dead or dying, with someone sure to happen by soon. The longer they waited, the worse their prospects became.

Jordan broke from his doorway, running toward two parked cars, hoping to draw fire and expose Kerrigan's position.

No shots came.

He darted from between the cars, heading away from the church to create a crossfire with Andrioli. He stopped beside a small van opposite Andrioli's perch, and they exchanged quick nods. Jordan signaled that they should both break for the corner.

Andrioli gave him the thumbs-up and Jordan did not hesitate. He moved first, rounding the corner in a tight, swift stride, Andrioli soon behind. Still there were no shots, no sign of the tall American. The only sound was a woman's scream from somewhere in the small square. She had discovered the body of the first man lying in the street.

The two men raced the length of the Rue des Beaux-Arts, each taking a side of the narrow street, then turned up towards the Seine. There, they rested together in another entranceway, another unavailing haven from a danger that may or may not yet be in pursuit.

Andrioli was panting. "Man, am I outta shape."

"The American," Jordan said. "The one still out there. He shot Dan Peters and the cop in Woodstock. And McHugh."

Andrioli nodded, still searching for air. "We could use a little extra motivation right now. Revenge is good." He smiled, but his eyes were still alert. "But I don't think he's out there anymore. He's a paid hit man doing a job, not a fanatic on a religious mission. He knows they blew their chance. He's gone by now."

"Maybe," Jordan said, still watching the street. "Let's take a minute and wait."

THEY STEPPED BACK into the vestibule of the apartment house overlooking the river. Andrioli leaned against the stone wall, and Jordan watched him, smiling at the attaché case he still had clutched under his left arm and had carried like a football as they dashed through the streets of Paris.

"Fond of that thing, are you?"

"You can laugh, if you want," he said, "but this baby is going to be the difference in us making it or not, believe me."

"Okay, so now what?"

"There are two guys who might help. I need to get with at least one of them. Word's out that I'm back in town, so we should move fast. But first I gotta ask you something."

"Go ahead."

"How deep are you into this mess? I mean, really."

Jordan sighed. "I'm in for the long haul. Let's leave it at that."

Andrioli nodded his understanding that this was all he would be getting, and that for now it was enough.

Jordan said, "Mind if I ask you something?"

"Why not?"

"Did you meet Christine when she came to see McHugh in Paris?"

"Yeah," Andrioli said. "Why?"

"He ever tell you she was his sister?"

"Hey, that's two questions. I only got one."

"I owe you one."

"I'll remember that. Yeah, sure. He said she was his half sister, something like that. That's what he said, anyway."

Jordan nodded. "Okay."

"So," Andrioli asked, "where'd you send her?"

"Fouquet's."

He stuck out his lower lip and nodded. "*Très touriste*, no?"

"Only place I could think of at the moment. I told her we'd meet her in an hour. Otherwise, she should get herself to the embassy."

"And call in the cavalry, I suppose."

"Nuclear strike force."

"We can't let her do that now, can we?"

Jordan smiled. "Not yet." He paused. "But I do think it's time to cut her loose, don't you?"

The sound of footsteps reached them before Andrioli could respond. They tensed, ready for action. Andrioli leveled his automatic just as a young Frenchman and his girlfriend happened by, arm in arm, the barrel of the gun pointed at his head.

The youngsters froze.

"Sorry," Jordan said, offering them an apologetic grin as he reached out and gently pushed Andrioli's gun to his side.

The boy made some remark about crazy Americans then hurried away.

Jordan laughed. "You really are out of shape."

"I guess I am," Andrioli conceded as he stuck the automatic under his jacket.

"So what do you think? About Christine, I mean?"

"Were you serious about letting her go to the embassy?"

"Of course. If we don't make it, what else is she going to do?"

Andrioli shook his head. "I don't like that sonuvabitch Covington, I gotta tell you."

"Neither do I," Jordan admitted. "Come on, let's go get her before she leaves, then we'll figure out what's next."

FORTY-THREE

Christine looked at her watch again and had another sip of coffee.

The waiter came by and asked if she would like something else. She had been playing with a brioche and a cup of coffee for the past half hour.

No, she insisted, she was waiting for someone.

Of course you are, the waiter seemed to say when he responded with a sympathetic look.

Christine ignored him and checked her watch one more time before lighting another cigarette. She didn't smoke, but this morning she found herself anxiously working through a pack of Gauloises.

SANDOR AND ANDRIOLI arrived at Fouquet's, having taken the precaution of changing cabs in front of the Hotel Crillon, then asking the second driver to travel around L'Etoile and back to the other side of the Champs-Elysées. When they stepped onto the street, they spotted Christine at a small table inside the glass-walled café, nervously puffing on a cigarette. She saw them and stood up.

Inside the restaurant she embraced each man as if she had not seen them in years. The waiter, obviously surprised to find that not one, but two gentlemen had joined her, came by to take their order. Jordan asked for a round of cognacs and, although none of them had an appetite for food, ordered sandwiches. Fouquet's more elegant cuisine would be wasted on them today.

After they told Christine everything that had happened on the Left Bank, Andrioli wrote down the name and address of a hotel on the Rue de Rivoli. It was an elegant place, he told them, and they would be well insulated there. When they instructed the front desk that they were not to be disturbed, they would not be disturbed. Andrioli would call and make the arrangements in the name of Jordan's alias, Scott Kerr.

"What about you?" Christine asked.

"I've got to pay a surprise visit to one of my friends." He thought that over as he sipped his cognac. "Might not be much of a surprise at this point."

Jordan agreed. "We've got to assume they're watching every one of your contacts."

"Yeah, well, nothin' to be done about that now. I gotta see him if we want the information we need."

"If you say so. But be careful."

"I'll be careful. I'll call the Pas de Tour, see what messages they have for Mr. Forest. Now that they know we're in town, Traiman'll probably have them try to set a meeting."

Jordan smiled. "Bet that clerk'll be happy to hear from you."

"Don't you worry about that clerk. He gets paid by all sides. Typical Frenchman. Love the one you're with."

"Is that what this was all about?" Christine asked. "You risked your lives so this man Traiman would set up a meeting?"

Andrioli and Sandor shared a quick look.

"It's more complicated than that," was all that Andrioli would say.

"You said you had two friends you wanted to reach," Sandor reminded him.

"Yeah," Andrioli said, then took a bite of the ham and cheese baguette they'd been served. "I got a backup if Jackson doesn't come through."

They were quiet for a while, each of them sifting through their personal ordeal. Then Christine said, "I wish you'd killed the other man."

The two men looked at her.

"It doesn't matter," Jordan said. "They're all interchangeable parts of the same machine."

Christine shook her head. "He killed Jimmy. The big one killed Jimmy. You said so yourself."

"I did, yes. But it might have been the little Arab who was there that day. What difference does it make which one of them pulled the trigger?"

Andrioli put down his sandwich and looked across the table at them, his eyes ghostly sad, the eyes of a man with a terminal illness. "He didn't pull the trigger," he said quietly. "Jimmy pulled the trigger. Just like I did. Sometimes the gun doesn't go off right away, that's all. It's only a matter of time."

Jordan reached out and gave Andrioli a friendly slap on the shoulder. "Don't get all preachy on us now."

"Sorry, but I don't want Christine walking around all full of hate about this for the rest of her life. Truth is, Jimmy and I were stupid and greedy and selfish, and we created everything we became. We couldn't see tomorrow for today. We were little boys playing soldier, just like a lot of little boys. Except most of us grow up. Take responsibility. Care about something or someone other than ourselves."

"What about us?" Christine asked him. "You're helping us, aren't you?"

"Helping you do what? Get yourselves killed? Jimmy never should have gotten you mixed up in all this to start with. Now you're stuck with me, a condemned man who wants to repent for his sins. If you two had an ounce of sense, you'd get up right now and walk straight to the embassy. Period. You're nuts if you don't."

Jordan looked him in the eye and said, "That's not an option. You know it, and I know it. There's too much at stake here for us to stop now, not to mention that we've aided and abetted a fugitive, traveled on forged passports and shot up the streets of Fort Lauderdale and Paris."

Andrioli could not resist a crooked grin. "Good point."

Sandor nodded slowly. "There really is too much at stake."

"More than you know," Andrioli agreed.

"So tell us."

"I will. After I find Jackson."

"Okay," Jordan agreed. He looked down at the drinks and food on their table. "It's been a while since I've flown to Paris for cognac and baguettes."

The three of them lifted their glasses in a silent toast.

COVINGTON AND FOUR of his men, including Todd Nealon, were on their way to France. He had just received an e-mail via satellite describing the shootings near the Cathedral Saint-German-des-Près. It was not yet clear what had

222

happened, but one man had been found dead. Interpol identified him as a known terrorist. No one at the scene had been apprehended.

The deputy director told Covington it was time to shorten the leash on Andrioli and Sandor. Regardless of what Andrioli managed to find in Paris, he should be taken in for questioning. If Sandor was with him, Covington was instructed to bring him in as well.

Covington had other plans, however. But for now he would follow instructions.

FORTY-FOUR

On the way to their new hotel, Jordan and Christine stopped to purchase a few items. The suitcases and clothing they had picked up in Atlanta were abandoned in Room 57 of the Pas de Tour. Andrioli suggested the shops just off the Rue de Rivoli, on a small street featuring an assortment of boutiques.

The shopping provided a welcome diversion. They visited a number of stores, replacing Christine's cosmetics and personals, choosing a couple of outfits for her, slacks and shirts for Jordan. By the time they were done, the two of them were laden with shopping bags and a large, signature khaki Longchamps tote for Christine.

"I don't think I can carry anything else," Jordan told her.

The spree over, they found their way to the small but elegant hotel Andrioli had chosen for them just a couple of blocks away.

The desk clerk greeted Jordan with a polite nod.

"I'm Mr. Kerr," Jordan told him. "I believe you have a reservation for us."

"Yes," the clerk said, "we received the call a short time ago." He asked for a passport and credit card. Jordan signed the register and American Express voucher as Scott Kerr, then they followed the bellboy who took their bags, led them to the lift and escorted them upstairs.

The room was generously sized, with French provincial furniture and appointments, a view of the street below and a large bed that beckoned as they felt a wave of exhaustion wash over them.

Jordan tipped the bellboy and locked the door behind him. When he turned back, he found Christine had already pulled back the comforter, kicked off her shoes and was lying on the bed.

"I'm going to take a shower," Jordan said. "You want to go first?"

Christine shook her head. "I can't move."

"I won't be a minute," he said.

Inside the marble-walled bathroom he removed the toiletry kit from his leather bag and had a shave, then stepped into a warm, steaming shower. He let the water wash over him, relaxing his tense muscles and tired mind for a long time. He toweled off and pulled on the plush, terrycloth robe provided by the hotel.

Back in the room, he found Christine had removed her slacks and blouse and was curled up under the beige coverlet, fast asleep.

He watched her for a moment, realizing that in the three days he had known her, it was the first time he had ever seen her lovely face truly at peace. He leaned over and straightened out the duvet to make her more comfortable.

Jordan considered dialing the front desk for a wake-up call, but thought better of it. He knew he would not sleep for long, and if Andrioli needed him, he knew where to find them. He took off the robe and slid under the cover, doing his best not to wake Christine. The satiny texture of the comforter felt good against his skin and, as he turned on his side, he was surprised to find that her eyes had opened. She was watching him.

"We need some rest," he said.

She nodded.

"You all right?"

She nodded again then moved closer to him, placing her arm around his neck.

"Danger is an aphrodisiac," he warned her, reaching out to stroke her sandy-colored hair.

"Is it?"

He nodded. "Wouldn't be fair to take advantage of the situation."

She smiled, maybe the best of the smiles she had shown him up to then. "So if you frighten a girl to death, then what? Is that like getting her drunk at a party?"

"Never thought of it that way," he said, taking her by the shoulders and gently drawing her towards him. "I guess it's the right analogy, though. Just isn't done."

She kissed him tenderly on the lips, her legs now eagerly entwined in his. He pulled back slightly and looked into her pale, blue eyes and saw a resolve that would have surprised him that evening when he had first met her at the cocktail lounge in New York.

Jordan held her, his emotions a mix of desire and doubt, passionate instinct and clinical analysis, wanting to trust her, but knowing he should not.

She reached up to kiss him again, pressing herself against him as she became lost in the moment, her hands searching his strong form. She pulled away from him slightly, remaining under the coverlet as she slipped off her panties and tossed them to the floor. Then she took his face in her hands and looked into his eyes. "You don't have to worry," she said with a slight smile, "this isn't because I'm afraid."

Their lips met again, mouths open, immersing them in a warm, moist flood of sensations, an enveloping wave that permitted no other experience but this embrace. He reacted to the feel of her firm breasts pressed against his chest, the taste of her, the reassuring suppleness of her body next to his. He felt her fingers dig into his back, pulling him closer and closer, until they were together. Lost in the grand illusion for the time being.

ANTHONY ANDRIOLI BELIEVED he understood things that his new partners in espionage had no way of knowing.

He understood the brutality of their adversary, Vincent Traiman, and how difficult that would make it for them to prevail. Even to survive.

He understood that life cares not at all what you think of it, that life rolls on with unremitting determination and uncaring inevitability, requiring no approval, unaffected by the intent or purpose of a man's deeds. He understood that life itself ultimately becomes the greatest teacher of how to live.

He also understood that for him, all that was left to him was the opportunity to stop Traiman, even if there was no valor in the deed. He had sacrificed his ideals long ago, saw them bleed to death with his friends in Vietnam, watched them tormented out of existence when he discovered how little remained for him back in the States. He had taken a handful of peculiar skills and become a traitor without a cause, a heretic with no religion to betray.

Now, after his years with Traiman, there was nowhere left for him to go. He had hidden in Florida too long. The corpses left beside the New River Canal in Fort Lauderdale was proof of that.

Now, at least, he had a reason to go on. He knew some of what Traiman meant to do, and he was determined to discover the rest. He gazed into the bathroom mirror in his small hotel room in Montmartre, his dark brown eyes staring back at him, wondering how far he would get—how far they would get—before Traiman stopped them. *What the hell*, he thought as he trimmed the edges of his beard, *we've come this far. What else is there for me to do?*

He turned on the shower, the rush of water quickly turning warm. He had very little sleep in the past couple of days, and he needed to wake up. He stepped into the tub, the Parisian shower fixture no higher than his neck. He bent forward, letting the soothing water cascade over his head and down his shoulders and back. He cupped his hands and splashed his face and hair, ducking his head beneath the shower again until he felt renewed and alert and ready.

He dressed quickly in his wrinkled clothes, then managed to smile at himself in the mirror. His rumpled appearance would be considered *très chic* in Montmartre. He picked up his attaché case and made his way out of the hotel, stopping at a public telephone on the Rue Lepic.

NIGHT HAD FALLEN, and Montmartre was alive with people bumping and bustling their way to the Metro, scurrying along the café lined streets, stopping to admire the local artists who displayed their work against the stone walls that climbed the hills of the area. Andrioli dialed a number and waited.

"Hello," the familiar voice answered.

"*Bonsoir*, Steve. This is Forest."

"What the—" Steve Jackson gasped. "Forest?"

"Yes," Andrioli said calmly. "Meet me in five minutes at the Sacred Heart Church," he told him, using the English name of the famous cathedral.

There was a pause on the other end. "Better make it ten."

Andrioli didn't bother to answer. He replaced the phone on its hook and walked away.

He hadn't seen or spoken with Steve Jackson in more than two months, but he was still the only man in Paris Andrioli trusted enough to call. He knew that

Jackson would not speak on the phone, that they would have to meet, which increased the danger. Any contact with Jackson was a calculated risk, but it was unavoidable. Andrioli had used his code name to tell him that his situation was serious, both men realizing it was a superfluous gesture under the circumstances. Most agents in the system knew that their friends, Jimmy and Tony, had disappeared. They probably knew that McHugh was now dead, and they had certainly been told that Traiman had declared open season on Andrioli.

Jackson received this information sooner than most. He worked the communications detail from Paris, the link between the free Western world and the dark operations that existed behind the veil of Arab protection. Jackson was a key man in the exchange of intelligence within Traiman's organization. That was another reason Andrioli wanted to see him.

Andrioli never believed the story Traiman was selling, the placement of overseas assassination teams. He didn't believe it any more than he believed that Qaddafi had become a moderate force for peace, or that Saddam Hussein had ever been committed to the dismantling of his weapons of mass destruction. There was another level to the missions Traiman had initiated. Andrioli had heard enough about the Loubar shipments to know that.

Jackson was the logical connection, the man who should be able to give him vital information to piece it together.

Why, then, Andrioli wondered, *had Jackson seem so surprised to receive his call?* After the shooting this morning, a systems coordinator in Jackson's position would surely have heard that Andrioli was in Paris. And that he had survived the incident. Jordan had left the name Forest with the clerk at the Pas de Tour. Jackson would have heard about that as well, probably would have been the man to relay the message to Libya. *What was so shocking about the call, then? Who else would I contact in Paris?*

Andrioli had chosen a hotel two blocks from Jackson's apartment, both of which were near the foot of the Sacred Heart steps. *Why would Steve need an additional five minutes to get there?*

These questions nagged at Andrioli as he climbed the mountain of steps that led to the imposing Basilique du Sacre Coeur.

When he reached the top, he paused to view the surrounding area. This was a good meeting place. It was wide open, and now that he had ascended the long hill of stone stairs, he was afforded a fine vantage point for any possible approaches. As he looked around, he gave a subtle impersonation of a curious tourist. He pretended to be absorbed in the majestic view of Paris that stretches out below this centuries-old cathedral, which is perched atop one of the city's highest points. He allowed himself a brief glimpse at those far reaches before he returned to the immediate area below.

He had arrived first but had purposely given Jackson very little time to meet him there. Even with the additional five minutes, there was no opportunity for any covert placement of snipers. They would have to come directly at him, and so he turned and made his way up the final flight of stairs to the front of the basilica.

He positioned himself beneath one of the cupolas, shielded from view by a large column and protected from the cold winds that whipped across the church's façade.

He stood there, opened the hardshell attaché case, and waited.

FORTY-FIVE

Vincent R. Traiman made ready for his voyage north across the Mediterranean to meet with Martin Koppel. Everything was arranged. All precautions had been taken. The timing of his operation meant he could not delay his appointment. The trouble in Paris had to be addressed, of course, but he would rely on his men there to handle Andrioli and Sandor. If they could not, Traiman had an insurance policy in place that made his position fail-safe.

The most important thing was to finalize his financial arrangements with Koppel.

Even though he had fallen from grace, Koppel still had an impressive background and a world of experience in the financial markets. His credibility could easily be restored, given the appropriate economic backing. His new company would be funded through an investment firm he would create with Traiman's money. After Nine Eleven, the United States regulatory agencies had become vigilant about suspicious foreign investments. Koppel was decidedly American. He was a man with a reputation, someone who had enjoyed great wealth.

Now, through a series of sanitized financial transactions, Koppel would be bankrolled and given an opportunity to repeat the success of his past. Except this time, his principal sponsor would be betting on failure. Koppel was as desperate as a man can become, and his cooperation was easily purchased, even if he would not comprehend the extent of his complicity in Traiman's scheme until it was too late.

Even as his Arab compatriots pressed Traiman for action on a series of assassinations that would never really take place, his men would complete their true missions, in the United States, England and Italy. The resulting panic would drive the financial markets to new lows. France and Germany, America's faithless allies, would be rewarded for their weakness by being spared these strikes. This would create an even larger rift between the Western powers, while generating a marked disparity in the economic reaction to these new terrorist assaults. Consumer and institutional confidence would plummet.

ANDRIOLI SCANNED THE scene below from the long stretch of ascending steps that rose from the street to the side entrances of the terraces just beneath him. He smiled at the irony of making his second visit to a church since arriving in Paris, reflecting on the grim reality that the first ended with a body lying in the street. Steve Jackson was his friend, and he hoped their meeting did not suffer a similar fate. Still, there was no way of knowing who might have detected his call or learned of their meeting.

As Andrioli worried over these dangers he spotted him. Jackson had begun climbing the stairs, steadily, slowly, off to the right. He appeared to be alone.

He was younger than Andrioli, not yet forty. He was tall and slim, his long, dark hair combed straight back in a fashionable Parisian style. He moved cautiously and, when he reached the terrace level, stopped and had a look around. His motions were deliberate, as if checking to see if he was being followed.

Andrioli was just above him now, standing beside a huge, marble pillar. He did not move, did not show himself. The section of terrace below was empty. For a moment the two men stood in place, waiting. Then Jackson turned and began up the last set of steps leading to the church entrance. He was near the center of the wide staircase, still to Andrioli's right. When he had climbed to the top, nearly reaching the tall doors of the basilica, Andrioli quietly called out, "Steve."

Jackson did not break stride. He continued toward the entrance of the cathedral, turning around to look behind him again. Then he turned and moved slowly until he disappeared from any view below and faced his friend behind the width of the stone column.

"You think you'll need that?" Jackson asked, pointing to the automatic that Andrioli had drawn and ready.

"You never know," Andrioli said with a smile, then shoved the Colt back into his waistband.

"If I was going to turn on you, I wouldn't even be here. You'd be in someone's crosshairs by now."

Andrioli realized he was right. "Yeah, well, I guess I should tell you thanks for coming."

Jackson took a moment to look at him. "What you should tell me is what the hell you're doing in Paris?"

"Good question. Wish I had a good answer for you."

Jackson hesitated then said, "Well I've got some good advice for you, buddy. Get out of here, and fast."

"And go where?"

"What do I know? China. Brazil. Look Tony, you ran out on Traiman, wasted two guys in Florida, then took out one of his favorite Arabs this morning."

"Who was the other guy, the one who skipped?"

"Kerrigan. You ever meet him?"

Andrioli shook his head.

"Tall, blond guy, right?"

Andrioli nodded.

"IQ about fifty-four," Jackson told him, "and vicious as a snake. He was the one got to McHugh."

"So I heard." When Jackson responded with a quizzical look, Andrioli said, "Not important. I just heard it."

"What is this, Tony, you on a one man crusade?"

"Not one man, no."

"Don't tell me you're still dragging around the girl and that CIA washout."

Andrioli's eyes narrowed, then he determined to forego any pretense, instead giving a quick nod. "Yeah," he admitted. "When did you find out Sandor reached me?"

"When I was keeping them off your ass in Florida."

"What?"

"I screwed up a transmission when they first made you there a few days ago. Rode them off your tail for a little while."

"Thanks."

"Don't mention it. Sorry I couldn't get word to you."

"I understand. You guys in ground ops know how to play it safe."

"Communications is the place to be, man. No danger. Nice clean work."

"Yeah."

"Look, Traiman has offered to meet with you. Didn't you get that message?"

"Oh sure, I got it when they blew up my friggen boat."

"No, that was only after Jimmy held out on them. He had a ticket back here, then changed his mind. He was supposed to get to you, set up a meeting."

Andrioli shook his head, wondering once more about McHugh's intentions. He found it hard to believe his friend was going to flip again, but maybe Jimmy really did think about coming back here alone, hanging him out to dry.

"Look, Tony, you're a big boy. You do what you want, but this is too dangerous for me to be standing around having a chat with you. You asked me to come here, and I did. Now tell me what you want and let me go inside the church to pray for your immortal soul."

Andrioli uttered a hollow laugh. "I want to know what Traiman's got cooked up with these teams he's placing. And don't give me any bullshit about assassinations."

Jackson shook his head. "I'm here for old time's sake, but I'm not crazy enough to cut my own throat."

"Come on, cowboy, time to give it up."

Jackson said, "Take a vacation in South America, will you?" Then he turned to walk away.

Andrioli grabbed him by the arm with his left hand and pulled out the automatic with his right. "I always liked you, Steve, but I got nothing left to lose. Now answer my question."

Jackson made a slight move with his free hand, but Andrioli jammed the barrel of the Colt into his ribs. Jackson stared into his friend's eyes. "You wouldn't kill me Tony. Even if you figure you're dead already, you wouldn't shoot me."

"I'll tell you, Steve, I'm not so sure myself anymore, and I don't wanna have to find out."

They stood there in silence, each man measuring the other.

"All right," Jackson said, "for all the good it'll do you. It's Traiman's VX scheme."

"Get outta here."

"I'd love to, if you'd let go of my arm."

"Traiman's going with VX gas? That's insanity."

"That's what I hear, and that's all I can tell you. Now get outta town, will you?"

Two gunshots, spit from a silencer, caromed off the stone wall behind them. Without the loud report, Andrioli couldn't determine the placement of the shooter. When those rounds were followed immediately by two more shots that blew chunks out of the marble column, Andrioli figured they were coming from just behind the balustrade off to their right. He yanked Jackson's arm and the two of them hit the cold, marble ground.

Andrioli turned to Jackson to ask him if he had a gun. Then he saw the thick blood oozing from the side of his friend's head.

He wiped at the source of the bleeding to see how bad Jackson had been hit. "Steve, I'm gonna take a run at him. It may only be one guy." Jackson's eyes were nearly shut. "Can you hear me, Steve?"

Jackson made a low, guttural sound. Then he muttered, "Must've followed me."

Andrioli had a quick look above the stone railing, then ducked again as another two shots took pieces out of the pillar. "I'm sweeping wide then coming back up the stairs at him. We need to get you help fast, and he probably has backup on the way."

Jackson's eyes opened now. They were the eyes of death. "Go on, Tony," he urged him in a barely audible voice. "Just go."

The shooting had stopped, their attacker likely on the move. "Traiman," Andrioli said. "Is the VX assault for real?"

Jackson nodded weakly and managed to say, "Go home."

"There's no way home for me. When is Traiman coming out again?"

Their eyes met for the last time. "Portofino," the dying man said in a raspy whisper. "Tomorrow. On the *Halaby*." Jackson tried to draw a breath, to say something else but a gunshot, from closer range now, hit him in the chest as he lay there. His body convulsed. Then he was dead.

Andrioli wheeled around, but it was too late. The sniper had come up the stairs on the far end, and Andrioli took the crippling blow of a bullet to the left side of his chest before sheer reflex caused him to squeeze off three rounds from his .45. The first shot went high, but Jackson's killer was staggered by the second and third. Then Andrioli fired a fourth, dropping the man to the ground.

Andrioli struggled to his feet. He stood there for a moment, leaning with his back against the pillar, bracketed by the bodies of Steve Jackson and his murderer. Both dead. But he was still alive, even as the searing pain of his wound nearly paralyzed him. He wasn't certain how badly he'd been hit himself. He worried about maintaining consciousness long enough to get the hell out of there.

People were screaming, the loud *crack* of the gunshots from Andrioli's automatic having created mayhem along the steps and terraces below. He pulled out his handkerchief, reached inside his shirt and pressed it against his left side. He shoved the Colt in his belt, closed his jacket, then picked up his attaché case and made his way off to the left, wary of any other shooters that might already be in place. He moved quickly despite the staggering pain, somehow making his way down the stairs, and headed to the row of cabs near the Place du Tertre.

FORTY-SIX

Jordan and Christine were up and dressed when the clerk at the front desk rang them.

"*Monsieur* Kerr," the man said, "a Mr. Forest to see you."

"Right," Jordan said. "Send him up."

Jordan reached for the gun.

"What is it?" Christine asked.

"Mr. Forest is coming up to see us."

"Wouldn't that be Tony?"

"Maybe," he said.

She nodded then stood off to the side.

Jordan checked the clip in the automatic and chambered a round. Then he unlocked the door and moved against the wall, checking for the best line of sight. "Lock yourself in the bathroom," he told Christine. "Don't make a sound until you hear from me."

Christine nodded again, then disappeared inside. Jordan took his position and waited.

He heard the knock and said, "Come in," ready to take out at least the first two men through. The door swung open, and Andrioli stumbled in.

"What happened?" Jordan said, helping him onto the bed as he called for Christine.

THEY INSISTED ON taking him to a hospital, but Andrioli wanted to straighten some things out first.

He began to tell them what Jackson had said, but his narrative coming in short bursts punctuated by long gasps for air and a look of pain that etched his features in dark relief.

Christine stopped him, pleading for them to get help.

"Listen, you take a foreigner to the hospital with a gunshot wound and they call the Sûreté, Interpol, the embassy. I'll be finished."

Jordan looked down at him. "You'll be finished if we don't stop the bleeding."

Andrioli motioned for his attaché case. Christine brought it to him, and he pulled out a number. "Call this doctor. Tell him you have a friend with acute gastric distress. He's got to come at once. He'll know what that means. He'll come."

Sandor nodded and dialed the number. "What about the desk clerk? Did he suspect anything?"

Andrioli offered a wan smile in response. "Whatever he noticed, a couple of five hundred euro notes made him forget."

While they waited for the doctor, Andrioli did his best to explain what Jackson had told him.

"VX is a nerve gas—"

"VX?" Jordan interrupted.

"Shut up and listen," he said, clenching his jaw until another wave of pain passed. "Yeah. VX. It's a nerve gas developed by the British about fifty years ago. It has the consistency of oil, and it's totally lethal. If you inhale it or touch it, you're dead. You can spray it, explode it, whatever. It'll wipe out a crowd in a minute."

"I know all about it," Jordan admitted.

"That company, Loubar, they've helped with the delivery system. They might even be the means for transporting it."

"Where?"

"Who the hell knows? The US for sure."

"Where in the US? Did he say?"

"If he knew the targets, he didn't have a chance to tell me. Any place they can expose a lot of people at one time. Think of it, hit a major city, kill forty or fifty thousand people in one shot."

"And it's already in process?"

"So he said. I can't believe they'd go that far. Can you imagine the American response?"

"Yes," Jordan agreed. "It would take things to another level."

"As in . . . all-out war. Even a measured nuclear response is possible."

"Against who?"

"I don't know, but you're going to Italy to find out. Your old friend Traiman is on his way to Portofino tomorrow. He's going there to work out the final details."

"Portofino?"

"Yeah. And Sandor. They all know who you are."

MAHMOUD RAHMAD WAS feeling rather pleased with himself as he strolled down Fifth Avenue. He glanced at window displays of the familiar stores, the upcoming holiday season another opportunity to treat himself to the finest of what New York had to offer. Bergdorf, Tiffany, Gucci, Cartier.

The meetings in Tripoli went better than he had anticipated. His failure to deal with the American, Sandor, had not been the problem he feared it might, and he certainly could not be held accountable for the failure of Traiman's men to resolve the issue of Andrioli down in Florida. In fact, if the rumors were correct, Traiman was falling out of favor with their Arab associates. The debacle in Fort Lauderdale might be another nail in his coffin.

On the other hand, the New York operations were proceeding smartly. It was true that he had exceeded his budget during the past few months, but he could not concern himself with those details. Results were all that mattered.

He had successfully coordinated the placement of the extraordinary team that had been hand-picked by Traiman himself. Two men were already in New York, and the rest of the team would gain entrance to the country through Canada. Of those additional men, four would be sent to San Francisco. Two others were to be assigned to St. Louis and the final two would replace the men assigned to the mission in Florida, the two who had been killed in Fort Lauderdale. They would act as rovers. Together, these men would be the vanguard of the attack.

Now that the Loubar Corporation was back on line, the return of the containers to the Port of New York would be as easy as sending an overnight package by Federal Express. The inspectors would never guess that they would be facilitating a transfer of VX from Europe back to the United States.

The disinformation being circulated, of assassination teams dedicated to the murder of key government officials, had fooled the others in Libya, but Rahmad had already uncovered Traiman's real plan. The Americans would also be kept busy with their useless Homeland Security efforts, moving ever further in the wrong direction. The team that had been arrested in Washington would resist any attempts to uncover the purpose of their mission. However, after a dose of sodium pentathol or some other cocktail mixed at the CTC, these zealots would reveal what they knew about an assassination plot. They knew nothing of Operation VX.

Rahmad wondered whether Traiman had been the one behind the exposure of the Washington team. He was certainly capable of such treachery, and Rahmad had long suspected that Traiman was responsible for the capture of Khalid Sheikh Mohammed in Pakistan. That betrayal dealt a crippling blow to al-Qaeda operations at the time, temporarily restoring Traiman's importance to the extremists. If either suspicion proved to be true, Rahmad acknowledged to himself if to no one else, they were brilliant ploys.

Yet, even as Rahmad reviewed the progress of these plans, he knew he had one more hurdle to overcome. The meeting that awaited him at his office was not to be a mere debriefing session. It was, in fact, an important strategy session with representatives of Ibrahim Abass, his direct link to al-Qaeda.

When Rahmad arrived, his aides had already admitted their guests into the office. One was a Saudi in his mid-twenties, the other appeared to be Lebanese, about forty years old. They had come, they announced, from Washington. There they had attempted to gather information on the apprehension of the three-man team. There was great dissatisfaction about their capture.

The younger of the two emissaries explained this to Rahmad.

"I see," Rahmad replied, although it was not clear why they had come to him with this report. The team in DC and its exposure had nothing to do with him.

"Good," the man continued, "because we are here to discuss this recent interference with our activities."

Rahmad seated himself behind his desk. "Please, gentlemen, make yourselves comfortable." He nodded to his two aides, who were standing behind these visitors, but no one sat other than Rahmad.

"We would prefer to stand," the young man said without apology. "What we have to tell you will not take long."

Rahmad looked beyond him, to his older assistant. "Interference?" Rahmad repeated the young man's word.

"Our team in Washington was betrayed," the young man continued. "We have been compromised by someone within our organization."

"How can that be?" Rahmad asked.

"It can be," the young man said, "when one of our own forsakes the integrity of Allah's mission in exchange for the excesses of Western comforts and depravity."

Rahmad felt himself stiffen. "Who?" he asked weakly. "Who would have done such a thing?"

"We think you know."

Now Rahmad sat up and nodded vigorously. "Yes," he said. "The American."

The older man, who had not spoken yet, broke into a smile, revealing a mouthful of stained, uneven teeth. "Why would Traiman destroy his own efforts?" His accent was much heavier than his younger companion's.

Traiman's intentional sacrifice of his own team seemed far-fetched, even to Rahmad. Still, he had long ago decided that Traiman could not be trusted. "I suspect these men were sacrificed in the name of a larger mission," he told them.

"What utter nonsense is this?"

"I'm certain of it. It was part of Traiman's plan. Don't you see? He is not one of us, after all." He attempted to go on, but the older man stopped him.

"No, Rahmad, we have learned the source of this treachery. Your name must now be added to the *Sijjin*."

The mere utterance of that word, the scroll bearing the names of those Muslims going to hell, resolved any doubt or hope for the Saudi. Rahmad's epiphany was complete. Traiman had engineered things perfectly, arranging for the removal of anyone who was privy to or even suspected his real motives.

"Wait," he said, "let me explain. You're making a mistake." But it was too late.

The next few seconds, the last moments of Rahmad's life, seemed to unfold in slow motion. He watched as the younger man drew a revolver, spun around, and fired shots into the chests of Rahmad's two aides.

The older Lebanese said, "*Allahu Akbar.*" God is great. Then he pulled out his weapon, smiled his filthy smile, and fired repeatedly at Rahmad as his body was thrown back in his chair and then sprawled forward, lifeless, across his large desk.

FORTY-SEVEN

The French physician summoned by Andrioli confirmed what they had suspected. The slug had passed through Andrioli's side. The loss of blood was serious. If they did not get him to a hospital soon, he could slip into unconsciousness and die.

The doctor was a distinguished looking gentleman, short and slender, with a thin mustache. He removed his jacket, folded back his sleeves and worked with meticulous care to treat the wound. First he swabbed the area, then injected Andrioli with a local anesthetic and then with an antibiotic. Andrioli almost passed out twice from the pain and blood loss.

The doctor gave Jordan more than a couple of looks, telling him he needed to get his friend proper care as soon as possible. After he closed the area with sutures, he handed Jordan a small vial of morphine capsules.

Andrioli had explained that the doctor was well known to his old cronies, so Jordan paid the man with a fistful of five-hundred franc notes from the attaché case and told him to keep his mouth shut.

"*Monsieur,*" he said to Andrioli, "you know my reputation well enough to believe that I will exercise discretion."

"And you know me well enough to believe that I'll find you if you don't," Andrioli told him.

The doctor responded with a knowing smile. They realized he could only be counted on to stay quiet for a few hours at best. They hoped that would be enough.

Christine showed the doctor out. When he was gone, Jordan told them he had a plan.

ANDRIOLI WAS IN desperate need of a transfusion, and Jordan knew the first thing he had to do was contact John Covington. Since there was no reason for further pretense, Sandor pulled out his secure reach number. The operator promptly referred him to the United States Embassy in Paris.

After being shunted from one level of bureaucracy to the next, he heard the familiar voice say, "Well, well, well. Jordan Sandor."

"Hello, Covington."

"Good to hear from you again. I trust you and your friends are enjoying France."

Jordan was seated at the writing table. "One of my friends wants to say hello."

Christine handed Andrioli the phone from the extension beside the bed. "Covington," he said into the extension.

"Ah, Mr. Andrioli. Finding Paris to your liking this time around?"

"Actually," Jordan said, "my friends are finding Paris a little tough to take. Thought we might get out of town."

"That so?"

"It is. And I'm going to make your life easy, so you can drop the trace on this call. We'd like to see you before we leave. This way, when you're trying to follow us, you won't be two days behind."

"How kind of you."

"I don't want you to think we're not flattered by the attention, but you're just not giving us much help, is all. We keep getting shot at, and there's no one around to cover our backs."

"That's not my job, gentlemen."

"We noticed," Andrioli said.

"You three are fugitives wanted by the United States government," Covington said. "You're also wanted for questioning by the French authorities for a shooting that took place here in Paris today."

"Four shootings," Jordan interrupted, "just to keep your scorecard straight."

"Four?"

"That's right. Three dead, one injured. Check the evening news if you want an update. Look, you want to see us or not?"

Covington said he would be pleased to meet with them, so Jordan gave him the name of their hotel and hung up.

THEY PACKED CHRISTINE'S tote and Jordan's black leather bag.

"Get going," Andrioli said. "They'll be here any minute."

Jordan stood at the side of the bed, placing his hand on Andrioli's shoulder. "You're sure you're up to this?"

"Go, will you?"

Christine went over and kissed Andrioli on the forehead.

"I'll be all right, as long as Covington gets here before Traiman's people do." He looked up at Jordan. "Right?"

Jordan nodded solemnly. "Either way, I'm worried."

"The government boys won't pull anything with me, not till I tell them what you're up to. I'll keep talking long enough to give you a head start."

Christine said, "Make sure they take good care of you."

"Sure thing." He pointed to his battered attaché case. "Remember that thing. And what I told you about the explosives."

Jordan nodded again.

"I guess you know more about those gimmicks in there than I do."

"We'll find out," Jordan said.

"So, you track him your way, and I'll have the cavalry right behind."

"That's the idea. I just want a little lead time."

Andrioli grabbed a cigarette from the nightstand and fumbled as he tried to light one. Sandor took the pack of matches and fired it up for him.

"Not a great idea," Jordan said.

"What the hell." Andrioli took a long drag and blew it out. "Too late to be worried about my health." He looked at Christine. "You sure you don't want to sit this one out with me? Be a lot safer for you."

"He's right," Jordan said.

"No. If I stay, they'll just take me into custody when they get here. I'm seeing this through."

Jordan nodded. "Let's go then."

Andrioli gave them a weak, narcotic influenced smile, then patted the Colt automatic that sat in his lap. "I feel kind of like Jim Bowie at the Alamo, you know? When Davy Crockett sets him up in bed for the final battle with a brace of pistolas."

Jordan nodded. "I remember. Hold a better thought for the outcome. Okay, cowboy?"

Andrioli smiled. "See you in Portofino."

Then Jordan and Christine left him alone in the room to wait.

ABOUT TEN MINUTES later, the door burst open with a loud crash. Two agents lunged forward, guns drawn, ready to fire.

Andrioli was sitting on the bed, puffing away on another cigarette. He raised his head slightly and said, "Doesn't anyone just knock anymore?" He looked pale and, although the doctor had stopped the bleeding, was badly in need of plasma. The gash in his side was throbbing, and he had yet to take any additional morphine, afraid to dull his senses before he knew who would get to him first.

The two agents remained poised and silent as John Covington and Todd Nealon came in behind them. Having a look at Andrioli's condition, Covington said, "Take his gun, but don't move him."

The first agent removed the automatic from Andrioli's lap and backed off. Covington pulled up the desk chair and sat down beside the bed. Nealon stood behind him.

"Seems you got the worst of the action in Montmartre."

Andrioli slowly crushed his cigarette in the ashtray and lit another. "Not really. The worst of it is dead already."

Covington nodded. "You look better in your dossier photo."

"That so? Well, I probably hadn't been shot the day they took it."

"So where are your friends? Got tired of playing with you? No, hold on. Let me guess. They turned you in because they thought they'd be doing you a big favor. We'd get you a doctor and have that nasty little cut taken care of, is that your play?"

"That's it." Andrioli shifted uncomfortably. "My medical plan doesn't cover foreign gunshot wounds, and Sandor told me what a sweetheart you are."

"Bad judge of character, Sandor."

"I'm not so sure."

"I think you'll have a chance to find out. We should have a little chat."

"Suit yourself," Andrioli said. He was in no rush. He offered Covington a cigarette.

"No thanks. Not one of my vices."

Andrioli felt the room starting to spin and planted his right hand on the bed to brace himself in case he was about to pass out. "I sure could use a doctor, I'll tell you. Lost enough blood to be a Red Cross poster boy."

"We'll get to that in due course. First, tell me where Sandor's going."

"I'm too weak to remember."

The CIA man glanced at Andrioli's bloody shirt. "Maybe Nealon here could poke a finger into your side, perk you up a bit."

Andrioli took an uneven drag on his cigarette and then coughed a small cloud of gray brown smoke into Covington's face. "This your tough guy routine?"

"I thought you were the tough guy here," Covington said.

"Not me, not anymore."

"So, what do you have to sell me today?"

"Depends what you're after. I can give you Sandor. I can give you my life story as a bad guy in Libya. I can give you Vincent Traiman."

The last comment caused Covington a nearly imperceptible flinch. "You can't give me anything I don't already have."

"If I got nothing you need, what the hell are you doing here?"

"Maybe I'm here to arrest you."

"You're a cop now? Hey, go ahead and arrest me, man. A prison infirmary sounds pretty good about now." He reached down and touched the bandage on his side. "I've got some stories to tell, if you're interested, but I'm running out of steam."

"You're just another sorry case of Vietnam burnout run wild. That's an old story, mister."

"You're not wrong about me, but you're wrong if you think I don't have something to deal."

"Suppose we're interested in your fairy tales? What do you want, other than the Congressional Medal of Honor?"

"I don't know. Immunity. Federal protection. A new identity. A girl with really big—"

"Come on Andrioli, we sit here much longer you're liable to die in that bed. Where's Sandor?"

Andrioli took a deep, painful breath. "He's on his way to find Traiman."

"You're crazy."

"Maybe so, but here's what I really need. I need you to arrange a piece in the papers and on the wire services. Say two international businessmen and an American ex-pat were slain this evening in Montmartre in an exchange of gunfire.

Something like that. Give them a good description of me. Make sure they list me as dead. Got it?"

"I got it, but why should we do it?"

"Traiman's got to believe that I died with those two guys. This way I'd have no way of telling you what his man said, about where he's going."

"One of his people told you that Traiman is on the move?"

"Sandor told me you were an asshole. He never said you were slow."

Covington ignored the taunt. "So what if I have Interpol make a release, the news services run the piece. Then what? Where's Sandor off to?"

"Not so fast. The immunity, protection—all that bullshit. I want it in writing. Official-like. For Sandor and Christine too."

"We'll get it, but right now my patience is running thin. Where are they?" Covington had his own information. He had to know if Sandor was headed in the right direction.

But Andrioli refused to answer. "Just a little while more, then I'll tell you." He took another puff of the cigarette and dropped it in the ashtray. "Meantime," he said, "get me to a hospital." Then he fell to his side, face down on the bed. He was unconscious.

FORTY-EIGHT

Early the next morning, as Andrioli was recuperating in the infirmary of the United States Embassy, Jordan and Christine were traveling to the port town of Santa Margherita on the Italian Riviera. They had taken an evening train from Paris, spent the night together in the Hotel Meridien in Nice, and now they proceeded by rail into Italy.

The train rolled southeast along the coastline, racing past rocky beaches below and hurtling through cavernous tunnels that had been gouged from the sides of craggy mountains that rose defiantly above the blue Mediterranean. Jordan and Christine, alone in their compartment, paid little attention to the passing scenery. They were reviewing, yet again, the plans for their arrival in the village of Portofino.

"Maybe we should have listened to Captain Reynolds," Christine said with a wistful smile.

"What did he tell you?"

"He told me to stay out of it. He said I should leave town and let the authorities handle everything."

Jordan reached across and took her hand. "Well, you certainly left town."

Christine laughed. "I don't think this is what he had in mind."

"It's not too late," he told her. "You can turn around when we get there, leave this to me. Or just wait in Santa Margherita."

She shook her head, never taking her eyes from his. "I told you before, I'm in this to the end."

"I know, but by now Andrioli has told them everything we know. Covington and his men will fly down here this morning, maybe even get there before we do. You don't need to do this."

"I really do."

Jordan sat back in his seat and studied her face, the pale blue eyes that had not smiled enough in these past several days. "Since everyone has fessed up, as Andrioli would say, how about you tell me the truth now?"

Christine also sat back. They were as far away from each other as they could be in the small compartment. She looked out the window for a moment, seemingly lost in the majesty of the passing mountain range. When she turned back to him, some of the sadness had returned. "I'm not Jimmy's sister," she said.

Jordan nodded slowly. Whatever she was going to say next, whoever she was, regardless of the intimacy they had shared the past two days, his instincts were now in control. He thought about the Colt in his waistband, then felt his mind racing back to catalogue her movements since they left Paris. Did she have a weapon? Was she an enemy? He hated himself for the inability to escape his own training, his innate suspicions. Still looking at her, he said, "I know."

"You know?"

Her surprise seemed genuine. "Yes. I've known since the airport in Atlanta."

Her wonder at his admission turned quickly to anger and she leaned forward. "You knew, but you never said anything?"

Jordan responded with a puzzled look. "That's a strange reaction, don't you think? After all, you were the one who lied."

"I had my reasons."

"Really? Then you'll have to believe I had my reasons too."

She appeared to be considering what he said, then waved it away. "You made love to me."

"Damn," Jordan said with a slight smile, "and I thought there were two of us there."

Christine responded with an embarrassed smile. "I guess we're a couple of liars," she conceded. "But mine was just a white lie. You never told me you worked for the government or any of that."

"Uh huh. And telling everyone you're Jimmy McHugh's sister . . . that was a white lie?"

"You wouldn't understand."

"Try me," he said.

She shook her head. "It all sounds so crazy, even when I say it to myself. I mean, I really hadn't heard from Jimmy in years. That was true. But I'm not his sister."

"I got that part. So who are you?"

"I told you, I'm an assistant art history professor at Penn State." She sighed. "Jimmy and I grew up together in Wilkes Barre. In Pennsylvania. He was much older. We were from the same town, neighbors sort of, and our families knew each other. Not much good to say about our families," she added with a dismissive shake of her head. "Anyway, he went off to Vietnam."

She was staring out the window again, remembering.

"I'm listening," Jordan said.

"He started writing to me from over there, chatty kind of letters, the kind soldiers write home. Jimmy never had a lot of friends and, like I say, his family wasn't worth writing to. So I wrote back. We knew each other for so long, it was no big deal for me to send him a note every now and then, tell him about this guy or that girl or what was new in town. But then his letters changed. They started sounding, I don't know, romantic or something. Not really romantic, that's not it, but he was writing to me as if we were, well, lovers."

"And you weren't?"

"No. Never. I mean, he was like an older brother to me, or a cousin or something. I don't think he ever really had a girlfriend before he went away, so he began making up this fantasy relationship between us that didn't exist."

"So what happened, you wrote him a Dear John letter?"

She turned back to him. "No. I should have. I realized that later, but I didn't. I was a kid, and it was nice having this guy overseas sending me these beautiful letters. I thought, if it made him feel better, what was it to me? I mean, he was fighting in Vietnam. From one letter to the next, I never knew if I'd ever hear from him again."

"So you led him on."

"No, I never did. I would keep writing letters that were like local news reports." She sighed. "But I guess I never told him to stop being serious in his letters to me. I guess I liked the attention. If that's leading him on, then I suppose I did."

Jordan watched as she remembered.

"Then one day he came home."

She nodded, not looking at him. "He stayed in the service, stationed some-place overseas for a while. But yes, then one day he was back, thinking we had this great romance and that I was going to marry him or something. It was crazy. I mean, I was still in high school."

"How did he take it?"

"Not very well. And I guess I didn't handle it the right way." She paused, and Jordan waited. "He became demanding, angry. It got really uncomfortable. He threatened my boyfriend. The police were involved. It was a real mess."

She hesitated again.

"Then what happened?"

"You know what happened," she said. "That's when he left, went back over-seas. Disappeared."

"Which solved your problems with him."

"That makes me sound so horrible," she said. "I felt responsible. I still do. He was heartbroken when he left, and it was all my fault. It was like I cheated a friend, a friend who really loved me."

"Even if you didn't love him."

"Yes."

"But you were just one of the reasons McHugh left the States again."

"I know that, in here," she said, pointing at her head, "but not here." She held the palm of her hand over her heart.

"Guilt and affection are a lethal combination," Jordan said, thinking of Dan Peters and Beth, among many others. "So what's the rest of the story?"

"The rest of it you pretty much know. After some years went by Jimmy began writing to me again. I don't even know how he found me. I was at Penn State by then. He apologized for everything, wanted us to be friends and all that. I was really careful this time, very particular about what I said."

"So, when did you decide to become his sister?"

"When he invited me to Paris. He offered to pay for the entire trip, insisting it would be a 'brother-sister' visit. I felt like I owed it to him. He made it sound so important. When I got there he explained what he was doing.

"It was only when I arrived that he told me all of his friends believed I was his younger half-sister. He said that if those people thought I was any sort of girlfriend, they might be concerned about him wanting to go home with me. So I agreed to be his half-sister. It didn't seem like a big deal to me."

"So he admitted it to you—that he was using you as cover to get him to Paris and then back to the States."

"Yes. He introduced me to Tony and some other guys. I can't even remember their names. After a couple of days, he shipped me off to Madrid and disappeared."

"Until you heard from him again, when he was holed up in Woodstock."

She shook her head. "No, I heard from Tony. He wanted me to go to Jimmy, said he might need my help to get to Florida. I never spoke to Jimmy again."

"Didn't you have any idea how dangerous it could be?"

"Not then." She uttered a short laugh. "You people, you seem to live with all of this killing and craziness. It wasn't real to me, not until I got to Woodstock and found out Jimmy had been murdered and they took me down to New York like I was some sort of criminal. Up to then, I actually thought Jimmy had been exaggerating, to make it all seem more romantic or heroic."

"Heroic?"

"You know what I mean."

Jordan watched her as she settled back in her seat.

"That's it, and that's why I'm here."

"Paying a debt to a dead man."

"It sounds morbid, I know, but I guess that's it. Yes."

"And you want me to believe all of this."

"Everything I'm saying is the absolute truth."

He stared at her for a while. "Then go back home. This isn't your fight. Go back as soon as we get to Santa Margherita."

She shook her head, very slowly. "No," she said. "I told you—"

"I know. You're in this to end."

She smiled. "So now you know who I really am. And whoever you really are, Jordan Sandor, I feel like I'm part of the reason you've gotten mixed up in this, and I'm not leaving until we're done doing whatever it is we need to do."

"Right," he said quietly. "But remember, this may be your last chance to walk away."

"Do you want me to walk away?" she asked him.

Jordan turned away from her, gazing out at the hypnotic dance of the ever moving sea, the train swaying gently as it climbed another stretch of mountainside. He knew the answer he should give, but he said nothing at all.

"It's okay," she said. "The history of art will still be there when I get back."

FORTY-NINE

When Andrioli regained consciousness, the first thing he did was ask for John Covington. A few minutes later, the CIA operative strolled into Andrioli's private room at the embassy clinic.

"What time is it?" Andrioli wanted to know.

Covington told him it was almost seven in the morning. "How do you feel?"

"Seven? We better get going, man."

"I'm having some trouble getting those guarantees you wanted. It could take some time."

"Screw the guarantees." Andrioli was in no mood for an argument today. He was sore and drugged and worried about his friends. "They're on their way already," he said, searching his groggy mind for a sense of how far Jordan and Christine would have gotten by now. He had trouble clearing away the morphine haze. "No, they wouldn't be there yet."

Covington looked down at him, his thin lips approximating a smile. "When you say 'there,' do you mean Portofino?"

Andrioli tried to sit up, a painful attempt that failed. As he grew more alert, the ache in his side became more acute. "Where'd you get that?"

"After a narcotic cocktail, a man can become more talkative than you think. Don't worry yourself. You only confirmed what we already knew. We're getting ready to leave now."

"Good. Gimme a minute to get dressed," Andrioli said, having another try at pushing himself up.

"I don't think so."

"Why not? What'd the doctor say?"

"Said you'll be fine, eventually. Some muscle damage, a fractured rib. Nothing that won't heal. Your biggest problem is the loss of blood."

"Fine. Get me something for the pain. I'm going back in the game."

"Why would I allow that?"

He made another attempt to sit up. "I can think of three reasons. First, I know exactly where Sandor is going and what he's doing, and I won't tell you unless you take me along. Second, I know Traiman's operation better than you do." He paused to take a breath, still trying to steady his thinking. "Third, I know what Traiman is up to."

Covington walked to the foot of the bed, where the two men had a good look at each other. "If I move you, you're likely to die before we get to Italy."

"Whatever. Let's get going." Andrioli again tried to raise himself but buckled under the effort.

"I congratulate you on your tenacity, I really do. Your determination has exceeded my wildest expectations. Learning Traiman's destination was very resourceful. And then, having us plant that story with the press so he wouldn't interrupt his plans. That was very clever."

"Is it in the paper today?"

"Of course. Just as you asked. Two international businessmen slain by an unidentified American who was also killed in the shooting. The description in the article didn't do you justice, but we included your name."

Andrioli drew a deep, uneven breath that hurt more than he would admit. The cracked rib, he thought. "You just told me you knew it already, that Traiman is headed for Italy."

"Let's just say our intelligence department does a fair job on its own. We planted the story for the same reason you requested it. We didn't want your clumsy interference to disrupt his appointment. We also happen to be quite anxious to have Traiman in Portofino."

Andrioli's numbed look phrased the question he could not ask.

"We owe you an apology, Mr. Andrioli. It seems you have been used. You, that is, and your two accomplices. You've all played important parts in moving this forward. Unfortunately, you became more successful than we had anticipated."

"Sorry to screw up your plans. Were we supposed to get ourselves killed along the way?"

"It was a considered risk but no, that wasn't it. We simply never expected you to learn of the meeting in Portofino. We never anticipated you and your friends getting in our way there."

Andrioli nodded. "Sorry to outlive our usefulness."

"So, when will they arrive?"

"I'm not sure. They should reach Santa Margherita later this morning."

"Damnit," Covington said, expressing more annoyance than anger.

As he turned and started for the door, Andrioli finally managed to sit all the way up, ignoring the searing pain that radiated from his side. "You said we were used, that you knew Traiman was heading for Portofino."

Covington stopped and turned back to him. "Yes."

"Without my help, Jordan and Christine might be a problem."

"I hope not. We're flying to Genoa right now. We'll find them and back them off."

"Sandor won't back off. You know that."

Covington hesitated. Then he walked towards the door. "I'll see you later," he said over his shoulder.

"No good," Andrioli hollered after him. "You need me there. You hear me Covington?"

Covington heard him, even as the door to Andrioli's room eased its way closed behind him.

THROUGHOUT HIS PROFESSIONAL life, Vincent R. Traiman had always been just that—a professional. In his ability to separate emotion from reason, he was as clinical as a surgeon.

His current passage across the Mediterranean was part of a plan shared with only a select few in his organization. His preparations and purpose were carefully guarded secrets. The death of Steve Jackson on the steps of the Sacre Coeur, therefore, caused concern among Traiman's closest aides.

The accounts of the shooting were sketchy at best. Jackson, Andrioli and the assassin who followed them to the cathedral were all dead. Traiman had to assume that Jackson, in his role as communications coordinator, would have been able to decipher some information about the planned trip to Portofino. If Andrioli had extracted that information from Jackson before he died, and if Andrioli had an opportunity to pass it on before he was killed, the mission might be compromised. Traiman therefore knew the Americans might be coming for him. He also suspected that Jordan Sandor would be part of the welcoming party, a collateral issue that could make for an interesting reunion.

And yet, Traiman went ahead with his plans.

His top assistant, Nelson, who accompanied him on the cruise, suggested the meetings in Portofino be postponed, but Traiman overrode his advice. He kept his own counsel, realizing that time had grown short, particularly after the explosion at Loubar and these violent incidents in New York, Florida and Paris. Matters had intensified, and the resultant scrutiny was also increasing. Traiman, however, had already arranged to minimize the risks.

As the luxurious, 132-foot yacht cut through the blue-green waters of the calm sea, Traiman satisfied himself that he had taken the appropriate precautions and had made the prudent decision. Martin Koppel would be in Portofino. It was an important meeting and, even if John Covington was bringing his men, Traiman already had his insurance policy in place.

Traiman saw himself as a consummate tactician, not offended when others compared him to a cold-blooded reptile who thrived in the ever changing environment of the desert. He felt flattered by the comparison and viewed his personal pleasures in much the same way. Not inclined to the liquor or drugs favored by his subordinates, and utterly immune to romance, he enjoyed the anonymous privileges of his position, especially on those occasions when he traveled outside Libya. On the *Halaby*, the yacht owned by their man Faridz that had taken him northward across the Mediterranean, Traiman could indulge his own preferred forms of relaxation.

"Come in," he said to the knock at his stateroom door. He was reclining on a large bed in the richly appointed owner's suite. It was decorated in an opulent mixture of Western and Arabian motifs, featuring rich fabrics, hammered brass and gold accents.

"Hello, sir," the steward said. "We should be arriving in less than two hours. The captain is holding a conservative speed, as you requested."

"Good."

"Would you like to be entertained in here, sir, or will you be using another cabin?"

Traiman's thin mouth turned up in his imitation of a smile. "This will be fine. Just send them in."

"Very well, sir." The steward gave a short bow and retreated, off to fetch Traiman's entertainment, two women who had been brought along for the ride.

Traiman got up and undressed, then slipped into a dark red satin lounging robe. When he heard another knock at the door, he was back on the king-sized bed. "Yes," he called out, and the two young women entered.

Someone closed the door behind them. Slowly they approached the bed. One was an Egyptian girl of no more than twenty. A tall, slim young woman dressed in a black silk dressing gown. She had smooth, olive skin, long, dark hair and a nervous look in her onyx eyes. The other girl was a black African of no more than eighteen, her voluptuous shape clad only in a red peignoir. The black girl had been with Traiman before; her apprehension was therefore all the more apparent.

Traiman believed that power was the key to sexual fulfillment. For him, violent rape was the most satisfying form of sexual expression. Even with these young women, who had no choice but to submit to his whims, he would engage in a brutal rite of passion, pursuing his illusions of sadistic conquest.

With a flick of his wrists he directed them to let their robes fall away. They followed his silent instruction, revealing the firm, naked sensuality of their youth. The Egyptian was petite with small breasts, a lovely shape and silky skin. The African was a study in ebony, with a full bosom, rounded hips and narrow waist.

There was fear in their eyes as Traiman beckoned them forward. His pugilist's features were frightening enough, but from everything the black girl had seen and what the Egyptian girl had been told, their dread of what was to come was real. They wanted to recoil, to run, to escape, but they had no choice, nowhere to go. They knew, regardless of their anxiety, they were there to provide whatever he demanded. Whatever pain or humiliation they were made to endure, they were there to suffer. The alternative, the consequence of his displeasure, was a far graver risk, not just for them, but for their families.

So they joined him on the bed, wordlessly attending to him, removing his robe, caressing him, clawing him, feigning resistance and then desire. The three of them acted out a deranged pantomime of his devise, the girls only praying that they would not be made to suffer too much pain as his excitement blended with anger.

They scratched at his thighs, rubbed his back, moistened him with their tongues, eager to rouse him and have it over with. He pinched them and then slapped them, abusing their firm asses, tender breasts and frightened faces. As his fury grew with his excitement, so did the viciousness of the assault. It was sex without intimacy or tenderness or compassion, culminating only when he had given full vent to the degrading cruelty and subjugation he chose to inflict upon them. Only then would he be relieved. Only then would his entertainment be complete.

FIFTY

The path along the coastline from Santa Margherita to Portofino is a craggy run, a picturesque strip of narrow, twisting roadway. Small homes and large villas populate the green hillside in the distance. Small fishing boats and large yachts rock gently on their moorings in the harbor, or sit quietly against the docks tucked along the shoreline. It is at once provincial and affluent.

"You have been before to Portofino?" the Italian driver asked.

"No," Christine said. "I suppose this isn't the best time of year to visit."

"Ah, but you are wrong *signora*. This is the very best. Quiet. Not so many *turisti*."

"Like us, you mean?"

The driver laughed. "No no, *signore*."

"It's okay," Jordan said. "We could use some quiet."

The taxi hugged the sharp curves that ran above the coast en route to their destination, the Hotel Continental, chosen for them by Andrioli.

When they arrived, they found it to be a square, squat structure, considerably more modest than the promise of its title. It was located on one of the cobblestone streets toward the rear of the village, away from the sea.

Portofino is small, its compact geography defined by a tiny, horseshoe shaped seaport. Situated on the edge of the Mediterranean, the front of the town faces the water, an inlet sheltered by the semi-circular protrusion of surrounding mountains. Adjacent to the modest harbor is a plaza paved in stone, ringed by a variety of restaurants, cafés and specialty shops. Behind these one and two story buildings are hotels and inns, each of which is more proximate to the real action, and with better views than the Hotel Continental.

Further inland, at the foot of the mountains, away from the *trattorias* and boutiques, are the local merchants and private homes that stand in the shadows of the larger villas above. At the highest reaches, above the crowded quarters of the native Italians below, atop the overlooking hills, are the exclusive estates of the very wealthy, with views of the town, the sea and the beautiful yachts anchored outside the small harbor.

Jordan paid the taxi driver, and they entered the lobby of the Continental. It was surprisingly airy, almost tropical. There were a couple of wicker chairs and a desk arranged in a sitting area. A large wooden table seemed to serve as the registration desk. No one was there. Jordan rang the brass bell on the table, and a young man appeared through a side door.

"*Buon giorno*," he greeted them with a smile.

"Scott Kerr," Jordan said. "You should have a reservation for us."

The young man opened a cabinet off to the side of the desk, revealing a computer, a master telephone and some related office equipment. "*Si, signore*," he said, after punching a few keys. "*Signore e Signora* Kerr."

Jordan registered, then held up his black leather bag, Andrioli's attaché, and pointed to Christine's large tote from Paris, showing the young man that they could handle their own luggage.

The clerk frowned and shrugged his shoulders. He was obviously a one man operation, which included check-in, bellhop and room service. When he handed Jordan his key, Sandor gave him a hundred dollar bill.

"Haven't had time to make change into euros yet."

The clerk's smile made it clear he didn't care.

"If anyone calls for me, put it through right away."

"*Si signore*," he said, still grinning as he pointed to the stairs.

BY THE TIME Jordan and Christine made it to the Hotel Continental, several Company field agents were converging on the area. Three were already in Portofino, another two waiting for instructions at an inn near the center of a neighboring town, Rapallo. These were not Covington's men. This team had been sent on the direct order of Deputy Director Byrnes.

Martin Koppel had also arrived. He was safely, if nervously, ensconced in a luxurious suite at the renowned Splendido, Portofino's finest hotel. He was alone, but not far from the watchful eyes of the three operatives dispatched by Byrnes. Koppel was instructed to stay in his suite and await his summons from Vincent Traiman.

Byrnes had taken great pains to inform Koppel of the risks. *What the hell*, the financier thought as he paced the generous living room, waiting for the phone to ring. He had done everything, seen everything, run as far up and down the ladder as any man could travel. This was the ultimate challenge, dealing with stakes so high that life and death were part of the equation. *What the hell*, he told himself again. With all the financial deals he had created and produced, he would once again be the star of the show, produced and directed by the Central Intelligence Agency.

JOHN COVINGTON KNEW nothing of Koppel. At the moment, his concern was Traiman and the terrorist teams that were moving into position throughout the United States and Europe.

He had flown from Paris to Genoa and was now riding in the front of a car driven by Todd Nealon. Another agent, Paul Betram, sat in the back seat beside Andrioli.

Covington had no choice but to bring Andrioli along. There was no way he could risk leaving him behind, not with what he knew, not with everything that would be happening in Portofino. The doctors had another look at Andrioli's side, re-dressed the wound, filled his pocket with painkillers and authorized him to fly. The turbulence over the Appennino mountain range was painful, but Andrioli popped another pill and suffered through. Now they were traveling together by car toward the coast.

"Just so you're clear on this," Covington said over his shoulder, "I'm going to say it one more time. First, you're going to talk to Sandor. He might listen to you and get the hell out of our way before he screws up the entire operation. Second, we need to keep Traiman off guard. And since you're so willing to get in his line of fire again, you're volunteering for that assignment too. You got that?"

"I got it."

Now Covington turned to face him. "Good," he said sharply. "Just remember, you're not here to redeem yourself. You're here to do as you're told. Got it?"

"I got it."

"Good. Sandor's at the Continental, right?"

Andrioli was slumped in the back seat, trying to find a comfortable angle as the car jostled him painfully to and fro. He nodded.

"Okay." Covington faced forward again.

"Mind if I ask you something?"

"What is it?" Covington didn't bother to look back.

"How were you so sure Traiman was going to be here?"

"We have our sources. And you confirmed what we suspected."

"No," Andrioli said. "I've been listening to you guys. The way you have this set up, it was more than a suspicion. You were sure of it before I told you anything. How is that?"

Covington turned back to him now, looking him square in the eyes. "You're here on a pass, not a fact-finding mission. Any trouble from you, and I'll deliver you back to Traiman myself."

Andrioli answered with a grim smile.

Covington did not respond. He returned his gaze to the road in front of them, leaving Andrioli to stare silently at the back of his head.

FIFTY-ONE

Christine stood beside him as Jordan sorted through the contents of Andrioli's attaché. In addition to the Colt automatic and the extra ammunition, there were still two small blocks of C-4 wrapped in paper.

"So, what kind of agent, or whatever it's called, were you?"

He looked up from the material he was organizing. "Am," he corrected her.

Christine shook her head, a mystified look crossing her face.

Jordan took her by the shoulders and sat her on the bed. He pulled up a chair to face her. "I'm not here because of you. You're here because of me. I work for Central Intelligence."

"But I thought you said you left there, or something."

"Or something, is more accurate. I've been working on this mission for the past few months."

"So, what does that mean, then? You were pretending to be a reporter all that time?"

"Journalist. And yes. Tony had it right. After a mission went bad in Bahrain, I officially left the Company. Unofficially, I began working on a couple of different assignments."

"So when you agreed to go with me to Florida . . ."

"Yes, that was part of the deal. I needed to find Tony, and I needed to get here."

"So you lied to me. You were lying all along."

"Yes," he said.

"But you could have trusted me. You had to know that."

Jordan broke into a wide grin. "I do now," he said, "which is why I'm telling you. If you want out, you're out. If you still want to help, we need to get to work." He stood up and went back to the two small blocks of putty-like substance. He held one up for her to see. "Things are going to get bad very quickly. This explosive may be our last chance, depending how things play out."

"Isn't it dangerous, holding it like that?"

"No. Not at all. It has to be detonated."

"Like in the hotel?"

"Not exactly. When the time comes, I don't think we're going to be using any long burning fuses. Meantime, the tough part will be holding onto it if they take us and search us."

"Take us?"

"Yes. Assuming we even get that far. It all depends how Traiman reacts. My guess is he already knows I'm here. My hope is he won't be able to resist the chance to meet with me."

"Then what?"

"Well, he isn't likely to be feeling very hospitable by then, I can tell you that. So, if you have any other questions, now's the time to ask."

She looked up at him. "Paris," she said, her voice softer now. "Was that, I don't know, was that part of—"

"No," he said. "That was about you and me."

She stood up and he took her in his arms.

"I told you to turn back," he whispered then kissed her softly on the cheek. "You can still get out of here. It's not too late."

"I won't. Especially not now." She managed one of those prize winning smiles, then held him to her. "You may need me."

"I might at that," he agreed. "Okay then. Let's go for a walk, take in some of the local color. Drop a few names."

He felt her nod, her head nestled in the crook of his shoulder.

"I don't know how much advertising we'll need to do, but word should travel pretty fast around here today."

JORDAN PLACED THEIR key on the front desk and told the young clerk they were going out for a stroll around town. The boy replied with an uncomprehending look that Sandor figured was just a pose. Andrioli had chosen this hotel for a reason, and whatever that turned out to be, Sandor was beyond trusting anyone at this point.

He took Christine by the hand and led her into the fading, autumn afternoon sun. They headed on foot toward the main plaza, searching for a *caffe* Andrioli had named. The streets were virtually empty at this hour. They walked slowly towards the harbor, checking various locations until they found the place along the main wharf. They sat at a table inside and waited.

When their waiter approached, Jordan was pleased to find he spoke English, a bit of good fortune in a resort frequented more by Europeans than Americans. He ordered Camparis with soda and two *panini*.

"Beautiful ships here," Jordan said to the burly man as he returned with their drinks and set their glasses on the table.

"*Si*, from all over the world."

"Yes. We noticed the different flags."

The waiter did not reply. He went to the service bar and began working on the setups for dinner.

"Might have been too subtle, huh?"

Christine forced a smile.

There was only one other couple there. They looked to be Italian and were very involved in a quiet discussion at their table in the back of the room. Jordan watched as the waiter sliced lemons and limes. A couple of minutes later, he disappeared into the kitchen and returned with their sandwiches.

"Maybe you can help me," Sandor said to the man. "I'm supposed to meet some friends in town tonight. They're coming in on a yacht."

The man set their plates on the table not looking at Jordan.

"They tell me it comes to Portofino quite often. I think it's called the *Halaby*."

Now the waiter glanced at him.

"I was wondering if you knew which boat it is. I wouldn't recognize it. I've never even seen it." Jordan offered a short laugh as apology for his ignorance. "I'd like to know when it gets here, or if it's here already, for that matter."

The man just shook his head, saying nothing.

"That's too bad. I'd really like to know when it arrives."

"I am sorry, *signore*. Your friends, they will look for you, I am sure." He turned to leave them, but Jordan reached out and touched his arm. The waiter looked down at Jordan's hand like it was something dirty that had just soiled his sleeve.

"I suppose you're right," Sandor said, keeping his tone friendly. "But just in case they stop in here, you can tell them I'm in town." Jordan held out a fifty dollar bill. "Jordan Sandor," he said. "At the Hotel Continental. Just in case anyone asks for me."

The waiter began protesting in rapid Italian, pushing the money away, saying something about never having heard of the *Halaby* yacht. An older man emerged from the kitchen. He could have been the waiter's father by the looks of him. He strode towards the table and stepped in front of the younger man. Without speaking, he took the fifty dollar bill from Sandor's hand and placed it on the table.

"We know nothing about this *Halaby*, *signore*. We don't know who comes in and goes out. This is not our business." His countenance bore a severe look that told Sandor the conversation was at an end.

"That's too bad," Jordan persisted. "This was the place my friend told me to come." He waited, but there was no further response in the offing. The waiter had already walked back to the bar, and now the older man turned and went back into the kitchen.

"What now?" Christine asked quietly.

"I didn't make much of an impression."

She forced a smile.

"We did just fine," he assured her. "I may run for mayor here when this is all over."

They finished their drinks and sandwiches and left, leaving the fifty dollars on the table to cover the bill.

They stopped at two more *caffes* along the dock, and each time Jordan asked about the *Halaby* he received the same sort of reaction. If anything, the responses were even stiffer. As soon as the name of the yacht was mentioned, it was clear Jordan was no longer a welcome patron. He knew that, by now, his own name would already be burning up the local telephone lines.

"At this point," he told Christine, "they'll know where to come for us."

"Jordan," she said as they walked back to the hotel, "I feel like we're being followed already. I suppose you're going to tell me that's good. I mean, that's what you want, isn't it?"

Sandor shrugged. "Depends on who's doing the following."

THEY RETRIEVED THEIR key at the front desk and found their way back to the small room upstairs. Jordan went to work immediately, first closing the shutters and pulling the drapes tight, then moving the table and two chairs.

He answered Christine's puzzled look by saying, "If we're going to have company, we better see them before they see us."

He went about rearranging the pillows on the bed, adding two from the closet and using a chair cushion, lining them up, then plumping them and pulling the covers over them. In the darkened room, his soft sculpture appeared to be two bodies between the sheets.

"That's supposed to be us?"

"Go ahead and laugh," Jordan said as he fluffed the pillows again. "Art was never my strong subject."

"And where are we going to sleep tonight?"

He looked up. "We won't be doing any sleeping in bed, not for a while. For now, let's just sit here and see who shows up." He put down a blanket and pillow on the floor, then sat beside her, their backs to the wall, out of view from the door.

"It's siesta time for you," he said.

She moved close to him, resting her head on his shoulder. "I am a little tired."

"Let's be quiet, then. See who comes for a visit."

FIFTY-TWO

As soon as the imposing *Halaby* dropped anchor in sight of the Portofino harbor, four of Traiman's men set off in the power launch. Once ashore, they split up. The first team would make contact at a few locations in the center of town. The other two men would generally canvass the area.

All four quickly learned that an American couple had been making the rounds, asking for the *Halaby*. The man had identified himself as Jordan Sandor.

The town seemed otherwise quiet, exuding its normal level of casual charm and studied indifference, particularly in the middle of autumn. Sandor intended his brazen arrival to distract attention from the other, more covert, activities initiated by Byrnes' agents. The three advance men Byrnes dispatched had not caused a ripple in the placid waters of the peaceful village or, if they had, it was obscured by the loud splash made by Jordan. Meanwhile, Jordan hoped that Traiman's men would be left to worry over why and how Sandor had come to Portofino.

Precisely one hour after their arrival on shore, the four Traiman scouts regrouped at their launch. The two men who made a general survey of the area reported that Koppel had checked into the Splendido. They also shared the news that Sandor was in town, staying at the Hotel Continental. He and the girl had been announcing their presence and leaving his name, asking for the *Halaby*, claiming it carried an old friend, acting as if they expected to be invited aboard. The second pair of Traiman's scouts confirmed the information.

As they motored back to the yacht to report their findings, they debated how Sandor's presence might affect Traiman's plans. He had proved himself an elusive target up to now, but Andrioli was dead, and that might make it easier to take him out. They had heard enough about Sandor, and they were eager to be rid of him as soon as possible.

ANDRIOLI WAS NOT dead, however. He was seated in the back room of a small restaurant in Rapallo under the close watch of Covington, Nealon and Betram, all of whom were keeping a close watch over him. The two other operatives who had been waiting now joined the group.

"Let me get this straight," Covington said. "He's going to try and get to Traiman himself?"

"That's the plan of last resort, if he doesn't hear from me."

"He's going to board the yacht and take Traiman alone?"

"Not exactly. We discussed some variations on that theme."

"Wonderful."

"Look," Andrioli said, "we came after Traiman. It's that simple. How were we supposed to know what you expected us to do?"

"I expected you to get yourselves arrested in Paris."

"Sorry. You might have given us a better signal that we were on the same side, you know."

Covington shook his head, worried he might have misplayed his hand. "All right, tell me how he expects to get on the boat."

"Don't know. He said I should leave that to him."

"I see. And I don't suppose, then, he gave you any idea about how he intends to get off."

Andrioli shook his head. He was not going to explain any of the details, not to Covington. He reached into his pocket and popped one of the painkillers they had given him at the embassy.

"Better go easy on those."

Andrioli smiled. "Yeah. Like it matters."

Covington watched him for a moment, thinking. "We've got to stop him," he said. "He'll never make it alone."

Andrioli shook his head. "That's the funny part, isn't it?"

"What is?"

"He really is alone. I mean, you used us to get here, I understand that. But now that we're here, you have no use for any of us anymore."

Covington did not answer.

"It's a little late for you to be worrying about that, unless you're going to help us move Sandor out of the way."

Andrioli muttered to himself.

"What's that?"

Andrioli grinned. "I said it's not like me."

"What isn't like you?"

"Worrying about someone else."

AN HOUR OR so after Jordan and Christine had returned to their hotel, the desk clerk received a call. It was a familiar voice, one of the local men who specialized in providing personal services to wealthy tourists. His instructions to the clerk were clear—do not put through any incoming calls to the American claiming to be Mr. Kerr. Get the caller's name then say you have instructions not to disturb their room. Notify me of any calls. And notify me immediately if either the man or the girl leaves the hotel.

The clerk knew he would receive an appropriate reward for his cooperation. More important, there would be no recriminations, so long as he complied.

As Jordan and Christine waited in their room, the clerk intercepted Andrioli's third phone call in the past twenty minutes, telling him that Mr. and Mrs. Kerr were not to be disturbed. Once again, the caller refused to leave a message.

The clerk recognized the caller to be the same all three times. He did not have a name, but he picked up the switchboard phone to report it each time. Just in case.

"DAMNIT," ANDRIOLI SAID as he slammed the phone down. "They won't put the call through."

Covington turned to Nealon. "Come on," he said, "three strikes and you're out. Let's go."

FIFTY-THREE

Darkness was descending on the Mediterranean coast, and Jordan knew it was time to make his move. They had waited long enough for Andrioli's phone call. They were on their own.

Christine had dozed off, curled up on the floor with her head in his lap. He gently roused her. They needed to get ready to leave.

"It's time," Jordan told her.

She sat up and rubbed her eyes.

"Come with me," he said.

He took Andrioli's attaché case and she followed him into the bathroom. He placed the case on the counter and removed the two packets of explosives. He removed the paper and carefully molded two pieces of the C-4 plastique. He smoothed the first piece and taped it against the small of Christine's back. The second he fixed with adhesive along the inside of his upper thigh.

Hiding the detonators was more difficult—the remote electronic device in Andrioli's case would be found in the most cursory frisking, leading to strip searches and discovery of the plastique. So the remote would have to be left behind. Sandor needed to rely on the magnesium strips. Not as reliable, more difficult to gauge the response time, but certainly easier to conceal. He placed two strips in the lining of his jacket and wove two under the collar of Christine's blouse.

When he was done, Jordan checked the clip on the Colt and pocketed two spares. At some point he expected to be taken by Traiman's men. Once captured, he knew the gun would be the first thing they would take from him. When they searched him and found the extra ammunition clips, it might be enough to satisfy his captors that Jordan was otherwise clean.

It was a theory, anyway.

"What about me?" Christine asked as he jammed the automatic into his waistband.

"What about you?"

"You know, like in *The Wizard of Oz*. Don't you have anything in there for me?"

Jordan smiled. "Are you looking for courage, my dear?"

"I was thinking more about a gun."

"Sorry, Tony only brought the two from Paris, and he's got the other one."

She nodded, forcing a brave smile. "I'll be right behind you then. All the way."

"Oh, you'll be doing more than trailing me around." Jordan told her what to do when they left the room, then took the remote detonator and hid it between the towels that were stacked on the ledge of the tub. Then he went back to the bedroom and placed the attaché case in the closet. When he turned around, she was standing there watching him.

"Well, it's time to go for it."

Christine walked towards him slowly, the unsteady rhythm of fear. "I'm ready," she said, then held herself against him.

"Don't worry," he told her. "We'll just have a quick drink on Traiman's yacht, then I'll get you home early so your mother's not upset." He stepped back and looked into her pale blue eyes. "You know what to do?"

She nodded.

"It'll be all right. Come on."

"I'm ready."

They stepped into the quiet corridor just above the small lobby. Christine handed Jordan her jacket and then, as calmly as she could, descended the steps leading to the front desk.

As she walked downstairs, Jordan took a small piece of paper and wedged it against the jamb at the lowest hinge, closing the door on it. He moved to the edge of the landing and listened.

Christine was doing her best to explain to the clerk that they were expecting a package that should have come already, doing everything she could to give the young man a reason to check in the back room for a delivery. "Maybe it came yesterday. Or before you got to work today."

She was at her most charming, even trying some Italian as the clerk pretended to struggle with his broken English, insisting there was no package. *Not a very polite young man*, Jordan thought, as the unhelpful clerk refused to check for her. It confirmed Jordan's suspicions that the boy was on watch and that he had probably intercepted Andrioli's phone calls.

The clerk finally relented. "*Aspete, aspete.*"

Christine nodded, which was Jordan's cue. As the clerk disappeared for a moment into the storage room behind his desk, Sandor stole down the stairs and hurried into the street.

A moment later, when the clerk returned empty handed, Christine expressed her disappointment, but thanked him all the same.

"*Si, si signora. Prego.*"

Christine showed him her smile and then turned towards the stairs. As soon as she rounded the corner, she stopped and listened. She heard the young man making a phone call, which meant he had his back to the front door. She turned and hurried across the small, carpeted lobby and outside.

The clerk spun around, having heard something, but she was already gone.

Jordan was waiting at the corner. "All right?" he asked as he helped her on with her jacket.

She nodded, although her heart was beating faster than she would have liked. "I think so. He seemed so nervous. I was just asking him to check for a package."

"I noticed. I don't know what he's up to, but I think it'll help if he believes we're still in the room." He placed his arm around her shoulder, felt her trembling as they began to walk.

"You think he saw you leave?"

She shook her head.

"Good. Let's take a stroll." He led her down the stairs, around the perimeter of town toward the private docks where they arrange daily rentals of small power boats. "Take a couple of slow, deep breaths," he told her. "The night is young."

MARTIN KOPPEL RECEIVED a phone call from Mr. Groat. There was a change in plans. The dinner, scheduled for a cozy restaurant in town, had now been arranged on the yacht. Two of Mr. Groat's associates would be by at seven to pick him up and take him by launch to the *Halaby*.

He nervously put down the phone, standing there, numb.

This was not the deal. He was supposed to have dinner at a restaurant, where he would be watched. And protected.

Koppel felt he should call someone, but he was warned not to make any phone calls. They would contact him, they said, and he reminded himself that they had his line tapped. They had certainly heard the call, and they would tell him what to do next. Otherwise, he would be having dinner on Traiman's yacht in less than an hour.

FIFTY-FOUR

Traiman was standing beside the bed in the teak lined stateroom. The comforter and pillows were on the floor, the sheets in disarray. He pulled on his robe, giving the two young women a last, dispassionate look. They were naked, lying face down, their fleshy, rounded asses bearing the marks of the lashes he had inflicted on each of them in turn, while the other was obliged to attend to him, until he became bored and forced them to assume new positions.

"Get up," he ordered them, having spent himself, knowing he had already wasted too much time at these games.

The women slowly turned and rose. The face of the Egyptian girl was marked and red, the mouth of the African woman swollen and slightly bloodied. Traiman took no notice. He waved them towards their dressing gowns and dismissed them, sending them off to another cabin where they might rest and heal. He was having guests, and their services might be needed again.

After bathing and dressing, Traiman met with his four scouts in the main salon, where they briefed him on their reconnaissance in town.

"And is that all?" Traiman asked.

"Sir?"

"Is that all you know?"

The men from the advance party looked from one to the other, then back at Traiman. "Yes," the senior agent replied. "That's all we learned so far. There doesn't seem to be any other unusual activity. Sandor and the woman are still in the hotel. No calls are being allowed in or out of their room. We know that someone was trying to get through to them from a location in Rapallo. We've been waiting for you, sir, for further instructions."

Traiman responded with a malevolent smile. "That's always a safe bet, isn't it? 'We've come back for orders.' What an excellent way to shun responsibility. 'We were awaiting your pleasure, sir.'" He mocked them, but they offered no reaction. "Get Kerrigan in here."

They waited through an uncomfortable silence until Kerrigan was shown into the room. The tall, blond American was usually one of Traiman's favorites. Formerly Special Ops in the US military. Recently the murderer of James McHugh.

"I hope you enjoyed your trip to the City of Lights," Traiman said. "It's been a long time since I've been able to promenade along the Champs-Elysées."

"It's the same," Kerrigan replied sullenly.

"Well, that's good to hear. We were just having an unscheduled convention of incompetents, and I felt such a gathering wouldn't be complete without you. Please," Traiman said, pointing to a chair, "sit down." He waited for Kerrigan to ease his large frame into the seat. "Now then. It appears fate has provided you an opportunity to atone for your failures."

"How's that?"

Traiman stood and began slowly pacing the large salon. "Your inability to resolve a nagging problem will be tested once again. My old friend Jordan Sandor seems to be visiting us here in Portofino."

Kerrigan's eyes widened, but he did not interrupt.

"Isn't it amazing? My former comrade-in-arms, the man with the most annoying, overdeveloped sense of patriotism I have ever seen, he haunts me still." He looked around the room at his five men. "Sandor's morality can be an insufferable pain in the ass, let me tell you, but he's worth more than all of you combined. I have to admit, it'll be good to see him again. Pity it'll be such a brief get-together."

He paused again. "All right, here's the situation. Our associate, Faisal Ridaya, has contacted me from Paris. It seems that Anthony Andrioli was picked up there yesterday morning by his own countrymen." He let that sink in for a moment. "Yes, gentlemen, Faisal's inside source assures him that Mr. Andrioli is quite alive, although wounded. The shooting at the Sacre Coeur was apparently not fatal. At least not to him. In any case, he is yet another burr under our saddle. In fact, at this moment he is also en route to Portofino."

Kerrigan spoke up. "You should weigh anchor and leave right now," he said. "It makes no sense for you to risk being here another minute. Leave this to us. We'll handle it."

"Thank you, Mr. Kerrigan, I appreciate your concern. However, I have already anticipated certain of these developments, and I can assure you that there is no need for us to leave this lovely setting. Not yet." Traiman seated himself behind the captain's table again, his eyes moving from one to the other of these five men.

"Before we act, we must consider each of the distressing possibilities we face." He picked up the phone and called the steward, ordering sparkling water to be served. "Jordan Sandor left the Agency after he had a difference of opinion with his superiors over the operation in Bahrain. You remember Bahrain, Mr. Kerrigan."

The American nodded.

"It is conceivable that Mr. Sandor has by now learned his true adversary in those proceedings was none other than his former partner. Add to that the death of Mr. Peters in Woodstock and the unfortunate assault on his lady friend in New York, and one might believe that he is bent on revenge. In short, he may have journeyed all this way to find me for personal reasons."

None of the five spoke.

"As appealing as that theory may be, it is the least likely of the three I have considered. Jordan Sandor is an able and tenacious operative, not a reckless fool. It is more likely that he is in league with Mr. Andrioli, attempting some maneuver we have yet to fully discern."

Four of the agents were nodding their heads, but Kerrigan was not.

"What is it, Mr. Kerrigan? Aren't you enjoying my speculation?"

"You said there was a third alternative."

"Option, Mr. Kerrigan, option. There can only be one alternative to a proposition, but there can be many options."

"Option, then," the American said with a disgusted look.

"And so there is. Care to have a guess?"

Kerrigan had enough of Traiman's pedagogy. "Sandor is still an American agent."

"Very good," Traiman said, slowly clapping his hands. "Go to the head of the class."

"If that's what you think, why stay here in Portofino?"

"If this is a CIA trap, you mean? Because, gentlemen, when you play chess, the key to success is planning several moves ahead. In this case, I have taken precautions to protect our position. What we need to determine is whether the financial arrangements I have put in place with our friend Martin Koppel are authentic or part of this so-called trap. That is an answer I do not yet possess."

They listened in silence.

"As a consequence," Traiman continued, "I have insisted that the meeting with Mr. Koppel take place here, on the *Halaby*."

They waited for more, but Traiman was done. Only Kerrigan, of the five men, knew of the plans with Koppel. Only Kerrigan understood what Traiman knew—that their days as trusted allies of the Arab extremists were at an end. The successful completion of Operation VX was not only critical to Traiman's personal financial scheme, but also necessary to an amicable parting from their Islamic hosts. If all went well, it would be an agreeable, but final, parting.

"Should we go ashore and take out Sandor?" Kerrigan asked.

"You have not managed that up to now. We might as well make use of your failure. You will take him alive and bring him here. Perhaps he can supply some of the information we need. You two, start at the hotel. Find Sandor and bring him to me. Mr. Kerrigan, you take Mr. Fraser and revisit the issue of whether there is other surveillance in town. I need to know if Sandor is truly alone. Then you can bring Mr. Koppel for his dinner. And you," he said, pointing to the fifth man, "you stay with the launch unless we radio you other instructions."

"What about the woman?" one of the men assigned to the hotel asked.

"She's of no use to us, except as leverage." He offered his thin smile again. "Jordan always had a weak spot in that regard, so she might provide some opportunity for persuasion if he is still his old, stubborn self."

"So we should bring her too, then?"

"Yes," Traiman said, "that would be best. But if she gets in your way, kill her."

*

AS TRAIMAN'S MEN were heading for shore, Jordan and Christine were negotiating with a local man for the use of his small boat and outboard. The man was finishing up for the day and was not pleased to be bothered with them.

"No, no to start at night," the man said in his best English.

Jordan gave him a wink, then nodded in Christine's direction. "It's romantic at night," he said with a smile.

The Italian shook his head. He was short, with unruly black hair and an unhappy look on his face. "*Freddo*, no? Cold."

Jordan pulled out his cash and peeled off five one hundred dollar bills. "Just a couple of hours," he promised.

The boatman looked from Jordan's money to the small wooden vessel. "No. No at night. You get killed. *Domani. Domani.*"

Jordan pulled out another five bills from his sport coat and placed them beside the five he was already holding. "This is it," he said, peering over the man's shoulder. "For a thousand dollars, I'll buy a boat from someone else. Just two hours."

The man snatched the money and shoved it in his pocket. "*Due oras,*" the man repeated.

"That's all," Jordan said. "We'll come back for it in a little while. Just leave it right here."

The man looked confused.

"I've got to buy a little wine. You know, *vino.*"

The man shook his head, as if to say he felt crazier than the American for allowing this. Then he showed Jordan where he would leave the ignition key, beneath the board that served as the aft bench in the boat.

"No," Jordan said, bending over and grabbing the key. "I paid in advance, right. This way I know I have the key, *capisce?* Wouldn't want someone to steal it before we get back." He smiled. "Don't worry, I'll leave it under there when we get back."

The man frowned and said, "*Due oras*, eh?"

Sandor nodded. "We'll be back in less than an hour," he assured him, then looked at his watch. "We'll take a quick ride, *tutto finito en due oras.*"

"*Bene,*" the man said, then turned and walked away, up the hill past the concrete reinforcement that ran beside the dock.

Jordan made a pretense of taking Christine back into town. Once he was certain the fisherman was out of view, they doubled back to the spot where the small boats were set aground.

"Now what?" Christine asked. "We've got ourselves a little dinghy for a thousand dollars, and pretty soon everyone in town is going to know about it."

"Exactly," he said. "That's just what we want." He gazed out into the moonlit night, the sea lapping gently at the shore just a few yards from where they stood.

"We want them to come here thinking they'll get the drop on us, expecting us to be gone for the next hour."

He led her to a spot behind some dry-docked skiffs, and they made themselves as comfortable as they could for another long wait ahead.

FIFTY-FIVE

Traiman's men came ashore at the main wharf, on the end of the harbor opposite from where Jordan and Christine were waiting on the rocky beach. They tied up the launch and prepared to split into two groups as instructed.

Kerrigan told Fraser they would start in the main plaza. Fraser was also American, an athletic looking man with the bow-legged stride of a horseman that belied his New Jersey upbringing. Like Kerrigan, he was a veteran of the Gulf War and had been in Traiman's employ for the past three years. He had never seen Sandor, but he had met Andrioli.

"We'll see you back here in an hour," Kerrigan told the others.

The two men assigned to the hotel were Iraqis, survivors of the American war of liberation in their homeland. Having been members of Saddam Hussein's Republican Guard, they did not remain in their country to celebrate their new freedom. They recently joined forces with al-Qaeda, presently taking their orders from Traiman. The taller of them was Zayn. He was carrying a canvass duffle bag with their automatic weapons and extra rounds of ammunition inside.

"We'll start at the Hotel Continental," he told Kerrigan in his heavily accented English.

The fifth man in the group had been appointed to stay with the motorboat. He was a short, trimly built Syrian, whom Traiman often used as a lookout. He found a bench on the pier, where he sat down and placed his cellular radio beside him. He lit a cigarette and prepared to wait.

A SHORT TIME later, Covington arrived in Portofino with Andrioli, Nealon and Bertram. They had driven along the same winding route Jordan and Christine had traveled earlier in the day. They parked away from the Hotel Continental and set off on foot. Covington had left his other two men back in Rapallo, as their control team.

Covington and Nealon walked ahead, Bertram guarding Andrioli as the wounded man limped along, trying to keep pace.

"You going to make it?" Betram asked.

Andrioli made an effort to steady his gait. "Probably not."

"How's the side?"

"Sore." The surgery on his chest seemed a long time ago, mainly because he was in a continual fog induced by the painkillers. "I almost forgot about it, till you reminded me. Thanks."

"Don't mention it."

They trudged down a hilly walkway where Andrioli pointed to a set of ancient stone steps. "That's the place, right around the corner."

Covington held up his hand, and the four men came to a stop. "Andrioli goes in first. Nealon and I right after him. You stay outside and back us up, Bertram."

Bertram nodded, happy to be relieved of trailing Andrioli.

"I'm not even armed," Andrioli said. "Why should I lead?"

"Sandor's your friend. He's not going to shoot you, is he?"

"What if Sandor's not in there?"

"Don't worry. We'll be right behind you."

Lemme have a gun, for chrissakes. You afraid I'll take the three of you out?"

Nealon and Bertram looked to Covington, but he shook his head. "You've got your orders," Covington said. "Now let's go."

They negotiated the steps, Bertram lagging farther behind now. When they reached the street, Bertram took a position against the stone wall. He watched as Andrioli, Covington and Nealon entered the hotel.

Inside, the three men found the young clerk behind the desk.

"We're looking for our friends, Mr. and Mrs. Kerr," Andrioli told him.

The young man eyed them suspiciously then said something in Italian none of them understood.

"Kerr," Andrioli repeated. Then, in response to the look in the clerk's eyes, he leaned forward slightly and said, "Now, fella."

The clerk stared into Andrioli's eyes and saw the man meant business. He nodded slightly and told him the room number. Then, in his broken English, he explained nervously that he didn't think *Signore* and *Signora* Kerr were in their room. Two men came by just a little while ago and went upstairs, but there was no answer.

"Where are those two men?" Andrioli asked.

The boy told them they were gone, but the way he said it caused Andrioli to turn to his two companions. "I don't believe him."

"Ring their room," Covington said.

The clerk shrugged. "I try before," he said. "No answer."

"Try again."

The three men watched as the boy placed a call. There was no answer.

INSIDE JORDAN'S ROOM, Zayn and the other Iraqi were waiting. They had already removed the two H&K MP5 submachine guns from their satchel and chambered the first rounds. The guns carried 9mm shells, with the option of single shot, three round bursts or continuous firing. The SMG was designed for a magazine with 30 rounds and an attached replacement clip carrying the same load.

Each man occupied one of the far corners of the room, facing the door. When the phone rang, they tensed, glancing quickly at each other as they brought their weapons into position.

WHEN THE CLERK finally hung up the phone after half a dozen rings, Covington asked, "You been at this desk all evening?"

The young man became agitated, insisting that he never leaves the desk. He was just like a good soldier, he told them, ever at his post.

"I think he's full of shit," Andrioli said.

"We'll have a look for ourselves," Covington agreed.

The clerk understood their comments, as well as the demand. He was definite in his refusal. "No, *signore. Impossibile.*"

Now Nealon stepped forward, pulled out his 9mm and pointed it at the clerk's face. "Key," he said in plain English.

The clerk turned slowly to his side and grabbed a spare key to the room, then held it out in a trembling hand.

"*Grazie*," Andrioli said.

Nealon stepped behind the desk and grabbed the young man by the arm, pulling him forward. He held his finger to his lips and motioned with the gun for the clerk to lead them up the stairs. The four of them proceeded in single file up to the first landing. Once again, Nealon put his finger to his mouth. This time the clerk pressed his lips tightly together to show that he understood.

Andrioli held out his hands, palms upraised, and shrugged his shoulders. The clerk pointed across the corridor to one of the doors.

Nealon took the clerk by the shoulders and spun him around, facing him against the wall. "Shhh," he whispered in his ear.

Andrioli noticed the small strip of paper on the floor near Sandor's door. When Covington motioned him forward, Andrioli shook his head and pointed to the paper.

Covington nodded his understanding then mouthed the words, "Call his name." Nealon had walked silently past the door. Covington stood on the near side, beside Andrioli.

"Jordan," Andrioli called out. It was a raspy whisper, but in the quiet of the hallway it was like a shout, sure to be heard inside. "Jordan," he said again. "It's Tony."

There was no answer.

Covington motioned for Andrioli to open the door with the key. Andrioli responded with a look that told him he must be out of his mind. Covington reached out and took hold of the knob. He could feel it was unlocked. He turned it and pushed at the door as he moved quickly two steps back down the hall.

A splintering crash of gunfire erupted before the door had come all the way open, shattering the wood and piercing the opposite wall. The fusillade, coming at crossing angles, struck Andrioli and dropped him to the floor before he could move aside. Covington and Nealon refrained from firing, just for an instant, giving the shooters enough time to think that Andrioli might have been alone. Then Nealon took a step forward and began firing.

The men inside responded with another hail of shots. The walls of the hotel were old and wooden and easily gave in to the powerful explosions launched from the automatic weapons. Nealon was hit in the side of the face, spinning him sideways as another series of shots killed him before he hit the floor.

As Nealon's lifeless body collapsed at his feet, Covington hollered out, "Hold your fire. It's Covington." He had yet to fire a shot.

Traiman's man, Zayn, who was off to the right, hunkered down behind the bed and took a quick look, his weapon at the ready.

"It's Covington," the CIA man repeated as he stepped into view in the open doorway. "Hold your fire."

The two men inside the room stood up.

The sound of the gunshots had already brought Bertram racing in from the street. He took the stairs two at a time, coming around the turn in the corridor at a crouch, just in time to hear Covington use his own name to bring the exchange to a halt. He froze, gun in hand, staring at his operations chief.

He saw that Nealon and Andrioli were down, the clerk was huddled against the wall, and Covington was standing in the middle of the corridor with his weapon at his side.

There was no time for Bertram to comprehend the treachery. Covington answered the agent's startled look by raising his automatic and firing three rounds into his chest. Bertram crumpled to the floor.

Traiman's men came slowly to the door, their SMG's still in position.

"It's all right," Covington told them. "That's everyone. They're done."

The second Iraqi followed Zayn into the hallway.

"What the hell are you guys doing here?" Covington asked. "Where's Sandor?"

"We don't know," Zayn said. "We came here looking for him. We had an hour before we had to meet Kerrigan, so we waited here, in case he came back."

"What about him?" Covington asked, pointing to the Italian clerk who was crouched against the wall, not looking towards them.

"He works for the locals," Zayn said. "Let him go."

"No," Covington said. He turned, extended his arm, and fired two shots into the back of the boy's head. "We're not leaving any loose ends this time."

Traiman's men stepped over Nealon's body to stand alongside Covington. He was staring down at Andrioli.

Andrioli was covered in blood, his breathing uneven and shallow, his eyes still open. He had fallen with his head propped against the baseboard of the corridor wall. He stared up at Covington.

Covington smiled down at him. "You just refuse to die, don't you?"

Andrioli struggled for air. "It was you all along."

Covington said nothing.

"You miserable traitor," Andrioli managed to gasp.

"That's kind of the pot calling the kettle black, don't you think?" Covington said. Then he took the H&K from Zayn and fired a three-round burst into Andrioli's chest.

FIFTY-SIX

Jordan and Christine had no way of knowing what had occurred at the Continental. They were still waiting near the shore in the cold, damp evening, Jordan sensing that the time for action was near.

A few minutes later, they heard footsteps coming down the long wharf, firm and unhurried. It was the confident gait of men who believed they were too early to be concerned about concealing their arrival. They had obviously learned of Sandor's renting the boat and bought the story he had fed the local about going for wine. These men probably assumed he was going for help, and they intended to get there first.

The sound of the water sloshing against the rocky beach made it difficult for Sandor to determine how many there were. It was certainly more than one. Three or more coming for them would be a problem. All he had was the one pistol. And the advantage of surprise.

As the men drew nearer, he was able to distinguish their steps. There were two men approaching and, as they came into view, Sandor could make out their silhouettes against the misty backdrop of the growing darkness. One man appeared to be broad, of average height, with an athlete's bearing. The other was tall, the swagger of his stride now recognizable as Kerrigan.

Jordan and Christine were silent as they watched the men slow, then step down onto the beach. They passed directly in front of them, just a few yards from the stacked skiffs that provided their cover. They watched as the men turned toward the water trying to identify which of the boats Jordan had rented.

"This might be it," one of them said.

Jordan stood, rising above the pile of inverted boats, his hand gripping Andrioli's Colt .45. "Sorry boys, you guessed wrong, but thanks for playing. Now, under the rules of our little game, if either of you so much as twitch, I'll shoot you both."

Kerrigan wasn't waiting to find out what came next. He dove to the ground, reaching for his gun.

Fraser, with no warning that Kerrigan was going to make a move, was a split second late in reacting. As he turned to his side, trying to pull out his weapon, Sandor squeezed off two shots, both finding their mark.

As Fraser collapsed onto the sand, Jordan turned to Kerrigan, getting a bead on the large man as he scampered on his hands and knees to find cover behind a nearby rowboat. Kerrigan had unholstered his pistol, but Jordan fired, hitting him with a shot in the back of the thigh, a second ripping through his side. Kerrigan lurched forward, sprawling face down on a rocky outcropping, his gun skittering out of his reach.

Sandor stepped cautiously from behind his makeshift barricade of wooden boats, his Colt trained on Kerrigan's back. He had a quick look at the other man. He appeared to be dead.

"I said I'd shoot you if you moved. You've got to learn to trust what people tell you, Kerrigan. Now I've got this gun pointed at the back of your ugly head. You move again, you die."

Kerrigan groaned some obscenity Sandor could not quite make out.

"Whatever," Jordan said as he circled slowly, keeping his distance as he retrieved the Glock 9mm and shoved it into his waistband. "If you want to have any chance at all of living through the next few minutes, you'll have to tell me where I can find Andrioli."

Kerrigan made a move, trying to roll onto his side.

"No no no," Jordan said. "Talk first, move later."

Kerrigan fell back on his face, uttering another painful moan. Then, as he attempted to speak, Christine cried out, "Jordan."

Sandor turned to see Fraser raising himself, gun in hand.

Jordan's instincts prevailed. He fired three rapid shots, one after the other causing the man to jerk back in a convulsive pantomime of death.

Jordan swiftly returned his attention back to Kerrigan and, in one deft motion, released the spent clip from the Colt and replaced it with a new magazine. "I asked you a question."

"Dead," Kerrigan grunted.

Sandor glanced briefly at Christine then asked, "When?"

"Tonight." Kerrigan managed to turn so he could look up at Sandor. "You just can't seem to keep your friends alive, can you?"

Sandor resisted the impulse to kick him in the head. "Where?"

"Right here, in Portofino," Kerrigan said. Then his face twisted up in a contortion of pain.

"Does it hurt?"

"Kiss my ass," Kerrigan spat at him.

"Witty reply. So, where's Traiman?"

Kerrigan managed a grin. "Traiman? He's having a little party on his yacht tonight. And his guest of honor is another friend of yours."

Jordan kneeled down, so Kerrigan could have a good look at the barrel of the Colt pointing at his face from just a few feet away. "Do tell."

"Yeah, once they buried that rat bastard Andrioli they took your pal Covington as an insurance policy."

"Bullshit."

"You think it's bullshit?" Kerrigan started coughing. It was not clear how bad he had been hit, and Jordan didn't want to lose him before he got some more answers.

"Covington?"

Kerrigan took a couple of uneven breaths and said, "That's right. Traiman's got your CIA man. What are you gonna do about it?"

"Where's your launch?"

He hesitated, so Jordan waved the gun at him. "I asked you a question."

"Main dock."

"Which yacht out there is the *Halaby*?"

"I'm bleeding to death here."

"Which one is the *Halaby*?" Jordan repeated.

Kerrigan said, "Go to hell," then made a show of trying to hold his wounded side with his right hand as he slid his left arm down towards his ankle.

Jordan saw the move and, as Kerrigan nearly reached his ankle holster, Sandor said, "Nice try," then fired two shots into his face.

Christine turned away, but Jordan watched the man's head snap back in a bloody spasm and then fall forward onto the rocks.

FIFTY-SEVEN

Jordan checked the magazine in Kerrigan's Glock. It was full, a cartridge already in the breech. The man had never gotten a shot off. He handed the gun to Christine.

"You're going to tell me you've never shot one of these, right?"

She nodded, holding the butt of the gun like it was covered with slime.

"All you've got to do is point and pull the trigger." He turned it in her hand so she was holding it properly. Then he gently pointed the barrel to the ground. "But you probably won't have to. If they take us, you just need to have a weapon. Once they find it, they probably won't search you beyond a frisking."

She responded with a look of fear and confusion.

"Trust me," he said. Then he took her by the hand and started off for the center of town.

THE GUNFIRE AT the Hotel Continental had caused neighbors to call the police. The shootings of Kerrigan and his partner were going to excite even more local activity.

Sandor hurried along with Christine at his side. He had no way of knowing whether any of the things Kerrigan had said were true. He only knew that he needed to get to Traiman.

As they neared the center of the town, he stopped beside a short brick building. "Come here," he said.

She followed him into the shadows, where he took her by the shoulders and looked into her frightened eyes. "We've got to split up. I'm heading for the main dock. I want you to go into the café near there, the one closest to the water. Go inside, order something and don't come out unless I signal you." He took the Glock from her and placed it inside her bag.

"You're going to leave me behind," she said.

"No," he lied, "but I need to try and get to the launch alone. If they see us together, they'll make us from a hundred yards away. If I'm on my own, I'll have a chance."

She stared into his dark eyes, understanding. "I've told you the truth. Do you know that?"

He nodded.

"No, really Jordan. I need to know that you believe me."

He took her in his arms and kissed her tenderly on the cheek. "I believe you," he said. "Now please believe me when I say that I know what I'm doing."

"You're going out there alone."

"Please," he said, "leave it to me."

She lowered her head and nodded.

"Good. Now wait here just one minute, then go right to the café, the first one we visited today. And hold onto that gun, we may need it."

He kissed her again, and she held herself against him for what she feared would be the last time. Then she watched as he walked towards the sea and disappeared from view.

JORDAN STOLE HIS way around a row of powered skiffs, sunfish and rowboats that had been pulled ashore for the night. As he came closer to the pier, he could see in the distance a man seated on a bench, directly across from what he assumed would be the *Halaby* launch. Traiman's lookout.

Jordan had taken the radio from Kerrigan's pocket to see if he could listen in and confirm what he'd been told about Andrioli and Covington, but whoever else was in town was obviously now observing radio silence. He turned the two-way off and headed for the underside of the quay.

He mounted a support post beneath the dock, then climbed from strut to strut. The old wooden beams were wide and round and slippery with years of the ebb and flow of the sea. He moved carefully and quietly, making his way by stepping in the joints of the crossbeams. When he reached the white power boat marked *Halaby,* he continued past it, carefully traversing the interior supports to the outside piling, where he climbed atop the dock behind the man standing guard.

He pulled himself up, finding that he was just beyond the bench where the guard was seated. He placed his foot on a rounded wood brace and drew the Colt from his belt. Then he yanked himself higher, slipping over the railing, his weapon pointed at the back of the man's head.

"*Buona sera,*" Sandor said.

Traiman's scout turned, his hand about to drawn his weapon.

"Uh uh uh," Jordan said. "Stay right there."

The Syrian did not move.

"I'm going to need your help," Jordan said, "but first I'm going to need your gun."

The man smiled, his white teeth in stark contrast to his swarthy complexion. "I don't think so," he said, motioning with his head at what he had been watching when Jordan appeared.

Sandor glanced down the length of the pier. Coming towards them were four men and a woman.

The Syrian said, "I think you better give me your gun instead."

Jordan had another look at the approaching group. Two men he did not recognize were walking close behind Christine, John Covington and a man Jordan imagined to be Martin Koppel.

He bowed his head at the sight and exhaled slowly as he released the butt of his automatic, the pistol now hanging from his index finger by the trigger guard. He extended his hand, and the Syrian stepped forward and took the gun.

"Now you will get in the boat," the man ordered.

"Not without her," he said, "and him," gesturing to Covington.

"Don't be concerned, Mr. Sandor. Everyone is invited."

The party of five had almost reached them. The only one speaking was Martin Koppel.

"What is this with guns?" he demanded nervously. "I'm a businessman. I'm here for a business meeting."

No one was paying any attention to Koppel. When they were only a few paces from Jordan, one of Traiman's men told the group they had gone far enough.

"Who are you?" Koppel asked Sandor.

Jordan ignored him. "Hello, Covington," Jordan said. "I see you're also having a bad night."

"Extremely," he replied grimly. "Lost both of my agents. And Andrioli."

"I heard," Jordan said. "Where?"

"At your hotel, where you should have been."

"I'm not sure how to take that, John."

Zayn barked at them, "Enough. No more talking." He turned to the Syrian, who was now holding out his Glock as well as Jordan's Colt. "Any sign of Kerrigan and Fraser?'

The man shook his head.

Jordan said, "I'm afraid they won't be joining us, if that's what you're waiting for."

Everyone looked at Sandor.

"Yes," he said. "I'm afraid they've gone off to join the foreign legion in the sky."

Zayn raised his hand to strike Sandor with the butt of his pistol, but his partner stepped forward and stopped him. "Not now. We'll have time for everything. Let's get them on the boat."

THE FIRST THREE men dispatched to Portofino by Deputy Director Byrnes were now gathered in the room they had taken at the small hotel just behind the shops on the edge of the harbor. One of them had been on watch and saw Traiman's man come and collect Koppel from the Hotel Splendido for his meeting. The agent then followed at a safe distance into the center of town. There, the other two CIA agents, who had taken a position in the café near the main dock, witnessed a second Traiman henchman arrive, accompanied by John Covington. They joined Koppel and his escort, and the four of them proceeded to the dock. It was near the entrance to the pier that they had encountered Christine Frank, who was standing alone, gazing out at the dock. They took her just moments before Sandor appeared on the wharf and went face to face with Traiman's operative at the power launch.

The three agents then hustled back to their hotel where they convened to make arrangements for their next move.

As two of the agents stood at the window, using binoculars to monitor the activities at the power boat, the third called Byrnes and reported these developments.

"They have Covington, then?"

"Yes sir."

"And the girl?"

"Yes. They're with Koppel now. And two of Traiman's men. They also have Sandor."

"Good," Byrnes said.

The agent asked if it was time for them to move.

"Not yet," the deputy director told him.

"Sir, I must report the situation is grave."

"I know," Byrnes replied.

"The risks are extreme, sir. If I may say—" he attempted to go on, but the DD cut him off.

"We all appreciate the risks."

"Yes sir."

"You go to the fallback position as we planned. And remember what's at stake. We need the information more than we need the kill. Sandor is exactly where we need him."

FIFTY-EIGHT

Any prospects for a celebration on the *Halaby*, with Martin Koppel as the guest of honor, had evaporated with the radio transmission from the launch. Traiman, however, was not entirely displeased. He was disappointed perhaps, that his conference with Koppel would not go as smoothly as he would have liked, but he was determined to conclude their financial venture. Or to discover that it was a ruse.

Traiman was in the main salon, accompanied only by his top aide, Nelson, a former British commando with broad shoulders, a thick neck and a bald, bullet-shaped head.

"Once they're aboard," Nelson was saying, "we should weigh anchor and leave."

"There appears to be no sign of backup. This is Covington's mission, and he's on his way here. Where's the concern?"

"What if there is backup? What if Koppel was followed? If we move right now, they'd never chance an attack in open waters."

"Perhaps not," Traiman said. "I'm not so sure."

"The Americans would never be that reckless, not without confirmation that you're aboard. And how will they get that confirmation? If they do, they'll also know we have Covington, Sandor and the girl."

"You may be right. On the other hand, they don't need to launch missiles or torpedoes to mount an attack."

Nelson shook his head.

"We need to conclude our business with Koppel," Traiman said, "then put him safely ashore. If there's any sign of a problem, we can make the appropriate arrangements then. Meantime, our security details are in place."

There was a knock at the salon door, followed by the entrance of one of his guards. "They're approaching, Mr. Traiman."

"Good, good." Traiman remained seated while his man went back to meet the boat. Traiman turned again to Nelson. "If we run, we'll surely be at risk. Consider it. As long as we stay right here, the chance of an assault is less likely and more manageable."

"And if it isn't? Time will work against us."

"Perhaps so, but I think our guests will ensure a measure of safety. Remember, our Arab clients will prove an even bigger problem if we fail to deliver."

Nelson knew he was right. He knew that this was Traiman's final opportunity to square himself with those who believed he had betrayed Khalid Sheikh Mohammed in Pakistan and the assault team in Washington—which, of course, he had.

There was another knock at the door. The same guard appeared. "They're aboard."

"Fine," said Traiman. "They've been disarmed?"

"Yes sir."

"Show them in."

He and Nelson waited a few moments. Then Jordan walked into the spacious salon, stopped, and had a look around at the modern décor, a combination of teak and glass and saddle leather upholstery. "I'm glad to see you're doing so well for yourself, Vincent."

Sandor was followed by Christine, Koppel, Covington, and the three men who had been ashore. Two more from Traiman's security force joined them.

Traiman remained seated as they entered. He pressed his hands together and brought them to his lips. "Jordan. You can't imagine what a pleasure it is to see you again. And Miss Frank. Your photograph doesn't do you justice."

It was Koppel who spoke first, demanding once again to know what the hell was going on.

Traiman ignored him, looking instead to his men. "You say they've been searched."

All five men nodded.

"My friend Jordan has carried some interesting toys with him, from time to time."

One of the men from the shore detail said, "Yes sir." He had searched them, but so far had not discovered the C-4 Jordan had molded and taped to the small of Christine's back and the inside of his thigh. The man held out his hand to Traiman. "We took their guns and an extra clip. He had one of our radios. Here are the papers and other things we found on them."

Traiman took what the man offered and placed it on the table, waving a careless hand without bothering to have a look. "No portable laser beams, Jordan? No nuclear devices? What a disappointment." He turned away and faced his other guests. "John Covington. So good to see you again, too. And you, sir, you must be Mr. Koppel."

"Damn right I am. See here—"

Traiman held up his hand, palm forward, and then rose from his chair. He was dressed in a dark suit, white shirt with French cuffs bearing gold links, and a gray silk tie. He appeared every bit the successful businessman. "I truly apologize for all of these theatrics, but you see, a man in my position has many enemies. I'm sure you understand. Corporate espionage has become a ruthless game." Traiman's congenial tone seemed to nonplus Koppel, if only long enough for Traiman to add, "I assure you, our meeting will proceed as scheduled. Gentlemen, please show Mr. Koppel to the forward dining salon, and get him anything he wants."

"What the hell—?" Koppel started up again, but he stopped as Traiman once more raised his hand.

"Please indulge me, sir. I'll only be a few minutes," he said, and two of the security detail politely, if firmly, escorted Martin Koppel from the cabin.

As soon as Koppel was gone and the door closed behind him, Traiman's tone became more severe. "Where are Kerrigan and Fraser?"

The dark-skinned Syrian, who had acted as scout on the pier, said, "They never made it back. He," gesturing toward Sandor, "claims they're gone."

"Gone?"

"Afraid so," Jordan told his old mentor. "A Viking funeral may be in order."

Traiman turned his steely gaze on Sandor. "I was very fond of Kerrigan. He was a good soldier."

"Only the good die young, Vincent."

Traiman responded by issuing several commands. Covington was to be detained in one of the guest cabins and kept under guard. They were to make ready for the dinner with Koppel. He would take a few minutes with Sandor and the girl, and then they would also be held for further interrogation.

Two men grabbed Covington roughly by the arms and led him away. That left only Traiman, Nelson, and one security guard with Jordan and Christine.

"Sit down," Traiman told his two guests. "And Jordan, please believe me when I say that in the event you make even the slightest untoward move, these men will kill you without another warning."

The guard lifted the submachine gun he was holding and pointed it at Sandor, just to reinforce the warning. Nelson removed a pistol from his shoulder holster and laid it on the table before him.

"You see, Jordan, in addition to the loyalty I command from these men, several of them were quite friendly with Mr. Kerrigan and Mr. Fraser."

"Thanks for the tender moment Vincent."

Traiman responded with a disapproving frown. "Do me a favor, please," he said as he resumed his seat. "Begin by explaining why on earth you're here. Other than a burning desire to get together with me to reminisce."

"I'd have to say it all began when your people started shooting at me in Woodstock—by the way, how far back do you want me to go? You want me to talk about how you screwed me when we were in Kuwait? Should I get into the Manama gambit?"

"No Jordan, not that far back. Truth being told, I don't have all that much time for this interview, and if you insist on wasting it on the tiresome sarcasm you find so amusing, I'll be left no choice but to turn you over to more persuasive members of my staff. Am I clear?"

"As always."

"So then, let's conduct ourselves as professionals and get to the point."

"Professionals?"

"Oh no, I feel it coming. We're about to move from sarcasm to jingoism, am I right?"

Jordan stared across the cabin without giving a response.

"Ah yes, Jordan Sandor, fighting for paychecks and patriotism while I, the mercenary, opted for wealth and power."

Jordan still refused to reply.

"Propaganda and peanuts, that's what you've risked your life for, Jordan. You've always been supremely talented, but incredibly naïve."

"You consider morality naïve?"

"Ah, morality. Tell me, Jordan, what gives the United States the moral high ground? It aids and abets the assassination of leaders in third world nations, promotes civil war in those countries, then invades them when their internal politics become distasteful to the American administration *du jour*. How many have died in the fields of Afghanistan or the streets of Baghdad? How many are slaughtered every day in the wars that rage endlessly in Africa, places where none of those bleeding hearts in New York or Los Angeles could begin to find on a map? No one cares about those tens of thousands that die of poverty, starvation, and internecine battles. Not really.

"So where is it written that only the United States cannot be attacked or invaded without provoking a world conflict? Why, when someone blows up a building in the United States in protest against its policies in the Middle East, must the entire world be made to pay? Spare me your sanctimonious patriotism, Jordan. Tell me, which of us is the mercenary here?"

"In answer to your first question," Jordan said slowly, "I came here because I wanted to see you again. And to kill you."

No one in the room moved.

Then Traiman began to laugh. "You see," he said to Nelson, "do you see why I've always loved this man so?"

No one else seemed to find it funny, except Sandor. He was smiling.

"So that's why you let my men take you without a fight. You actually did want to come aboard?"

"No. To be honest Vincent, I only gave up my weapon because they had Christine and Covington."

"Of course. You gave up your weapon to protect the damsel in distress and your old boss from the CIA, a man you don't even like, if memory serves."

"Not much. No."

"Always the hero. You just can't seem to help yourself, can you?"

Jordan watched him without answering.

"All right. And now that you're here, and we still have your lady friend and our old crony from the Agency—not to mention you, dear man—what did you really want to see me about? Before you killed me, that is."

"One of the items is moot, since I understand Tony Andrioli is already dead."

"I see. You came to argue for clemency."

"That's true, yes."

"What else, then?"

"I would like you to leave Christine alone."

Traiman turned his attention to her now. "I am sorry about Mr. McHugh. Not about his death, you understand. That became unavoidable. It is his disloyalty I regret."

Christine did not speak. She stared at him with obvious loathing.

"So then," Traiman said as he got to his feet again. "You have set your sights rather low, Jordan, and failed in all respects. Mr. Andrioli is dead, and there is nothing you can do to save Miss Frank or Mr. Covington. You should never have left the game, Jordan—it appears you've lost your edge."

"There is something else."

"Yes?"

"I want to know why you betrayed your own people?"

"Why I left the CIA?"

"No, of course not. I mean the people you work with now. I mean, I thought I had you all figured out, Vincent. The money, the power. That whole cynical speech you made. It all fits. But then you torpedo your own team of hit men in Washington. For the life of me, I can't figure out why."

Traiman could feel the gaze of his Syrian security man bear down on him as he stood there. "Don't be ridiculous."

"Ridiculous?" Jordan smiled again. "Look, everyone in the business knows you've worn out your welcome in Libya. Qaddafi is playing the moderate now, and he's giving you the heave ho. He might even turn you over to us, offered the right deal. So why risk your chance at a safe haven somewhere among your Arab friends by screwing them now? Especially when you're about to launch your VX project?

The Syrian turned from Sandor to Traiman.

Traiman's eyes flashed with anger as he said, "Nonsense".

"I don't think so," Sandor replied with a knowing smile. "Vincent Traiman, always the traitor. I guess you just can't help yourself."

"This discussion is at an end," Traiman said. "Mr. Nelson, take them to the library and keep them there. I'm going to meet with Mr. Koppel. I'll deal with them later."

"Leaving so soon?" Jordan asked as Traiman made for the door.

"Don't worry, Jordan. I'll be back."

FIFTY-NINE

Deputy Director Byrnes gave the order to move out. His agents, who had been waiting for instructions in Rapallo, were now on board a 37-foot, Italian made Cranchi Smeraldo speed boat that would travel a course around the point on a southeastern bearing into the Mediterranean. The three men in Portofino were taking a larger craft, cruising at a slower speed, due south.

A Black Hawk helicopter crew had taken off from Genoa, and remained out of sight and earshot from the *Halaby*, just beyond the ridge of the Appennino mountain range.

Meanwhile, the *Halaby* was anchored in the distance, gently rocking on the calm sea.

TRAIMAN WAS IN the private dining salon, doing his best to calm Martin Koppel's frayed nerves. He explained that the man and woman who had come aboard were rivals of his, and his bodyguard had been overzealous in protecting him. "Their presence here has nothing whatever to do with our arrangements."

Koppel told him that he did not buy any part of that story. "What about the other guy?" Koppel asked, referring to Covington.

"He's an associate of mine," Traiman told him confidently. "United States government official."

"Is he involved with our project?"

"No. Knows nothing of our plans."

"Why is that?" Koppel asked.

Traiman leaned back and had a good look at his guest. The more they spoke, the more relaxed Koppel appeared. "I have always made it a policy to segregate the data and people involved in the different aspects of my business life."

"Need-to-know basis, eh?"

"That's one way to put it." Traiman lifted his glass of Pellegrino water and took a sip. "So, I assume that by now you've researched the matrix set up by Montana Management in Switzerland."

"Yes, I have. You know whose money that is?"

Traiman's thin lips parted in his imitation of a smile. "Of course, Mr. Koppel. Together with the MidCo Finance group, these companies possess the riches stolen from the people of Iraq by Saddam Hussein and his minions."

Koppel nodded.

"My aspirations are not that grand, Mr. Koppel. Have you organized the investment funds we discussed?"

"Everything is set to go," Koppel told him. "But I don't like all this gun-toting nonsense. What kind of man are you? Are you kidnapping your competitors? Is that what's going on here?"

Traiman liked the questions Koppel was asking. They were the logical questions of a man who was here to do business, not a CIA plant. He was particularly relieved to have witnessed the fact that Covington and Koppel did not know each other, or about each other. Traiman had never entrusted Covington with any information about his investment plans with Koppel. Covington had simply been told that there was a scheme in place that would generate enormous profits in which he would share. He was on a need-to-know basis, just as Koppel said. If Koppel was part of a CIA gambit, Traiman reasoned that Covington would surely have known about that.

"Please, Mr. Koppel, don't allow your Hollywood-inspired imagination to run wild. There's nothing so dramatic at play here as kidnapping. Save those creative inspirations for the wealth we will produce together. After we have dinner and conclude our business, we will put you ashore. My associates and I will then address the matters we have to discuss with these . . . competitors. It's as harmless as that."

"Whatever," Koppel replied, proud of the acting job he was doing. "It's none of my business, anyway? I just don't like all these guns. Let's wrap up the details so I can get the hell out of here."

"Of course." Traiman held up his glass again. "We are going to be very wealthy men, you and I, and very soon."

JORDAN AND CHRISTINE were sitting side by side in the library. The walls of the cabin were lined with oiled walnut bookshelves, many of the volumes bound in leather. There was a campaign-style captain's table in the center of the room, several club chairs set around the table and a settee against the wall that Jordan and Christine occupied. Directly across from them, Nelson was comfortably seated in one of the armchairs, his weapon resting in his lap. The security guard had stepped outside, waiting on deck near the door.

"Hey Nelson," Jordan said. "That's your name, right? Nelson?"

He did not answer.

"All right if I have a cigarette?"

"You move your hand and I'll shoot your arm off."

Sandor nodded. "That's okay, I don't really smoke."

Nelson glared at him. "Traiman said he wants you alive for now, but he didn't say anything about what condition you need to be in. Don't press your luck."

Jordan nodded again, studying the man, taking the measure of his options and gauging the eight feet or so that separated them.

THE FIRST MATE, noticing something on the radar screen in the wheelhouse of the *Halaby*, was the first to see them. The speedboat was just a blip on the screen, but it was moving quickly. He radioed the man on the foredeck and asked him to have a look through his night-vision binoculars. The man obliged, scanning the dark sea to the west. The boat was not yet in view.

The lookout on the port side of the stern deck heard the radio communication from the wheelhouse and signaled back that a cruiser was moving slowly south from the Portofino harbor, still a long way off.

Neither activity was unusual in this area, but with Traiman aboard the yacht, the security detail was on high alert. When the cabin cruiser began to circle on a course slightly to the east, the man on the port side of the ship hurried to the dining salon. He knocked and then entered at Traiman's bidding.

"Yes?"

"Sir, may I speak with you, please? Privately."

Traiman was annoyed by the interruption, but his team was well trained and would not have intruded if it was not important. "I'm sorry, Mr. Koppel. I'll be right back."

Traiman followed the guard onto the deck, closing the door behind him.

"I'm sorry sir, but there seems to be movement. It may be nothing, but—"

"Details," Traiman demanded.

The man explained what they had noticed to the west and the north.

"Stay here," Traiman told him, then hurried forward along the teak deck.

JOHN COVINGTON WAS enjoying a drink in a guest cabin with one of Traiman's men, the man who sometimes called himself Groat. His real name was Richard Dombroski.

Covington was having a scotch. Dombroski was having mineral water. The two men knew each other, but they were not friends. Theirs was an association forced upon them by circumstances.

"That was a rather dramatic exit you arranged for David Fryar at Loubar, wouldn't you say?"

"We needed to make a point," Dombroski replied in his monotone.

"You certainly accomplished that." Covington took a sip of the fine, aged single malt scotch. "So, who is this Koppel character? Isn't he that financier, lost his shirt a few years back?"

Dombroski looked at Covington, his hooded gaze giving the impression that he might be falling asleep. "I don't ask questions," he replied in his flat affect.

Once he arrived on the yacht, Covington was looking forward to abandoning his role as a double agent, anticipating a warm greeting from Traiman. He expected to be the true guest of honor, the completion of the mission in Portofino his coming out party. Covington's days as a mole within the CIA were over, and he was disappointed to have his reunion with Traiman upstaged by Jordan Sandor and a broken-down Wall Street investor.

He was obliged to continue playing his part a little while longer.

He took another drink of the smooth, oaky-tasting scotch, left to bide his time with the man he knew to be Traiman's number one enforcer, wondering why Vincent had chosen Richard Dombroski as his chaperone.

DEPUTY DIRECTOR BYRNES arrived in Portofino to coordinate the mission himself. He already had word from the men on the water that they would be circling near the *Halaby* within a few minutes. They would be approaching the yacht from two directions.

Byrnes warned them again that the *Halaby* was likely to be well armed and staffed with experienced military personnel.

The crew on the attack helicopter was standing by, but the DD wanted to hold them off as long as possible. If there was any chance at all that Sandor could get the information they needed, Byrnes was going to wait.

SIXTY

Traiman threw open the door to the cabin where Covington and Dombroski were waiting. If Covington was expecting this to be the moment for an appreciative greeting, he was wrong.

"What goes on here, John?"

Covington was too dumbstruck by the anger in Traiman's voice to frame a suitable reply.

"There are two boats approaching."

"What?"

"You told me your detail was the only one trailing Sandor, that it was clean behind you."

Covington nodded. "Of course."

"Then who the hell is out there?"

"Out where?" He stood as if to go see for himself.

Traiman shook his head. "No. It's better if you continue to pretend you're our prisoner. We may still get some mileage out of that." Traiman was thinking now, calculating the probabilities of his situation. "Koppel. You never met him before?"

"Never."

"Never saw a file on him at the Agency, no mention of him?"

"Nothing."

Traiman nodded to himself. "Fine," he said. "You wait here. Richard, you come with me."

Dombroski followed Traiman out onto the deck, pulling the door closed behind him.

"We may be going seaside," Traiman said to Dombroski. It was all the man needed to know. Traiman had an emergency escape plan that was arranged for only two. Below decks were scuba gear and two motorized underwater props fitted with lights and a range of more than an hour. In the event all other options were foreclosed, he and Dombroski would enter the water through the transom hatch and head for safety.

Dombroski nodded his thick head in understanding.

"Hopefully it won't be necessary, but get it ready all the same."

As Dombroski went below to make the preparations, Traiman hurried aft along the teak catwalk. When he passed the guard and burst into the library, his entrance was so abrupt that Nelson quickly came to his feet, his automatic aimed at the door.

"Sorry sir," he said.

Traiman waved at him with the back of his hand and Nelson sat down. "What the hell is going on here, Jordan?"

"Not much. We were just in the middle of a staring contest."

Traiman turned to Nelson. "The next wisecrack he makes, shoot the girl's knee. Shatter it completely. One shot, you understand?"

Nelson responded with a satisfied smile as Christine took hold of Jordan's wrist, digging her nails into his flesh.

"Now," Traiman said, turning back to Sandor, "let's have it. What are you doing here?"

Jordan looked from Traiman to Nelson and then back again. "I told you my reasons for being here. What else do you want to know?"

"There are two boats approaching. Your friend Covington knows nothing about them. What do you know?"

Jordan had never told Christine anything about Deputy Director Byrnes or their plans to take Traiman. Her look of astonishment was therefore genuine. Sandor did his best to look just as bewildered.

"I was with Andrioli and Christine. You knew that. I figured Covington was on our tail, but you know I wouldn't count on him from here to there," he said, pointing across the cabin with the hand Christine was not squeezing.

"Watch it," Nelson told him.

"Right," Jordan said, placing his palm back on the sofa. "Look Vincent, Andrioli told me about your plans to place hit teams in the States and in Europe. That's as much as I know."

"You're lying, Jordan. You mentioned VX. Tell me what you know about Operation VX."

"VX? I don't know much. Somebody mentioned it to Andrioli in Paris."

"Shoot the girl," Traiman said.

Christine screamed.

Jordan hollered, "Wait," as Nelson leveled the automatic at her leg.

Traiman raised his hand to his aide. "Well then?"

"I've heard rumors about a terrorist assault involving VX. I realized later that's what McHugh wanted to talk with me about." Sandor gave a look that suggested he had just pieced together the last part of a puzzle. "That's it, isn't it Vincent? That's what Andrioli was after. The assassinations are bogus. The team they took down in DC, that's a disinformation ploy."

"Yes yes yes," Traiman intoned impatiently. "But what about you? What have you cooked up for me, my old protégé?"

"I told you, Vincent. I wanted to see you, face to face."

"Well then, you have your wish."

"Look, if those boats were heading for this yacht, what would I be doing here now? What kind of idiocy would that be?"

Traiman thought that over. "I wonder."

"So what are you really up to? VX nerve gas, that's not your style, Vincent. And Martin Koppel, what's that all that about?"

Traiman scrutinized him closely, Jordan's gaze never leaving him.

"I recognized him, of course." Jordan said. "Big time Wall Street at one time, right? What would you be doing with him?"

Traiman took a step back and sat in the armchair to the side of Nelson. "I'm afraid, if you insist you have nothing more to tell me, Miss Frank will have to serve as a human lie detector test."

Christine felt all the breath go out of her.

"I told you," Sandor said quickly, eying Nelson who was still aiming at Christine's leg. "I know you have a plan involving VX nerve gas, that's it."

Traiman nodded. "A fascinating substance. Unctuous, like motor oil, more toxic than sarin, with a longer effective life. Vaporize a few canisters in Grand Central Station or Times Square at rush hour and thousands upon thousands will die. Then New York will come to a standstill—even more so than after Nine Eleven. The destruction of those towers was a devastation to be sure, the deaths of two thousand people a catastrophe. But remember what happened next. In a couple of days everyone else went back to work. The tragedy lingered in the American consciousness, but the actual terror was remote to most people. My goal is to reach further, you see? Take away the hub of a city's transportation system, what have you got? You have hundreds of thousands, maybe millions, of people not willing to go to work for fear of their lives."

Jordan shook his head slowly, the solemn look in his eyes not lost on Traiman.

"You see it, Jordan. We'll have the same result in the BART in San Francisco, Paddington Station in London, the center of Rome. And on and on," he said, as if the subject was beginning to bore him.

"How do you get that much VX into the country?"

Traiman smiled. "You're always on duty, my old friend. Well," he said with a slight shrug, "since you have very little time left, regardless of the exploits being planned out there on the water, I suppose there is no harm in sharing the cleverness of my plan with you. You are one of the few men I know who can appreciate the genius of my approach."

Sandor responded with a grateful nod.

"You recall the explosion at the offices of the Loubar Corporation the other day?"

"Of course."

"Such a tragedy. A nice man, Fryar, but no character. In any event, an investigation into his company had begun, all of that bureaucratic rot you and I so despise. After the explosion, which I arranged, the authorities increased their vigilance. The government demanded that all shipments from Loubar that arrived in France last week be impounded and returned to the United States. What they don't know, however, is that these shipments, which were already at dockside in Marseilles, have now been fitted with this chemical solvent that will wreak devastation across the United States."

"I love the French."

"Yes, *quel dommage*. So you see, your own government is going to import the VX for me."

"How will they get it through customs? Those shipments are going to be examined left, right, and sideways."

"Of course they will. That is, once they've arrived and are taken off the container ship. But before that the barrels containing the VX will be separated and set aside, marked as lubricants. We don't need much of it, believe me. And as you and I often told those dolts in Washington, the harbors of the United States are the most vulnerable access points in America, not the airports. We told them that for years. But does anyone listen?" Traiman stood up, a professor having concluded his lecture.

Sandor's eyes narrowed as he carefully studied his old colleague. "So the team that was arrested a couple of days ago in Washington, they really weren't part of it at all, were they? They were just a decoy you set up, then sold out. Am I right?"

"Bravo," Traiman exclaimed. "And not even my hosts in Tripoli know my true intentions."

"So where are the real hit teams?" Jordan asked. "Where are the men who are going to plant the VX?"

"You're asking for names and addresses, I presume."

"It would be a start."

Traiman allowed himself a heartfelt laugh as he turned back to his man Nelson. "You see, yet another example of why I've always adored this man. Not only a patriot, not only brilliant, but one of the world's great optimists. Just moments away from death, and he's still planning to save the world. Ah, Jordan, if only you were ruled by a little more sense and a little less emotion."

They stared at each other for a moment. "I don't suppose there's any sense to my mentioning the loss of innocent lives or any of that."

"Don't be absurd."

"It's like you said, Vincent, I just can't help myself."

"Yes, I realize it's true. It may be your epitaph." He looked to Christine and said, "Miss Frank, I am truly sorry you have to be involved in this, but you should have chosen your friends more wisely. Now I must go. I cannot be here to see a lovely young woman and my old comrade face such grisly deaths." He turned for the door, then looked back at Nelson. "Dombroski is below decks. He'll be back in a moment if you need him. And Mr. Nelson, please handle this outside, where you won't make a mess of the library."

Traiman was almost at the door when they heard a knock. He opened it, and his lookout from the port side said, "They've thrown a floodlight on us, off the bow."

"How far off are they?"

"A couple hundred yards. The cabin cruiser is off to the west, but seems to be circling towards us."

"Prepare for an assault," Traiman snapped. He was standing in the doorway when he turned back. "You were the most talented agent I ever had the privilege to work with, on this side or that, Jordan. Even though you've become a horrible nuisance, I will truly miss you."

SIXTY-ONE

Traiman pulled the door shut behind him. Jordan could hear his voice trail off as he walked forward, barking orders to his men. Whatever the outcome of the action going on outside, Jordan knew he and Christine had little chance of surviving unless he moved now.

"You heard the man," Nelson said. "Stand up. Nice and slow."

Nelson was already lifting himself out of his chair when a burst of automatic weapons sounded from the front of the ship. In that instant, as Nelson's eyes momentarily moved toward the direction of the gunfire, Jordan had his opening.

He grabbed Christine's sleeve, dragging her to the floor as he lunged at Nelson.

Nelson tried to retain his balance as he squeezed off three rounds, all of them high. "Hold it," he hollered, "I'll kill—" But Jordan had already rolled into Nelson's shins, knocking him backward onto the chair. Sandor sprung up, driving the heel of his right hand into the point of the man's nose, breaking it with a single blow, blood covering Nelson's mouth and chin. Nelson still clutched the automatic, but Jordan came up with his left hand, hitting Nelson under the chin, snapping his head back and sending the gun clattering to the floor.

Sandor hit him twice more, short chops to his throat that left Nelson gasping for air. The door swung open, and Jordan pushed himself backwards, falling to the floor again as the armchair flipped over with a thud. The guard from outside stepped forward, measuring his shot as Jordan rolled to his side. Christine, kneeling off to the side, grabbed a heavy ashtray and flung it towards the door. It glanced off the guard's arm, but it was enough to give Jordan the split-second he needed to reach Nelson's gun, turn, and fire.

Bullets flew back and forth, the guard taking cover behind the bulkhead, outside the door. Christine yelled out a warning as Nelson made an effort to get to his feet. Jordan aimed the over his shoulder and shot Nelson once in the chest, sending him reeling against the bookcase and then falling across the table. The guard sent another barrage of rounds into the library, but he was still hidden. Jordan had no clean shot at him, but neither could the guard get a line of sight inside the cabin.

Sandor motioned for Christine to stay off to the side, behind one of the chairs. He clambered behind Nelson's body, using him for cover as he searched his pockets for another clip. A replacement magazine in hand, he fired a series of shots through the wall, then stopped and cursed under his breath as though he had emptied his clip. The guard chanced a quick peek into the room. Jordan fired two shots, but the first one was enough. It caught him in the forehead, killing him instantly.

"Get ready to go," he called to Christine. "I just need a minute."

"What?"

The din of gunfire at the front of the yacht had increased, which made it unlikely anyone would be checking on them. Jordan went through Nelson's jacket and came up with another magazine. "What a boy scout," he said as he dropped the nearly empty clip to the ground with a press of the release button and replaced it with the fresh one, then disengaged the slide lock, allowing it to ram a fresh round into the breech.

Then he went to the captain's table and lifted the top, exposing various nautical charts, maps, and information on the tides. There was also in a translucent yellow plastic cover holding several sheets of paper. Jordan smiled.

"What are you doing?" she asked anxiously.

"Old habits die hard," he told her. "I've known him a long time. He still writes everything out by hand."

"Traiman?"

He nodded, quickly rifling through the pages before sticking them back in the folder. "Doesn't trust computers. Doesn't trust anyone."

"What is it?"

"Whatever he was going to put in place tonight," he said, holding up the file. "Looks like it's right here."

She watched as he rummaged through the desk, pulling out a waterproof chart cover. He placed the file inside, zipped it tight, opened his jacket, and slipped it inside.

"Jordan," she cried, noticing the growing stain of blood on the side of his shirt.

He looked down. "No time for that now," he said.

Panic was etched across her clear features.

"Hey, you did a pretty nifty job with that ashtray." Then he paused. "You feel that?" Traiman was weighing anchor and starting up the engines. "They're moving out."

"What should we do?"

"If we don't jump now," he said, "we won't have a chance later."

"Jump? The water's freezing. We'll drown."

"Maybe. But if we stay here they'll kill us for sure. Turn around."

She obliged and he pulled her blouse out from her slacks. Then he tore off the C-4 he had placed there.

She let out a painful yelp.

"Sorry." He reached under her collar and took out two fuses. "I've got to get below decks to plant this."

"What about me?"

"I told you. Jump in the water and head for one of those other boats at anchor. You won't need to get all the way to shore."

She looked up at him and said, "I'm staying."

They went to the door, where Jordan had a quick look outside. Then he pulled the body of the guard inside, together with his Uzi submachine gun, and closed the door.

He took the automatic from the dead man, checked it, then handed it to her. "If you need to fire, just point and shoot—but not anywhere near me."

She gave him a look, as if to say she was not totally incompetent.

"It's not very accurate, is what I mean. Now keep low, and if I say jump, you go for a swim. Agreed?"

She nodded.

Jordan switched off the lights in the library and opened the door again. They heard action to the stern. He could feel the boat moving. They bent down and hurried along the walkway toward the bow. For the first time, the gash in his side began to ache. He couldn't even remember being hit, what with the hand-to-hand struggle with Nelson and diving back and forth across the library. He wasn't concerned about the pain—he was worried about becoming lightheaded from a loss of blood. He also knew that if he stayed aboard too much longer, with the yacht heading out to sea, he would not manage the swim back.

He stopped and listened at the next cabin. Hearing nothing he quickly opened the door and stepped inside. He found John Covington standing there alone. Drink in hand. Covington could do nothing to conceal his astonishment. He recovered enough to say, "Jordan, thank God it's you. I thought you were dead."

Sandor made a quick survey of the cabin. "Keep that pointed at the door," he said to Christine. "Anyone walks in—anyone at all—you shoot them dead. We have no friends here. You got that?"

"Got it," she said nervously as she clutched the submachine gun.

"What's going on out there?" Covington asked.

"Not sure, John. At the moment I'm more interested in what's going on in here. I mean, no guard, the door unlocked, you standing here having a polite cocktail." Jordan's eyes settled on the glass. "Scotch? That still your beverage of choice?"

He nodded.

"Well, why not finish your drink so you and I can go outside and have a look?"

Covington placed his glass on the bar. Sandor's cold gaze told him everything he had to know. "You've been hit," he said casually, dropping his guise as the nervous prisoner.

"You worried about me, John?"

"Not really."

"I believe you." He watched as Covington's hand moved a little too close to his side. "Uh uh uh," Jordan said. "You make another move like that and I'll have to get nasty."

Covington's pressed his thin lips together and said, "So you know."

"Oh yes. I know—that is, I knew."

"You knew nothing."

"I knew you sold us out. Why do you think I'm here?"

Covington said nothing.

"You gave them McHugh. That's how Traiman's men found Tony in Florida."

"We didn't count on you becoming such a problem."

"You didn't count on me still working for the Company," Sandor said.

"No," he admitted grimly, "I didn't."

"What about Andrioli? Was it a fair fight, or did you give it to him in the back?"

"Collateral damage."

"Right, like my team in Bahrain. That was you and Traiman too, right?"

"Yes. And you'll be joining them shortly."

"Humor me, then. You came here to meet Traiman, get rid of Andrioli and me, tell the Agency that Traiman got away, and then you were going to take the information back to the States to set his Operation VX teams in motion. How am I doing?"

Covington said nothing.

"Come on, John, how long did you and Vincent think it could last?"

Covington said, "A lot longer than this." Then he spun quickly to his left, reaching for a pistol holstered at the small of his back.

Jordan reacted instantly, lashing out a vicious backhand with the automatic he had taken from Nelson, smashing the right side of Covington's jaw. Covington fell sideways, still trying to pull out his weapon as Jordan kicked him in the throat with the heel of his shoe.

He knelt down, took Covington's gun, and tossed it on a chair across the cabin. Covington was gagging. "Oh no, John, I didn't crack your windpipe, did I? Not with one kick."

Covington made an effort to lunge at him, but Jordan responded with another swift blow from the butt of the automatic, striking him squarely on the forehead. Covington fell backwards, gasping and moaning, still struggling to breathe.

"Don't be throwing up all over the place now, John. We don't have much time, and I need some answers."

Covington panted, panic in his bulging eyes. "You're going to kill me anyway," he wheezed.

"Not me, John. I'm one of the good guys, remember? You tell me what I need to know, and I'm gone. I'll leave you to Vincent and his merry men."

Covington's mouth was bloody, his jaw broken, and he was still having trouble getting a breath. He stared at Jordan's face. "I'm dead either way."

"Maybe," Jordan said with a nod, "but I can tell you, you don't answer me right now, you're dead for sure."

Covington stared at him without moving.

Christine said, "I think I hear someone."

"Keep that thing pointed at the door," he told her without taking his eyes off Covington. "So John, what are you trying to protect? Traiman's plans? He didn't even tell you about Koppel. Come on, I saw it on your face. You had no idea. You thought this was only about Andrioli and me."

Covington tried to look away, but Sandor grabbed him by the hair and yanked his head back.

"That's why Byrnes never let you in on the Koppel play. This way Traiman would buy the whole show and come out to make his plans."

Covington stared up at him, realizing the truth. He was just another Vincent Traiman casualty.

"So let's have it, John. When and where is Vincent making his move?"

Covington did not answer.

"John." Sandor pushed the barrel of the automatic against Covington's bloodied forehead. "I keep telling you, bench jocks shouldn't play field games. When and where?"

Covington looked up at him. "I'm not sure."

Sandor figured it was true. And now he had Traiman's papers. Hopefully, the answers were there. "Then who's been your go-between up to now?"

When Covington hesitated, Sandor pressed the metal a little harder against his head. "You and Traiman never would have risked direct contact. Who was it?"

·"Figueroa," he growled, giving Jordan the name of the other traitor inside the Agency.

"Thanks pal," Sandor said.

"Drop dead."

Jordan nodded. "Not yet, John." He pulled the gun back and stood up. "You hear anything else?" he asked Christine.

"Yes," she said, giving her head a nervous shake, still watching the door. "I think someone just ran past."

Sandor stood there for a moment, listening. The intermittent sound of gunfire outside had not relented. He turned back to Covington. "Just so you know, we had you in our sights the whole time I was on the move. The DD figured you were the leak. You iced it when you got the call, that anonymous message exposing Traiman's team in DC. Typical Vincent, that move, giving up his own men. The old Queen's sacrifice. I played too much chess with him to miss it."

"And he usually won, didn't he?" Covington voice was raspy with pain. "What makes you think you'll beat him this time? Traiman has every option covered. You'll never get off this boat."

"Maybe not, John. Maybe not."

A loud noise from outside caused Sandor to turn toward the door and Covington made his move, lunging for the gun Jordan had tossed aside.

Sandor did not hesitate, spinning and firing two shots. Then he watched as Covington struggled to draw his last breath before he fell over, dead.

SIXTY-TWO

Jordan led Christine out of the cabin and down the steps, below decks. The bleeding from his side had increased again after grappling with Covington, but he felt clear-headed enough and quickly found his way to an aft compartment. Most of the crew were above, so he moved swiftly to place the plastique against the bulkhead and set the makeshift fuses he had taken from Andrioli's attaché case.

"This is going to blow," he said. "Let's get the hell out of here."

TRAIMAN WAS ON the bridge, directing the captain on their course, as well as handling the radio, monitoring the flow of the action. He ordered his men to keep the smaller craft at bay while they made way out to sea. Thus far, neither had come close enough to attempt boarding. Heavy fire had kept them away.

He picked up the intercom and called Nelson in the main salon but received no answer. "Damn," he said, returning to the walkie-talkie.

"Dombroski, this is Traiman. Where the hell is Nelson? Come back."

Dombroski replied immediately. "Main salon with Sandor and the girl."

"I'm getting no answer. Check it out."

"Right away. Over," Dombroski said.

At that moment, the yacht was rocked by the explosion Jordan had set below.

Traiman grabbed a handrail and steadied himself as the captain was thrown against the control panel.

"What the hell was that?" Traiman hollered into his radio.

"We're not sure," his man on the foredeck responded. "Explosion below."

"Send two men down there to find out. And protect your flank. It could be a diversion."

"Yes sir," the man said. "Over."

Traiman stared out at the dark sea ahead.

"Stay the course?" the captain asked.

"Yes yes. Push it," he said. Then he slammed his fist down. "Damnit," he said. "Push it."

BYRNES' LEAD AGENT radioed back to shore. "We just heard an explosion on the *Halaby*, sir. How much longer?"

The DD knew that it would become more dangerous as the yacht led them further out to sea. He also knew that Sandor should be given as much time as possible to complete his mission.

"All right," Byrnes said reluctantly. "Call in the chopper. Give it three minutes, then get on the bullhorn."

JORDAN AND CHRISTINE were hiding in the companionway, just outside the entrance to the steps leading down to the engine room. They listened as Traiman's men scurried towards the site of the first blast.

"I'm going below one more level," he whispered. "Alone."

She began to say something, but he put his finger to his lips.

"I need you here. Anyone comes this way, you shoot them. I'll be right back."

Sandor did not wait for a response. He lowered himself down the metal steps, facing forward, one hand on the rail the other holding the automatic. He moved as quietly as he could, but as soon as he came into view from below, one of the ship's mates spotted him.

Jordan could not afford to hesitate. He fired, hitting the man in the shoulder, then leaped to the deck and dove for cover behind one of the huge diesel engines that powered the ship.

He heard men shouting and then the sound of feet scuffling on the other side of the room, but no answering gunfire came. He rigged the C-4 he had already removed from his leg with the detonator fuse and secured it against one of the engines.

Judging from the first charge, he would have less than sixty second to get clear. He looked towards the metal steps, listening to the movement of the others as they pulled the mate to safety.

Jordan started the fuse and bolted, firing his pistol behind him, under his left arm, as he moved to the metal stairs. He was half way up when a series of gunshots followed, one of which caught him in the right calf just as he made it to the top. He clung there for a moment, almost falling backward, then sprung upwards, collapsing beside a startled Christine.

"You've been shot," she said as he slammed the metal door behind them.

"Again," he said, trying to force a smile that didn't work. He struggled to his feet. "That charge is about to blow." He dropped the clip in his automatic to the floor and inserted the final replacement. "Let's go," he said, taking her hand and leading her back toward the set of steps to the main deck.

The second explosion was more powerful than the first, the C-4 positioned as it was beside the engine, sending a violent shudder thundering throughout the yacht. Jordan and Christine held on as the boat shook, then ran to the corner of the passageway where they came face to face with two more men.

Both men had their guns drawn. Sandor responded by shoving Christine back and diving atop her, the two of them tumbling behind the corner of the bulkhead as the guards opened fire. Jordan grabbed the Uzi from Christine, scrambled to his hands and knees, and then, pointing the weapon around the turn, answered their fire.

In the small area, Traiman's men had no chance, falling under a barrage of rapid and ricocheting shots as Jordan emptied the submachine gun at them. He got to his feet and, holding Nelson's automatic at the ready, made sure they were finished.

One of them was the tall Arab, Zayn.

"We owed him that one," Jordan said. "For Andrioli."

He leaned over and picked up the man's MP5.

"Come on," he called out to Christine, and they hurried to the main deck.

TRAIMAN WAS STILL in the wheelhouse. He ordered the captain to go full throttle, but the explosion in the engine room had slowed the boat to a few knots.

"Engine's shot," the captain told him after speaking to his engineer on the intercom.

Traiman got a call on his radio from Dombroski. "Nelson's dead," he reported.

"Damnit," Traiman said through clenched teeth. "Sandor." He knew it was getting close to the time when he would have to exercise his emergency escape plan.

"Prepare for seaside," Traiman said.

"Copy that," Dombroski said.

JORDAN LED CHRISTINE to the port deck. They were squatting below the steps to the pilot house. "I want to get Koppel out of here," he whispered.

Just beyond the main cabin structure, they could still hear gunfire on the starboard side.

"Where is he?"

"They said something about the dining salon. Come on."

He moved swiftly along the deck. As he threw each door open he was ready with the SMG. They finally found Koppel in the main dining room, hiding in a corner, beside a large breakfront.

"Come on," Jordan said. "You two are going for a swim."

Koppel responded with a stunned look. "What the hell is going on here?"

"Move it," Jordan growled at him. "I'm the good guy, so let's go. Now."

Koppel stood up, more dazed than afraid, and came to the door.

"Drop over the side here," Jordan told them. "Push as far out to sea as you can, away from the ship, and just tread water."

"What am I, Johnny Weissmuller?" Koppel demanded. "I'll drown in thirty seconds."

"You'll get shot for sure if you stay here. Look, this boat's still moving, it'll go by you pretty quickly. Then the cruiser to the rear should spot you."

"Should?" Koppel asked.

"Just do it."

"And if they don't see us?"

"Keep your head down as much as you can until this boat is gone, then swim for the lights on shore. And whatever you do, stay together."

"What about you?" Christine asked.

Jordan looked down at the large stain of blood on his shirt and gingerly touched his leg. "I'm okay. I've got some unfinished business here. Then it's man overboard for me too." He checked the magazine in the weapon he had taken from Zayn. There were several rounds left.

They were kneeling beside the main bulkhead. He pulled out the rubberized, waterproof chart cover that held Traiman's file. He turned Christine around, tucked it inside the waistband of her slacks at the small of her back, and pulled her blouse over it. "This is important."

"I know," she said, leaning towards him. "You're going after Traiman."

Jordan looked beyond her, down the length of deck. "Go on," he told her. "Don't make me push you overboard."

"Be careful," she said.

"Careful?" Koppel asked. "Believe me, this is so beyond careful—" The rest of his statement was lost in the sound of gunfire coming again from the stern.

Jordan kissed Christine on the forehead and said, "Go." He watched as she and Koppel climbed under the rail and slipped, feet first, into the dark Mediterranean.

SIXTY-THREE

Once Christine and Koppel were in the water, Jordan stole up the stairway in a crouch, staying so low he was practically crawling. The ache in his side was not as bad as the debilitating pain in his leg. He pushed himself, knowing there was only one more thing left for him to do. He nearly tumbled as he quickened his pace, but steadied himself with the heel of his left hand, the H&K SMG securely in his right.

If Traiman was still on board, Sandor knew he would be on the bridge. It was his old partner's style. Always in control.

As he came to the top of the companionway, he realized he had already gone too far. His head was in view of the glass wheelhouse. He froze, but it was too late. The captain spotted him and pointed. As Sandor pulled back, he caught a glimpse of Traiman.

Traiman responded with a rapid fire explosion from a MAC 10 automatic that shattered the glass and sent it in a spray across the foredeck and into the sea.

Jordan held his position, just beneath the sight line of the bridge. He extended his arm, peered up swiftly, then squeezed off two rounds. His shots were answered by another burst from Traiman's gun.

"Get to the wheelhouse. Port side," Traiman hollered at his men into the radio.

Sandor acted quickly, diving across the fiberglass foredeck, firing up at the pilot house, striking the captain, whom Traiman was now using as a human shield. As the captain slumped, Jordan ignored the blast from Traiman's gun, knowing this might be his best and last chance. He came up shooting, catching Traiman in the shoulder and side of the neck, sending him reeling backward against the wall on the starboard side of the pilot house.

Jordan, on his feet again, moved cautiously forward. Traiman was barely standing, leaning against the control panel, his submachine gun now lying nearby on the deck. Sandor moved slowly inside, checking behind him, and kicked the door shut.

"What a bore you can be, Jordan." Traiman coughed.

"Every party has a pooper."

"I hope you don't expect me to answer any more of your endless questions."

"No Vincent. As it turns out, I got everything else I needed from Covington."

"That sniveling bureaucrat?"

"I never liked him."

"Neither did I," Traiman said with a slight laugh that became a throaty cough. When he caught his breath, he said, "Dead?"

"Very," Jordan told him.

Traiman nodded slowly. "Probably deserved it."

"That's how I saw it."

Traiman had a look at Jordan's blood stained shirt and trousers. "My men will be here in a few moments, but it appears I may not need their help. You're already done for."

Sandor steadied himself, grabbing hold of a handrail. "Maybe. You're not looking too swift yourself."

"So then, we old comrades end up dying together."

"Don't flatter yourself, Vincent. We're not comrades, and we're not going to die together."

In that instant, Jordan saw the flicker in Traiman's eyes, even before he heard the movement behind him. Sandor spun and slid to the side in one fluid step, firing a long burst at Dombroski. The man staggered backwards, down the steps to the wheelhouse, and over the railing. Given the moment, Traiman dove for the MAC 10 that had fallen to the deck. He looked up as he strained to reach the weapon, his gaze now met by Jordan's.

"I can't say I'll miss you, Vincent."

Traiman forced a grim smile. "I suppose not, old friend." Then he lunged forward the last foot or so. Jordan did not hesitate. He fired a burst of shots that sent Traiman sprawling face first across the deck of the bridge.

Sandor leaned over to make certain he was dead. He kicked aside the SMG, stood up, and stared down at Traiman one last time. He shook his head sadly and then made his way to the foredeck.

THE *HALABY* HELD its course, cruising slowly through the calm waters of the indifferent Mediterranean, the speed cut well back due to the damage Sandor had caused in the engine room. The sound of gunfire had subsided, the two crafts piloted by Byrnes' men having moved out of range. The remaining force on the yacht heard the helicopter before they saw it approaching from the east.

Jordan also spotted the Black Hawk as it emerged through the darkness, realizing that if Traiman's men refused to surrender in the next few moments, the *Halaby* would be pulverized, along with everyone on it.

Sandor had reached the foredeck and was kneeling in the cool night air in front of the enclosed bridge. He heard two men running fast along the starboard walkway. He was too weak now to chance another battle, especially if a second team followed them forward, along the port side, which was more than likely.

Jordan held the MP5 out, beyond the cover of the wheelhouse, and sent a barrage of shots at the two approaching gunman, holding them off for the moment. Then he hobbled to the railing and dropped himself overboard.

THE BLACK HAWK attempted to radio the yacht, but the two men who had been on the bridge, Traiman and the captain, were both dead. The American agents aboard the helicopter watched as the yacht limped slowly through the calm sea, its course set, its engines damaged.

Their next option would have been to send a warning shot across the bow, a small charge that would explode in the sea, sending a huge spray of water high into the air.

Instead, Byrnes ordered the co-pilot to hold off, instructing him to train two large spotlights on the deck of the ship. Then, using the high-powered loudspeaker, he directed him to tell the men remaining on the *Halaby* that they had exactly ten seconds to kill the engines and come on deck with their arms raised. The Black Hawk had to be concerned about the launch of a shoulder-mounted rocket, so no further warning would be given.

By now, the men aboard had spread the word that Traiman was gone. They also knew the Black Hawk could fire a charge smack into the center of the ship that would end the debate in one shot. One of the men argued that they could use a Stinger to take out the chopper, but the others shut him up. Even if they got lucky and took out the chopper, there was more artillery where this Black Hawk came from. If they missed, they would be annihilated in seconds.

So, without further argument, they marched onto the main deck, threw down their weapons, and held up their hands.

"Into the spotlight," the loudspeaker ordered them. "You will be boarded now. A hostile move by anyone on the ship will be an act of war by all."

The co-pilot radioed the larger boat and told them to take the *Halaby*.

MEANWHILE, THE PILOT of the smaller, faster boat had spotted Christine and Koppel when they went over the side and had circled back to pick them up. Now he was looking for Sandor as the larger cabin cruiser headed straight towards the *Halaby*.

Even with the aid of their night-vision glasses, it was Christine who saw him first. "Jordan," she cried out, pointing at him.

The speedboat swung sharply to the port side and came around to where he was struggling to stay afloat. They motored swiftly to his position, reached over the side, and hauled Sandor to safety.

SIXTY-FOUR

Jordan Sandor, his left arm in a sling, a cane resting against his chair, sat at a small table in Doney's on the Via Veneto in Rome. He was sipping a cup of espresso with anisette, looking out the window at the stream of pedestrians that crowded this famous boulevard on a sunny afternoon.

"Listen to this," Christine said, reading from the *International Herald Tribune*. She recited another account of the capture of terrorists in New York and San Francisco. There were only a few details, including a reference to the interception of a shipment of potentially dangerous chemicals from Marseilles, but no mention of VX gas.

"Potentially dangerous," Jordan repeated with a shake of his head.

The deputy director walked through the front door, spotted them, and came to their table. He held out his hand to Christine. "Hello, Miss Frank. I'm Mark Byrnes."

"Excuse me, if I don't get up," Sandor said.

"Good to see you haven't lost your sense of humor."

"Along with the blood, you mean?"

The DD sat down, taking a chair across from them, his back to the street. "It was a good job, Jordan."

Sandor nodded. "Too bad about—" he began, but Byrnes cut in.

"We stopped them. You stopped them. It was important, and you got it done."

"Yeah. Stopped them for now."

"We can only fight one battle at a time," the DD said. It was one of his favorite sayings.

"Koppel okay?"

"He's fine, thanks to you. And he'll wind up the hero, of course. Probably get someone to make a movie about him."

"One of life's sweet ironies."

"So it would seem."

"No glory for us though, right chief?"

The deputy director offered no response to Sandor's wry look.

When their waiter came by Byrnes said he would not be staying. The man ambled away, muttering something in Italian.

"I just wanted to meet Miss Frank, to thank her personally. And to tell you to take as much time as you need."

"And then?"

"And then you're coming back, aren't you?"

Jordan forced a smile. "Where else have I got to go?"

Byrnes looked at Christine now. "The world can be a pretty lousy place, young lady." He stood up and extended his hand. "Thank you for your courage."

Christine was not sure how to respond, so she shook his hand and said nothing at all.

"The name Covington gave me," Jordan said. "Was he telling the truth?"

"Unfortunately," Byrnes said. "Figueroa was a good agent, or so we thought. Smarter than Covington. We were onto Covington, but we had no idea Figueroa was involved. I'm surprised John gave him up."

"Covington was a coward," Jordan said.

"I suppose you're right."

"So what happens next?"

"After we take care of Traiman's last team, here in Rome, I'm going home and do my best to wrap up this whole mess."

"The VX?"

"Already have a team in possession of the shipments from Marseilles. It's all under control."

328

"Under control, sure."

"One battle at a time, Jordan." He turned to Christine. "Goodbye, Miss Frank. Sandor, I'll see you in DC."

Jordan sighed. "Yes sir," he said, "you will."

They watched as the deputy director walked through Doney's front door and strolled up the Via Veneto, quickly lost among the tourists and locals, on his way back to the embassy. When Jordan picked up his espresso again, it was cold. He signaled the waiter to bring them two more.

"You're thinking about your friends, about the people . . . all of that, aren't you?"

"Yes," he said.

"What you did," she said, "it needed to be done."

Jordan stared at her. "Yes," he said at last, "it did."

The waiter brought fresh coffee, and Christine topped them off from the bottle of anisette. "Let's make a toast," she said.

"To what? The end of tyranny for today? Or peace for all time?"

"To Anthony," she said solemnly.

Jordan nodded. "Sure, and to doing what needs to be done."

They touched cups before drinking and then sat silent for a while.

"Well, let's look on the bright side," he said. "At least we didn't catch pneumonia in the Med."

"Or drown."

"That's true."

"Next time we tour the world together, let's make our plans a little more carefully."

"Fair enough," he said.

He paid the check and they set off for their hotel, Jordan hobbling along on his cane as they slowly walked the ancient streets of Rome.

THE END

COMING SOON

"A.J. TATA IS THE NEW TOM CLANCY."
-- BRAD THOR, #1 NEW YORK TIMES BESTSELLING AUTHOR OF THE LAST PATRIOT

ROGUE THREAT

A.J. TATA

"Topical, frightening, possible, and riveting, A.J. Tata should be read by all fans of military fiction. Mixing Dale Brown's exacting detail with Stephen Coonts edge-of-the-seat pacing, here is a story that demands to be read."
-- James Rollins, New York Times bestselling author of THE DOOMSDAY KEY

AVAILABLE OCTOBER 20, 2009

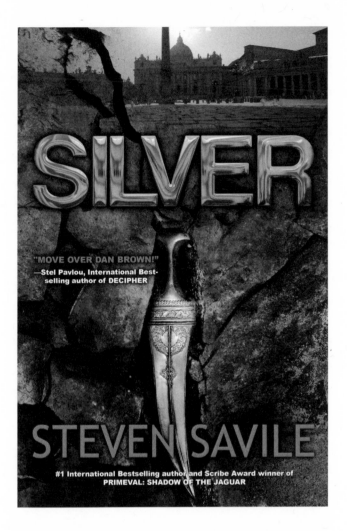

"SILVER is a wild combination of Indiana Jones, The Da Vinci Code, and The Omen. Read this book...before the world ends."
-- Kevin J Anderson, international bestselling author of THE SAGA OF SEVEN SUNS and co-author of PAUL OF DUNE

"Silver grabs you by the throat and doesn't let go. Silver is pure gold.
-- Debbie Viguie, co-author of the NY Times bestselling WICKED series

AVAILABLE JANUARY 19, 2010